THE BLACK RUSSIAN
AND THE
SERPENT'S STING

THE BLACK RUSSIAN AND THE SERPENT'S STING

A NOVEL BY

VLADIMIR ALEXANDROV

NIMCA Press
Brooklyn, New York

Published in the United States of America by NIMCA Press, Brooklyn, New York

Cover and book design by Damon Xavier Villard

ISBN: 979-8-9985758-0-8
Library of Congress Control Number: 2025908193

To the Memory of Frederick Bruce Thomas

ALSO BY VLADIMIR ALEXANDROV

Andrei Bely: The Major Symbolist Fiction

Nabokov's Otherworld

Limits to Interpretation: The Meanings of Anna Karenina

The Black Russian

To Break Russia's Chains: Boris Savinkov and His Wars against the Tsar and the Bolsheviks

CHAPTER ONE

Thursday, May 21, 1913, 3:50 p.m.
3rd Sushchevksy District
Moscow, Russian Empire

The shocking crime began quietly. An elegant black, horse-drawn coach rolled slowly down Bakhmetev Street toward the Fifth Municipal Elementary school, where the girl's little brother was a pupil. The driver pulled up to the dusty wooden sidewalk a short distance from the school and stopped.

It was a quiet time of the day in this working-class neighborhood. Few pedestrians were around, but the four men inside the coach raised the windows and drew the curtains anyway. After a few moments, the dimly lit red silk interior started growing warm and filling with the sour smell of their nervous tension. If they could have been kept in that coach for eternity, with the temperature rising and the smell growing ever stronger, it might have been just punishment for what they were about to do.

They were strangely mismatched to be in such close quarters. Two were young and thuggish, but their broad faces were clean-shaven, their work clothes new, and their big-knuckled hands well-scrubbed, as if they'd been promoted to a cleaner line of work. The third was tall, with a long face, a skinny moustache, and pomaded hair parted down the middle. He wore a straw boater, spats, and a yellow and brown checkered suit with a red carnation in his lapel, making him look like an office clerk about to go on a spree. The fourth man, the oldest, was very stout, with a jowly face and a meaty nose. Dressed all in somber black, with a stiff black silk cravat and a new black bowler pulled low over his ears, he still looked flushed with annoyance after rebuking one of the younger men for touching the curtains.

He held a gold pocket watch in his right hand and, because of his corpulence, wheezed whenever he brought it close to his eyes to check the time, which made the crowded space feel even more claustrophobic.

The girl emerged from the side street a few minutes before four o'clock, just as she had on each of the previous days, and was wearing the same faded, light blue muslin dress with the sleeves rolled up.

The bearded driver saw her from his high seat at the front of the coach as soon as she appeared. Twisting around, he slapped the lacquered roof twice, as he'd been instructed. He then pulled his cap low on his forehead, hoping it would help hide his face, and fixed his eyes on the girl's slender figure bobbing into view and disappearing among the carriages and wagons passing in the street. She walked up to the school's entrance, stopped near several adults and older siblings who were already waiting, and smiled shyly at them.

The driver knew the school's four o'clock dismissal bell was coming—he'd heard it twice before—but he still flinched when it rang. A moment later, the school's double doors were thrown open and a stream of boys poured out like a flock of liberated sparrows, their piping laughter and excited voices filling the bright spring air. One small, towheaded boy dressed in a patched, side-collared blue shirt, with a cloth satchel swinging from his arm, skipped up to the girl.

Bending gracefully at the waist, she brought her face so

close to his that a loose strand of her blond hair brushed his cheek as she said something. The little boy nodded, took her hand, and they started down the sidewalk. When they reached the corner and turned onto Lazarevsky street, the driver took a deep breath, twitched the reins, and started the two strong, well-groomed bays on a slow walk.

The traffic and pedestrians thinned even more by the time the girl and her brother got to the end of Lazarevsky Street, which was lined with soot-stained redbrick warehouses topped by signs announcing their owners' names and businesses in giant faded letters. The district's sidewalks ended here and rutted dirt roads began, adding to the street's dreary appearance. Just ahead lay the old Lazarev Cemetery, named for "Saint Lazarus," whom Russians revered as "The Four Days Dead."

The driver was sixty meters behind the girl and her brother when he saw them turn onto Voznesensky Lane, which ran between the low stone cemetery wall on the left and a grey, unpainted wooden fence that hid a little-used railway spur on the right. He turned the horses and followed.

It was the loneliest stretch of their route. The distant background noise of the city faded to a murmur. Crows cawed somewhere behind the fence. The still air smelled of sunbaked dust and rusting iron.

The bright sun did little to lighten the melancholy sight of the tilted crosses and neglected graves in the old cemetery, many of them overgrown with a tangle of field grasses, corn flowers, and nettles. Even some trees had taken root. A sturdy young birch grew out the middle of one grave, its white bark flecked with black, like pen strokes on parchment in some unknown language. It was so tall its roots must have penetrated the decayed coffin and remains of whoever had been buried there long ago.

The driver waited until the sister and her brother got part of the way down Voznesensky Lane and smacked his lips. The horses broke into a trot, the coach rocked back then forward as it picked up speed, and its rubber tires began to hiss across the hard-packed dirt. A black-gloved hand drew back the curtain on the right side and lowered the glass window. The gang's leader leaned out, his deep-set eyes squinting in the bright light.

The driver timed his approach so the girl and her brother would be halfway down Voznesensky Lane when the coach caught up with them. He rolled past for a half-dozen meters and stopped.

The man in black was staring openly at the girl and congratulated himself for deciding to dangle some extra cash in front of his foppishly dressed assistant.

"If it all play out like you *say*, my frien'," he'd promised four days ago in his Cajun-accented English, "an' you fin' me a prime, class-A Russian looker to replace dat other one, not only you gon' get a bonus, we gon' help you *celeb'ate* it. We'll have us a nice *shindig* at some swell place in town—maybe dat Aquarium Garden you keep goin' on about."

The girl and her brother stopped as well. They'd been absorbed in talking about their father's exciting plan to move the family to a bigger apartment, which he had announced last night at supper, and noticed the coach only as it passed them.

Both looked up at the round-faced man in the window with mild curiosity.

The man said something over his shoulder, ducked his head inside, there was shifting about that made the coach creak and rock, and the door on the right opened. A tall man, who seemed very handsome and well-dressed to the girl, stepped onto the ground, holding a piece of paper in his left hand.

"*Ska-zhí, mí-la-ya!*" (Sa-ay, swe-e-tie!) he called out to the girl, using the familiar form of address and drawing out his words with feigned casualness as he took a few strutting steps toward her.

"Come over here, would you?" he urged, smiling and raising the paper up, as if it would explain what he wanted from her.

That same moment, the door on the far side of the coach opened and the two workmen got out.

The girl looked uncertainly at the man with the paper but after a second's hesitation started to approach him. Her brother followed, still holding her hand, his little mouth round with surprise.

Then the girl noticed the two men coming from behind the coach and heading straight toward her.

Before she could say anything or even think, the man with the paper drew back his right hand, stepped up to her, and slapped her across the face with such force that her head was thrown sideways.

The girl's eyes went dark from the shock and pain, and she froze in horror. Her little brother gasped and dropped his satchel.

"Grab her, *now!*" the man with the paper shouted in Russian.

The two workmen moved with brutal efficiency. The first one wrapped his left arm around the girl's waist and clamped his right hand over her mouth; the second bent down and wound his arms around her knees and thighs. Picking her up as easily as if she were a rag doll, they shuffled to the coach, and with the tall man helping, began to push her onto the floor between the seats. No one noticed that a thin cord with a small silver cross had torn loose from her neck and was lying in the dirt near the coach.

Snapping out of his astonishment, the girl's little brother lunged at the nearest man, grabbed his left leg and yanked as hard as he could. The man, caught off guard, looked down and tried to shake him off. But when the boy tightened his grip, the man put his hand on the boy's head and pushed him away roughly. The boy stumbled backward, lost his balance, and hit the ground hard, landing on his back. The impact knocked the wind out of him.

The gang's leader was ready. When the three men finished stuffing the girl into the coach at his feet and climbed in after her, he tilted a brown glass bottle over a wad of stained rags, poured out a dollop of colorless, nauseatingly sweet-smelling liquid, and pressed the wad to her face. The girl gasped and tried to sit up, but he spread his gloved fingers across her nose and mouth and pushed down, grimacing, holding his breath, and twisting his head away as much as his fat neck would allow.

The two workmen leaned on the girl's arms and the tall man grabbed her knees to pin her legs. But the extra weight wasn't necessary. The shock of everything that had happened paralyzed the girl, and the suffocating fumes from the ether-based concoction went straight to her head. A shudder ran the length of her body and she went limp.

The driver had been crouching on his seat, glancing anxiously up and down the street as the men grabbed the girl, cursing himself under his breath for ever agreeing to take the job. As soon as everyone was back in the coach, he turned it around, whipped the reins sharply, and set the horses off at a quick trot back toward the center of the city.

It took the little boy several moments to come to his senses as he lay on the ground and struggled to catch his breath. When he saw the coach rolling away, he scrambled to his feet. But it was already too far away—he'd never catch it.

Overcoming the sharp pain in his back and feeling like he was going to throw up, he bolted down Voznesensky Lane toward home, his face soaked with tears, screaming "*Masha!* . . . *Masha!* . . . *Masha!*" between suffocating sobs.

When the carriage and the boy were gone and Vozne-sensky Lane was deserted again, the weather started to change. A breeze picked up and a band of grey clouds appeared in the west. Soon its leading edge covered the sun. Eddies of wind-swept dust began to curl down the empty street. One scudded over the cross the girl had lost, spun into a slender whirlwind that climbed into the darkening sky and disappeared. The birch growing out of the grave suddenly bowed, as though a strong gust had caught its branches, and a long shiver passed through its young, pale green leaves.

The black-clad leader of the gang took off his gloves and relaxed only when the coach was back on Bakhmetev street. He had waited impatiently for the smell of ether to dissipate before telling the workmen to raise the windows and draw the curtains again. Although it was getting uncomfortably hot inside, he was pleased with how smoothly everything had gone.

Looking down at the body of the girl on the floor in front of him, he leaned over and yanked down the hem of her dress, which had ridden up to her thighs. Then, sitting back to get more comfortable, he put his feet on the girl's stomach, being careful not to bruise her by pressing down too hard. "Our stable's complete wit' dis here lil' filly," he said, turning toward his foppish assistant with a satisfied grin.

CHAPTER TWO

Friday, May 22, 1913, 12:30 p.m.
Aquarium Garden, Bolshaya Sadovaya Boulevard
Moscow

The Russian inscription on the wooden door read in big gold letters:

ѲЕДОРЪ ѲЕДОРОВИЧЪ ТОМАСЪ
ДИРЕКТОРЪ

(FYODOR FYODOROVICH THOMAS
DIRECTOR)

Nikolay Ferapontovich Stepanov, Aquarium Garden's senior maître d'hôtel, a position to which he'd been promoted just two weeks earlier, paused outside the door, smoothed back his thinning grey hair with both hands, deliberately and firmly, and checked his tie before giving the varnished wood two discreet taps with a knuckle.

He had worked in the Garden for nearly a year and a half now, ever since Thomas and his partners took the place over and started to prepare for its first season. During this time, Stepanov had developed a great deal of respect for the *khozyain* (boss) as he and the other staff called Thomas in private. And he was grateful for his promotion to the top post because of the trust it implied as well as the generous salary. But he still wasn't sure how well he understood the man, so he thought it was best to be guarded in how he behaved around him. Thomas wasn't like anyone Stepanov had ever met before during thirty years of work in Moscow's restaurants and theaters.

It wasn't just because the *khozyain* was a foreigner. Stepanov was used to seeing people from all over the world in Moscow, and many who settled there modified their names to sound Russian.

The unusual thing about Thomas was that he came from the "United States of North America," as Russians called the country, and that he was a Black man whose name had originally been "Frederick Bruce Thomas." He also came from a place Stepanov had never heard of before that sounded as if it had been named for a woman, "Mee-sees Ippy." But what surprised Stepanov most, considering Thomas' wealth and position in Moscow, was his origin, because, as he mentioned once in passing—although he didn't make a fuss about it—his parents had been slaves.

Stepanov was well aware that his own background wasn't all that different, because his parents, his grandparents, and all his kin as far back as anyone could remember had been serfs on a nobleman's estate in the Yaroslavl Governorate three hundred kilometers from Moscow. And there were lots of others like him in the Russian Empire, since something like one-third of all Russians had been serfs until 1861, when they were freed. Stepanov was born three years after that momentous event and had often heard his parents reminiscing piously about the "Tsar Liberator," as people called Alexander II, the tsar responsible for the emancipation.

Nonetheless, meeting a descendant of Black slaves from the great American Republic was very unusual. For one thing, few Americans of any kind visited Russia, and Stepanov had met only a handful during the many years he had lived and worked in Moscow. For another, Black people were even rarer. Stepanov had seen some Black vaudeville performers on stage over the years who included Russia on their European tours, but he had never talked to a Black person before his job interview with Thomas in the winter of 1911.

So, his surprise was complete when he walked into the

Aquarium director's office on that cold and snowy December day. But Thomas either didn't notice how Stepanov had looked at him or pretended he didn't. Thomas spoke Russian surprisingly well, even though he made mistakes and clearly preferred to speak French. He also sized Stepanov up very quickly and after reading his recommendations offered him the job then and there.

"*Come in, come in, Nikolay Ferapontovich!*" Thomas exclaimed in his hearty baritone when he opened the door, extending his right hand and smiling warmly. The greeting was so infectious that a small grin appeared on Stepanov's dignified, sallow face, even though this kind of easy and effusive manner didn't quite fit with his idea of how an important businessman like the *khozyain* ought to behave.

Thomas was a bit taller than average, trimly built, and around forty years old. He was handsome and distinguished, Stepanov had to admit, even if he didn't look at all like a European. And it wasn't just because of the rich dark brown color of his skin. Everything about Thomas's features seemed exaggerated: his nose was long and broad, his cheekbones high, his mouth wide, and his eyes large, oval, and slanted a bit. He was bald on top but made up for it with an impressively wide and bushy moustache that stuck out a good three centimeters on either side.

Thomas also looked vigorous for a man of his age and profession, and evidence of his interest in sport was all over his office. This also struck Stepanov as not entirely appropriate, considering that an office is a place for work, and leisure pastimes should take place elsewhere. Hunting scenes and signed photographs of American and British boxers hung on the wood-paneled walls, and racks near the door leading to the small bedroom suite behind the office held Indian clubs and kettlebells. The *khozyain's* Borzoi, Strelka (Little Arrow), was in her usual spot in the back, lying in an elegant curve under a long, heavy, leather cylinder hanging from the ceiling. Stepanov had seen Thomas pummel it with his fists when he was doing his exercises. The dog's presence in the office was another of the *khozyain*'s eccentricities that Stepanov filed it away in a mental folder he kept for his own amusement.

But if Stepanov had reservations about Thomas's easy manner, which he understood from newspaper stories was typical of Americans in general, he had none about his dress. He noted with appreciation that today he had on a beautifully tailored navy wool suit from MacPherson, a cream-colored silk cravat with a pearl stick pin, a pink rose boutonniere, and a diamond ring on the little finger of each hand. A hint of good, sober French cologne completed the impression of elegance and success.

"So, how are things shaping up for this evening?" Thomas asked, gesturing to one of a pair of leather armchairs to the side of a large desk which held neat stacks of paper, ledger books, and two gleaming brass telephones. Stepanov appreciated the nuance that the boss no longer had him sit in one of the wooden chairs in front of the desk, which had been the case until the promotion.

"Everything looks good, Fyodor Fyodorovich," he replied, using the polite Russian form of address with first name and patronymic. He then sat down, but without leaning back, and pulled a small notebook out of a breast pocket to consult several lists.

Managing a business the size of Aquarium Garden required constant attention to myriad details. The place resembled a private park and consisted of two hectares of land with a half-dozen buildings near the center of Moscow—the Kremlin was less than two kilometers away. Over a hundred and fifty regular employees worked there in various capacities in addition to the dozens of performers who appeared on its stages during any given week. Stepanov's job was to keep track of everything that went on in the place, and he began each workday with a detailed report to the *khozyain*.

"We got word from the Kazan Train Station that the Chinese acrobats have arrived today. It's the last vaudeville act for the new lineup we were waiting for," he added, looking up at Thomas, to see how he was taking this. The boss nodded. It was obvious that he remembered the detail, as he seemed to remember everything that had to do with running Aquarium. The place became so successful during its first season that it was now beginning to compete with Hermitage for the title of most popular entertainment garden in the city.

Stepanov continued with a smile of pleasure at what he was about to report: "And the dressing room for Signora Lina Cavalieri is nearly finished."

Cavalieri was an Italian operatic diva with an enormous following in Europe and the United States and was admired as much for her beauty and acting as her lovely soprano voice. She was often called the world's most beautiful woman, and she was surely the most photographed. Russian and European businesses vied for permission to put her face on everything from match boxes to fancy chocolates.

For Thomas to have gotten her to commit to concerts at Aquarium next month was a coup and would be the envy of the city's other theater owners. His decision to rebuild a dressing room for her and equip it like a luxurious hotel with floor-to-ceiling mirrors, silk-upholstered furniture, and a marble bath was sure to impress even a star who had seen everything. It cost a fortune, and her contract was the most expensive he'd ever offered anyone. But if Cavalieri brought in the crowds to Aquarium that Thomas hoped she would, she would be worth every kopek.

"I'll take a look today," Thomas promised.

Stepanov flipped to another page, and continued: "Yes, the water pipe in the summer kitchen has been fixed . . . and Eliseyev Brothers sorted out the issue with shipments of Flensburg oysters. So that's all done."

Stepanov closed his notebook but then hesitated. Thomas cocked an eyebrow.

"There's a problem with one of the waiters in the Tango Salon," Stepanov said and paused, uncertain if the matter was worth bringing up since it didn't directly affect Aquarium's operations. But Thomas was paying attention.

"It seems Boris Nikitin's daughter has been kidnapped or something."

Thomas leaned forward in his chair. "Kidnapped? What do you mean?" he asked, sounding surprised and trying to remember who Nikitin was.

"Well, Nikitin told Matvey Alexandrovich that the girl disappeared yesterday," Stepanov explained, referring to the headwaiter in charge of the Tango Salon, "and Matvey Alexandrovich mentioned it to me when I was making the rounds just before I came up here to see you. I didn't have a chance to ask Nikitin himself."

Thomas nodded, still running the Tango Salon's staff members through his mind as he listened. Like most people, he remembered faces. But unlike most, he also had a knack for linking them to their names.

"Nikitin came in today anyway?" Thomas asked, and as he spoke the man's face crystalized in his mind's eye. He remembered his name and patronymic, Boris Frolovich, and that Nikitin was a good waiter—punctual, sober, well-groomed, diligent. A man to keep and encourage.

Thomas felt a stir of resentment at the idea that someone had harmed one of his people. "I'd like to talk to him, Nikolay Ferapontovich," he continued. "Could you please have him come up?"

Stepanov rose to his feet: "Yes sir, I'll fetch him."

As Stepanov went down the new, wrought iron stairs Thomas installed as a fire precaution, the treads resounding under his feet, he realized that he had gotten used to such things as the boss taking an interest in a single waiter even when he employed dozens of them. And it wasn't just Thomas's attention to detail, although this was a big reason for Aquarium's success. Rather, as Stepanov understood after watching how Thomas encouraged, admonished, praised, and rewarded employees, he was trying to build personal loyalty by treating everyone who worked for him generously and humanely, but without dropping standards. The payoff was that there were few departures from Aquarium's staff during the last year, unlike what happened with their competitors.

Five minutes later Stepanov was back with Nikitin. Thomas got up from behind his desk and walked over to him. The waiter was neatly dressed in his short, black uniform jacket, vest, and ankle-length white apron, he was freshly shaved, his blonde hair was parted down the middle, and he held himself erect despite looking frightened and pale. But although he was holding his head up and the office was brightly lit by an electric ceiling light, it seemed to Thomas as if there was a dull, gray sheen like a faint shadow around the man's face.

The waiter looked close to tears. Whatever was troubling him must have been made even worse by the summons to the director's office.

"Tell me what happened, Boris Frolovich," Thomas asked in a kindly tone.

Stepanov flicked a glance at his boss.

Who addresses a waiter so politely? he wondered. Bosses, like restaurant patrons, used *"ty,"* or the familiar "you" with them, the way one addresses an underling, instead of the polite *"vy." And how did he manage to remember the waiter's patronymic? Maybe he looked it up in his records,* Stepanov guessed.

"My Mashenka—I mean, my daughter, Maria . . . she was, she disappeared . . . from us . . . Fyodor Fyodorovich," Nikitin stammered, his lower lip beginning to tremble and tears welling up in his red-rimmed eyes.

Thomas walked up to Nikitin and gently rested his left hand on his shoulder. With his right he pulled a white handkerchief out of an inside breast pocket and handed it to the man, who pressed it to his eyes. Nikitin's shoulders began to shake.

"Don't . . . don't cry," Thomas said, trying to console him and squeezing his shoulder. "Tell me what happened, maybe I can help."

Thomas's attention flowed toward the man and enveloped him, until all he could see and feel was his heartbreaking pain and fear. It seemed to Thomas that he already knew something the man hadn't told him yet.

Strelka sensed it as well, rose gracefully on her long legs, and ambled over to her master's side. Her head came to his waist, and she looked up at the crying man with her widely spaced, intelligent eyes.

Nikitin wiped his face and mouth with the handkerchief and tried to suppress the trembling of his lips.

And then it all poured out. He was at work yesterday when Petya, their little boy, dashed into the kitchen after school, weeping and screaming that "some men grabbed Mashenka and put her in a big carriage and pushed me so hard I fell." After getting Petya to say where, Nikitin's wife ran all the way to Voznesensky Lane by the cemetery, but she was too late of course. All she found was her son's satchel and the string with a cross her daughter wore around her neck. She then left Petya with neighbors who rushed over to see why he was sobbing and ran to the local police post which was ten minutes away. But all the officer on duty told her was that she should calm herself and that he would make a report at the station house.

When Nikitin got home from his shift at Aquarium late last night, he found his wife sitting by Petya's bed, weeping softly as the boy slept. It was a terrible night—they didn't know what to do, where to go, whom to tell. In the morning, Nikitin went to the district police station, but the haughty officer on duty told him he would have to wait for the official investigation. He then suggested with a smirk, "your girl might turn up by herself—maybe she just went on a spree!"

"Mashenka is our oldest . . . our pride and joy," Nikitin cried, still shocked by the suggestion. "She's a good, obedient, and helpful girl, and wouldn't ever do what the policeman said!"

Thomas drew Nikitin closer and put his other arm around his shoulder.

"You'll have her back," he said. "She'll be all right, I'll help, I promise."

Then he added, bringing his face close to Nikitin's and looking into his eyes to emphasize what he was saying, "Right now, we'll put you in a cab, you're going to go home, and you'll stay with your family until all this is sorted out." Thomas glanced at Stepanov, who nodded that he understood.

When Nikitin began to object feebly, saying he needed to work, Thomas told him not to worry about it. He pulled out his wallet and handed him two ten-ruble notes—two weeks good wages and tips at Aquarium—and forced them into Nikitin's hand when he tried to refuse.

After Stepanov and Nikitin left, Thomas bent down to stroke Strelka's head, and ran his hand over the long, silky, white and brown fur on her back. She looked up at him with what looked like understanding. Going to his desk, Thomas picked up the internal telephone's receiver from its cradle and asked to be connected to the office of his head of security.

Sergey Sergeyevich Markov had come to work at Aquarium after retiring from the Okhrana (The Defense), the national police force charged with protecting the imperial family, important government figures, and the regime as a whole. He also had useful connections in the Moscow city police.

Markov listened carefully—the scratching of his pen as he took notes was audible over the telephone line's hiss—and promised to find out what he could about the case of the waiter's missing daughter.

Thomas sat up and pulled out his pocket watch. The workday was just beginning, and he had to get through a thick stack of correspondence and bills on his desk before the garden opened at 6 p.m., when he would start making his rounds.

CHAPTER THREE

Thomas started by picking up a folder containing a dozen light blue telegrams from the Heimat Talent Agency in Berlin. He was reading the first one—about a new American cowboy act they were recommending called "The Youngman Trio"—when there was a loud knock on the door.

He looked up. Before he could say anything, the door swung open and a big man with a rakishly tilted homburg on his head strode in, his loose black overcoat billowing behind him.

"Matvey Filippovich!" Thomas exclaimed. It was one of his partners, Martynov.

"It's a nice surprise to see you," Thomas said in a cheerful tone, putting down the telegram and concealing his annoyance at the way the man had barged into his office.

Martynov flashed his toothy smile as he shook hands, but the rest of his big, pale face was impassive. It seemed to Thomas as if his closely spaced eyes were coated with a thin grey film, as if he was trying to hide something.

It's about money again, Thomas thought with distaste. *Always about money with him.*

Two years ago, he had formed a partnership with Martynov and a third man, Mikhail Prokofyevich Tsarev, to reopen Aquarium Garden, which went bankrupt under its previous owners. Each put up the same amount of cash, but since it was a full-time job to run the place and Thomas was the only one with the experience, foreign languages, and international contacts, they had agreed he would get fifty percent of the net profits while Tsarev and Martynov would be passive investors and split the rest. To reflect the arrangement, the partnership was registered in Moscow's City Hall as "Thomas and

Company."

"Thank you. Happy to see you too," Martynov drawled, stressing the "*a*"s in his characteristic Moscow accent.

But his grin faded even before he finished his stock response. Like Tsarev, he had lived in the city all his life, came from a petty merchant background, and pulled himself up by his bootstraps. Thomas had thought this would help create a bond among the three of them. Unfortunately, it turned out to be more complicated.

"I won't pretend I just happened to be passing by," Martynov announced. Then, without waiting for an invitation, he dropped his bulk into one of the armchairs by Thomas's desk and tossed his hat onto the other one.

"I went to Stasov's yesterday to look at the books for the last two quarters," he began, "and I have to say . . . I discovered some serious *problems* . . .." Martynov let his voice trail off and looked away as was his habit, letting his eyes wander over the paintings and prints on the office's walls.

"Yes?" Thomas asked calmly. The Stasov Brothers were Aquarium's accountants, and Martynov was in his rights to ask them for whatever information he wanted.

But that's not the way a partner does it, without talking to me first, Thomas thought.

"Yes," Martynov repeated firmly and looked back at Thomas. "The staff expenses are too high, Fyodor Fyodo'rch," he said, casually swallowing the middle syllables in Thomas's patronymic. "You're spoiling people and paying them too much. You're also not getting any commissions from new employees, are you? Or collecting breakage fees from the waiters? And your payments for some of the acts you've hired are *absurd*! Especially that Cavalieri woman! All completely out of line if you look at our competition—Hermitage, Yar, Apollo."

"You don't like our profits, Matvey Filippovich?" Thomas asked. "We all got twelve percent on our money in the first year. Not bad, I'd say. In fact, hard to find another business where . . ."

"Yes, well . . .," Martynov interrupted, crossing his thick

right leg over the left and looking down at his knee as he plucked at the light-colored gabardine. "That was just the first year," he continued, raising his eyes. "If you hadn't thrown money at the waiters and the others, the return would've been closer to fifteen, maybe seventeen."

"The wages I pay are fair for the work," Thomas replied in an even tone, although his gaze hardened. "I'm not going to sell jobs to new employees or punish people for accidents. It's wrong and unfair, and I won't do it while I'm in charge. And big stars bring in big crowds. I explained all this to you and Mikhail Prokofyevich way back."

Martynov's constant harping about profits and his obtuseness about what it took to run a place like Aquarium had worn down Thomas's patience during the past year. Thomas was also disappointed with himself because he hadn't dug deeply enough into Martynov's character or his past when they first began to talk about working together. But Martynov had the money to invest, Aquarium had suddenly become available, and Thomas wanted it too much. In all his other jobs in Russia and before that in France and Germany, he had worked for someone else. Aquarium was his first chance to build something of his own since he'd left the United States nineteen years ago, and his eagerness had blinded him.

"The result of how I treat the staff is that they're very loyal," Thomas continued, enunciating clearly but still trying to sound agreeable. "And because I don't have to bother finding replacements all the time, I can focus on the shows and the restaurants, which are the keys to our success. This is one of the reasons Aquarium is doing so well, despite what you say."

"Well, it's only been the first year, Fyodor Fyodo'rch," Martynov repeated with a dismissive wave of his hand. "You don't know how fickle our fellow Muscovites can be. One month Aquarium's the favorite, next one it's someplace else."

Thomas felt the blood rise to his face. *Damn him! He thinks I don't know what I'm doing because I'm not a native of the city or a Russian like him!*

"I'm building . . . for the future . . . Matvey Filippovich," Thomas explained, slowly and pointedly. "For the long term .

. . We all agreed that's what we wanted."

Martynov looked away again. Then, as if he'd made up his mind, he turned back to Thomas. "Well, no matter what you say, Aquarium's finances are thin. And that's dangerous. It's not just that profits should be higher. The Italian diva's contract is so expensive I can't imagine how her ticket sales will cover the cost, even if she sells out every time! And the capital and reserve funds are so small that if we have a bad month we'll have to dig into our own pockets."

"I really don't think it'll come to that," Thomas replied quickly, trying to ignore what Martynov said about Cavalieri.

But Martynov heard the uncertainty in Thomas's voice, and that was all he needed. He rose to his feet, picked up his hat, and ran his fingers along the curved brim before putting it on.

"We need to have a meeting. All three of us," Martynov said with finality when he looked up. "We need to reconsider our partnership. See if we can change some things, fix some things. Tsarev's in Kiev now but he'll be back in a couple of weeks. I'll set it up."

The insult was obvious, but Thomas realized there was no point in aggravating things. "Please do, Matvey Filippovich, please do," Thomas replied, managing to sound affable again. "Always happy to talk with you both. Any time."

When Martynov left, Thomas sat at his desk for several minutes, waiting until he calmed down. He knew he blushed easily, and it was a relief that it wasn't readily visible.

Thomas didn't like admitting it, but what Martynov said about Aquarium's financial reserves was true. They were thin, and Thomas worried about them himself.

But how can you grow a new business without taking risks? he asked, trying to reassure himself. He thought of Cavalieri. *Did I gamble too much because I wanted to make my mark in this city?*

Thomas leaned back in his chair and ran through all the reasons he'd decided to spend so much to engage her. He'd done this a hundred times before and the numbers still appeared to add up. But because of Martynov he couldn't silence a small voice of doubt.

CHAPTER FOUR

Friday, May 22, 6:30 p. m.
Aquarium Garden

Markov, Thomas's head of security, spent the afternoon at Moscow police headquarters talking with the clerks in the statistics department and reviewing their records of kidnappings and disappearances of children, focusing on the past few days but also going back two months.

When he returned to Aquarium, he found Thomas in the white and gold columned foyer of the Garden's Winter Theater, where he was checking on patrons arriving for *The Gypsy Baron*, Strauss's popular operetta, which was going to be performed by a traveling Viennese troupe. Evenings in May were still too cold for the open-air theater and band shell to operate, which limited overall attendance at the Garden, but a line of well-dressed people was queuing up for Strauss and it looked like the performance might sell out.

Markov was a portly, grandfatherly type with red-veined cheeks, light-blue eyes, and a thick silver watch chain across his belly. But despite his genial appearance, he had a deeply cynical view of human nature that he acquired during his years in the Okhrana. He also carried a .45 British Bull Dog revolver in a well-worn shoulder holster and kept a good eye out for the grifters and pickpockets who tried to prey on Aquarium's clients.

In general, Markov thought Thomas was a bit naïve in his approach to people, but he had to admit that this didn't prevent him from being a good employer. For his part, Thomas found Markov's self-confidence amusing, but valued his honesty, diligence, and connections in the city police.

Markov's report about the kidnapping was grim. He found out that during the past month alone, 147 children were reported missing in the city. It could be assumed more hadn't been reported, and of those that were, most were probably runaways who had quarreled with their parents and would eventually turn up. However, two of the 147 resembled the abduction of Masha Nikitina, judging by what her brother Petya had been able to tell the police when they got around to questioning him.

One victim was a Tatar boy around thirteen years old who worked in a small leather goods shop owned by his uncle on Little Ordynka Street in the old, southern part of the city, on the other side of the Moscow River. He was sweeping the sidewalk six days ago when several men grabbed him, shoved him into a black coach that had stopped nearby and took off. The uncle caught a glimpse of the coach but didn't see its registration number.

The second case was a fifteen-year-old girl from an Armenian family living in the Presnya District in the industrial, northwestern part of the city, where the father worked in a furniture factory. Thirteen days ago, a male passerby saw her struggling with two men as she was returning home with a string bag of groceries. They overpowered her and carried her to a waiting black coach, but he was too far away to make out any other details or to help.

Markov sighed and shook his head when he finished his summary. He paused for a moment, as if mulling something over, then looked up: "Black coaches are hardly rare in Moscow, of course, but what both kidnappings had in common was the way they were carried out. Also, sir, it's important to note that the two children are exceptionally good looking, according to what the police learned from people who knew them."

Thomas didn't understand and looked questioningly at him.

"You told me the waiter's daughter, Masha, was also very pretty, didn't you, sir? A fair-skinned blonde?" Markov asked.

Thomas nodded, trying to remember. He'd never met the girl, but Stepanov told him about her after he put her father in a cab. He'd seen Nikitin's family once during the past year when they came for a puppet show at the Garden and he remembered her because of how beautiful she was.

"This doesn't seem random," Markov continued with a frown, "and there may've been others, in addition to the three we know now. The gang carried out the abductions in broad daylight. But they did it in places where they had little chance of being seen. And they chose children from humble families that can't raise a stink. Also, please note, sir, they were all different national types."

Markov paused to see how Thomas was taking this, then added: "They're collecting them, I think. Means the children are probably being held for something. Nothing good, obviously. Neither family reported any kind of ransom demand. Nikitin didn't either. And what sort of money could the parents have? They're barely scraping by as it is."

"What a nightmare," Thomas replied. He was thinking of his own three children—Olga, going on twelve, Mikhail seven, and little Irma, who just turned four.

Then something his father once told him long ago surfaced in his memory. It was evening, they had finished the day's chores and were sitting by the fireplace in their cabin on the farm back in Coahoma County. Lewis was talking about slave catchers in Mississippi before the war, how they would go anywhere to abduct slaves who had escaped, even to northern states, and do anything to bring them back to their owners, even if it meant beating them half to death and crippling them.

The image of Olga, his oldest, being grabbed by several men and forced into a black coach appeared in his mind's eye with such vividness that he started. He thought he could hear Olga's screams and his heart began to race. It took him several seconds to shake off the vision and return his attention to Markov, who was looking at him quizzically, wondering why the boss was taking this news so hard.

"The police are taking this seriously and investigating?"

24

Thomas asked hopefully.

"They will . . . investigate . . . it . . . sir," Markov replied slowly, underscoring the uncertainty. "But what with the imperial family's visit in two weeks and all, the entire detective bureau is up to its ears in security preparations. There are threats from the Socialist Revolutionaries, the Anarchists, and the other terrorist scum," he emphasized with a rising note of anger in his voice.

Thomas noted Markov's vehemence but said nothing. Terrorist attacks had become so common in Russia that it was difficult not to become inured to them.

But Thomas had forgotten that the entire imperial family—the tsar, the tsaritsa, the four daughters and the poor, hemophiliac tsarevich—as well as many royal relatives and other dignitaries from home and abroad, would arrive in Moscow on June 6th. It was part of their nation-wide tour celebrating the 300th anniversary of their dynasty. The imperial family would stay in Moscow until the 9th, and several weeks ago Thomas had discussed with the director of the Winter Theater the kind of patriotic program he would put on during those three days. The Aquarium's clientele expected it, and Thomas knew he'd have to accommodate his customers' tastes.

However, when Thomas first thought about the commemoration itself, he realized it left him cold. He was grateful for the kind of life he had been able to build for himself in Russia, which he could never have even imagined in Mississippi, or anywhere else in the United States for that matter. And he had genuine affection for Moscow because of the way its comfortable old ways blended with all that was new and modern. But he had no love for the tsar or his rule. During the thirteen years Thomas lived in Russia, he often witnessed the regime's stupidity and cruelty. The disasters of the Japanese War and the 1905 Revolution, when barricades were thrown up just outside Aquarium and there was artillery fire in the streets, showed that the country was also very ill.

And now, because the Romanov show is coming to town, Thomas thought with irritation, *the police can't help with something genuinely urgent.*

"What's going to happen to those children in the meantime?" he asked. "I shudder to think why they were kidnapped." Again, the faces of his three children arose in his mind's eye.

"Yes, waiting is dangerous," Markov agreed. "The Head of Detectives, Arkady Frantsevich Koshko, will be back from Saint Petersburg tomorrow. I'll try to speak with him in person. Maybe he'll be able to put a man or two on this after all. The case is very unusual. I, at least, have never heard of anything like this here. Maybe in France, Germany, or England . . .," he ended, implying Russia did not share Europe's perversions.

Something else occurred to him, and the corners of his mouth turned down with displeasure: "I'll also get a few of my friends in the criminal police to question some of their informants in the prostitution business. Just to see if anyone has heard anything."

"I understand," Thomas replied, feeling a chill because of what Markov implied. "Thank you, Sergey Sergeyevich," he added and extended his hand. "Let me know if there's anything I can do. I feel for poor Nikitin. This matter is important to me."

Thomas took out his pocket watch to check the time.

"Things look like they're going to be quiet in the Garden tonight," he said. "And Ilyushin can handle anything that comes up if you have to be away on this matter."

CHAPTER FIVE

But Thomas's intuition, usually reliable to such a degree that others found it uncanny, betrayed him on this occasion and the evening at Aquarium didn't turn out to be quiet at all.

An hour after Markov left to look up his old police contacts, Thomas was in the middle of his usual rounds of the Garden's different venues. He had stopped to talk with the ticket booth attendant in the Variety Theater when he saw an elegant young man in a frock coat and with brilliantined hair clattering down the marble stairs from the second floor. It was the theater restaurant's maître d'hôtel, Viktor Aristarkhovich Prokopenko. His pale, high-cheekboned face was flushed, his eyes wide, his expression indignant.

"Thank God you're here, Fyodor Fyodorovich!" he cried out when he saw Thomas and rushed up to him to explain.

Prokopenko was new to his job—Thomas had recently promoted him from senior waiter—and had encountered a problem in a private dining room that he didn't know how to handle.

There was a dozen of these rooms on the Variety Theater's second floor, all richly decorated with watered silk wallpaper, oil paintings, thick rugs, and mahogany furniture. Because their large internal windows were angled and curtained in a way that shielded those inside from public view but not from the stage, they were popular with people who had money and liked privacy.

Booking a private room also gave clients a place to entertain a performer they liked. This was a well-established practice in Moscow's vaudeville theaters, and managements encouraged it because guests would try to impress artists they admired with lavish orders of food and drink. The profits were split between the performer and the restaurant.

Prokopenko could barely contain his agitation as he explained that the problem in Room 3 began when the party of four who reserved it invited Natasha Solovyova, a young singer who just finished her performance, to join them and then tried to get her drunk.

Prokopenko had kept an eye on the room when Natasha went in, as he was supposed to, and when he saw that the two men in the party started to ply her with champagne, he employed the ruse Thomas introduced at Aquarium: Prokopenko swooped in and replaced her full glass with what he announced was her "special" brand, which was actually mineral water colored with a bit of tea. The clients weren't charged for this, the performer was out of danger, and she still got her cut from the rest of the tab.

However, on this occasion, the oldest man in the party, a foreigner of some sort, would have none of it and kept insisting Natasha had to drink what they poured her. Prokopenko could see that Natasha was getting very nervous. But she was also anxious not to upset the guests by leaving. So Prokopenko used another standard ploy: he came into the room to "remind" her that she had another "appointment." To his consternation, however, the foreigner and the other man laughed at him, said they were just getting started, and rudely told him, "Clear off!"

Thomas listened to the sordid story with annoyance. Natasha was a delicate young woman with blue eyes and pink cheeks who dreamed of enrolling in the Moscow Conservatory and becoming an opera singer. She had a sweet voice, was only eighteen, looked even younger, and still lived with her parents. Although Thomas didn't think her voice was strong enough for opera, he was touched by her ambition and decided to give her a break so she could earn some money. He put her in the vaudeville program, which included everything from acrobats to trained dog acts, to comedians, dancers, jugglers, and musicians. And having taken her on, he felt responsible for her.

He wasn't that protective of all the performers in Aquarium. Some of them had worked on stages all over Europe for years and knew the ways of the world. And although Thomas was strict about what he would and would not allow to happen in a private room in Aquarium, if the performer knew what she was doing and left with the guests willingly, it wasn't his business. This case was obviously different.

Telling Prokopenko to follow and watch him, Thomas trotted up the stairs and knocked on the door of Room 3. He had been in these kinds of situations many times before. The client probably had too much to drink and simply needed to be reined in. Thomas also knew that the color of his skin got people's attention and that Russians weren't very good at resisting authority.

There were no locks on the private rooms and Thomas didn't wait for an invitation. He put on a smile, opened the door wide and strode in. For a second or two he surveyed the people around the table to size up what he was facing and so they could all get a good look at him. He noticed that the heavy maroon curtain had been pulled over the window overlooking the stage.

Two men were in the room, the older short and heavyset, the younger tall and gangly. With them were two women, one in her thirties and the other in her fifties, wearing evening gowns and combs with ostrich feathers in their hair, the first one rose pink, the second black. The singer, Natasha Solovyova, in her short stage dress that reached to her mid-calves was sitting with her back to the door. She twisted around when Thomas came in and started to get up with an expression of relief on her face.

Thomas was on the verge of announcing who he was when the fat man, who had a napkin tied around his neck, stopped chewing the oyster he'd just slurped from a shell in his right hand and goggled at the intruder. Swallowing hard, he exclaimed in Cajun-flavored English:

"Well, ah'll be *dam'd*! Nevuh dreamt I'd see a *n* . . . . . heah!"

To Thomas it seemed as if an explosion went off in the room. He wasn't even sure he heard right. That word hadn't been uttered within his earshot since he'd shipped out of New York nearly twenty years ago.

But after a second, he felt the blood rush to his head and his heart begin to pound. He realized he had heard it after all. His smile faded, but he made an effort and managed to keep his composure. Looking straight at the fat man, who was grinning insolently at him as he wiped his mouth, Thomas replied in his deepest and slowest Black Delta drawl:

"Suh! It's a genuine plesha' to meet a real southe'n gentleman!"

The fat man's face dropped, his grin fading into open-mouthed astonishment. He hadn't expected this Black man to understand English, much less to hear a reply in the familiar tones of the American Deep South. The two women in the party looked completely bewildered as they glanced from Thomas to their companion. But the tall and gangly man at the table stared at him and frowned.

Thomas was gratified by the effect he produced. Then, dropping the "cottonfield" style of speech, he continued in his usual dignified tone with a trace of the South: "Allow me to introduce myself, I'm Frederick Thomas, an owner and the director of Aquarium."

He paused and looked at each of the four guests in turn, so no one felt left out of the developing drama.

"I've been told there's a problem with Miss Solovyova here," he continued, glancing at her and then at the older man, who, he realized, must have been the main culprit. Thomas spoke politely but didn't smile and intentionally raised his voice more than was necessary for the size of the room.

"*And I'm Cá-leb Fór-rest Díck-er-man!*" the fat man hammered out the syllables loudly. He hadn't recovered from his initial shock, but he had been made to look foolish and felt insulted by the Black man's bearing and manner.

"And I don't know what you're talkin' about, saying there's a problem," Dickerman continued with a sneer, "we're just having ou'selves a little *party*."

Thomas glanced at Natasha, who got up and was standing near Prokopenko by the door. Her nose was pink, and her eyes were glistening. She looked as if she would start crying any second. Her state clinched it for Thomas.

"Your party's over," he announced to Dickerman, dropping his voice to signal the finality of his decision. He repeated the same phrase in Russian to the others at the table, to be sure everyone got it.

Turning toward Prokopenko, Thomas curtly instructed him: "Prepare their bill, they're leaving."

The gangly young man at the table jumped up from his seat when he heard this and translated into English for Dickerman.

"The sonofabitch is throwing us out?" Dickerman shouted in disbelief, then turned toward Thomas: "You can't do dat! We ain't even finished yet!" he exclaimed, gesturing at the dishes and bottles crowding the table.

"Yes, I can. And yes, you are," Thomas replied firmly, "because I know what you were up to with this young lady!"

Prokopenko stepped back into the room from the hallway with the party's bill. Thomas glanced at it and gestured for him to give it to Dickerman.

"Here's your tab. Pay up and get out. And don't make me call the police," Thomas added, knowing how insulting this sounded and abandoning any pretense at politeness.

Prokopenko placed the bill on the table next to Dickerman, who remained seated, his eyes fixed on Thomas and burning with hatred.

Suddenly Dickerman bent sideways, and wheezing from the effort, picked up something lying on the carpet by his chair. A sly expression appeared on the older woman's face, and she glanced at Thomas. When Dickerman straightened up, his face flushed from the strain, Thomas saw that he was holding a thick wooden walking stick with a brass handle in the shape of what looked like a rattlesnake head. Thomas had seen enough timber rattlers in Coahoma to recognize the characteristic triangular shape.

Holding onto the edge of the table, Dickerman began to get to his feet, his girth slowing him down as he pushed his chair back. Thomas noticed an unpleasant, greenish yellow sheen hovering over the sour expression on his face.

Is this dumb cracker going to try to use that on me? he wondered.

The ends of Thomas's moustache rose as he smiled. He casually unbuttoned his jacket, let his arms drop by his sides, and shifted his weight to the balls of his feet so he could move quickly if he had to.

The younger man's eyes widened when Thomas mentioned the police. Seeing that Dickerman was lingering with his stick, and knowing his explosive temper, he took him by the arm and began to urge him in his accented English: "To hell wid' it boss, let's get outta this dump! It ain't worth dealin' with the cops!"

Dickerman looked at the younger man, began to say something, and abruptly closed his mouth. Without even glancing at the bill on the table, he pulled a thick wallet out of the inside pocket of his jacket, selected two one-hundred-ruble notes and threw them on the floor. But instead of leaving, he paused and surveyed the table for a moment. Reaching across it, he knocked over an uncorked bottle with a demonstrative flourish. The amber-colored liquid poured out, spreading across the white tablecloth in a wide stain. The room began to fill with the heady aroma of spirits.

Dickerman looked at Thomas and smiled sourly.

"Thank you-all for a most memorable evening. I can assure you, suh, I will *nevuh* forget it!" he squeezed out in a high voice trembling with injury.

Making an exaggerated bow, he gave his arm to the older woman, who was a head taller than him, and headed for the door, trying to walk with as much slow dignity as he could muster. Neither made eye contact with Thomas, but as the woman floated past him in her black silks, he noticed that her face and neck were heavily powdered.

The tall lanky fellow strode by with an angry expression, followed by the younger woman. She had been pretty once but now looked faded and worn, with brittle, ginger-dyed hair and dark red lips. Her rose-colored dress looked too youthful for her. As she passed Thomas, she glanced at him and smiled. He saw that her pupils were wide open and she walked with exaggerated care.

She's on cocaine, flashed through his mind.

He'd seen enough of these "frost" addicts over the years to recognize the signs. It was a scourge in Russia like everywhere else, and things had gotten so bad that newspapers were reporting American and German plans to start restricting its sale.

After the four left, Thomas calmed Natasha as best he could, gave her a fresh handkerchief so she could dab at her eyes, and told Prokopenko to put her in a cab for home.

He watched for a moment as a waiter began to clean up the mess in the room, which filled with the smell of the spilled liquor. He recognized it as American bourbon. Few customers ever ordered it, but Thomas kept one brand he liked on the list of spirits at Aquarium because it reminded him of home. He picked up the bill Dickerman left on the table and saw that the two hundred rubles more than covered the cost of what the party had ordered. Thomas decided he would add the entire sum to Natasha's pay for the week.

CHAPTER SIX

As soon as he stepped out of the Variety Theater's lobby onto the broad central allée leading to Aquarium's entrance, Dickerman exploded. Thrusting his stick at the gangly young man he shouted: "You told me the director of this place was an American, but you didn't tell me *what goddamn kind!*"

"I didn't know, boss!" the young man protested. He spoke English fluently but with a Polish accent. Born "Marek Bartkowiak" in Warsaw, he had simplified his name to "Mark Bartkow" after seven years in Chicago.

"He's famous in this town but no one told me he wasn't white," he continued. "It was always Mister Thomas this and Frederick Thomas that. And who could've imagined it? That jockey we saw, 'Wink' or whatever his name is, who won at the Hippodrome last week, is the only other Black I've ever seen in Moscow! Thomas was a surprise to me too when he appeared out of nowhere!"

Hilda Weber, the older woman in the party, saw how upset Dickerman was. She decided it was her duty to try to calm him, in light of what had developed between them.

"Well, actually," she said, also speaking English but adding some German words, which she thought made her remarks more expressive, "if you think about it, Caleb, dear, it is rather fitting that a *Schwarze* (Black man) would be in such a position here in *Russland* (Russia). As the Bible tells us, the descendants of Noah's son Ham include Africans and these semi-Asiatic Russians. So, you see, it is natural for Thomas to make his home in a backward country like this because, as you Americans might say, Russians and Blacks are birds of the same feather."

Bartkow sniggered at the woman's explanation, which

pleased him. He'd despised Russians for their high-handed ways ever since his youth in Poland, and other Polish émigrés he met in Chicago taught him to hate Blacks.

Dickerman forced himself to smile. He had to show he understood what Hilda was trying to do and appreciated her deft turn of phrase. He also didn't want her to see how grievously he felt insulted. But his smile was unhappy, and he was far from feeling mollified.

Hilda drew him closer, pulling his arm into her waist, and patted him on the shoulder. She would make an extra effort to calm him tonight. When she drew near, he caught a whiff of something unpleasant beneath her sweet perfume. He couldn't tell if it came from her mouth or was something else but ignored it and looked up at her with gratitude.

By the time they reached their black coach, which was parked in a line with carriages, cabs, and a few automobiles along the curving driveway in front of the Aquarium's grand, colonnaded entrance, Dickerman's anger with Bartkow had cooled. Now, all he could think of was vengeance.

The mere thought that the Black piece of shit dared to throw him out made him tremble. He needed to be punished, soon and hard, the way he would be back home in the South. Images of the last lynching Dickerman saw in Louisiana flooded into his memory—the torch flames convulsing the night, the hooting and whistling crowd, the limp corpse dangling from a branch.

When they reached their black coach, Dickerman turned toward the two women, urging them, "Get in, get in!" and gestured impatiently with his plump hand. Once they were inside and out of earshot, he took Bartkow by the lapel of his dress suit and pulled him close.

"I'm going to get that uppity Black bastard if it's the last thing I do," he hissed. "And you're going find out about this high and mighty sonofabitch for me. How'd he get here? Where'd he get the money for his place? Where's he live? Has he got a family? And I want to know *quick*!"

Bartkow's expression became unhappy: "It ain't worth it boss! Forget the bastard! We got big plans and don't need to

bother with him. We have our whole stable now!" he emphasized, repeating what the boss said earlier. "Why waste time
on something that's going to slow us down and not make us
any money?"

But Dickerman wouldn't listen. As he hauled himself onto
the coach's step, making the entire cabin tilt toward him, he
ordered Bartkow brusquely to do what he was told and not to
argue. There was no way he'd let this Thomas get away with
the insult.

We have time, he thought. *The house is almost set, and
we'll open soon.*

Once seated, he thumped the ceiling with his cane.

The bearded driver Matvey tugged the reins, released
them, and commanded the horses, "Start!"

CHAPTER SEVEN

Thomas was sitting at his desk in his office and reliving his run-in with Dickerman, which had soured his mood. It didn't help that it happened on the same day as the awful news about the Nikitina girl and Martynov's nasty visit.

Thomas knew he'd gotten the better of that peckerwood, and it felt good to put him in his place and see him leave speechless. But the attempt he and his filthy gang made to get young Natasha drunk was a dirty business, and the encounter with Dickerman awakened bad old memories of white men in the South, their faces contorted, spitting hatred.

Thomas hadn't run into many other Americans during the years he'd lived in Moscow. The few tourists—all white, of course—who showed up at Aquarium were reasonably polite, or at least pretended to be, even though they were always either surprised, shocked, or disappointed when they saw he was Black. Not one ever reacted with pleasure at meeting a fellow countryman so far from home. That happened only with touring Black American performers, who appeared on Aquarium's stages from time to time. The American vice-consul in Moscow, Nathan Smythe, was also racist, that was clear. But at least he kept his attitude in check whenever Thomas came on official matters because of the prominent position Thomas had in the city's entertainment business.

This Dickerman was something else. What on earth was he doing in Moscow with his sleazy entourage? And why did he have to come to Aquarium? Thomas wondered with

37

annoyance.

The encounter made him feel as if he'd been soiled by touching something repulsive.

Suddenly, he remembered how his father once had him pull a dead racoon out of Hopson Bayou near the family's cabin so it wouldn't spoil the water downstream, and how the swollen carcass split apart on the stick he used, spilling its awful black innards on the bank.

Thomas sighed, took out his pocket watch, thumbed the latch and saw it was almost 10 p. m. It was still early for Moscow's night owls, who would only be starting their evenings now. Many of the most popular restaurants with music and stage shows stayed open until dawn. Parts of Aquarium did as well.

Thomas decided he needed to do something to clear his mind. He moved from his desk to one of the leather armchairs and reached for his pipe and tobacco pouch on a side table, near a mother-of-pearl frame with a photograph of Hedwig, his first wife. As he lit up, filling the room with aromatic billows of his favorite Perique, he decided he needed to take the night off and that Stepanov and the others could handle things without him. He hadn't had any kind of break in over a week.

For a moment he thought he might just go home and spend a quiet evening. But then decided against it. He just couldn't endure seeing Valli's wounded expression and tear-filled eyes, and he didn't want to deal with her cow-like devotion.

They had been married for only eleven months, although they had known each other far longer, and he realized shortly after their wedding that he made a terrible mistake. Valli originally entered his and Hedwig's lives as the children's nanny when he was so overwhelmed with getting ready to open Aquarium, he barely had time to sleep. Then Hedwig fell ill. The doctor said it was double pneumonia and there was nothing he could do. Thomas sat helplessly by Hedwig's bed for four days and nights as she fell into delirium, her fever rising, her chest heaving as she struggled to breath in ragged gasps. Valli had already taken over supervising the household in addition to taking care of the children. When Hedwig died Thomas was so devastated, he didn't know if he would succeed in keeping his life together. But Valli was still there, efficient, running things, offering support. The children had grown attached to her, and Thomas was very grateful.

However, he soon realized gratitude wasn't enough. He saw the way Valli looked at him, and he felt guilty toward her, but he also knew he couldn't make himself love her. The shape of Hedwig's soul had fit his the way a right hand meets the left. Valli's didn't even come close.

And now, when the success he had first dreamt of with Hedwig seemed to be in hand, his life was poorer and more uncertain than when he first met her a dozen years ago. He was just a waiter then, newly arrived in Moscow from Saint Petersburg and working in a restaurant catering to office workers, and she was a clerk in an uncle's dry goods shop near the Arbat where he bought his clothes. Most of her family lived in East Prussia, where her father was a telegraph operator. She was pretty and smart, his German was good enough for him to joke with her, and they fell in love despite the differences between the worlds from which they came. Their tie grew deeper with the birth of each child.

Moscow was the first place where Thomas put down roots since he left the South in 1890. He still had his children and loved them dearly, but because of Valli he felt his family was broken. Divorce was difficult in Russia because the Church was involved, although the lawyer Thomas talked to explained it was much simpler for a foreigner.

As he watched the curls of smoke spread along the ceiling, Thomas decided to put off going to his apartment and seeing the children until tomorrow—it was already late. He called Strelka over, stroked her long muzzle as she looked up at him, then went to his desk to call the young clerk on night duty. He wanted to make sure the clerk took her for a good walk along Tverskoy Boulevard and fed and watered her.

He had thought of another way to distract himself.

Two days ago, Prince Vladimir Vladimirovich Istomin, Thomas's closest friend in Moscow, telephoned him that he had reserved a table for Friday at Yar, where he was planning to watch his latest romantic interest perform with her Gypsy choir and have dinner with her. He invited Thomas to join him if he was free, and Thomas just now decided he was. He also decided he should try to find a companion for himself. If he succeeded, Istomin could give more attention to his Gypsy and Thomas wouldn't feel like a third wheel.

For the last two months Thomas found his thoughts returning quite often to the owner of a fashionable ladies' boutique at 17 Kuznetsky Most, one of the toniest shopping streets in Moscow. He had met Mina Samoylovna Tsiffer a half-dozen times when he went to "*La Reine de Versailles*" (The Queen of Versailles) to buy special gifts—shawls, fans, handbags, parasols, gloves; all very beautiful and expensive—for the biggest stars who were going to perform on his stages. The gifts were small personal touches that the stars always appreciated, and he liked selecting them himself. Mina Samoylovna was Jewish, a widow in her mid-thirties who had inherited the business from her father, ran it initially with her husband, and then, when he died in a riding accident six years ago, even more successfully by herself.

She was beautiful and slender, with dark, almond-shaped eyes, a long, delicate nose and a birth mark perched above full, soft lips that naturally formed a slight pout. When he first saw her, Thomas was immediately stirred, and, to his amusement, felt an overwhelming desire to lean across the counter separating them and kiss her on the mouth. He could tell she liked him too, and when he came back on other occasions, she would gently send away whichever shop girl had approached and tend to him herself. The last time, a week ago, he tried to get a bit closer and felt a shiver of excitement when he tossed a ball of coquetry to her, she caught it in midair and tossed it right back.

Thomas looked at his watch again and decided it wasn't

too late.

Nothing ventured, nothing gained, he thought, trying to encourage himself. Mina had given him her "private" card, which listed her home number as well as the boutique's and he recited it to the telephone operator at the central exchange.

It had been a long time since he'd called a woman this way, and he felt a twinge of apprehension when the phone rang on her end. But when she picked up, she didn't sound surprised, which pleased him. She replied it wasn't too late for her and agreed to his proposal quickly and without affectation. He could hear her smiling as she spoke, which pleased him even more.

Forty-five minutes later, Thomas was waiting for her in the marble lobby of the new apartment building on Tverskaya Street where she lived, which was around the corner and a ten-minute walk from her boutique. Despite the long day he had already put in at Aquarium, he felt fresh and crisp after washing up and changing his linen in the suite attached to the back of his office. He had also put a touch of brilliantine on his moustache, got a fresh pink rosebud from the flower stand in the Variety Theater foyer, and inserted it into the lapel of his frock coat.

CHAPTER EIGHT

Friday, May 22, 9:25 p. m.

The scandal at Aquarium had forced Dickerman and his party to leave so early in the evening that traffic in the center of Moscow was still heavy, and it took their coach over an hour to drive to the mansion in the southern part of the city they used as their base.

Dickerman passed the trip fuming in silence. His humiliation by Thomas rankled badly and brought back a lot of unhappy memories. It also seemed to him as if every cart or wagon driven by a shabby peasant or workman in a torn caftan had been waiting for his coach to come near before it lurched out into the stream of vehicles and interrupted his progress. The ride was so uneven he kept having to grab the strap by his side to steady himself. His companions took their cue from his sour expression and tried to be as quiet as possible and not even move so they wouldn't reignite his volatile anger.

Dickerman hated Blacks because he thought they were to blame for the War Between the States—as he always insisted on calling it—which, in his mind, had caused all the ills that befell his family. The Yankees had burned Ophite Hall, the great manor house in St. Landry Parish, Louisiana, that his grandfather had built on his sugar cane plantation. The family had sunk into humiliating poverty during the Union Army's occupation. And in 1872, his father had been killed while leading a KKK raid on Black sharecroppers in the Mamsella Bayou neighborhood—sharecroppers who, unexpectedly, had guns.

Caleb remembered with bitterness the hard-scrabble farm on which his mother and uncle tried to eke out a living by growing corn and raising hogs; their cramped shotgun shack with the uneven floors and leaking roof; the terrible summer of 1878 when three of his siblings—two older sisters and a younger brother—died during the yellow fever that swept through the Louisiana lowlands like a scythe. Before the War, the Dickermans and other rich planters used to escape the pestilential clouds of mosquitoes that came every summer by moving to cooler and safer uplands. But after the old South was destroyed, Caleb's family became as vulnerable to every kind of misery as the poorest Blacks.

One of Caleb's strongest memories from his childhood was sitting on the porch at dusk with his mother, her rocking chair creaking monotonously, and listening to her lament the "Lost Cause" and the family's fall from its antebellum heights. It pained him to see how worn and bitter she was. What she said also angered him, and he decided early on that the kind of life they were living now wasn't for him.

At twelve he began to accompany his uncle on trips to Opelousas, the St. Landry Parish seat. It made Caleb feel ashamed to see the stoop-shouldered, prematurely grey man pull off his torn hat even before he went up the courthouse steps to plead for a little more time in connection with a note coming due or a tax payment that was late.

Sometimes Caleb would have to wait for him for hours. To escape the sweltering sun, he'd pull their battered wagon under a live oak across the street from the courthouse. The old mule would doze and lazily twitch its ears to chase away the buzzing gadflies, and he would watch the townsfolk in their fine clothes and shiny carriages going from one fancy house to another.

At first, Caleb dreamed of becoming one of those self-assured gentlemen in white linen suits and broad-brimmed hats who smoked long, black cheroots. But he soon learned it took money to become a lawyer. And as he grew older, he decided he didn't have time for "honor," a notion he found hard to pin down but that occupied an outsized place in his mother's memories of the past. Instead, he began to look for occupations that paid quickly and well.

His success was swift. By the time he was sixteen he had moved to New Orleans, where he started out as a hustler on the docks moving contraband and helping to fence loot stolen from cargo ships—bags of coffee, bolts of fabric, liquor, tobacco. After a couple of years, he expanded to the brothels of Storyville, the city's red-light district, first as a bouncer—he was short but strong and fought dirty—then as a procurer and manager, and finally, at twenty-one, as the owner of his own small place with a half-dozen Black and mulatto "girls." The money was good, especially for a farm boy from Mamsella Bayou, and Caleb started to spend time at the city's racetrack. But although the action was exciting and he enjoyed being in the company of the other swells, he didn't like losing money by betting without an edge.

It was then that fate seemed to intervene, and it wouldn't be for the first time in his life. He met an old veterinarian at the track who was drinking himself to death and who mentioned in passing that he knew ways to make one's own "luck" at the races. Caleb befriended him, and in exchange for taking care of his bar tabs got him to impart everything he knew about doping horses. The man had ways to make horses run faster or slower, and how to make them push through injuries.

Initially, Caleb had some qualms about what he was doing. The more he learned about racehorses, the more he admired their beauty and strength, and it shocked him to see how many collapsed and died after being "doctored." But he steeled himself and persisted because the money was just too good to pass up. Some of the drugs he used at the track were popular in brothels as well, which made for efficiencies and economies.

By the time he turned twenty-four, Caleb was making decent money from his two businesses. But New Orleans was crowded with criminal gangs, the Sicilians were the worst, and no matter what Caleb tried, he couldn't break out of being a small player.

He decided to try his luck and rolled the dice. In 1903 he sold his interests in New Orleans and transplanted himself to Kentucky, the country's premiere venue for thoroughbred racing. The staggering amounts of money riding on the outcomes made his skills highly desirable. And the stable owners who paid him generously to make sure their horses won—or their opponents lost—also often became clients of the new, fancier brothel he opened in Lexington's Hill district. Everything went well until 1908, and Caleb was starting to think about a family and a maybe a horse estate of his own, when anti-gambling zealots started a campaign to shut down the racing industry, including the fabled Kentucky Derby. Profits began to drop and Dickerman realized he had to think of something else.

Once again, fate seemed to intervene. With the collapse of the domestic market, breeders of Kentucky thoroughbreds had to look for other places to sell hundreds of horses, often at steep discounts. They turned to England, France, even South America.

Buyers also came to the Bluegrass State, including one very well-heeled one from Russia, a certain Philipp Anastasovich Nevzorov, whose family had originally made its money in oil wells in Baku. He owned a 5,000-hectare estate near Rostov-on-Don in the south of Russia with over 600 horses as well as one of the biggest stables in Moscow. His lust for winning knew no bounds, and when he heard of Caleb Dickerman's specialized skills, he became very interested in meeting him.

Nevzorov hired the Pinkerton Detective Agency to investigate Dickerman, liked what he learned, invited him to dinner at Burrowes, Lexington's fanciest restaurant, and offered him a contract as a "trainer" at his stable in Moscow, with bonuses for every "win." When Caleb converted the sums in the contract from rubles to dollars, he realized he could make more in Russia in three years than he could have in Kentucky in a decade when things were still going well.

He agreed, even though he had to sell his properties in a down market and Russia was as remote and unknown to him as Timbuktu. Nevzorov also paid top dollar for a dozen horses in Lexington, and Dickerman accompanied them on the long trip via ship from Baltimore to Hamburg, by train to Berlin, and then on to Moscow.

The capital of the German Empire is where crooked fortune smiled on Dickerman even more broadly, as if she was waiting for him and determined to do whatever she could to draw him deeper into iniquity. He stopped in the city for a week to let the horses recuperate after the ocean voyage and so he could arrange shipments to Moscow from the city's pharmaceutical and chemical industries, which were the best in the world. During a visit to Stark GmbH, a leading drug manufacturer, he met, seemingly by accident, a well-mannered young man with good English who was affable, rich, and interested in discussing business opportunities in Russia.

He introduced himself as *Freiherr*, or Baron, Wolfgang von Stürmer, invited Dickerman to lunch at the famous Hotel Adlon, drove him there in his sleek black Mercedes, and ordered a lavish meal with champagne. As they talked, Dickerman hinted cautiously about his past in New Orleans and Kentucky and about what he was looking forward to in Moscow. Stürmer was neither shocked nor surprised. He confided he was a member of a "consortium of successful businessmen" and hinted broadly that profits and certainly not morals were what interested them. And, he added with a contemptuous sniff, as far as he and his colleagues were concerned, barbarous Russia was a wide-open field for ventures of many different kinds.

What Stürmer did not reveal, however, was that he was a captain in German Military Intelligence, that his "consortium" consisted not of businessmen but of several high-ranking officers on the German Imperial General Staff, and that he had been looking for a front man like Dickerman for the past two months.

46

Stürmer's immediate superior was the redoubtable Colonel Georg Michaelis, the head of the Königsberg branch of the General Staff's Abteilung IIIb, its intelligence service for the Russian Empire. Michaelis was also one of the leading figures in the faction of the German Army advocating war with Russia because of Germany's need for *Lebensraum* (living space). He believed war was both inevitable and imminent because of geopolitical and economic competition between the two empires. To prepare for it, he began to organize a broad range of operations—from having his agents compromise and blackmail senior civilian and military figures in the Russian government, to stealing military and industrial plans, to subsidizing Russian revolutionary groups so they would destabilize the country. The operations were all expensive, but the General Staff granted Abteilung IIIb a generous budget of 5 million gold marks a year.

On the day after they met, Stürmer continued to cultivate Dickerman, who appeared to be exactly the type of experienced, venal, and ruthless collaborator he needed. But being prudent, Stürmer decided to investigate further. Using the encrypted Hughes machine at the General Staff building on Königsplatz, he telegraphed the Imperial German Embassy in Washington, D. C., and asked the senior military attaché to make inquiries with the New Orleans and Lexington police departments about Dickerman.

The information he got forty-eight hours later regarding the few aspects of Dickerman's past known to the police—which were just the tip of the iceberg of Dickerman's achievements—reassured Stürmer that he had found his man. When they met again the day after, Stürmer suggested a joint venture that made the southerner's head spin.

One of the results of Dickerman's deal with Stürmer was the mansion at 17 Kochkinsky Lane that became his base in Moscow. It was on a quiet street in the Khamovniki district on the southern edge of the city, near the historic, sixteenth century Novodevichy Convent. A solid brick structure in a gloomy neo-Gothic style, with arched windows, gables, and sharp spires, it was built shortly after the great fire that destroyed much of Moscow during Napoleon's invasion in 1812. It had belonged to a rich merchant, whose family—as the nineteenth century progressed into the twentieth—gradually sank into moral dissipation and financial ruin.

For the kind of operation Dickerman was starting, the mansion was perfect. It was big, with two dozen rooms of different sizes, including grand reception rooms; it sat in the middle of a park over a hectare in size and was planted with old trees that shielded it from view; and the entire estate was surrounded by a tall wooden fence with solid gates at the main entrance and another, smaller set in the rear. Much of the Novodevichy neighborhood still consisted of large empty lots and gardens, which made it easy to come and go without being seen, especially at night.

Stürmer made a series of financial and legal arrangements in connection with the property that were like Chinese boxes stacked inside each other and concealed its connection to German Military Intelligence. It was also easy to conceal the connection from Dickerman, who was dazzled by how much Stürmer and his consortium were willing to spend on renovations of the property.

Work began as soon as the purchase was completed: repainting and re-wallpapering rooms; refinishing elaborately carved woodwork; adding major plumbing, heating, and electrical upgrades, including two telephone lines; replacing worn furniture and rugs; and installing some secret features. When the work was done, the place once again looked like a rich man's grand home. Stürmer also came up with the name "Convent" for the place. Considering what the mansion would be used for, the name's inappropriateness amused him.

CHAPTER NINE

Friday, May 22, 11:15 p. m
18 Tverskaya Street

When Mina stepped out of the brass cage of the elevator which the grey-haired, uniformed doorman opened for her with a bow, she looked up at Thomas from under her brows and smiled broadly. She was ravishing in a tightly fitted emerald dress, a short capelet covered her shoulders like wings, and a small, black top hat edged with lace perched charmingly over her right brow. When Thomas approached her and removed his Panama, she extended her right arm and arched her wrist with swan-like grace so he could kiss her hand. It was soft, manicured and smelled of good perfume—Guerlain, he guessed.

A long, dark green "Turcat-Méry" limousine—advertised by the French manufacturer as "The Automobile of the Connoisseur"—was parked at the curb. It was one of four automobiles Thomas maintained for use by Aquarium's most important patrons, and for himself when he wanted something special. Glancing at the driver standing by the rear door, Thomas tilted his head toward the front to signal that he was going to help the lady into the back himself. After they were seated on the supple, black leather seat, Thomas instructed the driver to take them to Yar and not to rush. Once the limousine pulled away onto Tverskaya Street he leaned back and looked at Mina.

For a second, he hesitated, feeling oddly constrained. He spent so much time on public view and interacting with people that he never had to search for words and believed he could speak to anyone, anytime, and about virtually anything. But this was different. He hadn't courted a woman in a long time and felt he should be careful. He didn't know Mina well enough to talk about anything very personal. And this certainly wasn't the time to allude to his failed marriage.

The Turcat-Méry passed rows of horse-drawn cabs, some other automobiles, and a few late delivery vans clattering across Strastnaya Square, then swung between the statue of Pushkin, who seemed lost in thought, and the pointed belfry of Strastnoy Monastery. Turning away from the window toward Mina, Thomas commented on the elaborate decorations going up on the streets and the facades of buildings in preparation for the imperial family's visit—flags, bunting, portraits, intertwined monograms illuminated with electric lights.

But Mina also seemed reserved and replied politely without showing any real interest in the subject. After a few initial phrases in Russian, Thomas switched to French, as he had previously when in her boutique. His French was better than his Russian and he preferred to use it when subtleties of wording were important. Mina also spoke French fluently, thanks to governesses, even though she had been born and raised in Moscow.

Thomas decided to try another tack. "I'm delighted you could come tonight, Mina Samoylovna," he began, continuing to address her by name and patronymic as was customary in Russia, "because I'll be able to introduce to you my dear friend, Prince Istomin, whom we will be joining, together with a new friend of his."

"Prince Istomin?" Mina asked, looking into Thomas's eyes, and pausing almost imperceptibly after the title.

Thomas understood immediately why Mina had hesitated, but he also knew what to tell her to ease her concerns.

"Yes, I'm sure you'll like Vladimir Vladimirovich," he replied. "He's the most liberal and charming Muscovite I know. He avoids using his title whenever he can, believes Russia needs to be transformed into a socialist democratic republic, and I suspect—although he hasn't admitted this to me, and I don't want to ask—that he gives money to the SRs."

"Really?" Mina responded, sounding genuinely surprised. The majority of the Russian nobility were monarchists, or at most in favor of modest political change in the empire. But "SR" was shorthand for the notorious Socialist Revolutionary Party, which was known as the party of "bombers," and was dedicated to overthrowing the imperial regime by violence.

"What an unusual man," Mina replied. "How ever did you meet someone like him?"

Thomas understood what was behind this question too, and that it also was personal for her.

Like anyone who had grown up and lived in Moscow, she knew how stratified Russian society was—by birthright, wealth, and social standing. Jews in particular were the target of official and unofficial discrimination (rather like Blacks in the United States, Thomas always thought). Mina alluded once to the difficulties her father had when he first came to Moscow from Minsk. And even now, when her boutique was well-known and attracted customers from the city's uppermost social ranks, Mina still noticed the superciliousness with which some members of the nobility, and even some from the merchant class, smiled at her when they left with their purchases. For Thomas to refer to Istomin as a "dear friend" was very unusual and revealed a lot about both men.

"It started with English," Thomas explained. He was both relieved and happy that he found something to talk about that interested her and reflected well on him.

"Vladimir Vladimirovich was with a group of friends having dinner, I stopped by to greet them, my appearance made him ask if I was an American, and when I said yes, he switched to English. We found other things in common later and became good friends. It turns out his mother was English, and she grew up near Kostroma on the Istomin family's estate."

"That's an unusual place for an Englishwoman to wind up in Russia," Mina observed, "they usually prefer Saint Petersburg, and even often dislike Moscow." What Mina would like to have said was that many of the Englishwomen she'd encountered in her business were dreadful snobs, worse than many of the men.

Thomas noticed the shimmer of antipathy in Mina's remark but knew what would dispel it.

"Her father was an engineer," he explained, "and brought his family with him from Manchester when Istomin's grandfather hired him to build a linen factory on his land and manage it. The English girl and the landowner's son fell in love. There was some initial opposition from his father, but they overcame it, married, and the result was Vladimir Vladimirovich. He learned English from his mother and probably inherited a lot of his political views from her too since she was a socialist and a suffragist."

"What a wonderful story!" Mina exclaimed, not expecting this twist. "And I know Kostroma linen, which is very fine, although there are many manufacturers."

"You may well have seen Istomin's. His factory won prizes, here and abroad, and is still quite profitable, which allows Vladimir Vladimirovich to live comfortably in Moscow."

"He lives for his . . . pleasure?" Mina asked. For someone like her and her father and others in their circle, living well was the reward for working hard for every ruble they earned. She liked that this was the case with Thomas too and had little respect for those who didn't have to lift a finger and were still rich.

"He does what he wants now, but he was an engineer by profession—he said it was his English grandfather's influence—then enlisted in the army when the war with Japan broke out in 1904, rose to the rank of major and saw some serious action in Manchuria. He's also a sportsman—loves hunting and fishing. And he's a good boxer. A Welsh foreman worked in the family's fabric mill and taught him when he was growing up."

Mina shifted in her seat and turned toward Thomas.

Gratified by her interest, Thomas added, "You know, we spar together quite regularly. There aren't many boxers in Moscow and I'm glad I found him."

"Fyodor Fyodorovich, now you're *teasing* me!" Mina exclaimed. "Do you mean to tell me you do this kind of fighting," she clenched her fists and circled them in front of her face.

The gesture was so charming and unlikely coming from her that Thomas burst out laughing. "Yes, indeed, and Vladimir Vladimirovich and I are well matched. It's a wonderful sport."

"I've never actually seen it . . . performed . . . is that what one says about it?" she asked.

"Well, we don't have boxing in Russia, although it's popular in Europe. And of course, in the United States. I've actually been thinking of trying to introduce it at Aquarium. You'll have to come and see us sometime—we're well matched."

"Isn't it dangerous? It must take courage to face another man who intends to beat you with his fists!"

"Oh, we use protection, gloves and padding of various kinds. There's no real risk. If you want to hear about real danger, you should ask Vladimir Vladimirovich about his adventure with a tiger in Siberia."

"Goodness, a *tiger*! . . ." she started.

But a flood of bright light distracted her and she stopped. The automobile was slowing in front of the soaring entrance to Yar.

When the restaurant's celebrated owner, Aleksey Akimovich Sudakov, rebuilt it a few years ago on its old location on Petersburg Highway near Petrovsky Park, he told his architect he wanted patrons to feel they had arrived at a destination that was nothing less than spectacular. The result was the new Yar—a modernist palace dedicated to pleasure with triple height ceilings, cupolas rising five stories, and giant torchères flanking the doors, each three times as tall as a man.

CHAPTER TEN

Friday, May 22, 11:45 p. m.
Yar Restaurant, Petersburg Highway

Two doormen in double-breasted black coats with gold piping on the lapels strode up to the limousine and doffed their caps as they opened its rear doors. Thomas instructed the chauffeur to come back at 3 a. m., joined Mina on the sidewalk, and offered her his arm.

The soaring white marble foyer of the restaurant was a foretaste of what lay ahead, and Thomas looked around with a connoisseur's appreciation. Tall bouquets of lilacs, the masses of flowers as thick as foam, poured out their sweet fragrance, which mingled with the sounds of a string orchestra in the dining room playing an airy Viennese waltz. Crystal pendants in the chandeliers overhead multiplied the bright electrical lights and filled the mirrored walls with trembling reflections.

Yar was not only one of the most famous restaurants in Russia, but well-known throughout Europe, and the famous Baedeker travel guide characterized it with Anglo-Saxon understatement as "much frequented in the evening (not cheap)." Thomas learned a great deal when he worked there for four years, until he left to take over Aquarium with his partners.

He barely had time to take everything in before the maître d'hôtel in charge of greeting guests was briskly walking toward him, a smile of welcome on his broad, smooth face, his eyes crinkling with pleasure.

"Fyodor Fyodorovich, *my dear sir!*" he exclaimed, then

adroitly paused to bow to Mina and murmur "Madame" before returning to Thomas. "It's wonderful to see you, you are our very own!" he went on with restrained enthusiasm. Like all of Aleksey Sudakov's senior employees, he knew how to balance a dignified, self-respecting manner with the utmost attention to a client. "I regret to say Aleksey Akimovich is not here tonight. He'll be very disappointed to hear he missed you!"

Mina glanced at Thomas when she heard this and resolved to ask him later what his connection with Sudakov and Yar was.

Thomas shook the man's hand. "It's good to see you Alexander Trofimovich," he greeted him warmly. "Yes, please give my best to Aleksey Akimovich," he said, pausing for a second before explaining, "We're joining Prince Istomin tonight."

The expression that appeared on the maître d'hôtel's face suggested this was the best possible news he could have hoped to hear this evening. He waited for a moment while Thomas deposited his hat on the coat check counter and Mina unpinned hers and gave it to the young woman attendant. Then, extending his left arm and letting Thomas and Mina precede him through the arched entrance into the warmly lit dining room, he skillfully slipped ahead of them and led the way to the front of the restaurant near the stage, half turning back toward them in a sign of respectful hospitality.

It was approaching midnight, but the evening was in full swing, and the dining room didn't have a single empty table. The familiar, infectious atmosphere of happy indulgence for which Yar was famous washed over Thomas: the clink and clatter of silverware over the sounds of the string orchestra, the hubbub of conversations, a woman's rippling laughter, the delectable pop of a cork being pulled. Thomas caught a whiff of one of his favorite dishes as he walked by a table, baked sterlet *au beurre blanc*—a house specialty: a small sturgeon cooked in a white butter sauce. He noticed with approval that the couple—a pink-faced fellow with muttonchops who looked like a banker, and his matronly wife, her elaborate coiffure adorned with a spray of orchids—had a bottle of Chablis sweating in a silver bucket by the table. As Thomas followed in Mina's wake, weaving with easy grace between the closely spaced tables, several of the women he passed watched his progress with an interest they tried to conceal from their companions.

Istomin rose to his feet when Thomas and Mina were only halfway to his table, in the row nearest the stage and second from the left. He stepped toward Mina as she approached, Thomas introduced them, and she gracefully offered him her hand. As Istomin inclined his head and simultaneously raised her hand to his lips, she noticed the frank admiration in his eyes. The maître d'hôtel was hovering behind Mina, so Istomin left her to be seated by him and turned to Thomas.

"*Golubchik!* (My dear fellow!) I'm delighted you decided to come," he said with enthusiasm, using his favorite folksy expression, and after shaking Thomas's hand drew him closer and leaned in. Thomas smelled Istomin's musky cologne as the bristles of his beard brushed his face and they exchanged three light kisses on the cheek. "God loves the Trinity," was how Istomin had jokingly explained the Russian practice the first time, when Thomas had stopped at two, in the French fashion. Before pulling away, Istomin squeezed Thomas's arm and whispered in English, "She's completely delightful!" Thomas smiled in response, pleased with his friend's reaction.

Istomin's warm manner put Mina at ease and her reservations faded. "It's very kind of you, . . ." she started, and was going to address him as "Prince," but remembered what Thomas had said, "Vladimir Vladimirovich, to invite us to share your table." She looked around, "The place is quite full, and we would not have gotten in. We might very well have starved!" she added with a laugh.

Istomin chuckled in response, happy she was comfortable enough to joke. "The pleasure is entirely mine, Mina Samoylovna," he replied, "I'm delighted to make your acquaintance. And I make it my mission tonight to ensure you do not go hungry!"

Istomin ordered a bottle of Veuve Cliquot, "to celebrate our acquaintance," as he gallantly said to Mina, and while the waiter filled their flutes, she examined their host more carefully. He was about Thomas's age or a few years younger, in his late 30s, and very handsome, with a long, oval face and large, strong features—widely spaced grey eyes, a chiseled nose, and a powerful chin. There was some grey in his temples, but he still had a full head of chestnut hair that matched his trimmed beard and moustache.

Turning to Thomas, and continuing to speak in French, as they had during the drive, Mina asked him how it happened that he was so well known at Yar. "I imagine it's because of your business dealings?" she suggested.

But Thomas explained in a straightforward manner, as if it wasn't anything unusual, that he had worked as the owner's assistant and senior maître d'hôtel at Yar before taking over Aquarium.

"So that's when you both met," Mina said, trying not to sound too surprised, and glanced at Istomin with curiosity. When Thomas told her during the drive that he had first met Istomin when he was having dinner, she assumed it was at Aquarium and Istomin had been a guest there. But it turned out that Istomin hadn't thought it was beneath him to befriend a man who was still an employee at Yar, even if a senior one.

"Yes," Istomin replied. "But I have to say that as wonderful as Yar still is, it's not quite at the same level as when Fyodor Fyodorovich was in charge of the dining room. It's not that the food and drink have gotten worse. Certainly not, as I hope you'll agree!" he said to Mina. "But I don't know anyone else who was as good at reading clients as Fyodor Fyodorovich was . . . and remains of course, although elsewhere!"

Thomas shook his head, grinning: "You exaggerate, my friend!"

"I do not!" Istomin protested. "It was amazing how he could tell instantly not only what a patron's mood was by just looking at him, but he also knew what to suggest the person should order to help adjust the mood in the right direction. Using both food and drink! And," he emphasized, "he never forgot a repeat customer's tastes. He was a mind reader and a magician!" Istomin said with finality.

"Well, I see you might be dangerous company, Fyodor Fyodorovich," Mina interjected with a sly smile.

"How so?" Thomas smiled back, pleased to hear the flirtatious note in her voice.

"A lady can have no secrets from you, you see right through people. And you know how to conjure them to do your bidding!"

Thomas laughed out loud, reached across the gleaming white tablecloth, and allowed himself to pat her hand.

"Mina Samoylovna, you have nothing to fear!" And then, in a teasing tone, "I assure you that whatever secrets I discover about you, I will keep strictly to myself."

Thomas decided that it was turning out to be a most enjoyable evening, unlike any he'd had in a long time. He hadn't expected Mina to engage in such playful relations and was happy to continue.

Valli surfaced in Thomas's mind only briefly. When he was following the maître d'hôtel to Istomin's table he realized there were probably people in the dining room who recognized him—this often happened to him in Moscow's restaurants, theaters, and the like—and some of them also probably knew that he had recently remarried. But the thought of Valli's dowdiness and doleful expression seemed so incongruous in Yar's high-spirited atmosphere that Thomas pushed it away.

Istomin noticed the waiter hovering nearby. It was time to order. After surveying the menu briefly, Mina asked for crayfish salad followed by roasted squab, which the waiter described, when she quizzed him, as "perfection." Istomin took his time, and after being assured the Flensburg oysters were first-rate and had been received the same day by the Eliseyev Brothers Emporium, chose them, to be followed by roast beef, which he specified had to be rare. Thomas remembered how much he liked the way they did the baked sterlet and asked for that. And since the others were having seafood to start, he ordered beluga caviar with toast points. A small carafe of frozen vodka to go with the caviar—which he preferred for its brilliant clarity to champagne—a bottle of Bâtard-Montrachet and another of a Nuit-Saint-Georges rounded out the order.

While they waited, Thomas decided not to continue with the "mind reading" and "magician" theme Istomin had introduced, even though the subject intrigued him. Dropping the theme also allowed him to move away from the flirtation with Mina, which although pleasurable for him could not be shared by his friend.

"I mentioned your encounter with the Siberian tiger to Mina Samoylovna," he said, glancing at Istomin and then at her. "Won't you tell her about it? Now that's an example of something genuinely uncanny."

"I'd be happy to," Istomin replied, and added politely to Mina, "if you don't think a hunting story would bore you."

The remark made Mina feel slightly miffed. She didn't like it when men assumed things about her "just because" she was a woman. But she concealed her reaction and answered brightly, "Not at all. Any true story about a man and a tiger is bound to be fascinating." As she said this, she looked straight into Istomin's eyes but couldn't tell if he had noticed the little barb in her reply.

"Well then," Istomin began, "I like to revisit this event because it's the most remarkable thing that's ever happened to me. Thus far, at any rate. In fact, in some important ways, it changed my life."

CHAPTER ELEVEN

Dickerman's coach passed through the gates of his estate and was pulling up to the mansion when he looked out his window and saw a long automobile parked beyond the porte-cochère. It was a Mercedes touring model, its polished black carapace reflecting the carriage lights by the front door.

Stürmer's here, he thought with annoyance. *That popinjay didn't warn me he was going to visit.*

Dickerman resented the surprise inspection, which he was certain this was.

Stürmer's visit also made Dickerman nervous because there had recently been trouble with two of the abducted children, and he didn't want the German to know or suspect anything about it. A month ago, Sergey, a quiet, soft-looking boy who seemed to acquiesce quickly to captivity, had been allowed to come downstairs as a reward for his good behavior and to listen to the phonograph in the living room with two other compliant children. But when the boy noticed that the front door of the mansion had been left ajar, he leapt up, dashed through it, and almost made it to the property's front gate before he was caught by one of the workmen who doubled as guards.

Hilda tried to persuade Dickerman to get trained dogs to prevent these kinds of things in the future. But Dickerman refused, his face twisting with disgust. He never explained, but he had been attacked by guard dogs early in his career on the New Orleans docks.

And then only two weeks ago, things got even worse. Dasha, a pale, blue-eyed, blonde Russian girl, who seemed meek and apathetic, suddenly exploded into a fit of hysterical sobbing and screaming when Bartkow came into the dining room. He grabbed her with one of the workmen and they managed to carry her upstairs, twisting and kicking, but she broke loose on the top landing and before anyone could stop her threw herself over the low banister and hit the marble floor headfirst. The two workmen buried her body at night on the estate's grounds and hid the grave with dead leaves and a cluster of small birches they dug up and replanted on it.

Both events shook Dickerman. If these two could pull such stunts, so could others. Maria Chernyshova, the younger woman in his gang, was so upset that she began to talk about pulling out, and he had to use threats and promises to keep her in line. He also had to get Bartkow to replace the dead Russian girl with another one like her to fill out the collection he had planned. And although grabbing the new one went smoothly the day before, she became difficult as soon as she woke up. Now, as Dickerman walked to the house, all he could do was hope there wouldn't be any more outbursts.

Stepan, one of the two Golub brothers who provided the gang's muscle, was on duty downstairs and unlocked the massive oak door with its wrought-iron hinges in the form of coiled serpents. Despite the bright electrical wall sconces and chandelier Dickerman installed in the high-ceilinged entry foyer, the space still looked somber. It was as if the slate floor and dark, wood-paneled walls swallowed whatever light fell on them. Inside the central hall it was even worse. There were deep shadows in the corners and under the grand double staircase, where the light didn't reach at all, creating the unpleasant impression of openings leading to narrow passages that disappeared somewhere into depths of the mansion.

We'll need to get palm trees or something and flowers to brighten things up more, Dickerman made a mental note to tell the housekeeper.

"Ask him," Dickerman said, taking off his hat and looking at Bartkow.

"How are the children?" Bartkow asked Stepan in Russian.

"Everything's quiet," the guard replied. "Boris is upstairs. A couple of them started crying when they woke up, but he gave them some more of the drink and they went back to sleep."

"OK, good," Dickerman replied after Bartkow translated.

"Stürmer?" he asked, turning toward Stepan.

The man gestured to the library across the hall. Dickerman told Bartkow and the two women to wait for him in the seating area between the halves of the staircase, screwed his face up into a smile and crossed the foyer to the library.

The German, dressed in a double-breasted black suit, was sitting stiffly in a leather armchair, and holding a book that he'd taken off a shelf. When Dickerman walked in, he set it aside and stood up with a smile he had rehearsed in front of a mirror until he'd gotten it right—a balance between politeness and hauteur.

Stürmer was a slight man with cropped blond hair, a narrow chest that accentuated his unusually broad pelvis, and a small mouth that he camouflaged with a wide moustache. His one striking feature was his large, dark eyes, which, as Dickerman noticed with surprise when they first met in Berlin, were touched up with black eyeliner. Dickerman later concluded Stürmer was trying to make his eyes look even bigger to produce the impression he was scrutinizing you intently.

But in the end Dickerman didn't care about the man's pretense or poses. The German had a lot of money and lived up to every one of his promises. Those were the only things that mattered.

"My dear baron, it's a surprise to see you here, but I'm pleased, *I'm pleased!*" Dickerman exclaimed, dragging out his words in theatrical bluegrass style and clasping the German's hand with both of his. When Dickerman wanted, he could be charming and his whole manner now exuded confidence and genial hospitality.

"I only wish you'd let me know so I could've had some refreshments ready for you. And I'd have rushed back earlier from our outing."

"I did not want to trouble you, Mister Dickerman," Stürmer replied in his precise, flat British English. He had only a trace of a German accent and made very few mistakes.

"But I thought it would be useful to see how you are progressing with everything." Stürmer saw no reason to reveal that he wanted to catch Dickerman unprepared.

Looking around the library and gesturing at the walls of books, he said: "From what I have seen here on the first floor, so far, you have done an admirable job of preparing the house, which looks very . . . superior, shall I say?"

"I'm pleased you like it," Dickerman responded enthusiastically, "and I'm happy to show you the rest too. You'll see how your gold was put to good use."

Stürmer smiled in response and inclined slightly from the waist in a kind of partial bow. Dickerman suspected he wore a corset under his clothes to ensure he had the proper carriage.

"In fact," Dickerman went on, "I'm sure you'll also be pleased that our, . . . um, . . .," he paused, making believe he was searching for the right word, "our stable is now complete as well."

"Indeed? You have truly made rapid progress!" Stürmer replied, allowing his voice to register a note of surprise.

"We have a total of eight fillies and colts . . .," Dickerman continued in the same vein, pleased with his wit, "and their training or, rather, their breaking in has been progressing well. Very well, indeed." He paused and raised his eyebrows to see if Stürmer understood.

Seeing Stürmer smile again, he continued: "My team is here now and would be pleased to greet you, and then we can take a look at what we've got."

Stepping aside with unexpected briskness for a heavy-set man, he gestured with his arm toward the central hall.

Bartkow and the two women stood up when Dickerman

and Stürmer walked in. Dickerman's manner was now entirely different from how he'd acted earlier that evening at Aquarium and on the drive back. He was quick, attentive, and gracious. And knowing how important the rich young German was for their operation, everyone followed Dickerman's lead in kowtowing to him.

The older woman in Dickerman's entourage, erect, willful-looking, and with clean, regular features that made her look like a schoolteacher was Hilda Ulrikhovna Weber. She was an experienced procuress and madam who ran an expensive brothel in Riga before Stürmer recruited her to work with Dickerman in Moscow. Even though she had lived all her life in the Livonian Governorate, a province of the Russian Empire on the Baltic Sea with a large ethnic German population, she accepted Stürmer's offer not only because of the money she could make but also out of her long-held, secret sympathy for Germany, the land of her ancestors.

She was impressed by Stürmer's title and wealth, and when he walked up to her, she curtsied. To his greeting in Russian, she replied in fluent German, adding that it was a special pleasure to be working with a *Landsmann* (compatriot). When Stürmer offered her his hand and smiled in response, his moustache moved, but his eyes did not change.

The faded younger woman, Maria Antonovna Chernyshova, spoke only Russian easily, but like others in her business had enough French, English and German to get by. She had been a prostitute in an expensive Moscow brothel for several years and was very popular with her clients because of her looks, sweet disposition, enthusiasm, and fondness for any kind of debauchery, which she liked to enhance with drugs. A rich Moscow industrialist decided that he liked her style and persuaded the owner of the brothel to sell it to him; then he put Maria in charge so he could be completely "at home" when he stopped by. Hilda heard about Maria Chernyshova's establishment from some of her own clients who had visited it, and after making inquiries, and with Stürmer's blessing, approached her on behalf of Dickerman's new venture. Chernyshova readily agreed to join—the money promised was too good to pass up.

Maria was by nature eager to please, and when she saw Hilda curtsey to the German, she decided to do it as well, thinking Dickerman would like it. But, in truth, what she felt most strongly at that moment was a growing craving because her cocaine-induced euphoria had started to fade on the drive back from Aquarium.

When Bartkow's turn came, he managed an awkward bow, and, to Dickerman's annoyance, thrust out his hand to Stürmer first, who took it with pointed condescension.

After the greetings and introductions were over, Dickerman invited Stürmer to follow him, beckoned to Bartkow, and led the way up the staircase. When they reached the second floor, Boris, the second Golub brother, rose from his chair in the hallway and placed his copy of the *Moskovskaya gazeta kopeyka* (Moscow Penny Paper) on the table next to him.

Turning to Bartkow, Dickerman lowered his voice to a whisper: "Tell him we want to see two or three of them, but quietly. We don't want to wake them. And make sure he chooses the right ones," he emphasized, to make sure Bartkow understood. "Just unlock each door so we can see in and then make sure to lock it up again."

To Stürmer Dickerman explained, "We're not going to turn on the overhead lights in the rooms of course."

Boris picked up the torch and ring of keys that were on the table and led the way down a long, carpeted corridor with doors on either side. There were polished brass electrical sconces between the doors, and the walls were hung with oil paintings of exotic landscapes, their surfaces glinting richly in the corridor's soft light. He stopped at the end on the right, and, after finding the right key, unlocked the door. A neatly lettered card on it read "Karina" in Cyrillic.

The lock was new, well-oiled, and hardly made a sound. Boris pushed the door halfway open, switched on the torch, which cast a pale, diffuse beam onto the room's parquet floor, and moved to the side.

Trying to be as quiet as possible, Dickerman stepped into the doorway and peered in. The smell of stale urine hit him and made him pause for a second. But he beckoned to Stürmer and then stood aside, thinking the German might as well get the whole experience.

As Stürmer leaned into the room, trying to make out what was on the bed, his heart started to beat faster. Visiting the Convent and actually seeing one of the captives was the culmination of a year's planning and work. He didn't notice the smell but reached out and moved Boris's hand up so the torch's faint beam fell on the bed.

A naked young girl lay across it, with the blanket and sheets bunched up against the wall and the pillows on the floor. A mass of long, curly black hair covered her face. Stürmer was so nervous he almost stopped breathing.

In secret, he had fantasized about such moments after launching Dickerman's operation, but he didn't anticipate he would react so strongly. He wanted to get closer, to see more—the girl was lying on her side, he could make out the curve of her narrow buttocks. The thought that he could reach out and run his hand along her thigh or her flank made him feel weak. But then fear welled up in him that he would wake her, that she would scream horribly or leap off the bed, and that the others would see the state he was in. He dropped his gaze to the floor and forced himself to pull away from the doorway.

Dickerman was watching him with what looked like an ironic expression. Stürmer noticed it, and the idea that he might seem ridiculous to this American plebian brought him to his senses.

"Hard to see very much," Stürmer said quietly after Boris locked the door. "Didn't want to wake her. What's her type?" he asked, trying to sound casual.

"They tell me she's Armenian, baron," Dickerman replied softly, quickly replacing his ironic expression with one of neutral politeness. "Oriental beauty . . . exotic, that sort of thing."

He gestured to the next door. "Would you like to see the others? Here we have Sergey, a Russian boy."

By then Stürmer had regained full control over himself

66

and replied matter-of-factly, "No need. Thank you. Too much trouble now, don't want to wake them. Just tell me who else you have."

But Dickerman wanted to toy with the German a bit longer: "Are you sure, baron? Perhaps you'd like to check a couple more? I'm happy to unlock . . .," and he gestured vaguely up the hall.

"No," Stürmer replied curtly and shook his head. He had already revealed too much interest and regretted it.

"We'll have photographs of all of them later, perhaps next week," Dickerman explained in a conciliatory tone, then started along the corridor, pausing in front of each door, and gesturing gracefully with his plump hand as if showing off a collection: "Duya—a Kalmyk girl . . . Fatima—Tatar girl . . . Ibrahim—Tatar. . . Masha—Russian . . . Sergey—Russian . . . Zina—Russian . . ."

"Sorry, sir—that's Anya," Boris corrected him in Russian, stressing the name.

Dickerman looked at him with annoyance, then at the card on the door.

"Right," he admitted. He could make out the Cyrillic script but forgot the girl's name. As if it makes a difference, he thought, they're not racehorses.

"Anya—Russian," he corrected himself. "And here, Dora— a Jewess, number eight," he concluded at the last door.

"Now, shall we go downstairs and talk?" Dickerman asked Stürmer.

When they were back in the library, the German declined a cognac, saying he would be driving that night. Dickerman poured four large, cut crystal snifters, kept one, and handed out the others. He and Stürmer took leather armchairs, and the two women shared a yellow, silk-upholstered couch with Bartkow.

Stürmer hesitated for a second, uncertain how to refer to what were no longer abstract elements in a cunning plot, but actual, abducted children.

"All eight . . . are from simple families, as we specified?" he asked. "Ones that cannot cause any troubles?"

"It was all very clean, baron, no one can identify us," Dickerman replied in a confident tone. "And in a city this size, believe you me, these families aren't going to get anywhere with the police." He then added with a smile, "Everything else has also gone smoothly, baron, very smoothly."

Stürmer nodded, then turned toward Hilda and Maria on the couch: "And the ladies, they approve how these youngsters look?"

Hilda smirked as she replied in English for Dickerman's benefit, saying they would all be highly desirable in the eyes of aficionados and that it would be possible to charge the highest prices. Then, following Dickerman's cue, she explained that all the children were "behaving just as we would like," and that she and "her colleague" had great experience in "making certain this continues."

"By employing cocaine . . . morphine . . . heroin?" Stürmer asked in an indifferent tone, even though his heart started to beat faster again.

"Yes, all three, as well as opium. In the right combinations," Hilda replied.

Maria didn't want to be left out and perked up at the subject, which was a specialty of hers. She volunteered that she had used this method, which was well tested, "to introduce" frightened young women to "the profession" and that it would not be a problem with the boys either. Eager to impress the German, she added that she could bring a half-dozen of her most popular women to the mansion when it was time. Even more could be added later, and there was no doubt that the mansion would the most attractive and selective brothel in the city.

"And the most expensive," she concluded with her throaty voice and seductive smile that was famous among dozens of clients.

Dickerman briefly described the rest of the Convent's staff and confirmed that they were also all in place. In addition to the senior members of the team, whom Stürmer had just met, there were Stepan and Boris Golub to provide "security," as well as a coachman, a housekeeper who doubled as a cook, and two maids. Their silence was insured by the money they were all paid and by their fear of retribution, which Dickerman instilled in them at length and in graphic detail, with Bartkow translating.

"And no trouble with anyone, no suspiciousness?" the German continued his quiz. "Your camouflage at the Hippodrome works well?"

"Everything's been as smooth as Kentucky bourbon going down a parched man's throat," Dickerman replied jauntily. He described how pleased the stable owner Philipp Nevzorov was with his results. A few other Americans worked as jockeys and trainers at the Moscow Hippodrome as well, so his presence there was entirely unremarkable.

No reason to bring up the run-in with that Black sonafabitch at Aquarium, Dickerman thought when he finished his summary. That was a personal matter, and he would settle it himself.

"Excellent, excellent," Stürmer answered. "I have with me the list of some of the clients we would like to visit here."

He pulled two sheets from his inside breast pocket and handed one to Dickerman. It was typed in German, but he assumed the American would be able to understand the names as he read some of them out loud, also adding who they were.

"My . . . partners compiled this from their . . . sources," he said, "and will help ensure that these gentlemen will know about our Convent."

Most of the names meant nothing to Dickerman, but he was impressed by the titles, ranks and positions in Stürmer's annotations. The list began with a *Grossfürst*, a grand duke or a senior member of the imperial family. A number of men had important positions in the Ministry of the Interior, the Foreign Ministry, and the Ministry of War. There were two generals and several colonels from elite guards' regiments in Saint Petersburg; bankers and newspaper editors; members of Moscow's City Council; and owners and directors of railroads and heavy industry factories, including the giant Putilov Steel

Works, which produced rolling stock and artillery for the imperial government.

"You see, most of these gentlemen are based in the capital and in Moscow, with some in Kiev and Warsaw. But even if they do not live in Moscow, we believe they might be interested in visiting. In fact, perhaps making a special trip to what is going to be the most . . .," Stürmer paused to choose the right words, "the most fashionable, and, shall we say, varied establishment in the Russian Empire. One that will be able to satisfy the most refined tastes."

He looked around the room, pleased that everyone was watching him attentively.

"We know, or, rather, have reason to suspect," he corrected himself, "that all these men have such establishments either visited before or have shown somewhat unusual tastes or proclivities, shall we say. It will be necessary simply to spread the word, discreetly, very discreetly of course, that there is a new place of great interest."

"In my own house, I've already started to hint something new is coming," Maria interjected eagerly.

"Quite right, word of mouth is the only way to do this," Hilda added. "But your partners as you call them, baron, and everyone else, are clear the Convent is a totally private establishment, yes?"

"Of course, or course, Frau Weber. They are very well instructed."

Stürmer understood her hint. Prostitution was legal in Moscow and was regulated by the police and a special medical board. But none of the best establishments in the city was registered officially, which made them far simpler to operate: no "yellow tickets" or age limits for the prostitutes, no restrictions about locations near churches and schools. Secrecy also made it possible to sidestep the accusation that pederasty was a unique abomination, which even some of the old-fashioned brothel owners made.

"As you see, baron, we'll be ready to start very soon, in a week or two," Dickerman said, setting down his empty glass and continuing in his genial tone. "And because I—because we, all of us," he added with an expansive gesture toward the others in the room, "have held up our end of the bargain . . . and I think you are pleased with the results, I believe this would be a good time to revisit the matter of . . . money."

"Oh, yes?" Stürmer replied, making believe he was surprised by this turn of events. In fact, he had anticipated it and discussed it with his superior when he was making plans for his surprise inspection.

"What do you propose?" he asked Dickerman calmly. "I believe we have been very generous and have a clear arrangement that satisfies everyone."

"Very generous, no question, very generous," Dickerman agreed quickly. "The money you provided for this house and for the . . . people, horses, . . . equipment, all that was very generous. And you deserve a return on your investment, that is only fair."

He paused and then said, emphasizing his words, "But considering that your return will be equal to ours, while we face far greater risks, I believe we deserve additional compensation for this, in the form of a greater percentage of the profits."

"How much, exactly?" Stürmer asked coolly.

"An increase from 50% to 60%."

That's not as much as I feared, Stürmer thought with smug satisfaction. He had anticipated two-thirds or even three-quarters.

But for the sake of sounding convincing, he hedged and made objections for a few minutes, and then agreed to a 60/40 split. The income from the Convent wasn't important to him or his "partners" anyway. What mattered was the threat of exposure and blackmail they would hold over the Convent's "clients," the photographs they would have to support the threats, and the power this would give them to paralyze or disrupt major sectors of the Russian Empire's war machine.

He's going to want more later anyway, Stürmer concluded, looking at the American's satisfied expression. But for now, the most important thing was that the plan he'd been working on for over a year was coming to fruition.

CHAPTER TWELVE

Saturday, May 23, 12:40 a. m.
Yar Restaurant

Istomin paused to take a sip of champagne and to gather his thoughts, then looked from Mina to Thomas, smiled, and began.

"The reason I remember my encounter with the tiger as vividly as if it happened yesterday is that it changed how I saw my life. In fact, how I started to see life in general.

It happened when I was with our army in Manchuria during the war with Japan. *What a disaster that was!* The ineptitude of the commanders and the thieving that went on behind the lines! . . . But I don't want to get started on that. In any event, I was in the engineering corps and working on repairing rail connections between the Trans-Siberian railroad and Mukden when the notorious battle broke out there in February 1905. We were completely outmatched, and I had to take command of an infantry company when every last one of its officers was killed. Every single one! But that, too, is another story. In any event, I was incredibly lucky and managed to get away without a scratch even though our army suffered a hundred thousand casualties—killed, wounded, and captured! Can you believe it? I'd never seen such carnage. It was what made me resign my commission when the war was over."

"Be that as it may, in early March, after our forces retreated from Mukden, there was a lull in the fighting, and I decided I simply had to get away for a while. I managed to get leave for a couple of weeks. I first went to Vladivostok and then to the Ussuri River basin to the north to do some hunting."

"I'd heard that this part of eastern Siberia was a paradise but had no idea of what it was really like until I saw it for myself. Pristine forests, gorgeous mountains, crystal-clear streams, lakes, all teeming with every kind of fish, bird, and animal! I was there in April and some snow was still on the ground in places. But the climate on the western slopes of the region is so temperate—it's shielded from the winds coming from Sea of Japan, you know—that wild cherry and apricot trees, and even grapes grow there."

"I went to a village that was recommended to me and asked around for a guide and soon found one. This was another surprise! My guide was a woman, the widow of a local Cossack who had worked as a guide for years, Zoya—Zoya Pavlovna Shchyogoleva, and she picked up her late husband's profession. He was much older than her and when he died, she was left alone. They didn't have any children. When I first met her, she was in her fifties and despite being tiny and looking like a wrinkled old granny, had amazing endurance. She could outwalk me any time and knew the entire wild region like her own backyard. I stayed for a week in a small room in her cabin and enjoyed her company very much. She was very simple in many ways and had little knowledge of the outside world. But I had the distinct impression that as far as some very important things in life are concerned, she knew much more than most priests, professors and philosophers ever suspected. My experience with her showed I was right."

"It was the afternoon of the third day. I was after pheasant and grouse and had had good luck the previous two days. Wandering with Zoya through the forests, climbing the hills, breathing the cool air fragrant with the sweet and spicy smells of spring was like bathing in a magical spring after the horrors of Mukden. On that fateful day, I remember Zoya and I had crossed a small clearing and entered a forest of pine, birch, and aspen covering a slope that rose before us. It had rained in the morning, a thin silvery mist hung in the air, but the sun was beginning to come out from behind the clouds. Zoya was always very quiet when we were walking this way, going first, and listening for the calls and those drumming sounds male grouse make with their wings. But on that occasion, she stopped dead in her tracks, turned around and softly whispered that we should go back. I was surprised and was about to ask her why . . . ."

Istomin stopped talking and looked up. Two waiters had appeared, one with the appetizers, the other with the carafe of vodka, wines, glasses, and an ice bucket, and began to arrange them on the table. They poured everyone some Bâtard-Montrachet and filled a small, stemmed glass with vodka for Thomas.

Although Thomas had heard Istomin's story before, the quiet intensity with which he told it was mesmerizing. Thomas had to force himself to turn his attention to the opalescent grey mound of caviar in the crystal dish before him. Mina was also being drawn into Istomin's tale. She watched him closely as he spoke and was slow to look down at her artfully arranged plate of crimson crayfish and yellow crescents of lemon.

"Look how lovely," Istomin gestured at the dozen freshly opened, large oysters glistening before him on a bed of ice. Picking up a shell he used a two-tined fork to pull out the plump, grey and tan flesh, and pop it into his mouth.

"Admirable," he said with enthusiasm when he finished chewing, "it really smells of the sea."

Istomin was as eager to continue with his tale as his companions were to hear it, but in his role as host he took pleasure in verifying that everything was to their liking. It was. Thomas downed his first pony of vodka and followed it with a generous dollop of caviar that he had spooned onto a small piece of toasted white bread. He smiled with pleasure as he ate, the sensation of the pure frozen liquor replaced by the lovely rich pop of the sturgeon eggs. Mina was working through her salad vigorously and replied to Istomin's question that all was wonderful.

Istomin didn't want to spoil his story by interrupting it while he ate and limited himself to answering some questions Mina had about the famous Gypsy troupe that was going to perform later. But after finishing his last oyster with relish, he refilled his glass of wine before the waiter could get to the table, drained it, and continued.

"Yes, so, as I was saying. Zoya began to insist that we should go no farther. She'd never acted this way before and I didn't understand why. There were still several hours of daylight left, I had room in my game bag, and I wanted to go on for a bit longer.

By then I had walked up to where she stopped. Zoya didn't answer me when I asked her again what was wrong and just shook her head. But I was a fool. I shrugged it off and took a few steps up the slope ahead of her. When I glanced back, I could see she was following me, and decided everything was all right."

"We went on this way for another couple of minutes, pausing once or twice to listen for grouse."

"I saw it when it was only some ten paces away. First, I spotted its enormous yellow-green eyes staring straight at me from under a small pine, and only then made out the black and orange of its massive head and muzzle.

Everything that followed couldn't have taken more than a second or two. I saw the tiger's head drop as it tensed for the attack, I twisted around to run, but it was too late of course, and I didn't even think of raising my shotgun. I heard a loud, terrifying snarl and felt a massive weight land on my back, a stabbing pain in my right shoulder, and I swear, the hot air of the tiger's breath on the back of my head and neck. I was sure I would feel the tiger's jaws next, and I knew there was nothing that could prevent it from crushing my skull."

"But then, an amazing thing happened. I suddenly heard a high-pitched voice chanting something. I opened my eyes, which I had shut in horror when the tiger knocked me down, and saw Zoya, not more than three paces away from me. She was kneeling, had bent down so her body was lying on the ground with her arms extended toward me and the tiger on top of me, and this extraordinary sound was coming out of her

75

mouth. It was like, it's hard to describe, like . . . a repeating musical phrase.

I watched her in amazement as she let her voice drop to a whisper, with her arms still extended toward me. As she chanted, I could still feel the crushing weight on my back but not the heat of the tiger's breath. Then, miraculously, the weight disappeared and a second later I heard the tiger snort from a distance behind me. I raised myself up a bit and twisted around in time to see it disappear into the forest where I had been heading."

"What an incredible story!" Mina exclaimed, clasping her hands together. So this old lady was able to save you from that beast by what . . .," Mina hesitated, not knowing what word to use, "talking to it? Singing to it?"

"I think she appealed, or prayed to its spirit, actually," Istomin said. "That's what she told me later. She apparently learned this from her mother, who was a member of the local Nanai people. Her father was Russian. The Nanai are like many of the other natives in Siberia and believe everything has a spirit—trees, rocks, water, animals, birds, and people of course—and you must know how to talk to them. In fact, it's necessary to talk to all the spirits to be able to live in harmony with them, in harmony with creation. This is what their shamanism is largely about, as I understand it. I talked to Zoya about this later, although she was reticent and didn't really like dwelling on it. She told me her mother taught her, and she also learned much by herself. There's a lot of Christianity in what Zoya believes too, probably from her father and her husband. Both were Old Believers."

The main courses arrived, the waiter poured the red wine for Istomin and Mina, and refilled Thomas's glass with the remainder of the Bâtard-Montrachet. Istomin began to order another bottle, but Thomas declined, gesturing to his empty vodka carafe to show he'd had enough. Mina replied that one glass of red would suit her perfectly.

Mina peppered Istomin with questions about the consequences of the encounter. He explained that although his back had been badly bruised by the tiger's paws and its claws left some deep scratches on it, no bones were broken, he wasn't injured seriously and made it back to Zoya's cabin in the village without too much difficulty.

In the days that followed she ministered to him in a way that was also remarkable because her treatments consisted of salves she made and spread on his back and included a session in a banya, or a traditional Russian sauna, that she fired up. She also made infusions with plants, mushrooms, bark, lichen, and other things she gathered in the forest and had him drink. The tiger was probably a female, Zoya told him, and its den and cubs must have been nearby. Otherwise, it wouldn't have attacked because Siberian tigers avoid people.

When Istomin asked Zoya what made her stop and try to dissuade him from proceeding, she seemed reluctant to say more than that it was a "feeling, like she could hear the tiger thinking."

Istomin ended by shaking his head and repeating that he was a "fool and a complete idiot" for not having taken Zoya's warning seriously.

"I'd love to meet someone like her someday," Mina said. She was thinking that because this was all so far outside the familiar borders of her life, it was also very appealing. "Somebody wise in ways we can't begin to understand."

Thomas looked at her when she said this. He'd been watching Istomin as he told the story, drawn in by its mystery, and was pleased that Mina seemed to be as enthralled by it as he was when he first heard it years ago. Not everyone reacted to it that way.

But the evening's surprises weren't over yet. Istomin replied to Mina that he'd be happy to arrange a meeting because Zoya had been living with him for the last six years.

He described how, after he left Siberia and resigned from the army in 1906, he didn't think much about Zoya for the first year. He bought a comfortable old house in Moscow in the

Patriarch's Ponds neighborhood and spent most of his time enjoying civilian life and the varied entertainments the city had to offer. During the summers, he went to his family estate near Kostroma, around 350 kilometers to the east of Moscow.

However, as time passed, thoughts of Zoya started to arise in his mind. He even began to dream about her and developed the nagging feeling he had left something unfinished in Siberia. The feeling of urgency kept increasing, so he wrote her a letter. He waited four months but got no response. When the spring of 1908 came, he bought a ticket on the Trans-Siberian Express to Vladivostok, hired a driver with a wagon and horses, and after four days on rutted roads that had been washed out in places by spring floods, and three nights in cabins with insatiable bedbugs, reached the village where Zoya still lived. She seemed genuinely happy to see him, but, oddly, not surprised. Things had gotten hard for her after the generous sum he left her ran out. With the end of the war, Zoya's work as a guide for officers on leave and others connected to the army had dried up. She never responded to his letter because it never reached her. That's when Istomin realized what the nagging feeling was that he'd had for months. In some way, Zoya had been asking him for help and he sensed it.

He now felt a new bond to her, didn't want to lose sight of her again, and offered to take her in so she could live in peace and security. He feared she might resist, but she agreed, without pretense or false humility, as if what he proposed was both good and just. Since Istomin was a bachelor, his Moscow house was much bigger than he needed, and he gave Zoya a wing which he never used. There was a large yard and garden as well.

"She's very undemanding," Istomin explained, "and tries to be helpful, so the servants accept her without complaint. She likes to make fruit preserves, pickle vegetables, and bake excellent *pirogi* (savory pies) with various fillings—meat, fish, vegetables, mushrooms."

"She's also very good with animals, and although she doesn't interfere with my groom's care for the two carriage horses and the two mares I keep for riding, she takes in stray cats and dogs and even nursed a turtle-dove chick that had fallen out of its nest. As a result, it now spends most of its time sitting on her shoulder."

"At first I thought she'd find it hard to put up with the noise and bustle of the city," Istomin continued, "but she managed. My home is in a quiet neighborhood, and she spends the summers in the country with me. She does miss the wilds of Ussuri. However, when I offered to arrange a visit, she shook her head and said the distance was too great. It's eight thousand kilometers!"

"She also found things about the city she likes, which pleased me very much. Old churches, monasteries, the Kremlin, historical places like that. She likes experiencing the past, as she explained."

"Yes, I'm fascinated by that in Moscow too, the deep roots people have here," Thomas commented, interrupting Istomin.

Except for his family's farm in Mississippi, he'd already lived in Moscow longer than anywhere else during his life. He'd often thought about how impossibly different this ancient city's history was from Coahoma's, where white planters brought slaves to settle a wilderness only forty years before he was born.

Learning about Moscow's past didn't make him feel it was his own, or make him like everything, but it was still a good way to get a feeling for the roots in the place. For his children, who were all born in Moscow, the situation would be entirely different.

"Zoya likes modern things in the city as well," Istomin went on, as if eager to defend her. He shifted his gaze from Thomas to Mina, who, judging by her expression, continued to follow what he was saying with attention, which he found flattering.

"I took her to Khodynka Field for an aeronautical exhibition a year ago, when Sikorsky was exhibiting one of his giant four-engine aeroplanes, and she loved it. I think she'd go up in one herself if it could be arranged."

"And there was another amusing development I certainly

didn't expect—she became very fond of moving pictures! She goes to see whatever is being shown in the city's cinema palaces, no matter whether it's one of these passionate melodramas with seductions and suicides, or an historical epic with bold warriors and ferocious enemies. Sometimes she'll sit through the same picture several times."

"It's remarkable that she would be so flexible after the life she led in Siberia," Mina commented.

"Yes, it is. But I also think she sees connections between what is new and what she's always known."

"Like what?" Mina asked.

"Well, with the moving pictures, when I asked her what she thought of them, she said seeing people who were only shadows was like the world of spirits that surrounds us but that we usually can't see. And as for the old churches in the city and the like, she said she liked to hear the voices and to talk . . . ."

Istomin stopped abruptly and looked down at his plate, as if he'd said too much and was embarrassed.

Mina and Thomas both noticed it, but what Istomin did was so unexpected that neither said anything.

After a moment, Istomin looked up, smiled, and changed the subject.

"Fyodor Fyodorovich visits Zoya," he said, looking into Mina's dark eyes, "and she enjoys meeting new people. She's very friendly, you know," he concluded.

"Yes, I like her very much," Thomas said, still thinking about what made Istomin stop. A confidence she'd shared with him, perhaps? Something he didn't want to betray?

"She reminds me of an old couple who lived on a farm near ours in Mississippi when I was a boy," Thomas went on. "I didn't know any of my grandparents," he added, looking at Mina and Istomin and paused, unsure if he should explain that this was because of the way enslaved Black families were broken up by their owners. But he decided against it. No point in getting into that now.

"So that old man and woman were sort of like the grandparents I never had. They loved children. And they were also mysterious about what they knew, like Zoya. We'd go to them for herbs and potions and things when we got sick since there weren't any real doctors around, not for us Black folk at any rate. And they told me and my brothers and sister wonderful stories about different animals, and even a spider, as I recall."

"Zoya likes to tell stories too," Istomin interjected, turning toward Mina again.

"Yes, I like to bring my children for visits because of this," Thomas said. "Zoya is also very sweet to them and likes to give them old-fashioned treats—simple things, like honey or apples. And the children respond. They sense something about her."

"I accept your invitation happily, Vladimir Vladimirovich, and can't wait to meet her!" Mina exclaimed energetically. "She sounds simply wonderful!"

"It's settled then," Istomin replied, sitting back in his chair with a contented expression on his face.

He fished out his pocket watch, raised his eyebrows at it, and announced the show would start in ten minutes.

They had all finished their dinners. Thomas was happy the sterlet was as good as he remembered it. No one wanted dessert, even though the aroma of blancmange with a fragrant raspberry sauce and fresh mint someone was having at a neighboring table was delectable. The men ordered coffee, Mina said she would love some tea and asked Istomin to order it as she got up to go to the powder room.

CHAPTER THIRTEEN

Thomas was feeling relaxed, and a bit flushed from the vodka and wine, and for a moment wished he could just go on this way, enjoying the restaurant's festive atmosphere and not change anything. But with Mina away from the table, memories of what happened that day began to seep back into his mind. Martynov and that Southerner weren't worth talking about because he could handle them by himself. Masha Nikitina's abduction was a different matter, however, and maybe Istomin could help in some way.

Thomas switched to English, as he and Istomin usually did when by themselves. Since it wasn't spoke as widely as French and German in Russia, it gave them a bit more privacy.

"I'm very glad to see you today," Thomas said. "I think I could use your help with something quite difficult. Difficult and upsetting."

Istomin wiped his moustache with his napkin, put it back on his lap, and leaned forward.

"I didn't want to bring this up with Mina Samoylovna here because it might be too troubling for her. You see, earlier today, one of my waiters told me his daughter was kidnapped. I had Markov look into it with his police friends."

"You remember Markov?" Thomas interrupted himself. Istomin nodded.

"He found out that a couple of other abductions of children in Moscow took place that look similar. He concluded it could be a gang collecting children."

"How do you mean collecting?" Istomin asked, his handsome face becoming serious.

"As far as Markov was able to find out, all the children were different national types, as he put it. My waiter's daughter is a blond and blue-eyed Russian girl. There was also a

Tatar boy and an Armenian girl. All about thirteen to fifteen and all described as exceptionally handsome children. Could be others, too, we just don't know because they might not have been reported to the police."

"What a *dreadful* thing to happen!" Istomin exclaimed, looking shocked. "What are the police doing?"

"That's a problem. Markov says all the detectives in the Moscow bureau have been dealing with security for the imperial visit in two weeks. Markov will see if Koshko might be able to spare a man."

"How ghastly!" Istomin said and shook his head, "*how positively ghastly*! I shudder to think what could happen to them."

"I've seen some of these horrors, you know," he went on. "When I was in Vladivostok during the war, I remember once taking a short cut through the notorious 'Millionka' neighborhood to get to the port. That was a mistake, I'll tell you! What a cesspool! I'm glad I had my service Nagant with me and that it was loaded. Among other memorable sights, there were children, nearly naked, standing outside some of the Chinese brothels and opium dens, trying to entice passersby. But I never imagined we could be facing anything like that here!"

Istomin reached for his glass and took a sip of wine as if to wash away the bitter memory.

"But how can I help?" he asked in a resolute tone. "Shall I see what I can do with the people I know in the Ministry of Justice and the Governor General's office?"

"Would you? That would help a great deal, I think. Markov is a good man, but he doesn't have your influence."

"Well, I'm not sure how much I . . . .." Istomin noticed Mina Samoylovna returning and let his voice trail off. Both men rose from their chairs.

"Just in time, it's almost one thirty and the show is about to begin," Istomin said as he rotated Mina's chair so she would have a better view of the stage.

He and Istomin opted to have cognac with their coffee after all, and a glass of tea in a silver holder was at Mina's place next to a small plate of crimson strawberry preserves.

They barely settled into their seats when the house lights dimmed, the curtain parted with a soft rustle, and Sokolovsky's Gypsy Ensemble filed out in a blaze of color.

In front were a dozen women in brightly patterned, long silk dresses shimmering in the stage lights—indigo, crimson, gold, emerald—with heavy necklaces and long fringed shawls. And behind them, like a dark background in a painting of a lush bouquet, a line of men wearing high-collared, black velvet tunics and black silk *sharovary*, or loose pants gathered at the ankles. The contrast was very striking, and a murmur of approval passed through the audience.

Half the men carried seven-string Russian guitars. One of them, old but still handsome, with thick, curly grey hair and the ends of his moustache twisted jauntily up, stepped to the front of the stage and bowed low to the audience, sweeping his right arm so it grazed the floor. He took a step back, raised his guitar, and slowly struck three plangent chords, pausing between each. The other guitars joined in, each with a slight hesitation, as if reluctantly, and then the chorus's voices rose and melded into a wave of harmonious sound that engulfed the dining room and everyone in it.

Thomas had heard Gypsies many times before in Moscow, where they were extremely popular, including in his own Aquarium, but he never tired of the beauty of their singing. The Sokolovsky chorus was a regular at Yar and had been famous for generations. It was a large clan consisting of several families in which the older members passed on their traditions to the young. Many of their songs were a mixture of Russian and Romani, the old Gypsy language, but even if you didn't understand all the words, the music still went straight to the heart. They sang about things that were eternal—love, loss, ecstasy, death. They sang with equal passion about joyful abandonment and the bitter sweetness of remembrance when happiness was gone.

The only kind of choral music Thomas had ever heard that moved him more, that had more "soul," and that remained a

living tradition for those who performed it—not just entertainment for others—was the Black spirituals of his childhood
and youth.

The coffee and cognac he had drunk spread a warmth
through his chest. Tears welled up in his eyes as the Gypsies'
ringing voices dropped, soared, then dropped again, sad and
happy at the same time.

He went back in memory to the Sunday mornings in the
log chapel his parents had built on the edge of their farm, the
bright sunlight flooding in through the windows, his sister and
brothers next to him on the bench, and the congregation filling the space with glorious songs of faith.

The Gypsies sang for half an hour, with one song leading
seamlessly into the next, and it was a shock, like coming out
of a trance, when they stopped.

The audience erupted in applause. Thomas looked at
Mina and saw she was dabbing her long eyelashes with a
handkerchief.

CHAPTER FOURTEEN

A few moments after the chorus left, a young woman in a crimson silk dress with a full skirt brushing the floor and a black flowered shawl over her bare shoulders appeared in the doorway to the left of the stage. Istomin had been watching for her and stood up. Thomas followed suit. It was Vera Sokolovskaya, a niece of the old man who ran the chorus. Beautiful, slender, and pale, with shining dark eyes and long black hair in ringlets that seemed to have a bluish sheen in the subdued light, she walked to the table as half the clients in the dining room followed her with their eyes.

She held herself very erect, the Gypsy *monisto*—a wide and long necklace of gold coins—that covered her breast trembling with every step, her knees pushing against the thick folds of her skirt. Istomin was beaming as he stepped toward her, then kissed her hand and escorted her to the table.

After making introductions, he busied himself for a few moments with what he could order for her. Thomas and Mina exchanged a few remarks about how much they enjoyed the performance, but mostly spent the time admiring the young woman, who was even more dazzling close up.

When the waiter left with her order, Vera and Istomin turned their attention to the others at the table, and the conversation switched to Russian in deference to her.

But it was not easy to engage young Vera, Thomas saw. In her throaty voice and faint Gypsy accent, she replied politely to his and Mina's compliments and questions about the choir, but also in a way that seemed detached, as if she wasn't really interested.

Her real focus was Istomin and herself. She moved her chair closer to his, leaned in, and kept touching him as she talked—his wrist, his arm, his shoulder, which she brushed possessively—all her gestures weaving an invisible barrier of intimacy around them that excluded everyone else. At one point when a loud burst of laughter at a neighboring table made Vera look away, Thomas exchanged glances with Mina, who smiled faintly at the beautiful young woman's self-centeredness.

Vera's open signs of affection pleased Istomin, but they also embarrassed him.

"Won't you tell us about the chorus's summer plans?" he asked, trying to steer her in a different direction. "Will you go to Warsaw and Berlin again?"

Vera visibly brightened at this.

But just as she was about to start, Alexander Butakov, the senior maître d'hôtel who had greeted Thomas when he arrived, suddenly appeared behind his chair.

"Excuse me, Fyodor Fyodorovich," he said, bending over and speaking softly so only the people at the table could hear, "but there's a telephone call for you . . . from a Mr. Markov. He said it's important," the maître d'hôtel added apologetically.

It took a second for Thomas to pull himself away from the company at the table. Getting a call from his director of security in the middle of the night and at a place like Yar was surprising. It was also uncanny because he had just mentioned Markov to Istomin.

Thomas's heart stumbled and then begin to beat more strongly.

"What? . . . Did he say what it was about?" Thomas asked, pushing his chair back as he got up, and staring at Butakov.

"No, sir," the maître d'hôtel replied, looking concerned, and thinking to himself that no call like this could be good news.

"I've put a telephone in the Blue Salon where you'll have complete privacy. If you would be so kind as to follow me," Butakov said, extending his right arm.

"I'm very sorry, Mina Samoylovna . . .," Thomas said hurriedly, tilting his head toward Butakov by way of explanation, then glanced at the others to include them in his apology.

Istomin looked worried, but Vera was smiling as blankly as if she was looking at herself in a mirror.

"Of course, of course—Fyodor Fyodorovich. Go. Please go!" Mina replied anxiously, making little waving gestures with her hands so he wouldn't delay.

"I hope you don't mind that I called you in this . . . unorthodox manner," Markov began as soon as he heard Thomas's voice. "Young Ivlev in the office told me where you were . . .." Markov stopped and cleared his throat before continuing.

"I regret to have to tell you this, Fyodor Fyodorovich, but I thought you should know right away . . . The police think they may have found Masha Nikitina's body."

Thomas felt as if a gust of freezing air hit him. He stopped breathing for several heartbeats and listened to the faint hiss in the receiver, thinking Markov might say something else. Somewhere, as if at a great distance, he could hear rasping noises on the line that sounded like snatches of conversation from which all meaning had been stripped.

"I know you took her father's grief very much to heart," Markov added quietly.

"How . . . Where did they . . .. They're sure it's her?" Thomas asked. He couldn't believe what he was hearing and pressed the receiver more tightly to his ear, as if this would make a difference in what he heard.

"I'm afraid it appears to be so. My contact in the detective bureau—he's a good man, knows what he's doing—said the girl is about fourteen or fifteen years of age, very pretty. He repeated this: very pretty, tall, long blond hair, faded light blue dress with rolled-up sleeves. She even has what looks like an old scar on her left hand. A bit hard to tell because there were cuts all over her arms and hands, like she'd been fighting off someone. But it's all like what her mother described to the police. A patrolman found the body on the Ustyinsky Embankment, near the bridge. And . . . she was . . . she had been violated, according to the look of things."

Thomas thought he could hear Markov's voice trembling.

"My God, my God," Thomas repeated, as the shock rever-berated through him. "That's near the Khitrovka, isn't it?"

"Yes, sir, near where the Yauza flows into the Moscow River. A nasty place. *Very nasty.* All kinds of criminals and foulness there."

"How can we be certain it's her? I mean, who can identify her? You told me Nikolay Ferapontovich knew her?"

"He only saw her once, and last year at that. I thought of him right away and called him before calling you, sir. Just to check, so we'd know where we stood. He said he wasn't sure if he could identify her. I'm afraid that leaves only her parents. We don't have anyone else who knows her . . . knew her well enough."

The thought that Nikitin or his wife would have to identify the dead girl horrified Thomas. His heart sank at the prospect of having to deal with this, and he looked away from the tele-phone for a moment, letting his eyes wander over the intricate baroque plasterwork decorating the blue walls of the high-ceilinged salon.

But then, as if a voice had called out to him, Thomas real-ized there was no choice, that it had to be done. It could not be delayed, and he was the one who had to do it.

"I need Nikitin's address," he said, his tone hollow. "Can you get it for me?"

The old police officer replied at once, as if he had antici-pated this moment too. "Let me come with you, sir. No need to do it alone. I've been through this kind of thing before and could help you. It'll be hard for everyone."

Thomas hesitated. But the prospect of having Markov with him was an enormous relief.

"Thank you, Sergey Sergeyevich. Thank you very much."

Thomas looked at the clock on the carved marble mantel-piece. "It's nearly two-thirty. I'll come back to Aquarium now, but I need to make a stop on the way," he added, remembering Mina. "I should be able to get to my office by . . . three o'clock. Could you go to Aquarium in the meantime and find Nikitin's address? Ivlev will know where to look in the files."

"Of course, sir. But let's agree that I'll be by the main

entrance at three. You won't have to come inside to find me. It'll make things quicker."

Thomas returned to the dining room in a daze, scarcely noticing the festive clamor around him which was growing as the night built to its culmination.

"Well, my friends," he said when he reached the table. He remained standing but put his hands on the back of his chair to steady himself.

"I'm sorry, but I've been called away. Apparently, there was . . . an accident . . . a very bad accident with one of the employees at Aquarium."

He couldn't imagine telling them anything approaching the truth and used the first excuse that occurred to him.

"Mina Samoylovna, I regret spoiling our evening," he said looking at her, then shifted his gaze to Istomin, "as well your generous hospitality, Vladimir Vladimirovich." He felt as if he had been split in two and was watching himself from a distance as he spoke.

"My dear fellow, don't give it another thought," Istomin replied, rising to his feet with a look of alarm on his face and still holding his crumpled napkin.

Mina was so shocked by Thomas' distraught expression that she reached out and clasped his right hand firmly with hers.

"Please, don't be concerned, Fyodor Fyodorovich," she said earnestly, looking up into his eyes. "I've had a wonderful evening, thanks to you and to Vladimir Vladimirovich," she glanced at Istomin and flashed a weak smile before turning back.

"You should go now, your matter is important. And please don't . . .," she interrupted herself, "I'll ask the restaurant to call me a cab."

Even beautiful Vera seemed sad when Thomas bowed to her. She'd been looking forward to telling everyone about her choir's command performance for one of the grand dukes during the imperial family's visit to the city.

"Thank you all," Thomas replied, touched by their concern but also feeling strangely dissociated from it as he struggled to make sense of what Markov had told him.

"However, if you'll allow me, Mina Samoylovna, I'll still take you home. I must get back to Aquarium and it's on the way. We may need to take a cab because . . ."

Thomas was about to say that he couldn't wait for his Turcat-Méry to come at three o'clock when Butakov, who had been watching attentively from a distance, walked up and whispered that the driver had returned early. The automobile was already at the entrance.

CHAPTER FIFTEEN

Saturday, May 23, 3:05 a. m.

Thomas's drive back from Yar with Mina was awkward. The prospect of having to wake Nikitin in the middle of the night and take him to identify the body of his murdered daughter filled Thomas with dread and he couldn't think of anything else. Mina saw how troubled Thomas was and felt sorry for him, but their acquaintance had been so brief that she was unsure about what kind of consolation she could offer. His silence and preoccupied air made her fear she might trivialize whatever dreadful news he had gotten.

Thomas glanced several times at Mina during the drive, her refined profile silhouetted against the drifting patterns of black and grey outside the automobile's window. But she didn't look back.

When they pulled up to her apartment building on Tverskaya Street he escorted her inside, and although a doorman was on duty in the lobby, waited with her until the elevator arrived. Only when the attendant opened the brass door did she look up at him with a sad smile.

"I hope everything will go as gently as possible . . . for you . . . and for . . . everyone . . .," she said in French.

"Thank you, Mina Samoylovna," Thomas replied, then added, "perhaps at a happier time . . .?"

Her eyes remained sad, and she smiled only with her lips, then nodded, and offered him her hand.

Markov was already at Aquarium's main entrance, standing in the white halo of a gas streetlight, when Thomas's automobile pulled up in front of the colonnade. He walked over briskly, opened the rear door himself before the chauffeur could do it, and dropped into the seat opposite Thomas. He switched on the electric light above his seat. A brown leather briefcase was on his lap. Despite the late hour, his eyes were alert and he looked determined.

"I took the liberty of gathering these things from the Aquarium's offices with Ivlev's help after he got the address," he started to explain without any preamble.

Placing the briefcase on the seat next to him, Markov pulled out a thick, tan, paper-bound volume.

"All Moscow, Address and Reference Book, 1912," he read out loud, squinting at the title on the cover. "We'll need it to find Nikitin's house."

Next were two small metal cylinders with hinged covers on one end. "Electric torches, so we can find the house number in the dark," Markov explained. "Not a lot of streetlights where we're going."

He held up a flat pewter flask. "Cognac, if we need it for poor Nikitin. To soften the blow a bit. Could help."

Lastly, Markov pulled back the left lapel of his suit jacket to show Thomas. "And I'm armed, just in case. Khitrovka is a nasty part of town. Even the local patrolmen are wary of it . . . in any event, those who aren't on the take," he added, shaking his grey head, and giving a contemptuous snort.

"You've thought of everything, Sergey Sergeyevich," Thomas said, feeling chastened by Markov's foresight in comparison to his own bewilderment.

"It'll be all right, Fyodor Fyodorovich," Markov said in an encouraging tone, and started to lean forward before stopping abruptly. He noticed Thomas's confusion and was going to reach over and pat his knee the way he would have a rookie's but thought better of it.

"We'll get through it together, step by step," he began and picked up the address book.

Holding the volume under the ceiling light as he flipped the pages, Markov located Nikitin's address, then unfolded a map of the Sushchevksy District in the back of the book, and after scrutinizing it for several seconds while muttering "Pokrov . . . Pokrov . . . Pokrov . . .," put his finger on a spot half a kilometer north of the Lazarev Cemetery.

"Here it is, 17 Pokrovskaya Alleyway!" he said. He then glanced toward the chauffeur sitting behind the glass partition. "We'll need him tonight, sir. For several more hours at least."

Thomas nodded and started to crank down the partition to tell the man.

The chauffeur kept pausing to look at the map he had spread across the steering wheel as the automobile crept through the unfamiliar neighborhood, its headlights bouncing up and down the rutted dirt road and illuminating sections of tall, weather-stained, grey wooden fences and gates shut for the night.

The address book indicated that Nikitin's home was on the eastern side of Pokrovskaya Alleyway, a short distance from where it branched from Voznesensky Lane. The chauffeur took what seemed to be a right turn—the area wasn't built up fully, and there were broad spaces between some of the properties that made it hard to tell where the road was—then stopped and turned off the engine.

Thomas and Markov got out and looked around, trying to orient themselves. The sky must have been overcast because it was so dark they had difficulty making out where the fences were on either side of the road. The air was cool, and Thomas felt a light breeze. As he took a step away from the automobile, he caught a whiff of manure. The only sound was the slow ticking of the engine as it started to cool.

Markov turned on his torch and walked along the wooden fence on the right until he came to a gate with a number, played the light over it, then moved to the next one. Thomas followed, his torch throwing a pale oval on the dusty, hard-packed earth of the street and the scraggly weeds growing along its edge.

"Here it is, number 17!" Markov said in a loud voice,

pointing his beam at the white, crudely painted numbers.

Then, to Thomas's shock, Markov walked up to the gate and began pounding on the boards with the side of his fist, shouting, "*Ni-ki-i-i-tin! Ni-ki-i-i-tin!*"

The booming noise and shouts were so unexpected that Thomas winced. He wanted to rush to Markov to make him stop when a dog on the other side of the fence began barking furiously. A moment later, another one started up somewhere behind them, then a third and a fourth farther down the street.

"*Have to do it, sir!*" Markov shouted to Thomas over the barking which was becoming louder and more hysterical as the other dogs joined in. "*Only way to get anyone up around here at this time of night!*"

Thomas froze, his torch pointing at the gate, and watched helplessly as it shook under Markov's blows.

It seemed to Thomas that the racket went on for an unbearably long time. But after a minute, a feeble light appeared on the other side of the gate, then grew in the gap between its two halves as someone approached.

Markov stopped pounding. When he leaned forward and peered into the gap, he saw a sliver of Nikitin's pale face and his right eye wide with fear.

"*It's me, Boris Frol'ych! Please open!*" Markov shouted.

Coming out of his stupor, Thomas also stepped forward. Raising his voice so he'd be heard over the dog, which now sounded as if it was choking with rage, he shouted "*Boris Frolovich! It's Thomas! I'm here too . . . with Sergey Sergeyevich!*"

Thomas heard Nikitin gasp and begin to fumble with the iron latch. A woman's voice, nearly drowned out by the dog's piercing howls, shouted behind him, "*Borya, Borya, what is it?*" and then a second later to the dog, "*Trezvonka! Trezvonka! Enough! Stop it!*"

The left half of the gate swung open, revealing Nikitin, wearing a ragged striped robe with untied shoes on his bare feet and holding a kerosene lantern. A short-haired, rust-colored mutt was panting at his side and wagging its tightly curled tail. A second later, a barefoot woman in a night shirt and a scarf over her head and shoulders ran up behind him.

Markov didn't wait. He pocketed his torch, stepped across the gate's threshold, and clasped both hands on Nikitin's shoulders, gave them a firm shake, then reached out with his right and drew the woman toward her husband.

"Come here, Marfa Savelyevna! Come!" he urged her. "Now hold your husband's hand," he instructed her and bent down to take her arm. "You must both be strong and help each other."

"*Okh! My God!*" the woman gasped. Her knees buckled, and she would have fallen to the ground if Thomas hadn't dashed forward and caught her.

Nikitin's panic changed to horror. He clutched Markov by the shoulder and peered into his face.

"Is it M . . . Ma . . . Ma . . . Masha?" he stammered, as if afraid to speak her name.

"Yes. I'm sorry. Yes. It may be," Markov replied, and glanced at Thomas, hoping he would understand that it would be better not to get the parents' hopes up.

"The police found a girl. Her description . . . Anyway, we need you to come with us . . .," Markov said, wrapping his left arm tightly around Nikitin's shoulders, bringing his face close to his, and nodding to emphasize what he was saying. "You need to see . . . to see if it's her . . . there's no one else who can do it . . .."

Nikitin's lips began to tremble, and his eyes filled with tears. Marfa twisted around with a sob and buried her face in Thomas's chest.

His heart swelled with her pain, and he gently put his hand on her back. He felt paralyzed by his helplessness, and all he could do was to embrace her with his pity.

The whole neighborhood had been awakened by the dogs, the banging and shouting, and a half-dozen neighbors rushed over, gathering by the gates of the Nikitins' yard with kerosene lanterns and candles in tin holders. They all knew what happened to Masha. It wasn't a good sign that the two important-looking men showed up in the middle of the night with their big automobile, the likes of which no one had ever seen in their neighborhood before.

Whispering among themselves, they watched as Markov walked Nikitin back to the door of his house, his arm still wrapped around his shoulders to support him. Thomas followed with Marfa, who stumbled several times on the hard-packed earth and leaned heavily on him.

Nikitin came out a few minutes later, fully dressed but alone. He looked dazed and his face wet with tears.

"Marfenka will stay with Petenka," he explained to Markov and Thomas in a quavering voice. "Petenka loves his sister very much . . . and she loves him. Marfenka will help Petenka pray for his sister to the Mother of God. They are kneeling together now . . . praying before our family icon . . . the icon of the Most Holy Mother of God of the Veil . . . she is our defender and our protectress."

Hearing Nikitin's words, a handsome, bearded old man leaning on a stick by the gate called out, "May She answer their prayers!"

A kerchiefed, round-faced woman next to him shook her head sadly and crossed herself.

"And don't worry, Frol'ych," the old man added, "we'll look out for Marfa and Petenka while you're gone!"

Others in the crowd nodded and murmured in approval, "We will, Frol'ych, we will! You can count on us!"

As Nikitin followed Markov and climbed into the back of the Turcat-Mery, the kerchiefed woman raised her right hand toward them and made the sign of the cross in the air.

The powerful automobile raced through the sleeping city. It passed a train of wagons loaded with bricks lumbering down the pavement on Bolshaya Presnenskaya Street and several cabs on Tverskoy Boulevard with revelers whose shrieks and laughter echoed in their wake. The other streets were empty. The windows in the surrounding buildings were dark. The widely spaced streetlights did little to dissipate the gloom and the rushing darkness swallowed the headlights' beams.

Thomas and Markov sat close on either side of Nikitin on the back seat and when the automobile went around turns, they let their shoulders press into his, as if wanting to remind him they were with him and to strengthen him for what lay ahead. Nikitin didn't seem to be aware of anything and stared blankly ahead, his lips moving as he whispered something over and over again that Thomas couldn't make out but decided must be a prayer.

The automobile turned left at the Kremlin, its red-brick walls and pointed towers barely visible against the dark sky, then skirted Theatrical Square with the Bolshoy Theater reduced to a blur of black and grey in the distance, and banked sharply across Lubyanka Square. The gloomy facades of the buildings on its far side were filled with gaping shadows, like the empty eye sockets of skulls.

The Turcat-Méry had to slow down when it entered Solyanka Street, which narrowed as it snaked down the hill into Khitrovka. Thin whisps of vapor began to appear in the headlights, thickening into a filthy yellow-grey fog as the automobile descended.

Unlike the rest of the city, Khitrovka wasn't asleep. Thomas peered through the windscreen at the dark-stained wooden walls and the peeling stucco of the low buildings and saw lights and movement in the windows. There were ratty taverns in many of the basements. Thick smells of burnt cooking oil and wood smoke filled the air. Ragged-looking people were going up and down the stairs, the doors flying open and releasing bursts of garish light, laughter, and rasping mechanical music. The automobile had to slow even more because of indistinct figures that kept staggering out of the fog. As it rolled by a trash-strewn alleyway, an emaciated young woman with disheveled blond hair and a bruise on her forehead stepped out and leered at Thomas.

The driver had never been in Khitrovka before, and it made him nervous. When Markov told him to take the next turn onto Ustyinsky Lane, which led to the river, he didn't notice a wide pothole. The front right wheel suddenly dropped into it, tilting the entire limousine, and splashing dirty water onto a wall near three rough-looking men huddled over something in a doorway. They turned around, glowering, as the automobile righted itself with a loud scraping sound. One of the men stepped forward and began to reach into his pocket.

Markov unbuttoned his jacket and slipped his hand onto the butt of his revolver.

"Faster," he ordered the driver. "Then turn onto the embankment down there on the left, by that streetlight. See it?"

"We're almost there," Markov said, turning toward Thomas. "We'll be all right. A couple of good men are waiting. And a detective is supposed to come as well."

When the Turcat-Méry reached the quay of the Yauza it made a sharp left turn and came to a stop parallel to the bank. Its headlights cut through the darkness and illuminated three figures standing under the stone archway of the Ustyinsky Bridge some fifty paces away. A kerosene lamp was on the ground between them and something long lying closer to the water. The light from the lamp dissolved in the gloom a few meters from the men. No one else was in sight and the windows in the redbrick warehouses lining the quay were dark.

Nikitin didn't seem to understand what was happening as Markov and Thomas helped him get out of the back seat. They each took him by an arm and started to walk with him toward the men under the bridge. Nikitin moved haltingly, his feet scraping on the cobblestones.

No one spoke. The Yauza made a soft plashing sound against its banks. A breeze brought the nauseating smell of raw sewage from its dark, glistening surface.

They were halfway to the men standing by the lamp when Nikitin noticed the long shape on the ground and went limp.

"Be strong, Frol'ych," Markov said in a hollow voice, pulling him up by his elbow.

Thomas wrapped his right arm around Nikitin's waist and brought his face so close to Nikitin's cheek that his moustache brushed it. *"We ... are ... with ... you!"* he said, emphasizing the words as if trying to push them into his mind.

They stopped a few steps from the shape on the ground. Although Thomas had seen it from the automobile, it was a shock to recognize what it was. Feet in thin cloth slippers, of the kind that were worn indoors, and the hem of a light blue dress protruded from under a sheet of stained canvas, and he could make out the shape of the body and the head.

Nikitin stared at the canvas with horror, leaning heavily on Thomas.

Markov nodded to the two patrolmen and walked up to the detective, a clean-shaven man in a suit and bowler with hollow cheeks and hard eyes.

"Stepan Vasil'ch. Here already," Markov said.

"Sergey Sergey'ch," the detective replied, then glanced at Nikitin. There was nothing else to be said.

The detective walked over to the body and bent over it. He picked up the lantern with his left hand, raising it so the light fell on the canvas, then took a corner of the canvas between the thumb and forefinger of his right hand and looked up at Thomas.

Thomas stepped closer, drawing Nikitin with him. Then he let go and moved to the side. The father had to do this alone.

Nikitin was trembling and hardly breathing, his tear-filled eyes riveted on the shape in front of him.

Thomas held his breath as the detective lifted the canvas and pulled it away, revealing the corpse's face.

"*No! No! No! Oh my God!*" Nikitin moaned, clasping his hands to his head, and falling to his knees.

"*It's not! It's not her! It's not my Mashenka!*" he shrieked *through sobs. "It's not her!*"

Thomas felt as if time stopped. He looked at Markov, who stood frozen, an expression of surprise on his face, his arm raised. The detective's mouth was open, and he had turned toward the patrolmen. But no sound came out, and no one moved.

Thomas bent over and looked at the dead girl. She was very young, no more than fourteen, with a Russian face—

wide-set, blue eyes, high cheekbones sprinkled with tiny freckles, a strong chin, and plump, pink lips that curved in at the corners of her mouth. Her golden hair was so thick it escaped her tight braid. An ugly purple and black bruise ran around her neck. Her left sleeve was torn, revealing a deep cut on her forearm, and her hands and fingers were covered with scrapes and dirt.

As Thomas gazed at the girl, his heart throbbing with sorrow, he heard footsteps and looked up. Markov was leaning over Nikitin and asking him something with an anxious expression on his face. Nikitin reacted with surprise and shook his head vigorously, then got to his feet and crossed himself three times, his lips moving rapidly. Thomas heard him repeating *"Slava Bogu! Slava Bogu! Slava Bogu!"* (Glory be to God!).

The detective walked over to Nikitin, took him by the arm, and started to lead him back toward the automobile. Markov bent over the girl's body and passed his fingers over her eyes to close them. He gestured to the patrolmen to cover her with the canvas, then waited for them to get out of earshot by the lantern.

"A police van will be here shortly," Markov said to Thomas. "They'll have to do an autopsy of course."

Then, glancing at the patrolmen, he added, "These two didn't follow procedures when they found her. They weren't supposed to touch anything, so's not to interfere with the detective's investigation. But . . . they admitted that they moved her . . . her legs . . . and . . . and pulled her dress down."

A patchy, uneven flush appeared on Markov's plump, wrinkled face, and he started blinking as he fought back tears.

"Can't really blame them," Markov said, his voice breaking. "They're both fathers. Who could think of harming a girl like this? And what of her poor parents? From the look of her, she must have a family that loves her . . . cares for her . . ."

Markov turned away, struggling to pull a handkerchief from an inside pocket.

Thomas stood up and waited for a moment. He had never seen Markov like this before.

Reaching out, Thomas clasped his right hand firmly on the older man's shoulder.

"Come, Sergey Sergeyevich, let's get Nikitin home. He needs to tell his family. There's still hope for his daughter. And he still needs us to help him. We'll do it together."

Markov finished wiping his eyes and looked at Thomas, then nodded.

"Thank you, sir. Quite right. We still have to see the poor fellow home."

"Yes," Thomas replied, "and I think a bit of your cognac will be very good for him now."

CHAPTER SIXTEEN

It was nearly five in the morning when the chauffeur dropped Thomas off at Aquarium, where he decided to spend what was left of the night in the small bedroom suite.

The drive back to Pokrovskaya Alleyway from the river had gone quickly. Nikitin was in a feverish state when he first climbed into the Turcat-Méry because of everything roiling in him—relief that it wasn't Masha, renewed hope about her fate, the burning need to tell his wife, horror about the dead girl, embarrassment before Markov and especially Thomas. But the big swallow of cognac that Markov made Nikitin drink from the flask took his breath away enough to distract him for the last part of the journey.

The moment the automobile pulled up to the gates of Nikitin's house his wife came running out, and when he told her, she threw her arms around his neck and sobbed. Several neighbors who had been keeping vigil on the porch surrounded them, then hurried off to tell their families the hopeful news.

Thomas and Markov didn't linger after assuring Nikitin and his wife that they would do all they could to get Masha back. It had been a long night for everyone, and after dropping off Markov, and arranging to meet with him the following day, Thomas dismissed the driver and told him he could take the next day off with pay.

He was exhausted, more from nervous tension than anything else, but couldn't fall asleep for a long time. Images from everything that happened during the previous day kept tumbling through his mind like a nightmarish kaleidoscope. The dinner at Yar and Mina seemed a distant memory.

When at last he drifted off, his sleep was troubled. He dreamt he was trying to get home from somewhere far away and was walking rapidly down an endless series of unfamiliar streets but couldn't find a cab or automobile or any other way of getting there.

When Thomas woke up the following morning, a band of white sunlight was streaming in along the edge of the maroon window curtain, making it look like it was on fire. He looked at his pocket watch—it was 9:35.

His first thoughts were about his children. After everything that happened last night, he needed to see them, to embrace them, to hear them talk. Today was Saturday, and because Olga and Mikhail had only half days at their schools, they would be home by noon. Thomas decided he would take all the children out to lunch. That way he could spend time with them before he had to come back to Aquarium in the late afternoon. And he would take a car, which always delighted them.

But first, he had to try to revive himself and clear his head.

When Thomas emerged from his suite wearing a British-made, blue silk track suit and soft black leather running shoes with cleats, Strelka, who slept in the corner of the office under the body bag, was already by the door, whimpering softly. He hurried to unlock it and she bounded down the stairs, heading for her spot behind the maintenance shed in the northwest corner of the Garden surrounded by a thick growth of lilacs.

Although the entire territory of Aquarium was only two hectares, numerous gravel paths meandered among the buildings, gazebos, and flower beds. Shortly after taking over the Garden, Thomas discovered that the paths could be used for some limited jogging and sprinting. This saved him the trouble of driving to Khodynka Field or other outlying area, which were the only other choices in Moscow. Running in the streets or any of the city's few parks simply wasn't done. Thomas had tried it a few times early on, but he didn't want to deal any more with policemen's whistles, or the open-mouthed gaping of passersby, or having to explain what he was running from, or where he was hurrying. He also discovered that having to change direction suddenly on Aquarium's twisting paths was good practice for the boxing ring. It reminded him of what Jack Johnson, who coached him in Chicago years ago—long before he became the first Black heavyweight champion of the world—told him about "movin' like a rabbit tryin' to outwit a hound dog."

Thomas started out slowly to warm up. After a few minutes Strelka joined him, trotting on his right side, as she always did, and occasionally looking up at him. As he picked up his pace, so did she, and when he broke into a sprint, she tore away, outdistancing him in a heartbeat, stretching out as she accelerated, and leaping over flower beds. It was a thrill to see her run. Borzois had been bred for hunting game in the open and Aquarium wasn't nearly big enough for her to hit her top speed. Thomas promised himself he'd take her out into the country one of these days for a proper run, maybe when he took Istomin up on his offer to do some hunting on his estate in Kostroma.

Half an hour later, Thomas was walking back to his office, breathing hard, bathed in sweat, and reveling in the cool spring air. He saw three men from the grounds crew digging a trench for a new drainpipe near the bandshell and greeted them. They doffed their caps, and as he passed, he heard one of them say something and the others laughed in response.

Probably can't get over the boss behaving or looking like this, Thomas thought. But their laughter wasn't malicious and he didn't mind.

There was one more important part to his exercise routine. When Thomas returned to his office, he put on boxing gloves and pounded the body bag hard for ten minutes, trying out several combinations and dancing around to attack the bag from different directions. He stopped once to catch his breath and then repeated the session. In conclusion, he worked with the speed bag for several minutes, varying the staccato rhythms until he had exhausted himself almost to the point of nausea.

After washing, shaving, and dressing he felt wonderfully refreshed and clear headed. Since it was so late in the day, he decided to skip breakfast. Before leaving, he telephoned the garage and asked the dispatcher to have the Turcat-Méry brought around to his apartment building in half an hour. He then told his secretary to confirm with Markov that they would meet at 6 o'clock.

Thomas's residence was an apartment on the first floor of a new, six-story building at 32 Malaya Bronnaya Street that was only a twenty-minute walk from Aquarium, which is why he snapped it up as soon as the building was completed the previous year. A fashionable architect had designed its exterior with a nod toward medieval Russian architectural features such as heavily pillared kokoshnik archways. But inside it was the height of modernity, with hot and cold running water, central heat, an elevator, electricity—with a generator for emergencies, a dumbwaiter, and telephones. It also faced a small, lovely park called "Patriarch's Ponds"—a traditional name despite there being only one rectangular pond left—that was a welcome oasis of green and a good place for the children to play year-round and go ice skating in the winter.

The apartment was big, with eight rooms, not counting the kitchen, and had three separate bathrooms, which was unusual. Because of its high ceilings and large windows, it seemed even more spacious, despite the heavy, carved mahogany furniture and maroon velvet drapes which Thomas ordered for it. The building towered over the surrounding neighborhood of mostly old, two-story wooden and stuccoed houses, with a few larger estates set amid gardens. It was home to successful lawyers, businessmen and senior officials in the city government. By happy coincidence, Prince Istomin lived only ten minutes away in his own townhouse on a large plot of land and both children's schools were also within walking distance.

It always saddened Thomas that Hedwig had not lived to see the luxurious new apartment. When she was alive, he couldn't have afforded it. But the last place they had, near Yar when he worked there, was comfortable enough and they had been very happy.

CHAPTER SEVENTEEN

Vasily, the porter who opened the building's front door for Thomas, replied cheerfully "The kiddies are indeed home-s," and then volunteered "Valentina Yakovlevna-s is home too."

Thomas glanced with mild surprise at the kindly old man, who still wore nineteenth-century styled muttonchops and always tacked on the old-fashioned, respectful "s"—an abbreviation for "sir"—to everything he said. Thomas hadn't asked him about Valli, but it seems the old busybody took an interest in the tenants' personal affairs and had noticed Thomas's increasing absences.

Rather than ring the doorbell for the maid, Thomas decided to let himself into the apartment and was rewarded with surprising seven-year-old Mikhail, who was scooting along the shiny parquet floor of the foyer on his knees with two toy horses, one white the other black, which he was making race each other.

"*Papa!*" the little boy shouted when he looked up, and dropping the toys rushed to his father. Thomas bent down, enveloping him in his arms and reveling in his familiar toasty smell and the touching fragility of his back and little shoulder blades.

"How's my boy?" Thomas asked in English, looking into his son's face, and stroking his soft, curly hair. "How's Mikey?" he repeated using his favorite, American name for him.

"*Vsyo khorosho, Papa*" (Everything is good, Papa), the boy replied hurriedly in Russian, and launched into what had been preoccupying him—the story of how he and his friend Vitya at school had almost gotten into a fight and how "Anisya Fyodorovna told us not to and made us stand in the corners and Vitya started to cry but I *didn't!*"

Thomas listened to his son's excited chatter as he kept

stroking his head. It didn't sound like anything serious, but he wondered if he should call on Anisya Fyodorovna. He remembered that she was a smart and dedicated teacher.

"Did Anisya Fyodorovna give you a note for me?" he asked, again in English.

"No, Papa," the boy replied in Russian again and looked up at him with his big, innocent brown eyes. He didn't even seem to notice they were speaking different languages.

Thomas decided that whatever had happened between the boys wasn't worth bothering with. However, he would have to do something about the children's English.

They need to be fluent in Russian, of course. How could it be otherwise? he thought. But English was their special tie to him and to his past, and he didn't want to lose it. He couldn't be around the children enough himself to keep the language alive in the family, and Valli, who spoke English fairly well, wasn't making much effort. *I'll have to find tutors for them*, he decided, and then thought it wouldn't be a bad idea to add some more French and German to what they were learning in school.

"*Zdravstvuy, Frederik*" (Hello, Frederick), he heard Valli say.

He looked up to see her standing in the arched doorway that led to the living room. Behind her the windows facing the park were filled with bright sunlight pouring through the lace curtains, and her face and broad figure were dimmed by shadow. Maybe because of how elegant Mina was, or because of Vera's remarkable beauty, Valli now looked even plainer to him than before with her big chin and wide mouth. Her eyes seemed to be rimmed with red and he noticed that she was clutching a crumpled handkerchief in her hand.

Crying again, and wants me to see it, Thomas thought with irritation. And because he was guilty for hurting her with his growing indifference while she remained doting and tried to be affectionate, he felt a stir of annoyance not only with himself but also with her.

"Hello, Valli," he replied in Russian and in what he wanted to be a neutral tone but that came out sounding cold.

He knew he should go up to her but could not bring himself to move. He seemed not to have any control over how he behaved toward her.

"All the children are healthy? . . . And all is well with you?" he asked in what sounded to him like a false and unnatural tone. Despite Valli's English, he now preferred speaking to her in Russian or German. He wanted to save English for his children.

"I'm sorry I didn't let you know . . . that I'd be working late last night," he lied, which made him even more unhappy with himself. "A lot was going on, there was some trouble . . . and it was a very busy night," he concluded lamely.

Valli didn't reply, but after looking at him for a moment turned toward the corridor where the children's rooms were located and called, "Olechka, Irmochka, your papa's here. Come!"

Olga appeared quickly, still wearing her school uniform, a long-sleeved brown dress to her ankles and a white apron with a bib. Thomas was struck by how much she resembled Hedwig, down to the delicate curve of her lips, determined chin, and steady gaze.

She's growing prettier all the time, he thought.

"Hello, sweetheart," he said as he kissed her warmly on the cheek and felt her arms wrap around his shoulders. Olga was maturing early, and although she was only twelve, she was already showing the beginnings of a bust and a gentle swelling of her hips.

Thomas looked around for his youngest, but she hadn't come out.

"Where's Irma?" he asked Valli, surprised. "Is she well?"

As he said this, he thought he saw something like a smug expression flit across Valli's face.

Once more, she didn't reply directly but instead called Irma again.

Just then, Thomas saw a movement behind the heavy maroon curtain gathered by the doorway to the children's corridor and realized Irma must be behind it. A second later, she peeked out. But she wasn't playing. She looked shy, wary almost, and instead of going to her father sidled over to Valli and leaned back into her legs and the folds of her dress. She too looked very much like Hedwig, but the four-year old's behavior shocked Thomas.

"Go to your papa, Irmochka," Valli said softly, putting her hands on the little girl's shoulders and urging her forward.

Mikhail got back down on his knees and was playing with his toy horses again, but Olga remained next to Thomas looking at her sister: "Come, Irmochka," she called to her affectionately and stretched out her hands.

Thomas squatted down and opened his arms wide. Only then did the little girl start inching toward him, dragging her feet. As he embraced her, gently and carefully, he looked up at Valli, who was now smiling tenderly.

Irma acts as if Valli is her mother, Thomas thought as he held his daughter, pressing his cheek to her head and stroking her back with his hand. *She spends all her time with her, doesn't remember Hedwig at all and I'm like a stranger.*

Then he remembered the smug expression on Valli's face when Irma didn't come right away.

Maybe she's trying to turn Irma against me, the thought came to him. *Or maybe she thinks this'll bring me back.* He felt himself getting angry at Valli but suppressed it. Things were just too confusing. He needed to understand more before jumping to any conclusions.

Thomas picked up Irma and rose to his feet, holding her in the crook of his arm. He relished having her close like this and realized he hadn't done it in a long time. Irma looked at him with curiosity from a few inches away but didn't resist or try to get down.

"I'm going to take the children out with me for the afternoon," he announced to Valli in a firm voice. "We'll be back before dinner."

Sounding resolute made him feel better. "It'll give you a break from all you do," he added, realizing that by saying this he was treating her like the nanny she had been before she became his wife.

Valli's face dropped. Thomas knew that excluding her this way was pointed and cruel, but he didn't care. They were his children, not hers. He needed to make that clear.

"Frederick . . .," she began, but stopped when she saw the expression on his face.

"We'll talk later," he replied, just to end the possibility of any discussion with her now, which was the last thing he wanted.

"Go, go, get your coats," he urged Mikhail and Olga, "we're going in the Turcat-Méry!"

When they heard this, Mikhail jumped up and down several times in excitement and Olga clapped her hands. A ride in the big limousine was one of their favorite treats, especially when the driver sounded the horn. Seeing their reaction, Irma began to squirm in Thomas's arms, trying to get down, and when Thomas set her on the floor she ran to her room and a moment later came back with a favorite doll.

Valli turned to what she saw as her duty with a resigned expression on her face. She put a light coat on Irma, and then, with a concerned expression, tied a small straw hat with an upturned brim and long ribbons under the little girl's chin. The effect was so adorable that Valli couldn't help smiling herself. Olga changed her school uniform and came out in a white dress with half-sleeves, a favorite of Thomas's because it brought out her rich, milk-chocolate complexion. Looking very much the young lady in the floppy hat and long shawl she put on, she offered her hand to Irma, who took it readily. Mikhail wanted to go as he was in the sailor suit he was wearing but reluctantly put on a hat and jacket when Valli insisted. When they trooped out the front door Thomas followed with a sense of relief. The apartment felt less and less like home, and he was glad to get away.

CHAPTER EIGHTEEN

It was sunny and quite warm for Moscow in May, and Thomas decided they would go to one of his favorite places— Krynkin's Restaurant on Sparrow Hills on the southwestern edge of the city—where they could sit outside. The owner was an acquaintance, the food was good, and the famous outdoor terrace hanging over a steep drop had a spectacular view of Moscow that extended a dozen kilometers or more.

The children eagerly piled into the limousine and sat facing each other in the back. Once they passed the city center and got to Khamovniki, Thomas asked the driver to sound the horn periodically, delighting the children. Later, as they approached Novodevichy Convent on Usachev Street, he asked the driver to open the muffler. The sudden leap in the automobile's speed and the engine's deafening roar made Mikhail and Olga squeal with delight, although the noise was so loud that little Irma look frightened until Thomas hugged her close and told her it was all right.

Thomas tried to speak only English with the children, and the results reinforced his conclusion that he had to get tutors: Olga understood almost everything he said and spoke reasonably well; Mikhail understood less and had trouble saying what he wanted to; and Irma seemed to know only a few phrases and isolated words. Thomas tried to comfort himself by thinking they were all still very young and there was time for them to learn. But he couldn't shake the painful feeling that he'd neglected them. Opening and running Aquarium had consumed him, and he'd relied too much on Valli.

Stepan Vasilyevich Krynkin, the owner, wasn't there when Thomas arrived with the children. He hadn't made a reservation and the restaurant was crowded with prosperous looking men in straw boaters and vested suits, and their female companions in what must have been the new fashion that season—a short, close-fitting jacket over a slim, high-waisted skirt, and a wide-brimmed hat with a giant bow, which, from distance made the lady look like a giant exotic flower.

But like every other maître d'hôtel in the city, the one on duty knew Thomas and took him and the children to a nice table right near the edge of the veranda. When Olga and Mikhail looked down, they had to draw back because of the frightening height, and Thomas put himself between Irma and the railing to hide the drop.

Children weren't commonly seen at a place like Krynkin's and Thomas drew some stares because of this and because his complexion was darker than theirs. As he passed one table, he heard an old woman in lace, holding a lorgnette to her close-set eyes, say with authority—and a bit too loudly—"Tatarin" (a Tatar) to the man sitting opposite her. However, no one looked back a second time at him or the children.

The meal passed pleasantly. Olga was a good older sister and helped Irma decide what she would eat. Thomas let Olga and Mikhail order whatever they liked for themselves, just making sure they didn't eat so much pie, pudding, tarts, and ice cream that they would get sick.

As they sat in the warm sun, with the white glass lanterns that were illuminated at night swinging gently above the wrought iron railing, and the festive clatter of silverware on china and snatches of happy voices rising and receding around them, Thomas's thoughts turned to Mina. He tried to imagine her in a different guise from the ones in which he had seen her in her boutique and then last night at Yar.

But it was difficult. The evening had been cut short very abruptly, just when Thomas thought he was getting to know Mina; and then what followed with that poor girl in Khitrovka cast a pall over it. And although Thomas felt he would like to see Mina again, the prospect of having to say something to her about Valli was unpleasant because he simply didn't know what he could say.

Could Mina be a wife to me and a stepmother to the children? he wondered.

Thomas tried to picture her sitting with all of them at this table, but despite finding it easy to evoke her elegant and attractive features, for some reason he couldn't see her helping Irma cut her portion of almond tart with a fork or reminding Mikhail not to lean on the table with his elbows.

The children and I, we all need the same unknown woman, he thought. *A woman who can be a wife and companion to me and a mother to them. Someone who will be an anchor for us all.*

But "anchor" didn't seem right because it wasn't alive. Thomas pictured a tree instead. The children were the branches, the ground was Russia, and he and the woman would be the trunk and roots tying them all together and connecting them to this place. Valli wasn't that woman, and he couldn't pretend she was.

I have to be honest with myself. I can't just put up with a sham marriage forever because of the mistake I made when I confused gratitude with love.

This thought made him feel better, but then another, troubling one occurred to him: *If I divorce Valli, how would the children take it, especially Irma?*

Thomas gazed over the vast expanse of Moscow before him with the sun burning on the golden cupolas of the churches dotting the city and the bends of the Moscow River gleaming like polished steel. The sweet scent of lilacs wafted over the terrace in sun-warmed waves from somewhere below. Skylarks swooped and soared through the sky, filling the air with their whistles and trills.

It was all deeply familiar after a dozen years. *But could Moscow ever be my real home?* Thomas wondered. *Or will I be able to go back to the United States someday, maybe even to Coahoma?*

Not if what I've been reading in the newspapers and all the rest is true, he answered himself.

The newspapers in Moscow reported the lynchings and racial violence that took place in the United States with depressing regularity. But Thomas also knew from talking to some of the Black American performers who appeared on his stages that it was actually far worse than the papers said.

He sighed, looked at his watch, and realized that it was time to get the children home and go to Aquarium.

CHAPTER NINETEEN

Saturdays were the biggest days for racing at the Moscow Hippodrome during the spring season. When Dickerman arrived mid-morning on Saturday, May 23rd, the sprawling territory was already alive with activity, and the stables, practice tracks, and paddocks were filled with horses and men. The familiar clamor and movement, the neighing, the rich barnyard smells of manure, and ringing of blacksmiths' hammers, all added to Dickerman's good mood.

His meeting with Stürmer the night before had gone well. The memory of being humiliated at Aquarium still stung, but it was just a matter of time before he figured out how to pay back "that uppity Black sonofabitch," as he told Hilda when they came down from their bedroom for breakfast in the Convent's kitchen. Everything else was moving along well too. Bartkow had gone out to search for information about Thomas, and Hilda and Maria were continuing to "break in" their eight captives with the help of the Golub brothers.

Dickerman felt full of energy. He hadn't been to the track in a week and was buoyed by the prospect of reimmersing himself in a world he knew intimately.

The Hippodrome complex, which had both flat and harness racing, was located across Petersburg Highway from Yar, on the edge of Khodynka Field. The vast sums of money at play in the world of Moscow horse racing became obvious as soon as you saw the palatial main pavilion, with its soaring neoclassical pediment surmounted by towers, above which sculptures of Nike, the goddess of victory, and two quadrigae of giant steeds were silhouetted against the sky. On the side of the pavilion facing the track itself, tiers of viewing stands rose six stories. Races at the Hippodrome attracted the cream of the city's society as well as its biggest gamblers. They were also an obligatory stop for racing aficionados from the rest of the Russian Empire and abroad.

Dickerman noted with pleasure that the half-dozen prizes announced for the races that day totaled 27,000 rubles, and as was his habit, divided the sum in half to get dollars. Just a piece of the sum would put anyone on the road to becoming rich. But there was also betting, and those sums far exceeded the official prizes. It was no wonder owners were willing to do almost anything to ensure their horses won, and that was where Dickerman was a master.

He left his cab by the members' entrance and walked through the Moorish-styled archway to the main stable, a long, barn-like structure with a stone foundation, wooden walls, and tile roof.

The Nevzorov stalls were at the end of the central corridor on the left. They were shielded from view by canvas curtains, but the two men guarding them nodded to Dickerman and let him through. Philipp Anastasovich was already there with several of his trainers, and all eight of his stalls were filled.

Nevzorov was a large man with a big head, a Roman nose, and protruding black eyes. He greeted Dickerman warmly. They were able to communicate adequately in French, which Nevzorov spoke well enough, although it had taken him some time to get used to Dickerman's Louisiana Cajun-flavored accent.

Racehorses were Nevzorov's passion, and he liked to repeat that he "loved them like they were my children." But he loved winning even more and was willing to take risks with the health of his "children" to make sure he did. He spent a fortune every year on buying, training, and maintaining the best horses he could find. He also didn't hesitate to have them run when they were injured, sick, or hadn't fully recovered from a previous race.

Dickerman's job was to concoct whatever it took to make the horses perform and win, and after he arrived, he transformed Nevzorov's stable into something like a pharmacy. The

results were very gratifying. The number of victories by Nevzorov's horses had grown since the season began, and he was
so pleased that he increased Dickerman's cut of the prize
money from twenty to twenty-five percent when a horse he
had "trained" won.

Today there were two horses with injuries. Timur, a beautiful bay Arabian with a deep, powerful chest, was entered in
the first race of the day and had a bucked shin that made him
limp. Dickerman examined the leg and decided it wasn't too
serious: all the horse needed was something to dull the pain.
He told Nevzorov to have his trainer give him a small injection
of procaine, a local anesthetic, and later, half an hour before
post time, another one of cocaine as a stimulant and for better
endurance.

The second horse was Tatarka, a chestnut Don mare with
strong legs and a white blaze on her forehead. She had bled a
little from her right nostril that morning and seemed tired after a trainer took her out for a short run.

"This happens," Dickerman told Nevzorov with a shrug after running his hand appreciatively over mare's neck; he was
especially fond of this Russian breed. The hemorrhage was
minor and would clear up by itself, he explained, but to help
the horse recover its strength more rapidly he prescribed what
he called a "milkshake," which was a favorite of his. This en-
tailed mixing up bicarbonate of soda in water with some
sugar, honey, milk, and salt and pouring the mixture down a
rubber tube inserted through the horse's nose and into its
stomach. Since Tatarka wouldn't be running until 4 p. m.,
Dickerman explained, the "milkshake" could be administered
to her at noon; she could also get an injection of cocaine thirty
minutes before post time.

Examining the other horses scheduled to run that day,
and questioning Nevzorov about their gaits, condition, endurance, and temperaments, Dickerman indicated what each
should be given. The idea of not intervening with some drug
or other concoction to affect a horse's performance hardly
ever occurred to him anymore, and he had trained himself not
to get attached to particular horses.

In two cases, he thought the horses were too nervous and prescribed small amounts of heroin as sedatives, enough to relax them so they could run their best. The others got different mixes of caffeine, cocaine, and strychnine to enhance their performance, although Dickerman had to caution Nevzorov about the strychnine because in larger doses it was also used as rat poison.

Dickerman's arrangement with Nevzorov was supposed to be secret. Nevertheless, word got out. The world of Moscow racing was too competitive and full of spies for other owners not to catch on, and whatever one of them did, the others tried to copy. The demand for doping experts and new drugs and methods was growing all the time. The numbers of guards hired by owners also increased, making it much more difficult to drug an opponent's horse, or to bribe someone in an opponent's stable to do it. The result was that more horses started to die because of how they were pushed, or their injuries masked.

But for Dickerman Russia had become a horn of plenty and he was rapidly fulfilling the dream that had brought him here. He had already made 7,500 dollars from Nevzorov, and the Convent promised to add a great deal more. He estimated that at this rate, in three or four years he would have enough to go back home to the South. By then, whatever advantage he had at the Hippodrome would be gone, the Convent would be thriving, and he could afford to leave.

The secret dream Dickerman nurtured, which he wouldn't have admitted to anyone, not even Hilda, was to rebuild the life his parents had lost in Louisiana.

He didn't think it would take all that much. After the Yankees came, the family's plantation had been broken up into twenty small farms that barely provided enough for their owners to live on, and he could buy all of them out. When his uncle died, his farm was sold for so little that it didn't even cover his debts.

Then there was the cemetery near Mamsella Bayou, in

what used to be the northeast corner of the plantation, where his uncle and his parents and all his other kin were buried. On his last visit many years ago, Dickerman could scarcely make out the graves amidst the cane and brambles. He would buy that piece of land too.

He could rebuild Ophite Hall, the old family mansion, just as his mother used to describe it, with the wide porch all around where you could sit at dusk and listen to the mourning doves, and a tall central hall that drew in the evening breezes. He could start growing sugarcane and cotton, both still good cash crops, maybe with the farmers he bought out working as his hands.

He could raise horses too. But he'd treat them differently from the ones at the track. He would breed them for pleasure and for improving bloodlines—maybe by importing some of the Russian Don stock he liked. He still remembered the pleasure he got in his early days at the track in Louisiana from seeing newborn foals tottering off on their spindly legs and yearlings kicking and gamboling in the fields.

He thought he might even marry a woman of substance and style. Someone who would appreciate all he accomplished. They could have children so there would be someone to leave it all to. Enough money would make anything possible.

By midday Dickerman finished his work in the stables and was ready to see the results. He placed bets on all the races where he figured he had an edge, then went up to one of the private terraces to watch together with Nevzorov and some of his team. One of his "nervous" horses won a 6,000-ruble prize, and the Arabian came in second in his race and won 750 rubles. Dickerson had also placed side bets on four horses, two to win and two to place, and won money on two of those. By the end of the afternoon, he was ahead 900 rubles, or 450 dollars. It was enough for an entire new wardrobe, he calculated. *Ten more days like this and I'll be able to buy myself one of those fancy new Packards.*

When Dickerman went to the winner's paddock after the last race to arrange his next session with Nevzorov, his wallet filled with a wad of crisp rubles, he passed through the crowd of well-dressed men, and a few women, who had gathered to see the day's champions.

There were businessmen in top hats and fedoras, stout senior military officers in uniforms with medals, younger ones in trim tunics with aiguillettes, foreigners speaking French and German. Some were smoking cigars, others were laughing. He heard a few snatches of British English from a pair of men in tweeds who were standing very erect and gazing at the crowd with haughty expressions. Most of those who had gathered here did so because they won today, and they all looked happy or complacent.

Dickerman took in the scene with satisfaction. He figured this was where he belonged too and didn't regret anything that he had done to get there.

CHAPTER TWENTY

Dickerman usually came to the Hippodrome only on race days and gave Nevzorov's men instructions about how to handle the horses during the week. The rest of the time he spent dealing with the myriad details necessary to get the Convent up and running.

He had finalized plans with Hilda and Maria about how they would "break in" their captives two months earlier, at the end of March, when they were getting ready to start their "collecting." All three had experience with one or another aspect of the process, and Dickerman increased his orders of drugs from Berlin.

The knockout potion Dickerman used on the children was one he first tried when he worked in brothels in New Orleans—chloroform mixed with tinctures of opium and barbiturate. It had been useful with some of the "girls" when they were being uncooperative, as well as with abusive customers who needed to be taught a lesson, even the biggest of them. The combination was also quicker than chloroform alone and lasted several hours, enough time to transport the captives to the Convent and for Stepan and Boris to carry them upstairs to their rooms.

However, the concoction wasn't without risk and Dickerman learned that he had to be careful about how long he kept the saturated rag pressed to the victim's face.

The first target Bartkow spotted in early April was a willowy street girl with ginger hair and green eyes who was loitering in front of a beer joint in the Khitrovka district. When the gang tried to grab her in an alleyway, she pulled a straight razor, cut Stepan's hand, and almost got away before Boris knocked her down. Either because of the blow or her weakened constitution, she didn't survive the chloroform mixture.

After that, Dickerman instructed his crew to focus only on children who lived with their families and weren't likely to be as street smart.

Once the captives were locked up, Maria and Hilda began by letting fear do its work. When the children woke up alone in their dark rooms feeling sick and dizzy from the sedative and unable to make sense of their surroundings, then suddenly remembered the attack on the street, they panicked. They would leap to their feet, start crying, try to open the locked door or the window shutters, hammer on the walls with their hands, and scream for help. Except for the made-up bed, a chamber pot, a chair, and a pedestal sink with a bar of soap and a towel, there was nothing else in the room. After a while, when the children realized they couldn't get out, they would collapse on the bed or the floor and curl up, trembling or sobbing.

Maria would listen through the door, or through the secret spy hole some of the rooms had, until the initial storm of despair passed. She would then begin the first act.

The light switch for each room was in the hallway. With Boris or Stepan waiting outside just in case, she would turn on the light, unlock the door, and come in with a radiant smile on her worn-looking but sweet face, dressed in a frilly, bright-colored dress, her hair done up, with bracelets and other jewelry, smelling of perfume. She would be carrying a tray with a glass of cranberry *mors*—a thick, sweet drink made of pureed fruit and water—and big pieces of white bread spread with butter and raspberry jam. All of the children were from poor families and the simple treats she brought were things they rarely saw.

She then began to play the role of the "good auntie," prattling on in a syrupy and affectionate tone as she comforted the children, calling them "dearie" or "lovey," helping them onto the bed or covering them up if necessary, hugging them, giving them little kisses, and saying everything would be fine, and they would go home "very soon," but without giving any details. The bewildered children first gaped at her with wide-open and tear-filled eyes, but quickly fell under her sway because even if they didn't understand what had happened to them, she was at least comforting. Maria also urged the children to eat and, especially, to drink the cranberry *mors*, which was laced with heroin.

They were invariably hungry by then, the white bread with butter and jam was delicious, and the *mors* was sweet and easy to drink. Maria would sit with the children and watch them until the first drug-induced euphoria set in and a smile spread over their flushed faces. She wouldn't leave until their eyes began to roll, their limbs relaxed, and they sank into the bed and fell asleep.

Over the course of the next several days Maria would return at mealtimes with different tasty things to eat and drink, and every day at lunchtime she brought a glass of *mors*, always reminding the children they would be going home "soon." The doses of heroin were small but regular and dulled the children's anxieties. They also soon began to look forward to the glasses of the viscous pink liquid because of how it made them feel.

Once the addiction started to take hold, Maria would let the children out of their rooms for short periods so they could bathe in the marble hallway bathrooms with hot and cold running water, a luxury many had never seen before. The maids would use their absence to change their linen and clean their rooms. Maria also began to allow small groups of children to take meals together in the dining room downstairs or to listen to music on a gramophone in the sitting room so they could get used to the public spaces and to each other. However, this always happened under the watchful eyes of one of the Golub brothers, Hilda, Mark, or herself.

It took nearly a month and a half to find and abduct all eight children. Those who were seized first were usually also the first to become addicted and compliant, whereas the more recent captives, because they were still in the early stages of their "training," remained somewhat "shy," as Maria put it.

She was used to a staggered process like this, and also knew from past experience that different children, and adults as well, responded differently to the same doses of heroin and other drugs.

However, her system did not always work smoothly because of her own addiction to cocaine. At times, Maria's attention to detail wavered, and this is what allowed two of the children to escape briefly from under her control. Chastened by this lapse, and by Dickerman's fury and threats, she and the others took additional precautions, including varying the doses of the drugs they put in the *mors*.

But they still underestimated the resourcefulness and courage of their captives and neither she nor anyone else realized that two other children had caught on to what was being done to them and began to dissimulate and plot rebellion.

Ibrahim, the sloe-eyed, olive-skinned Tatar boy, was the first. He noticed after the first glass that the *mors* made him feel very strange. He knew nothing about narcotics but had been raised in a strict Muslim household and taught from his earliest childhood that alcohol was evil because it made people forget God.

He decided that Maria was trying to get him drunk. He had seen many drunk Christians on Moscow's streets and resolved that he would rather die than be like them. And considering Maria's attractive appearance, he concluded she must be one of those demons who disguise themselves as human beings and who often figured in the Tatar folktales his grandfather told him. He also knew the demons were cunning and had to be deceived and fought.

When Maria brought his *mors* the second time, Ibrahim emptied the entire glass, licked his lips, and assured her "it was very tasty." But as soon as she left, he stuck his fingers down his throat, vomited into the sink in his room, and ran the tap until all traces were gone. The next time he took a sip while she was watching, and when she left, satisfied that he was coming along nicely, poured the rest down the sink. He also remembered how the drink made him feel the first time, and after every lunch pretended he was dozing, in case she came back to check.

Ibrahim's ruse worked and he graduated to having his meals downstairs with two other children. Watching them both, Ibrahim concluded that Sergey, a soft-looking, red-haired boy with slender arms and legs, had succumbed to the drink, and tried to remember his listlessness so he could imitate it. The other child was Anya, a beautiful girl with pale skin, black hair and blue eyes who had been abducted shortly after Ibrahim. He noticed that she crossed herself whenever she sat down for a meal, and her piety made him feel he could trust her.

The following day, near the end of dinner, when Maria turned away from the table to talk to the housekeeper, Ibrahim managed to whisper to Anya about what he was doing and told her she shouldn't drink the *mors* because it would make her drunk. She blushed when he leaned too close but then confided that she was already pouring it out because she came from an Old Believer family and saw drinking alcohol as sinful. She added that she ate the food they were served and used the plates only because she had no choice.

Ibrahim didn't really understand what she meant by this except that it sounded like *haram*—forbidden food or practice according to Islamic law. This made him trust her even more. The next time the two talked surreptitiously, they resolved to try to escape together.

Most of the other captives who had been in the Convent the longest became accustomed to the daily doses quickly. But some of the newer ones, like the blond Russian girl Masha, did as well.

When each of them got to the stage of reaching for the glass of *mors* as soon as Maria brought it in, she took the next step in her malignant "training" process.

She would wait for the drug's rush to fill them. When it did, she would slip her hand under their clothes and first barely touch, then lightly brush, and finally massage them gently in increasingly intimate ways. The first time she stopped as soon as she saw that they were beginning to respond. The second time, she went farther. The third time she waited until their bodies began to stiffen, they started to breathe more rapidly, and she felt herself drawn into their growing excitement. With Sergey and Karina, who became her favorites, she had to stop herself from continuing to the end. Even so, on some occasions she got so carried away that when she went to wash her hands and put her rings back on, she looked up at her reflection in the mirror above the sink and didn't immediately recognize herself.

This is the stage when Hilda took over. Her role was to play the "bad aunt" and to shatter the drug-induced passivity into which the children had drifted and to finish bending them to the Convent's malevolent purpose.

Looking angry, dressed in a severely cut, dark dress with her hair pulled back into a bun, no jewelry or perfume, and a steel-framed pince-nez glinting above her long, narrow nose, she shocked the children when she strode into their rooms without warning for the first time. In a stern and intentionally harsh tone, she proclaimed that they "would have to *work*" if they ever wanted to see their families again and that there would soon be "rich gentlemen" who would come "to see them" and who would be "*very angry*" if they were not pleased with "how you behaved."

Four of the children broke into tears and capitulated, promising they would obey. But two others assumed sullen expressions and didn't respond, and Ibrahim and Anya, who had not yet progressed to Maria's sexual initiation, went even further, and glared at Hilda with open resentment.

To cow them into obedience, Hilda called Boris and Stepan. The brothers would begin by offering to beat the rebellious children, but Hilda made a show of stopping them, explaining, "we don't want them bruised." The brothers would then grab the defiant children by the shoulders and shake them while she screamed her message at them until they collapsed in terror or in tears. She also took over the task of bringing the resisting captives their food, but instead of *mors* gave them plain, sugarless tea.

When Ibrahim and Anya first warily tasted theirs, they were shrewd enough to understand they were being punished by being deprived of what they thought was alcohol. Determined to continue to deceive their captors, they pretended to be angry and started to whine and demand the *mors*. This satisfied Maria and Hilda, who were becoming suspicious about their behavior and had delayed their "initiation."

But the other children's craving for the drug became a gnawing torment by the morning after they missed the first dose. After missing the next one they became agitated, tossing restlessly on their beds, complaining about feeling nauseous, some of them throwing up and scrabbling at their arms and legs because of the unbearable itching that began with withdrawal.

This is when Maria returned with the glasses of pink liquid. The addicted children responded to her as if she was their savior, swallowing the sweet and tart *mors* as if it was the elixir of life, throwing their arms around her, weeping, and begging her to protect them "from the other one."

The contrast worked equally well with the girls and the boys. And Maria promised each one she would protect them, and each would continue to get the delicious *mors*, and soon rich gentlemen would caress them the way she had, and if they did what the rich gentlemen wanted, they would see their parents very soon.

CHAPTER TWENTY-ONE

The longer Bartkow worked for Dickerman, the more he resented him. Despite all his efforts—contracting the Convent's complex renovations, hiring staff, planning the abductions, and serving as Dickerman's translator and guide to all things Russian—Dickerman's manner grew increasingly harsh and insulting.

Recently Bartkow noticed that Dickerman started taking him for granted as well, as if he was a lackey whose job was to serve the master's every whim. But since Dickerman paid well, and the Convent promised to be a gold mine, Bartkow swallowed his pride and did what he was told.

As a result, all he replied was "OK, boss!" and didn't argue when Dickerman called him into the kitchen before leaving for the Hippodrome on Saturday morning and ordered him to start digging into Thomas's life right away.

However, Bartkow's long face looked unhappy and Dickerman noticed it. This reminded him of how they'd been thrown out of Aquarium—it made him feel as if he'd been scalded whenever he thought of it—and how Bartkow had started whining that there wasn't any money in getting back at Thomas.

"It wasn't ever about the money, *you dumb Polak*!" Dickerman exclaimed angrily, as if Bartkow had just mentioned it again.

Bartkow stopped and winced.

"It's about the *insult*! That Black bastard *insulted* me!" Dickerman shouted. "And I'm not going to let him get away with it! Thinking he's so high and mighty because he's so far from home. He would never have dared treat me that way, not in the South, not even in the goddamned North, because he would've known that I'd string him up and gut him. And I'd have help from other men who'd back me up! So don't give me any of this let's-not-bother-shit of yours."

Even though Bartkow carried out Dickerman's instructions reluctantly, he found out what Dickerman wanted to know about Thomas without difficulty.

Pretending to be a journalist writing an article about Thomas for a well-known trade magazine, *Teatralnaya zhizn* (Theatrical Life), Bartkow got most of what he needed from Vasily, the nosy and talkative old porter in Thomas's apartment building. He then spent parts of the morning and the afternoon on Monday the 25th on a park bench in Patriarchs' Ponds across the street from the building, hiding behind a newspaper and watching as members of Thomas's family, who were easy to pick out, came and went. When Bartkow saw a girl who must have been his older daughter leave in the morning, he followed her as she walked to school. He also followed her home when she returned in the afternoon.

By Monday evening Bartkow had gathered enough information to make his report. He found Dickerman in the dining room with Hilda. It was one of the important "public" rooms and had been redecorated at considerable expense, with luxurious pink and green striped French silk wallpaper, carved rosewood furniture, and several giant, glossy paintings on "appropriate" themes—satyrs chasing nymphs through a forest, Bacchus imbibing with a retinue of pink-cheeked and pink-bottomed youths, and shepherds hiding behind tall reeds and spying on maidens bathing in a pond. Maria had commissioned the paintings for her own establishment and brought them to the Convent "on loan."

Dickerman had a notebook in front of him, Hilda was checking receipts, and they were going over the list of alcohol and drugs he had ordered for the grand opening, which had been set for Wednesday, June 4th, only nine days away. The Convent would offer "refreshments" to the select and demanding clientele expected to attend—everything from fine French champagnes, wines, cognacs, and liqueurs to tinctures of opium, morphine, and heroin. Cocaine would be available as well but would be served in its usual powdered form.

Seeing the self-satisfied smile on Dickerman's face, Bartkow concluded he was in a good mood. He cleared his throat to make his presence known.

Dickerman looked up. "So, what do you have for me?" he demanded.

Bartkow summed up what the doorman told him. Thomas and his wife didn't spend much time together, which meant his tie to her wasn't strong enough to use. But Thomas was attached to his children and had three of them. The youngest stayed at home with her mother; the seven-year-old boy went to school and was always escorted by someone—the mother, the maid, even the cook sometimes. But the oldest child, a twelve-year old girl, was allowed to go to her school by herself, and it was only a fifteen-minute walk away.

As soon as he said this, Bartkow saw Dickerman's eyes flash.

"Did you follow her?" he asked. "Where's her school at and what time does she get out?"

"Yeah, I did, today, both ways. It's a private gymnasium for girls at 22 Khlebnyi Lane—expensive, fancy, in its own building, not far from Nikitsky Boulevard. She gets out at 4. Her route is down quiet streets with big houses that are surrounded by gardens, which means there isn't a lot of traffic on the streets. There aren't a lot of pedestrians either in the afternoon."

A cunning expression appeared on Dickerman's face. "What's she like?" he asked.

"Tall, pretty, mulatto . . . looks older than she is. Developing early. Name's Olga."

"*That's it then, isn't it?*" Dickerman exulted, looking at Hilda, and slapped his hand on the table. "We'll add this Olga to the stable! It'll be good to add a Black gal, and my God won't it make her daddy stew!"

Bartkow had feared Dickerman would react exactly this way.

Screwing up his courage he decided to make a final try to

put Dickerman off, but not by arguing directly against hurting Thomas.

Trying to sound cool-headed and practical, Bartkow said it would be a good idea to track Olga for a few days longer to learn more about her. Her father was rich and knew people, and it paid to be really careful before trying to grab the girl so that nothing went wrong.

Bartkow was hoping that if Dickerman agreed, and it was possible to drag things out, the Convent opening would get so close they'd have to forget about Thomas.

But Dickerman told him not to talk nonsense. They knew all they needed to know.

"Set it up for after school tomorrow, got it?" he said curtly.

"Why wait?" he asked, looking at Hilda again, who returned his gaze calmly. He waved his hand at Bartkow, dismissing him, and turned back to the notebook.

CHAPTER TWENTY-TWO

When Thomas realized during his outing with the children that one of the reasons he'd been neglecting them was that he was trying to avoid Valli, he resolved not to let this happen again. The question became when and how to see them. His schedule at Aquarium rarely allowed him to get to bed before three or four in the morning, which meant he was still asleep when the two oldest went to school.

He decided the best time would be in the afternoon after school, which would be before the evening at Aquarium got under way. And he would start seeing them individually, beginning with his oldest, so he could focus on each one's different interests. Olga was becoming a young lady, whereas Irma was just learning to read, and neither one had any interest in Mikhail's toy soldiers and horses.

On Monday, May 25th, Thomas overcame his reluctance to talk to Valli and telephoned her from Aquarium. To his relief the maid answered, saying "Madame" was out on errand. Thomas left the message that he would be staying at Aquarium for the next several days because of work but would call again in a day or two.

He spent the rest of the afternoon in his office responding to letters and telegrams from booking agents in Paris and Vienna that had piled up. He also sent an inquiry to Berlin about the new act they had been recommended to him—the American cowboy trio, which was something Moscow audiences hadn't seen before and which sounded appealing. He wanted to clear his desk so he would have time for Olga and the other children in the coming week. He also knew that he would be busy during the next few days with plans for an addition to the Winter Theater he wanted to build.

Thomas then called Markov to check if he'd gotten any

news from the police about the Masha Nikitina abduction. Markov's reply was disappointing. He still didn't know when a detective would be assigned to the case, although he hoped it would be during the coming week. The detective who'd been at the Ustyinsky Embankment was still busy trying to identify the dead girl. It didn't seem she was from Moscow, which made it difficult.

Thomas then called Istomin to ask if he'd heard anything from his friends in the city government, but the valet who answered the telephone said "his excellency" was out and it wasn't clear when he would return.

At least, Thomas thought when he hung up, *Istomin would have called me if he had anything to report.*

Tuesday, May 26th, was sunny but cool, as May often was in Moscow, but it would be perfect weather for a walk. Thomas decided he wouldn't warn Olga but surprise her after school. She was growing up so quickly that he thought he might start talking to her about her future, or at least try to plant some ideas in her mind.

During their outing to Sparrow Hills, she had impressed him with how smart she was in ways that went beyond the good grades she always got in school. She seemed to understand people well, certainly better than he did at her age. This struck him when Olga remarked in passing how some of her girlfriends at school who came from well-to-do families quarreled about trifles "simply because they had so little to lose that was important." Olga had also made him happy when she said that she liked being able to speak Russian and English "because I can say things easily in one language that are hard to say in the other."

I'll have to try to introduce her to my business, Thomas thought, *and I hope she takes to it. Russia is the only home she's known . . . that any of them has known. I want them to feel this is where they belong. I want to grow my business and they can take it over when I'm gone.*

Thomas remembered Martynov's toothy smile and the

unpleasant meeting in his office about money and the risks Aquarium could face.

No, it'll be OK, Thomas concluded after reflecting for a moment. *I know I'm right. He's exaggerating because he's greedy. Cavalieri is going to make Aquarium number one this summer.*

Olga's school, "Stepanova's Institute for Young Women," was small, select, and private. It bore the name of its headmistress, Sophia Andreyevna Stepanova, who was a graduate of the teacher's program at the prestigious Smolny Institute for Young Noblewomen in Saint Petersburg and a well-respected pedagogue in Moscow's moneyed circles. The school was housed in its own one-story building painted a cheerful canary yellow at 22 Khlebny Lane in a quiet neighborhood about a twenty-minute walk from Thomas's apartment.

He was waiting outside on the sidewalk when Olga came out onto the columned portico with two other girls, all wearing their brown and white uniforms and hats and talking animatedly. The school drew girls from across the city and a row of carriages and several automobiles were waiting at the curb to pick up those who lived in the more distant parts. Others, like Olga, who lived nearby and were old enough, walked home alone. The neighborhood was quiet and safe.

When she saw her father, Olga greeted him with a happy smile and a wave of her hand. She then said something to the other girls, who looked with curiosity at the dark-skinned gentleman, and hurried over.

Thomas couldn't help thinking how much prettier she was than her friends. He immediately checked himself for being an overly admiring father, but after a moment's hesitation concluded he'd been right after all. Taking off his hat he embraced her warmly as she stood on tiptoe to plant a kiss on his cheek.

"What a lovely surprise, Pápa!" she said in English to please him but using the Russian form of address she knew he liked. Then a worried expression appeared on her face: "Has something happened?"

Thomas assured her that everyone was fine and that he simply wanted to spend some time with her since it was a nice day, and the walk would be enjoyable.

Their route home took them across Bolshaya Nikitskaya Street, then quite near Istomin's town house at 17 Malaya Nikitskaya Street, before they got to Patriarch's Ponds and their apartment building.

Dickerman and his gang were in their black carriage waiting for Olga around the bend in Spiridonovka Street just above Malaya Nikitskaya, which is where she would be coming from. Bartkow chose the location because of how quiet it was. The properties were large, there were few entrances off the street, and consequently fewer yardmen hanging or puttering around.

He told the coachman Matvey to pull up under the branches of a gnarly old oak tree that reached over a masonry garden wall running along the street, which gave the coach some cover. As before, Matvey had also been instructed to signal when he saw the girl and then start to drive toward her.

They hadn't been parked for more than five minutes when the driver suddenly began to rap repeatedly on the roof of the carriage instead of slapping it twice. Dickerman looked at Bartkow, who was sitting next to him, and jerked his head toward the side, indicating that he should see what was going on.

"*A man is with her!*" the driver whispered when Bartkow stuck his head out the window. "They're walking together, so it's not just some passerby!"

Bartkow got out of the coach on the right side where he couldn't be seen, planted his foot on a metal step and hauled himself up to the level of the coachman's seat, looking toward the intersection with Malaya Nikitskaya.

What he saw made him catch his breath. He jumped down from the step and clambered back inside.

"We've got to get out of here boss. She's not alone—

Thomas is with her!"

"Are you out of your mind, boy!" Dickerman exclaimed. "Are you sure?"

"I swear it's him. He's still a way off but I can see it's a Black man! And who else could it be? He wasn't around when I followed her, and the old doorman told me she went to school by herself. We'd better get out of here!"

The idea that he should run from that Black bastard after everything he'd endured from him infuriated Dickerman.

"Nobody's going anywhere," he hissed. "We're going through with it as we planned."

"But boss . . ." Bartkow tried to object.

"Don't be such a pigeon-livered coward," Bartkow snapped. "We're still going to get us that Black gal, and we're going to give her goddamn daddy a hiding he won't ever forget. Here's what we're going to do."

He told Bartkow to tell the Golubs that when the coach got near, they should come at the girl from the front and grab her before Thomas could do anything. At the same time, he and Bartkow would attack him from the rear.

"I'm going to use this," Dickerman said, hefting his snake-headed cane, "and you're going to use this," he told Bartkow as he pulled a black object from a compartment under his seat.

"Ever use a cosh before?" he asked with a contemptuous expression on his face as he held it up for Bartkow to see. The object was a thin leather pouch as long as a man's forearm and filled with lead shot.

Bartkow glowered back and replied curtly, "Yeah, lots of times," even though in truth he'd only held one in Chicago years ago and hadn't even come close to hitting anyone with it. But he had been angered by Dickerman's implication that he might be afraid to use it on Thomas and wanted to push back.

"Just give him a good smack on the head and that'll be the end of him," Dickerman explained. "All the Blacks I've ever seen have been cowards. And I've got a nice surprise," he added, brandishing his cane. "We'll give him a licking he won't ever forget."

By the time they had walked a few blocks from the school, Thomas decided he would take the plunge and ask Olga if she would like to learn a bit about running Aquarium. He wasn't sure if he should mention something so grownup to her now since she was only twelve. But the idea that he could gradually bring her into the world he was building excited him.

Maybe the little ones will want to follow her too, he mused, recalling how Mikey and Irmochka often tried to imitate Olga in what she said or did. What a dream that would be!

He gave Olga a sidelong glance.

The top of her head already comes to my shoulder. She's growing up fast, he thought, *but she's also still just a little girl.*

Feeling a flood of tenderness, he reached out, taking her hand in his. Olga looked up at him from under the brim of her hat and smiled.

And what a difference between us, he continued to think as they walked. *She's spent her entire life in this enormous, rich city, with its amazing mix of ancient Russia and modern Europe. But what did I know as a child? Only the family farm in Coahoma County, a few neighbors, and Clarksdale, the nearest town, which had a couple of stores and a maybe two hundred people, most of them Black and poor.*

He remembered that even Friar's Point, the county seat a dozen miles away as the crow flies, wasn't much different. *But you couldn't get there like a crow*, he thought.

The thick forests and swamps in Coahoma meant it could take several days to get from one town to the other and you had to go mostly by water. Farms were scattered through the Mississippi Delta's wilderness like islands across a vast green ocean. Olga's childhood bore no resemblance to anything like his. What did she know of a farmer's backbreaking work? Or of the rich brown smell of freshly tilled earth, the oscillating buzz of grasshoppers on hot summer days, the sweet smell of tangled honeysuckle?

That farm wasn't only where we were but what we were,

he thought. *Would Olga or the little ones ever be able to understand what all that was like?*

Thomas took a breath, paused, and speaking casually, in an everyday tone of voice, asked her if she'd like to know a bit about how Aquarium works. He didn't want to influence her by sounding too eager. And if she was indifferent, he feared sounding too crestfallen.

But to his delight, Olga responded with lively curiosity. Taking heart, he tried to paint a picture that was as entertaining as possible and launched into a description of how they might go about it—she could spend a day in the office with him, accompany him when he made his rounds of the venues at Aquarium in the evening. He'd show her the elaborate stage machinery in the Winter Theater, which would be fun to see in operation. If her school schedule allowed, she might even come with him when he went on one of his trips to other cities in Russia or abroad to recruit new acts.

The idea of a trip like that made Olga clasp her hands with excitement, and Thomas was so encouraged by her reaction and so absorbed in their conversation that he didn't notice the black coach coming toward them as they started up Spiridonovka Street.

Feeling uncomfortably exposed on his driver's seat, Matvey kept his head lowered and his eyes fixed on the Black man and his daughter as the gap between them and the coach closed.

Forty meters, thirty, twenty, ten.

A moment later, the driver pulled up on the reins, stopping the coach. He felt the four men pile out, with the Golub brothers on the street side and Dickerman and Bartkow on the other, along a neighboring property's fence, where the coach's cabin blocked them from view.

Thomas looked up, still absorbed in what he had been telling Olga about the charms of Vienna and Paris and saw two men in neat work clothing striding straight toward them. One of them was holding a piece of paper in his outstretched hand.

It flashed through Thomas's mind that the men were trying to find an address and had gotten lost. He was distracted just long enough not to notice Dickerman and Bartkow coming around the team of horses so that they could approach him from behind.

The man with the paper held it up and called out, "*Excuse me, sir!*"

Then, when he was only two paces away, and acting as if Thomas wasn't even there, the man stepped forward, reached out with both arms, and wrapped them around Olga's torso, making her gasp. At the same time, the other man bent down, enveloping her legs, and they started to lift her off the ground.

It was all so brazen and quick that Thomas froze for a second.

But then he reacted with lightning speed. He lurched forward, grabbed the nearest workman by the collar and drew back his right arm for a punch when he sensed someone behind him. Instinctively, he slipped his head to the left just in time to evade a blow from something heavy that hit the brim of his homburg and glanced off his right shoulder.

Thomas's years of practice took over. Continuing the feint to the left, he let go of the man's collar, pivoted in one smooth motion until he could see the attacker behind him and put the full momentum of his twisting torso into a right hook.

His fist landed squarely on Bartkow's jaw, breaking it with an audible crack, and sending him flying backwards, the black leather cosh spinning through the air like a child's pinwheel. Bartkow landed hard on his back on the cobblestone pavement. Thomas saw that another man was a few paces behind him, but he ignored him and spun back to face the two who had grabbed Olga. They backed away closer to the coach, their faces painted with shock at what the Black man had just done to their accomplice.

"*Take him!*" Boris yelled to Stepan, who dropped Olga's legs and stepped toward Thomas in the threatening manner of a Russian street brawler, facing him squarely, his knees bent, his arms spread wide, and his fists clenched.

He was an open target. Thomas danced up to him, feinted

a right to the head, and when Stepan automatically lifted his arms to defend himself, followed with a hard, straight left to the face and unleashed his right hook again. The blows staggered Stepan, and he stumbled backwards with a grunt of pain. Blood began to pour out of a cut on his brow, flooding his eyes and half blinding him. His nose looked broken, and it was all he could do to stay on his feet.

The skin on the first and second knuckles of Thomas's right hand had split from the punches he threw but he didn't notice. Only a few steps separated him from the man holding Olga, who was kicking her feet and trying to wriggle free, her face contorted by panic.

Thomas started toward the man with cold determination and fists raised and was almost on him when time seemed to slow down.

He heard himself breathing, his heart beating, and then a woman's voice behind him screamed "*Fred-d-d-y-y!*" The scream echoed as if it had been emitted in some vast vaulted space and he recognized it was India, his stepmother.

Thomas whipped around. The short fat man he'd thrown out of Aquarium, his face crimson and his mouth open wide, was coming at him with something long and thin. He'd been aiming it at Thomas's back, but because Thomas had unexpectedly turned around the weapon was now inches from his chest.

Thomas slipped to the right to dodge the point but wasn't quick enough to escape it entirely. It went through the fabric of his jacket, and he felt it pierce his skin and slide along a rib, cutting a long gash in his left side.

The pain was so sharp that Thomas moaned and dropped to one knee, pressing his left hand to the wound, and supporting himself with his right. His eyesight began to blur, and it was hard to breathe. When he looked up, he saw the man who grabbed Olga hauling her into the coach with the driver's help.

Thomas struggled to his feet but lost his balance and collapsed again after taking two staggering steps. He watched helplessly as Dickerman skittered around him, giving him a wide berth, still holding his sword cane in one hand and its shaft in the other, then ran to the coach and began to climb in.

The ground under Thomas was wobbling. He shook his head violently, trying to revive himself. He could see the driver lifting and pushing one of the men into the coach, while the other one was getting in on the other side.

A moment later, the doors of the coach slammed shut and it started down Spiridonovka toward Malaya Nikitskaya, the driver whipping the reins and the horses breaking into a gallop.

Bartkow chose the location for the abduction because he thought it was lonely and no one would be around. But a curious *dvornik* (yardman) raking leaves along the inside of a fence that separated an estate's backyard from Spiridonovka Street heard the scuffling and shouts as soon as they began. He dropped what he was doing and glued his eye to a gap between two weathered boards.

What he witnessed shocked him. "It was like nothing I've ever seen before under God's holy daylight," he described it later to his wife, the other servants, the master, the police, anyone who'd listen.

"A dark-skinned gentleman absolutely drubbed" the "hooligans" who seized "the pretty young miss" who'd been with him "and then collapsed in the middle of the street."

As soon as the coach was gone, the yardman unlatched a gate in the fence and ran over to Thomas, who was on his hands and knees.

Holy Mother of God, I've got to get him to the hospital, the yardman thought in a panic when he saw the big blood stain on the man's side.

But how? He didn't know how to help—there were no cab stands nearby, no police stations either. The master wasn't home and there was no telephone in the house.

Thomas saw something move and looked up at the man in a long, soiled apron standing next to him. Thomas's head was spinning, and he felt like he was going to pass out, but suddenly remembered where he was.

"Do you know . . . Prince Vla . . . dimir Vladimir'ch . . . Istomin?" he asked, gasping, the effort of speaking sending stabs of pain through his chest.

"*Why, yes*! I do, sir!" the yardman replied eagerly. "How can we not know such a fine gentleman? His house is right nearby, on Malaya Nikitskaya, number 17. We've seen it many times!"

Being asked about something he knew brought the *dvornik* to life. He took hold of Thomas's arm and began to try to help him get up on his feet, but he had to stop when Thomas groaned and shook his head.

"No. Help me lie down," he said, and groaned again when the yardman lowered his shoulders to the ground.

"Now, go to Istomin's house and tell him . . . or anyone . . . what happened. My name is 'Thomas,' tell them it's 'Thomas,' they'll understand. They have a telephone and tell them to get help . . . help to get me to his house . . . and they have to call a doctor."

This was something the yardman knew he could do.

Without hesitating, he left Thomas lying where he was on the cobblestones, turned the corner, ran the four hundred meters to Istomin's estate, and, panting so heavily he had difficulty speaking, managed to rouse the entire household, including the master himself who was in his study. Ten minutes later he was back with Istomin and Istomin's yardman.

Before running out of his house, Istomin had shouted instructions to his valet to telephone a doctor. He'd thought at first of taking his brougham because it was roomy and had a soft ride, but then realized it would take too long to harness the horses. He started up his new sporty automobile and rushed over in it instead.

Istomin became frightened when he saw how Thomas looked and the pool of blood that had spread under him. He remembered enough from his time in the Japanese War to push his hand with a wadded-up handkerchief under Thomas's jacket and press against his side to try to stanch the bleeding, then gestured to the two yardmen to help him.

CHAPTER TWENTY-THREE

Three minutes later, they were carrying Thomas's limp, sagging body from the automobile into Istomin's house. They put him down on a Caucasian tribal rug covering a leather couch in the drawing room. Istomin tried to question Thomas about what happened, bringing his ear close to his lips so he could hear, but all Thomas could manage was a slurred phrase in French about "Olga" and "*cet Américain*" (this American).

The doctor lived one street away and arrived a few minutes later. A grey-haired man with a neat goatee and a pince-nez on a ribbon that made him look like Chekhov, he had served in the same division as Istomin during the Japanese War. When he first saw Thomas and raised his eyelid with a finger, he pursed his lips and shook his head. He shook it again after he cut open his clothing and saw the wound.

Thomas's brown skin had a greyish cast because of the amount of blood he had lost. But that wasn't the worst of it. The thin cut on the left side of Thomas's ribcage was a dozen centimeters long, but it was shallow and there were no vital organs or blood vessels near it, which meant it shouldn't have been life threatening. And yet, the edges of the wound were inflamed and swollen, the swelling was spreading across Thomas's torso, and he had lost consciousness. His breathing was labored, and his heartbeat and pulse were irregular and weak. He seemed to be drifting toward death.

Thomas's symptoms made the doctor think there was poison on whatever had cut him, but he had no idea what it could be or how to treat it. Feeling helpless, he decided to take a chance by trying to revive Thomas's failing heart.

He prepared a hypodermic, inserted the shockingly long needle between Thomas's ribs—it looked to Istomin as if it would go right through him—and injected adrenaline directly into his heart. After a few seconds the heartbeat got stronger and everyone's hopes rose as it stayed steady for the next quarter of an hour. But then it began to fade again. Thomas's breathing became shallow and irregular.

Istomin watched the doctor with a feeling of impotent despair. Not knowing what else could be done, he asked if it was worth trying to move his friend to a hospital. But the doctor shook his head and replied he didn't think it would do any good or that he could survive the trip.

"*Bozhe moy, Bozhe moy!*" (My God, my God!) Istomin kept whispering as he leaned over his friend, listening to his faltering breathing. Tears began to fill his eyes. He couldn't believe that all he could do was to sit and watch helplessly as Thomas died.

The gaps between Thomas's breaths kept getting longer and Istomin was hanging on every one, fearing it would be the last, his eyes riveted to Thomas's face, when a movement to the side made him look up. To his surprise he saw Zoya approaching through the archway from the dining room. She rarely visited the drawing room, or any of the other "fancy" rooms in the house as she called them, and preferred to stay in her own wing or in the kitchen.

Zoya was hunched over but shuffled smoothly on her small feet, which made it seem as if she was floating over the floor rather than walking on it. A brightly colored kerchief was tied tightly around her head, which made her wrinkled, amber-colored face, with its narrow eyes, look like that of a kindly old doll. She looked very worried.

"*Barin, akh barin!*" (Master, oh master!) Zoya exclaimed, rocking her head from side to side, and using the old-fashioned term of respect that Istomin had not managed to get her to drop.

"*My God, what a dreadful horror, my God, what a dreadful horror!*" she repeated in her singsong manner as she looked at Thomas's prostrate body. "We've got to hurry now, hurry, my dear ones! *We have to hurry!*"

Istomin looked at her with amazement. Somewhere in the depths of his soul hope awoke.

Zoya beckoned to the yardman and valet who were standing uncertainly by the windows, and then made the same urgent gestures to the doctor and Istomin.

"Quickly, quickly, my dear ones, get him to the *banya*, to the *banya*!" she urged, and shuffled rapidly toward the door, leading the way.

Her simple actions and words had an electrifying effect. No one paused to question what she said, the four men grabbed the edges of the rug that Thomas was lying on, lifted it, and carried him out of the room.

The *banya* was in the back yard of Istomin's property. He had it built when Zoya came to live with him because he knew the importance it had in her life, as it did in the lives of the vast majority of folk who lived in the countryside.

It was a compact, two-room structure made of thick, tightly joined pine logs, and consisted of an anteroom and the bath proper, which was equipped with a cast-iron wood-burning stove on which sat a large metal pan filled with fist-sized river rocks. The floor was hard-packed earth—Zoya had asked for it specifically instead of wood. Three wooden benches rose in tiers toward the ceiling, and in the corner stood a big wooden tub filled with water in which various grasses and herbs Zoya had gathered at Istomin's estate in Kostroma were steeping. The walls and rafters of the bath were hung with more of her herbs as well as clusters of dried, thin birch branches.

Zoya hurriedly instructed the men carrying Thomas to put him down on the floor of the anteroom, leave the rug there and carry him into the *banya* itself, where they were to lay him directly on the earthen floor.

The small, windowless space was illuminated only by a flickering candle in a clear glass holder, and it was already hot, as if Zoya had fired it up knowing she would need it that day.

The doctor looked anxiously at Thomas's prostrate body.

The heat in the *banya* was so intense he wanted to object that it would further strain Thomas's failing heart. But then Thomas's right arm slipped off his chest and fell lifelessly to the ground, and the doctor decided it was too late to make any difference.

Zoya went to work, ignoring everything around her. A small sharp knife appeared in her hand, and she began to slice through the clothing on Thomas's arms, legs, and torso, exposing them as she stripped off the fabric and pulled it out from under him so that he was lying naked directly on the earthen floor.

She then rose, crossed herself rapidly three times, and splashed three full ladles of water onto the heated rocks, making them sputter and hiss as blasts of fresh steam rocketed through the small space, filling it with a pungent herbal smell and nearly extinguishing the candle flame before it danced back to life.

The heat in the room soared even higher, and Istomin felt that it got harder to breathe.

But Zoya didn't seem to notice. She reached up to the shelf with the candle and got a clay pot that was behind it. Using her fingers, she began to spread a dark, glistening poultice on the wound in Thomas's side and then all over the rest of his exposed body. The strong and sharp smell of pine and of something meaty, like mushrooms, filled the *banya*. Sweat was pouring down Istomin's face and starting to saturate his clothing, but he continued to watch, mesmerized.

Zoya stood up as straight as she could, gestured to everyone except Istomin to leave, and assumed a grave expression, as if what was going to happen now was the most important. When the doctor and the servants were gone, she reached under the lowest bench and pulled out two thick bundles Istomin hadn't noticed—one of animal skins and another of curved sheets of oak and birch bark.

She crossed herself three times again and began to chant quietly. Istomin recognized it was Old Church Slavonic, the liturgical language of the Russian Orthodox Church. After the first few seconds he made out a prayer to Saint Panteleimon, known as "the Healer" in Russian popular belief. Zoya was praying to him for help in saving "this sufferer."

At the same time, to Istomin's astonishment, she untied the two bundles and started to fit the curved pieces of oak and birch bark over Thomas's arms and legs, as if encasing them in armor. When she was done, she started to layer the animal skins over his entire body—Istomin recognized lynx, hare, sable, bear, martin, wolf, deer, wolverine—molding the pelts to his torso and limbs, tucking them under him, and even covering his face. When Zoya was finished, she got down on her knees facing Thomas, bent down so her forehead touched the floor, stretched out her arms and began to whisper something he couldn't understand.

In an instant, Istomin remembered the tiger in Ussuri. Zoya had prostrated herself and whispered in the same way then too.

A chill ran down Istomin's back despite the suffocating heat. As he listened to Zoya's whispering, the sibilant sounds melded with the quivering shadows on the walls from the candle. The smells of the poultice mixed with the scent of the herb-infused steam. Istomin's vision started to blur, and he began to feel light-headed. It seemed to him that everything was happening more slowly.

He took a deep breath, trying to overcome his dazed state, and looked at Zoya, who was still kneeling but had raised herself off the floor and put her hands on the pile of skins that concealed Thomas's body. She was whispering more insistently now, and as Istomin watched he thought he saw a white light appear under her palms. Incredulous, he blinked several times, but when his vision cleared the light was gone.

For several long moments the only sound in the *banya* was the clicking of the metal stove as it heated and the beating of his own heart. Zoya had abruptly stopped whispering.

She began to rise to her feet laboriously, the way old people do, pressing her left hand against the edge of the bench near which Thomas's shrouded body lay.

"*Nu, batyushka*" (Well, dear little father) she said, using another of her affectionate, old-fashioned forms of address, "now we can only wait and hope that the Mother of God, who watches over us with her protective veil, and Saint Panteleimon the Healer have heard our prayers."

She straightened the scarf on her head and sighed with fatigue. "Let's call the others, my dear, to get Fyodor Fyodorovich out of the *banya*. I'll warrant he's gotten all sweaty, the dear man."

When Istomin walked into the anteroom, the sun pouring in through the window was so bright he had to squint. He filled his lungs with the cool, fresh air, feeling as if he'd awakened from a trance. Taking out his watch, he looked at it uncertainly. It showed they had been in the *banya* for over an hour, but it seemed to him that just a few minutes had passed.

CHAPTER TWENTY-FOUR

When Dickerman's sword sliced through the skin and muscle on Thomas's side and glanced off a rib, the poisons coating the blade entered his bloodstream, and when he was brought to Istomin's house his consciousness was flickering like a dying candle flame. He remembered that something violent and painful had happened to him and could hear the distant voices and labored breathing of the men carrying him, but none of this concerned him any longer.

He felt as if he had awakened from a troubled sleep and was walking through dark rooms in an unfamiliar house, feeling the rough wooden walls with his fingertips. He knew he had to find something important but wasn't sure what and when he saw a thin band of light under a door, he stepped outside onto a plowed field with furrows running to the horizon.

It was dawn, everything was shrouded in lilac-tinged mist, the air was cool and smelled of honeysuckle, and as he walked, his feet sank into the soft earth. He heard the sound of running water ahead and started to walk faster. The sound kept getting louder until he came to a deep, rapidly flowing stream with sun gleams rippling on its surface.

This was what he was seeking and his heart filled with a joy he had never known before. He heard a ringing woman's voice call his name—*Fred-d-d-y-y!*—and when he looked up he saw all those he loved most and had never forgotten: his parents, India and Lewis; Hedwig, his wife; his brothers Yancy, John, and William; his sister Kate; and Mireille, the girl he was going to marry in Paris but who died.

They were on the opposite bank of the stream, standing pressed tightly together, with tall, feathery reeds rising around them. India and Hedwig were smiling at him, their eyes glistening with happy tears, Lewis raised his right hand in greeting, but the boys and Kate and Mireille stared at him with expressions of wonder.

The purling of the water changed to a whisper as Thomas looked at them. He couldn't understand what it was saying but knew it was important. He strained to make out what it was, but just when he thought he was beginning to catch a few words, the whisper began to fade.

There was nothing for him here and he had to return to the house. After a few steps in the soft earth, he looked back, but the stream was gone and the vast empty field with the furrows ran to the horizon.

Thomas was still dead to the world, but his heart was beating weakly and regularly when the four men carried him out of the *banya* into Istomin's house and up to one of the bedrooms on the second floor.

He didn't regain consciousness until dawn on the following day.

He felt he was lying on something soft and saw a dim light pass in front of his closed eyelids. When he opened them, Zoya was bending over him, shielding a candle with her hand, her kindly face silhouetted against the room's white ceiling.

Thomas's awakening caused a stir in the house. Istomin hurried into the bedroom and breathed a sigh of relief when he saw his friend's eyes were open and focused on him. The doctor, who had expected Thomas to die in the *banya*, was amazed by how much he'd improved: his skin color lost its deathly greyness, the wound in his side was less inflamed, and the swelling that began to spread over his torso receded.

When he put his stethoscope to Thomas's chest, he heard a calm and regular heartbeat and was honest enough to admit to himself that this couldn't have been due to the injection of adrenaline he had made.

For a few minutes Thomas luxuriated in the feeling of a hazy and unfocussed well-being as he lay in the cool, clean sheets. He smiled weakly at Istomin.

But when Istomin saw Thomas's smile, his heart sank.

The *dvornik* who helped Thomas in the street had told Istomin everything he'd seen, and Istomin knew he didn't have the right to withhold this from his friend, no matter what state he was in.

Putting his hand on Thomas's shoulder, he began by asking him if he remembered what happened to Olga.

When he heard her name, memory of the abduction crashed down on Thomas.

"*It was that Southerner, the one who came to Aquarium!*" he exclaimed in a hoarse voice, raising his head from the pillow. "I recognized him . . . and his accomplice too. He's an American from the South. They'd been in Aquarium the same night we met at Yar. I threw them out and they're the ones who kidnapped Olga!"

Istomin remembered what Thomas had told him about the abduction of Masha Nikitina, the daughter of one of his waiters, and how he'd asked for help in finding her.

"What do you mean? Are you saying these men who attacked you and Olga are the same gang you told me about, the ones kidnapping children in the city?"

"I don't know! *But don't you see?*" Thomas said, struggling to sit up, although the effort made him feel so dizzy he had to drop back onto the pillow: "It doesn't make any difference because I know who kidnapped Olga! He's an American, his name is Caleb something—Dicker . . . Dickerson or something . . . he told me what it was. Whether or not he's part of the gang that kidnapped the others doesn't matter. He's got Olga!"

"*My God, my God!*" Thomas exclaimed, as the thought of what they might do to his little girl sank in.

A wave of fatigue and nausea engulfed him, and he asked Istomin for a drink of water. Zoya had left a big glass covered with a clean white handkerchief and filled with something that looked like tea on the night table by the bed and had told Istomin it was important for Thomas to drink it. Thinking his friend would take only a few sips from the glass, Istomin carefully raised it to his lips, but Thomas drained all of it, stopping only once to catch his breath.

A good sign, Istomin thought to himself.

"We'll get her back, I'm certain we will," he tried to assure Thomas, sounding buoyant but concealing how much Olga's fate frightened him as well.

Then he remembered something that might be encouraging: "I phoned Markov, your security man, last night to tell him what happened to you, and he told me Koshko assigned someone good to the case of the waiter's daughter after all, a detective who's been on the force for twenty years, Vatslav Stanislavovich Fedukovich. And you know," he added as a new thought occurred to him, "that Southerner had to register with the city police when he came to Moscow, so there has to be a record of where he lives, where Olga might be!"

But Thomas was no longer listening. Whatever was in Zoya's drink suffused him with calm, he closed his eyes, and in another few seconds his face and mouth went slack.

Istomin leaned over him in alarm but saw that his friend was breathing regularly. He had fallen into a deep sleep.

For a few seconds Istomin listened to him breathe and watched his chest rise and fall. He checked the time and saw it was nearly 5 a. m. Taking a small notebook from a pocket in his vest, he wrote down the names Thomas mentioned, then went to his bedroom, thinking he had enough time to get a few hours' sleep himself before starting to search for this "Southerner."

CHAPTER TWENTY-FIVE

While the frightened yardman, his heart pounding from excitement and exertion, was running to get help for Thomas, Dickerman's black coach was clattering over the cobblestones of Nikitsky Boulevard toward Khamovniki and the sanctuary of the Convent.

Stepan and Bartkow sat slumped in their seats, bloodied and dazed, their heads rocking helplessly with every bump the coach hit. Dickerman's face was glistening with sweat. He was still breathing heavily from helping to haul the two men into the coach and struggling with the Black girl, who was now lying on the floor between their feet. She was stronger than she looked, and he had to use all his weight to keep the rag saturated with the chloroform mixture pressed to her face until she passed out.

Bartkow's face was swollen, a smear of blood was drying on his chin, and his long jaw was askew and turning purple. He could barely open his mouth to speak. After the coach started, he tried to mumble something about "a hospital," but Dickerman snarled at him, *"Forget it!"*

Stepan looked even worse because of the amount of blood congealing on his face from his cut brow and broken nose. He hadn't been able to stanch the flow with his sleeve and a lot had poured down over his mouth and chin onto his shirt and jacket. His eyes were rolling back in their sockets with only the whites showing, and he seemed close to losing consciousness.

What a goddamn mess, what a goddamn mess, Dickerman kept thinking as he looked at the two men. He glanced at Boris, who had gotten off unscathed, but the man sullenly avoided his gaze.

A hospital! Dickerman sneered, thinking of Bartkow's whining. *All I need is to go to some hospital and have a doctor*

155

ask me questions about what'd happened and who I am.

He imagined a busybody peering inside the coach and asking: "And who is that girl lying on the floor, sir?" The idea was so absurd that Dickerman snorted. *No, we'll get a goddam doctor for these dumb shits when we're safe at the house and not before.*

But at least I got the bastard! it occurred to him. *And we grabbed his little bitch!*

The thought that he'd succeeded after all, even with the beating his two men got, cheered Dickerman.

He ran through the details of the attack, savoring them. He remembered how he'd gotten ready to stab Thomas in the back with his sword cane after Bartkow smashed him with the cosh, and that it almost didn't work because of how surprisingly quick and strong that Black bastard turned out to be. It was an even greater shock when he whipped around at the last second, as if he'd sensed Dickerman was approaching.

But I was still too quick for him! Dickerman thrilled, reliving the feeling of his sword going through the man's jacket into his left side before it was stopped by bone.

He parted the window curtain to check where they were. The Novodevichy Convent's red and white bell tower and gold cupola were already visible above the trees ahead on the right, which meant the coach was almost at the mansion.

And he knew who sent him to hell! There ain't no one gonna survive what I put on the blade, Dickerman thought with satisfaction.

To make sure the sword cane would kill, he had coated the first foot of its razor-sharp tip with a thick mixture of rattlesnake venom and strychnine and allowed it to dry. It could last for months inside the cane, and there was enough on the blade to kill an ox.

Feeling more buoyant, Dickerman grinned, and in a rare gesture, reached over and slapped Boris on the shoulder.

"Don't you worry. We're going to be OK!" he said in a reassuring tone. "We'll fix up these fellas," he nodded at Stepan and Bartkow, "and we'll be back in business!"

Dickerman's touch startled Boris and he didn't

understand the English. But he could tell the boss was trying to be encouraging, which rarely happened, and a sheepish grin spread across his broad, thick-lipped mouth.

However, on this occasion fate did not intend for Dickerman's good mood to last very long. No sooner had the coach pulled up to the Convent and he had gone inside to get Hilda and Maria to help with Olga than Boris ran in shouting, "*Stürmer! Stürmer!*"

Dickerman looked out the parlor window, saw the long black automobile pulling under the porte cochère, and felt his throat constrict with panic.

The timing couldn't have been worse because the two bloodied men were in full view as the driver and Boris were helping them out of the coach.

"*Mein Gott!* (My God!) What happened here?" Stürmer exclaimed in a shocked voice when Dickerman hurried outside.

"There was a little accident, my dear baron, just a little accident," Dickerman replied as calmly as he could and in what he hoped was his most conciliatory tone.

"What sort of accident? A collision in traffic?" Stürmer asked uncertainly as he stepped toward at the coach, which did not seem to show any damage.

"No, baron, we ran into a bit of . . . eh, trouble when we were . . . collecting our last . . . our last filly."

"Collecting? But you told me you were finished! And in a few days, you are supposed to open!" Stürmer's exclaimed, his voice developing a shrill edge.

"There were . . . developments that changed our plans, just a bit. But all is well now. The man who did this," Dickerman gestured to Bartkow and Stepan as they were being helped to walk to the front door, "won't bother us anymore. And I saw to it that there would be no consequences."

Stürmer could not believe what he was hearing: "What do you mean, the man?" he cried in disbelief. "Only one man did this! Who? What happened to him? What did you do?"

Dickerman hesitated. He was torn between reluctance to tell Stürmer anything and wanting to brag so the German would know who he was dealing with. *And what's the difference?* he thought. *It's not as if that Black bastard matters or Stürmer's own hands are lily white.*

"I ran that sonofabitch through like a pig on a skewer!" he said, raising his chin proudly.

"You killed someone?" Stürmer gaped.

"It was self-defense, baron!" Dickerman said in a petulant tone. "He insulted me, and I paid him back. No one saw it. There were no witnesses."

"Insulted you! Who was it? And where is the body? Where did this happen?"

"We left it and got outa there. Believe you me, no one saw it, and no one will know what happened."

"I cannot believe you are telling me this!" Stürmer exclaimed and looked around nervously at the trees in front of the mansion, as if someone could be lurking behind them. The wall of secrecy and deniability he'd fashioned around the operation had been hideously breached. He felt all his self-possession slipping away.

"But who was it, I ask you?" Stürmer asked shrilly, raising his hands in frustration at Dickerman's evasiveness.

"Just the girl's pappy, baron—don't worry, a man of no importance," Dickerman lied, trying to sound matter of fact. Stürmer's growing panic was increasing his own, and he was beginning to feel that his attempt to control the situation was slipping.

Just then, Hilda and Maria, who had gone to the coach and paused to watch for a moment because of the loud argument between Dickerman and Stürmer, began to pull and lift Olga's limp body out of it.

"What is that? What . . . what is that?" Stürmer stammered, pointing with his trembling index finger.

"That's the filly I got to add to the . . . to our stable. I just told you."

"But what is she is wearing! That is a uniform of a private school!" Stürmer yelled, his command of English slipping

because of his agitation. "She is from of a family of property? Her father it was you killed?"

Stürmer walked hesitantly toward the two women and leaned over to peer into Olga's face as if he was afraid of what he would see.

"*She is not white!*" he shrieked so loudly that Dickerman cringed. "*Who was her father! Tell me!*"

"Let's go inside, baron. Inside . . . we'll discuss it there," Dickerman said, trying to sound ingratiating and gesturing with his right arm toward the mansion's door.

"No, no, no! I insist you tell me now, you . . . you stupid man! Tell me now!" Stürmer demanded.

The insult angered Dickerman. Despite his nervousness, he gathered himself up and hissed: "You watch how you talk to me! I ain't your flunky! Anyway, the man's name is Thomas, Frederick Thomas, although he uses a Russky name for some reason. He runs, or, rather, he used to run," Dickerman added with a twisted smile, "the Aquarium Garden."

"God in heaven, worse and worse it gets! I know that place! Everyone in Moscow knows it! The man is rich, and he is a foreigner! From where is he?"

"He is, or he was, an American Black," Dickerson spat out.

Hearing this, Stürmer clenched his fists. He wanted to grab the stupid fat American and slap him across the face the way he would a dense and clumsy private. He restrained himself with difficulty. It was more important to figure out what to do. He also had to report immediately what had happened to his superior, Colonel Michaelis.

His face twitching with emotion, Stürmer looked directly into Dickerman's eyes and ordered in a quiet, trembling voice: "You will stop now all preparations for the opening and wait for me to return with instructions. I am going to consult with my . . . consortium about how to proceed. Stay in the house. Do not go anywhere. Call a doctor to come here for those two and make up an excuse about what happened to them. Do you understand?"

Caleb bristled at Stürmer's tone and glowered at him but said nothing. He knew himself that he needed time to think about how he could save the situation, and he was planning to lie low for a while anyway.

CHAPTER TWENTY-SIX

Stürmer was too agitated to drive when he got into his automobile. He sat behind the wheel for several minutes, looking blankly at the windscreen in front of him and his wan reflection in it, which seemed to float against the green background of the garden's foliage like a pale ghost. He could scarcely believe the entire plan might have to be abandoned now after all the effort and money that had been expended on it. Even worse was that its failure would probably end his career.

So many unhappy thoughts were roiling in his mind he didn't notice the big black raven that flew in from somewhere and landed on a low branch of one of the old oaks near the mansion. It cawed once, and, flapping heavily, soared to the Gothic spire above the front door and cawed again. Turning its sharp, glossy beak back and forth several times, it seemed to eye the long black automobile and the man sitting in it. From the spire it flew up to the roof, cawed one last time and disappeared as suddenly if it had dropped into a fissure in the air.

Stürmer came to, started the engine, and began to drive through the heavy shadows of the tree-lined driveway, his automobile rocking softly as it rolled over the thick roots that had spread everywhere under the gravel, as if trying to block its passage. When he reached the street, he turned left and headed north, planning to take the Crimean Bridge over the Moscow River to the Yakimanka District.

Traffic along the riverbank road was backed up because of some religious procession or other at the giant, white marble Christ the Savior Cathedral up ahead and the trip took longer than Stürmer expected, which he found frustrating. He struggled to adjust to the constant disruptions of daily life in Moscow caused by church events and holidays. As far as he was concerned, this famous Russian religiosity was excessive and served only as additional evidence of the country's contemptible backwardness.

When Stürmer arrived at his destination, a nondescript two-story wooden building covered with peeling grey paint down the street from the gloomy First City Hospital near the Kaluzhsky Gate, he drove past it and parked the automobile around the corner behind a line of empty dray carts. He returned to the building on foot.

Looking around to see if anyone was following him, Stürmer turned into the dirt-covered alleyway between the building and its twin, ran up the short flight of stairs to the rear entrance and knocked on a door. It bore an enameled blue and white sign announcing in Russian and German, "Schmidt & Sons: Imports and Exports." The guard, a sergeant in civilian clothes, examined Stürmer through a peephole, snapped to attention when he let him into the shabby foyer, and opened an inner door for him on the right.

Stürmer entered, glancing at a table covered with samples of cloth, machine gears, tightly-wound spools of wire, and other hardware—all "samples" of German exports—before announcing to the duty officer, "*Hauptmann* Stürmer to see *Oberst* Michaelis."

The junior lieutenant, also in mufti, rose to his feet.

"One moment, please, captain," he replied, gestured to a row of chairs along the wall, knocked on the door behind his desk, and went in.

Stürmer took a seat beneath a photograph of a stern-looking Kaiser Wilhelm II, dressed in one of his gaudy guards' uniforms, the tips of his moustache twisted up like a boar's tusks. A minute later the lieutenant emerged, invited Stürmer to enter, and closed the door behind him.

Colonel Michaelis was at his desk with a neat stack of folders in front of him and looking at Stürmer with a faint smile. He had come to Moscow two weeks ago from his base in East Prussia to review several of his operations, including the Convent. He also wanted to see what he could learn about the state of preparedness of the Moscow Military District's five army corps, which had begun large-scale maneuvers in connection with the Romanov Tercentenary celebrations.

The Okhrana knew who he was; and he knew they knew. But the time for a visit was opportune because the police were so preoccupied with security for the celebrations, they could assign only a handful of *fileurs*, or spies, to follow him. Taking advantage of the lax security, Michaelis had recently made a short trip to Kiev, where, with the assistance of a German-born veterinarian, he developed a plan to spread the equine disease glanders in Moldova and Ukraine, which supplied mounts to the Russian Empire's vast cavalry forces.

Michaelis would have been a handsome man, with his high forehead, square jaw, and neatly trimmed moustache, were it not for a deep dueling scar under his left eye which he acquired while still a military cadet. It ran down his cheek, pulling on the lower eyelid and giving the left side of his face a permanent expression of surprise that was disconcerting. His interlocutors often didn't know which side of his face to look at or how to read his expression. By contrast, he found his disfigurement useful, especially during interrogations, and it added to his reputation as a very perspicacious judge of character.

Stürmer's unexpected arrival at the main safe house of German Military Intelligence in Moscow and the anxious expression on his pale, small-featured face told Michaelis he was in trouble. But since Stürmer was the son of a senior general on the German General Staff who had the Kaiser's confidence, he would have to be treated reasonably gently, at least initially. Nevertheless, rank was rank, and Michaelis let the young baron stand at attention for a few long moments before he addressed him.

"Captain, you have come to report about the Convent operation. What is the problem?"

Stürmer was already in awe of Michaelis' reputation as a spymaster, but the precision and directness of the question took him aback. He felt himself blush, which made him blush even more. Then, with the same feeling he had when he launched himself down a steep mountain slope on skis, he confessed everything he had just discovered.

Michaelis listened attentively, drawing his lips into a thin line as Stürmer poured out his story of "the disaster," as he called it. The news was certainly not good, but Michaelis' long experience with complex intelligence operations had taught him they rarely went as planned. That was simply the nature of the game, like the fog of war. Stürmer's only real fault, Michaelis decided, was his inexperience in choosing Dickerman to run the Convent without having probed his psychological weak spots more thoroughly.

But it is easy to make such a mistake, Michaelis mused as he watched Stürmer stand at awkward attention. *One can never anticipate how a recruit will react to an unexpected development. A seemingly brave man will crumble, but a weakling can show unexpected courage. And who could have imagined this American fool Dickerman would have a run-in with a rich Black American in Moscow, of all places!*

Michaelis now had to decide two questions. Could the Convent operation, which had cost a great deal of money and promised to be a powerful tool of blackmail and control over some leading figures in Russian society, still be saved? And was Stürmer, and therefore Michaelis himself, in danger from Russian counterintelligence?

Whatever happened to Dickerman and his gang or to their victims was of little concern. They were expendable because they were all merely tools of historical necessity—the coming great battle of the German Empire for living space and resources. And none of them knew anything about the much greater wheel that made their own little wheel spin.

"Yes, captain, a messy situation," Michaelis sighed.

"*Colonel, sir! It is my fault entirely!*" Stürmer proclaimed, raising his chin, and trying to stand even more erect. "I am prepared to be put under arrest!"

"Not so fast, captain, not so fast," Michaelis replied calmly. "Your task is not over yet. Things look troublesome from our perspective, yes. But how do they seem from the Russians' point of view? What do they know about any of this?"

Stürmer hardly dared to breathe as he stared at Michaelis.

He thought he was sinking, but now he felt like a shipwrecked sailor who sees search lights piercing the howling darkness and a lifeline being thrown to him across the white-capped waves.

Michaelis got up from behind his desk and walked to the dirt-streaked window that looked out over the backyard, which looked dreary and forlorn in the fading light. When he first leased the building, the yard was completely overgrown, and he had hired workmen with scythes to clear the field grasses and wildflowers that had taken root. They also cut down a dozen birch saplings that had sprouted, leaving their sharp ends protruding like spikes from the ground.

Michaelis thought for several minutes before turning around. He had decided to reveal something he had been keeping in reserve for just such a moment.

"At ease, *Hauptmann*," he said and watched as Stürmer relaxed awkwardly.

"I am going to reveal a secret to you. An important one. I have a man in the Moscow detective bureau. He is a strictly undercover asset and very valuable. You will contact him according to the instructions I will give you and will ask him to find out what, if anything, the police know about the Convent, or Dickerman, or this murdered Black man . . . Friedrich Thomas, you said? Once we find out, we will know what to do—what is possible and what is not."

"Yes, sir!"

"It is essential that our agent's identity be kept absolutely secret, do you understand? We will soon need him for bigger and more important matters."

"I understand, sir!"

"Are you sure you can handle this yourself?"

Stürmer blushed again at the new rebuke implied in the question: "I am certain, sir!"

"Because, you know, you can have Sergeants Rutschen, Gifter and Schlanger to help. I brought them with me from Königsberg. They are reliable and experienced with all forms of clandestine work." Michaelis scrutinized Stürmer's face to see that he understood.

"Thank you, sir! That is good to know, and I will bear it in mind. But I can handle the matter now by myself."

Michaelis waited a moment, just long enough to make the young officer feel uncomfortable if he was still holding anything back. But Stürmer remained silent, his eyes fixed on Michaelis and his whole body straining with attention.

Michaelis pulled a small notebook from an inside pocket, looked up something, took a blank sheet of paper from a desk drawer and wrote down a half dozen short lines on it in pencil. He explained to Stürmer that these were the secret agent's code name, the telephone number to call to arrange a meeting with him, and the code phrases to be used when specifying when and where the meeting was to take place. He handed the sheet to Stürmer and instructed him to go to the anteroom, memorize all the details and return the sheet to the duty officer so he could burn it.

"You may not leave with the sheet, understood?"

The reprieve and the thrill of the new mission transformed Stürmer. Being bare headed, he clicked his heels in lieu of a salute: "Thank you, colonel, for entrusting me with this! It will be done!" He turned about-face and strode out.

Michaelis returned to the papers on his desk. *Whatever happens,* he thought, *General Baron Baldur von Stürmer will think well of this chance I gave his son.*

CHAPTER TWENTY-SEVEN

Wednesday, May 27, 7 a.m.
Prince Vladimir Istomin's residence
17 Malaya Nikitskaya Street

Istomin tried to go to bed when Thomas fell asleep, but he was too upset by everything that had happened and gave up after an hour and a half of intermittent dozing and tossing. Kicking the sheets and blanket off himself in annoyance, he went to his bathroom and took a long, hot shower, then turned off the hot water and turned on the cold, forcing himself to endure the freezing stream for a count of fifteen. He was shaking and sputtering when he got out, but he felt awake. After getting dressed, he looked in on Thomas, who was breathing evenly, made tea himself in the kitchen because the cook wasn't up yet, and carrying a glass in a silver holder went to his study to plan how he would pursue the leads that had occurred to him. By 9 a. m. Istomin's patience ran out. When he heard his valet beginning to tidy up downstairs, he asked him to check in on Thomas periodically and left the house.

Istomin first thought of going to the central Moscow police registry to see if he could find out anything about the American Southerner who attacked Thomas and Olga. But knowing how slow the city bureaucracy was, he decided he had a better chance of getting a quick answer from the American diplomatic representative in Moscow, who also kept records of visitors and residents from the United States.

The American Consulate General occupied a suite of rooms on the first floor of an old, well-maintained, cream-colored apartment building at 9 Arkhangelskiy Lane, a short distance from Chistoprudny Boulevard and its linear park. Istomin drove over in time for its opening at 10 a. m. in his green Russo-Balt convertible, and since the weather was dry and sunny, he kept the top down. He bought it the previous fall after examining several more popular foreign automobiles and deciding it would be good to support domestic production. Taking off his hat and gloves, he presented his card to the young Russian clerk in the anteroom and asked to speak with the consul general himself.

A minute after disappearing through an inner door, the clerk returned, invited Istomin to follow him down a corridor, and ushered him into a high-ceilinged office filled with bookcases and filing cabinets. A large map of the Russian Empire covered the wall between the windows and a photograph of President Woodrow Wilson hung behind the consul's desk. A faint smell of good American tobacco permeated the room.

Consul-General John Harold Snodgrass, a tall, courtly man with a narrow, pale, Puritan face—rather like Wilson's, Istomin thought—came around from behind his cluttered desk. He shook Istomin's hand warmly and asked him to take one of a pair of facing armchairs, then sat in the other himself.

Snodgrass spoke Russian well, although with a typical American accent. He had worked in various commercial and diplomatic capacities in Russia for over a decade, liked the country, and made a point of addressing Istomin by his title, which he evidently enjoyed doing. His eyebrows shot up and he seemed impressed when Istomin switched to his fluent British English.

While driving to the consulate, Istomin thought he should invent a reason for asking for the consul-general's help in locating an American in Moscow. Otherwise, the request might seem to be an invasion of privacy and could be denied.

He came up with the idea that he was interested in discussing a business proposition, namely, exporting linen from his factory in Kostroma to the United States. He explained he had been told that a Mr. Caleb Dickerson, or Dickerman—he wasn't quite sure how the name ended—who recently arrived in the city was in the business and might be interested.

"What a fascinating possibility, prince," Snodgrass responded, skillfully concealing behind a polite smile his actual reaction, which was immediate skepticism.

Snodgrass spent most of his time dealing with trade issues between Russia and the United States and knew that something like Istomin's proposal was unlikely to succeed for any number of reasons, not the least of which was competition from the British textile industry.

But it wasn't his job to discourage trade relations or to disappoint a Russian nobleman. Smiling again, he agreed to check his register of Americans in Moscow for surnames beginning with "Dicker" and rang for the clerk.

Several minutes later, Istomin was back in his automobile with a slip of paper on which Snodgrass had written "Caleb Forrest Dickerman of St. Landry Parish, Louisiana, and Lexington, Kentucky; arrived Moscow July 17, 1912; professions—horse trainer, business man; Hollberg Pension, Lubyansky Passage 3."

When Snodgrass examined the registration card and saw what profession had brought Dickerman to Moscow, his skepticism about Istomin's proposed venture became total, although all he said in parting was "Good luck, your excellency!"

The address where Dickerman first stayed when he arrived in the city was nearby and Istomin drove there in five minutes. A plump, middle-aged German woman was sitting on a stool behind the counter in the pension's tidy foyer, placidly knitting. Istomin's question about "Amerikanets Kaleb Dikerman" who had been a guest ten months ago made her scratch her head with a needle. After a moment's thought she allowed as how she remembered him, vaguely, and only because Americans were rare visitors to her establishment. He hadn't stayed long, and she didn't know where he went. Nothing made him memorable.

Istomin left disappointed but not surprised. He had only one other lead, and an hour later pulled into the driveway of the Moscow Hippodrome. The sky started to darken, so he put up the convertible top on his automobile before entering the grounds.

He didn't know what Dickerman looked like, except that he was "short" and "fat," according to Thomas. Istomin also had no reason to think he would even be at the track in the middle of the week, or working there at all, for that matter. The biggest problem, however, would be to penetrate the closed club atmosphere of the racing world and to overcome its members' suspiciousness about inquisitive strangers.

Unable to think of any better way of going about it, Istomin spent the entire afternoon wandering around the vast territory near the stables, and in the towering Hippodrome Pavilion itself. He approached anyone who looked like he might work there in some capacity and asked him about an "Amerikansky trener Kaleb Dikerman."

It had started to drizzle steadily, Istomin hadn't brought an umbrella, and people were annoyed when he stopped them. Some of the older and more experienced-looking men shook their heads in response to his question, their eyes narrowing skeptically; others smiled ironically at his presumption and replied they had never heard of him. The only thing that saved Istomin from harsher reactions was his distinguished manner and that he didn't look like a detective.

When he tried to go inside the stables, guards politely but firmly turned him away, explaining, "It's not permitted by regulations, sir, unless you are an owner or have a pass from an owner." Istomin decided it wasn't worth trying to get one. It would take such elaborate invention he doubted he could carry off.

Only once did his heart leap when a pink-cheeked youth leading a chestnut mare to a practice track tried to be helpful. The young man's face brightened at the word "Amerikansky," and he pointed to a barn near the stables, saying he had just seen "him" behind it. Istomin walked over briskly, but when he turned the corner, he stopped. Supervising two grooms who were brushing a beautiful roan Arabian in an open-sided shed was a young, short, slender, and dapper Black man.

Istomin recognized him from photographs in newspapers. It was Jimmy Winkfield, the American jockey who had won the Kentucky Derby twice before leaving the United States (to escape racism, Istomin assumed). He was famous in Moscow for having won all the major races in Russia, including the Imperial Cup. Istomin smiled wryly at his mistake.

There was nothing left but to return home. His clothing was soaked, and it was time to check on Thomas.

CHAPTER TWENTY-EIGHT

Thursday, May 28, 8:30 a.m.
Captain Baron Wolfgang von Stürmer's apartment
71 Starosadsky Lane

Stürmer came from a rich Prussian Junker family with estates in Silesia and received a generous allowance from his parents to supplement his officer's pay. This allowed him to rent a comfortable, furnished apartment in Moscow by himself, with daily maid service, a telephone, and errand boys on call who brought him his meals from a restaurant around the corner. It was on the third floor of a new building across the street from the Saints Peter and Paul German Lutheran Church, a fifteen-minute walk east of the Kremlin.

Stürmer's "cover" in Russia was as a sales representative for Stark GmbH Pharmaceuticals in Berlin. He chose the neighborhood because other members of Moscow's large German colony lived there, and he made a point of attending services at the church every Sunday to add to his peaceable profile in case any *fileurs* were tailing him.

Shortly after getting up on Thursday morning, Stürmer began to prepare to telephone the secret German agent in the Moscow detective bureau. He'd never done anything like this before and it made him nervous.

For several minutes he sat on a couch, warily eyeing the brass apparatus glinting on his desk, and ran through the instructions Michaelis had given him. He decided it would be safer to call from his apartment than from a post office where he could be easily distracted or overheard. And he would be speaking in code, so there was no risk if his telephone line was tapped.

The information Michaelis instructed Stürmer to memorize was intricate, and even though he wasn't supposed to keep a copy of it, he wrote everything down as soon as he got home out of fear of forgetting some detail. He walked over to his desk, put the sheet in front of him and pulled the telephone closer. Taking a deep breath, he wiped his sweaty palms on his pants and rang the operator. When she replied, he tried to sound calm as he asked to be connected to 2638, which was the secret agent's office number.

A man's voice answered. Stürmer didn't know who it was—the agent or some chance co-worker—and, following his script, asked to speak with "Ni-ko-láy Ni-ko-lá-ye-vich Fe-dós-kin," enunciating the syllables very clearly. The agent's actual name was Pyotr Fyodorovich Ivanov, and this "wrong" name was the sign indicating that the call was from his contacts in German intelligence.

The man on the other end seemed to hesitate before replying, "there is no one here by that name." Stürmer pressed the receiver to his left ear more tightly and listened with bated breath to see if the man would say anything else. To his relief he did:

"My dear, sir!" the man added in an annoyed tone, "in the past three days I've gotten seven wrong calls!"

The response and the numbers "three" and "seven" constituted the countersign indicating it was indeed the agent Ivanov who had answered the telephone. Any other response would have led Stürmer to hang up and try again later.

Now Stürmer had to set the day and time of the meeting, and for this he needed to speak quickly to make the conversation sound realistic if anyone was listening in.

"I'm sorry, but is this number 528?" he asked, using the code for May 28, or, in other words, the same day. A second later he pretended to correct himself and said "Sorry, I meant 2813."

Moscow's telephone numbers were either three or four digits, and the last pair signified that Stürmer wanted to meet Ivanov that same day at 13:00 hours, or 1 p. m. It was not necessary to specify the location because it was understood the meeting would be in a particular section of the linear park near the northern end of Tverskoy Boulevard.

"No, it's neither," Ivanov replied testily and hung up. If the date and time were not convenient, Ivanov would have recited other numbers.

Stürmer leaned back in his desk chair and congratulated himself on arranging the meeting successfully. His hands felt cold and moist again, and he felt a trickle of sweat running from his armpit down his left side. Pulling out a handkerchief, he dabbed at the film of perspiration on his face and forehead.

Michaelis' procedures had seemed overly complex when he first tried to memorize them, but now Stürmer appreciated how ingenious they were. No one who might have been eavesdropping on the call could have guessed what it was actually about. And if any of the codes needed to be changed, it could be done easily during the meeting itself.

Detective Pyotr Ivanov sat for a minute at his desk in police headquarters after the German on the other end rang off. He knew it wasn't Michaelis, who had recruited him—the voice was different, although this man spoke Russian as well as Michaelis. Something was afoot with the Germans, and he was intrigued.

Ivanov noted the time and left his office. He walked down the green-painted corridor, which was illuminated by dim gas lights and smelled faintly of the carbolic acid the janitor used when cleaning the detention cells in the basement, trotted down a flight of stairs and knocked on the door of the Director of the Moscow Detective Bureau, Arkady Frantsevich Koshko.

"The Germans have taken the bait, Arkady Frantsevich!" he said excitedly after stepping inside and closing the door behind himself.

Koshko gestured to a chair in front of his desk and leaned forward expectantly as Ivanov described the call he had just gotten.

CHAPTER TWENTY-NINE

Thursday morning had started out brisk and sunny, but by noon the sky became overcast, the temperature dropped, and a steady rain began to fall. Despite the weather, Ivanov left the headquarters building of the Moscow police department at 12:30 so he could get some air and think as he walked to his meeting. He waited for a break in the continuous stream of wagons, cabs, and carriages on Tverskoy Boulevard, crossed its northern side from Sytinsky Lane, and entered the boulevard's median park ten minutes before the German agent was supposed to arrive.

Standing under his umbrella, he looked to the left and right at the benches spaced evenly along the yellow gravel walkway but saw no one. Linden trees grew in several parallel rows the length of the linear park and their water-stained black branches contrasted with the pale green, heart-shaped leaves that were beginning to cover them. The air was clean and smelled of wet earth. A light breeze made the leaves shiver, releasing the drops that had accumulated on them and letting them fall to the ground with a continuous melancholy patter.

Ivanov was an experienced detective who dealt mostly with financial crimes such as counterfeiting or embezzlement, although he had also collaborated with the Okhrana on crimes involving foreigners and their movements across the Russian frontier. When, half a year ago, the Okhrana's Moscow bureau chief, Leonid Pavlovich Menshikov, started getting reports that Colonel Georg Michaelis, who was well known to him, had begun to visit Moscow, he decided to try to infiltrate the Germans' local operation.

To do this Menshikov coordinated with Ivanov's superior, Koshko—a process that went more smoothly than he expected, given their occasional interdepartmental rivalries—and Koshko delegated Ivanov to try to get close to the Germans. The Detective Bureau knew the pulse of the city better than anyone else and had scores of informants in different locations and among the most different social groups. It didn't take long for Ivanov to learn where Michaelis and some of his underlings liked to spend their free time.

Ivanov began to frequent these places too, most often the Alpine Rose, a comfortable old restaurant near Theatrical Square that was a favorite with German businessmen. Playing the role of a tipsy and disgruntled windbag, Ivanov made a point of complaining to anyone who would listen about the lousy pay and poor working conditions in the Moscow Detective Bureau.

In time, this reached Michaelis' ears. He investigated Ivanov and learned he had been an exemplary detective for a dozen years, but that, according to his landlady (who was on the Moscow Detective Bureau's payroll), was living beyond his means.

When Michaelis finally approached him, Ivanov initially pretended to be shocked at the idea of working as an informant for the Germans. But after hemming and hawing convincingly for several weeks, he agreed to do it for a monthly retainer of two hundred rubles. His primary task, Michaelis explained, would simply be to pass on anything he heard about police interest in German activities in Moscow.

To test Ivanov, Michaelis had one of his regular agents, whose cover was attaché for economic affairs in the German Consulate General, begin to frequent a café near the Spassky Army Barracks in the northeastern part of the city that was popular with officers of the regiment billeted there. The agent befriended two junior lieutenants and pretended to be curious about army life, quizzing them about the regiment's strength, training, equipment, and planned deployment in case of war. The officers reported this to their commanding officer, who reported it to the Okhrana, and the Okhrana informed the Moscow police department. Ivanov then "leaked" to Michaelis that his spy had come to the notice of the police and would soon be arrested. Michaelis immediately ordered his compromised agent to leave Russia on his diplomatic passport. And as far as Michaelis was concerned, Ivanov had proven that he was trustworthy.

A minute before 1 p. m., *with German punctuality*, Ivanov noted wryly, a man in a long black raincoat, wide-brimmed hat, and carrying an umbrella appeared at the northern end of the park near Strastnaya Square and began to walk toward him. He occasionally varied his stride to step over puddles that had formed on the broad gravel path. The detective watched him approach and when he got nearer took a step toward him. They sized each other up before either said anything.

Ivanov noted that the German held himself erect like a soldier, not a civilian, but his features were small and undistinguished and he seemed nervous. To Stürmer, Ivanov's slanting eyes and dusky complexion made him look oriental. *Scratch a Russian and you'll find a Tatar*, Stürmer thought with distaste, recalling Napoleon's famous dictum.

"Nikolay Nikolayevich Fedoskin?" Stürmer asked, and holding his umbrella in his right hand, raised his hat with his left.

Ivanov tipped his bowler and replied "528, 2813," thus giving the necessary countersign.

This confirmed their identities and Ivanov suggested they stroll down the central lane of the median. He noticed Stürmer hesitate, as if he was uncertain how to behave.

Must be a beginner, Ivanov thought.

After walking a few paces over the softly crunching gravel, Stürmer cleared his throat. He had rehearsed what he was going to say and knew he needed to strike a balance between asking questions that were specific but that did not reveal more than was strictly necessary.

"We are interested in two matters," he said in his good Russian with only a trace of a German accent. "What do the police know about abductions of children in the city during the past few weeks? Also, what do they know about the murder of the entertainment impresario at the Aquarium Garden, the American Black man, Frederick Thomas?"

The questions surprised Ivanov and he examined the German's face more closely. Ivanov hadn't heard anything about either of these matters and couldn't understand what they could have to do with German espionage, which in the past always focused on military and economic topics.

He was careful to conceal his surprise, however, and replied, noncommittally, "I will make inquiries, of course." At the same time, he was thinking about what he could do to get the German to tell him more.

Make it seem I misunderstood the first question and keep him talking, he decided.

"The police naturally get many reports about missing children in a city this size. Can you tell me which children interest you, or where the abductions took place?"

Stürmer hesitated. He realized that Ivanov's question was a practical one but also that it would be dangerous to reveal any details.

He decided to speak abstractly: "We need to know about any patterns the police have noticed. And not regarding children who have gone missing but who have been abducted."

You bastards must be involved, Ivanov thought and felt himself getting angry.

But he hid his reaction with a cough, as if he was clearing his throat. "That may not be easy," he replied, "but I'll look into it. And this impresario who you said was killed," he added as if it was an afterthought, "do you know where this happened or when?"

"That's not important," Stürmer replied curtly. He understood that to reveal either fact would be like acknowledging complicity. "Just let me know what has been reported."

The two men had strolled to a point level with the Church of Saint John the Theologian, the gates to which were across from Tverskoy Boulevard. A movement at the top of its pink, faceted bell tower attracted Ivanov's attention and he looked up. Amid the suspended bells was a figure in a long dark garment looking toward the park, as if standing watch over him. Ivanov smiled to himself at the thought.

The steady rain became heavier, more puddles formed on the gravel walkway, and the patter of the raindrops falling to the ground from the lindens got louder. Ivanov put his collar up against the damp chill.

"I need to have answers by tomorrow," Stürmer said, looking at Ivanov with what he hoped was a stern mien. "So, I would like to meet across from Malaya Bronnaya tomorrow at 10 a.m."

"I'm not sure I'll be able to find out by then."

"You must try," Stürmer replied with finality, turned sharply, making the wet gravel crunch under his heels, and started walking back from where they had come.

On top of it all, the Krauts are in a terrible hurry! Ivanov thought to himself with annoyance.

It was clear something big was going on with them. As Ivanov headed out of the park, he imagined how pleased Koshko will be to hear what he had to report.

CHAPTER THIRTY

Director of Detectives Arkady Frantsevich Koshko had risen through the ranks over the course of twenty years of exemplary service. A tall, thick-chested man with a proud and shrewd expression on his broad and handsome face, he saw his department as his fiefdom and treated the men under him with gruff affection, as if he was their headmaster and they his often-unruly charges. He was a perfectionist, liked to give advice, and genuinely fretted if the junior detectives made mistakes, leading them to refer to him secretly as *"Ded"* (Gramps). Like all the other detectives, Ivanov admired Koshko, even if he was amused by some of his eccentricities.

"So, so, so," Koshko prompted Ivanov eagerly as soon as the detective sat down, "what can you tell me about our German friends?"

"My contact—whose real name I didn't learn, incidentally, but who is probably military—asked me about two strange, very strange matters."

Koshko leaned forward in anticipation: "For heaven's sake, out with it, *golubchik*, don't torment me!"

"They want to know about recent abductions of children in the city—if we've noticed any patterns," Ivanov emphasized, raising his eyebrows, "and if we know anything about the supposed murder of Thomas, the American Black man who directs Aquarium Garden."

Koshko looked stunned and threw himself back in his chair.

He remembered that a week ago, or even less, his old acquaintance Markov, who now worked for this Thomas at Aquarium, had come to him for help in connection with the abduction of a waiter's daughter. Markov had found several similar cases when he went through the police records for the last two months, and when he told Koshko about them, Koshko decided something bad was afoot. He had had even recently assigned Fedukovich to help with the case.

"The damned sausage grinders are somehow connected with these abductions!" Koshko exclaimed, slapping his hands on his desk.

"But what is this about Thomas? I haven't heard anything!" he said. "I don't go to Aquarium, but the place is popular, and we would have heard something."

Well, we'll find out right now," he announced, and reaching for the telephone pulled the apparatus toward him.

Two minutes later he cradled the receiver. "It gets better and better," he said in an irritated tone and looking up. "They told me Thomas hasn't been in for a day and they don't know why. What on earth is going on?"

Ivanov shook his head and shrugged.

"What's your arrangement with this German?" Koshko asked after thinking about something. "How're you supposed to give him answers? We need to figure out . . .."

A knock on the door interrupted him. The clerk apologized as he entered with an envelope: "An urgent telegram from Okhrana headquarters in Saint Petersburg, sir," he announced.

Koshko looked annoyed but took a birch-wood letter knife from a tray with other correspondence and slit the envelope open. As he read, his annoyed expression turned into a frown.

"A report from the Okhrana office in Paris claims that Savinkov may be heading for Moscow with the intention of assassinating the emperor," he said in a flat voice. "I'm supposed to detail every man I've got to increase security when the imperial family arrives on June 6th."

Like everyone in the Russian police, Ivanov recognized the name. Boris Savinkov was the notorious terrorist who orchestrated the assassinations of Minister of the Interior von Plehve in 1904 and Grand Duke Sergey, the emperor's uncle, in 1905. But during the last few years the reports from the Okhrana agents watching Savinkov in France had been that he was lying low on the Riviera.

"How can this be?" Ivanov asked. "I thought Savinkov went to ground and gave up terrorism after the scandal with that double agent, the provocateur Azef, a few years ago."

"So did I. So did everyone. But the Okhrana in Paris just raised the alarm, which means they may be on to something, and we have to drop everything and go on special alert. What happens if they're right and this bastard really is planning to attack the emperor? God forbid!" Koshko added, piously crossing himself and looking up at the ceiling. The thought that something like this could happen on his watch and in his city frightened and angered him.

"But what are we going to do about the Germans then?" Ivanov asked uncertainly. "I'm supposed to meet my contact tomorrow at 10 a.m., and I thought that one of the other men, Andreyev or Peshkov, could tail him after the meeting."

"No. No. That won't be possible, not now. We have to put aside the Germans and whatever nasty business they're up to with the children and with this Thomas fellow. The imperial visit is too important. I'm going to need all of you for this assignment, including you and Fedukovich."

Koshko thought for a moment, staring off to the side, thinking, then turned to face Ivanov again.

"When you meet your contact tomorrow, tell him the police know nothing about any disappearances of children, beyond the usual sort—runaways and the like. As for Thomas— tell them we haven't heard anything about his death. Let them investigate it themselves if they want. They're German after all, and they'll be thorough," he said with a wry expression.

"They're obviously worried about us, and we want them to feel secure so we can figure out later what they're up to. After the imperial visit, we can pick up this matter. In the meantime, Markov at Aquarium can look into it on his own. I'll call him now."

Koshko got up and offered his hand to Ivanov, signaling that their meeting was over.

When he left his chief's office, Ivanov walked down the corridor thinking it was unfortunate they couldn't pursue the Germans now because it gave them the freedom to do as much damage as they wanted.

CHAPTER THIRTY-ONE

Thursday, May 28, late afternoon
Prince Vladimir Istomin's residence

Istomin sped home from the Hippodrome, passing slow-moving carriages and wagons wherever he could on the heavily trafficked Petersburg Highway, Tverskaya Street, and Bolshaya Sadovaya. When he pulled into the driveway of his estate he slowed to a crawl and stopped the automobile some distance from the shed he built for it near the carriage house. The engine's rattle and the smell of the exhaust frightened the horses, and his groom and valet would take care of pushing the Russo-Balt the rest of the way.

He was impatient to know how Thomas was doing but had to change out of his wet clothes first. When he was done, he walked down the corridor from his bedroom, stepping lightly as he approached Thomas's door. He winced when a panel in the parquet creaked and peered through the narrow opening, weighing if he should enter or not.

The light was dim, but he could make out the shape of a body lying on the bed under the bedclothes and recognized his valet's legs in striped trousers just inside the door.

The valet heard the movement in the hallway and, holding a newspaper, got up from the easy chair. Seeing his master, he came outside.

"He's been sleeping soundly all the time, sir," the valet reported in a whisper. "The doctor came by about an hour ago, looked at him, and said to let him sleep. He said Mr. Thomas was doing very well, judging by his appearance."

"Very good, Evgeny, thank you. I'll sit with him for a few minutes now if you'd like to take a break."

Istomin settled into the upholstered armchair in the bedroom and sat very still. The small electric lamp on the side table shed a yellow cone of light onto his lap but the rest of the room was shadowed by the drawn curtains. He could hear the slow, steady sound of Thomas breathing and the soft ticking of the clock on the old armoire in the hallway. After a few moments, the two sounds began to interlace into a gentle syncopated rhythm. It drew him in, and as he listened to it, he remembered the strange feeling in the *banya* when time seemed to stretch out during Zoya's ritual. He felt that he needed to think about what had happened, to try to understand it, but there was too much running through his mind for him to be able to do it now.

Perhaps Zoya will say something about it all later, he thought as he pushed the idea aside. But then he also remembered that her explanations were always mysterious.

The two rhythms gradually separated and Istomin returned to the present. *What am I going to say when he wakes up*? he thought with a sinking feeling. *His sleep is healing him, but what about poor Olga*?

Istomin was very upset that he had failed his friend. During his visits to the hotel and the racetrack he hadn't picked up even a single clue about where Dickerman was. His hope that his comrades in the city would be able to help him was also fading. Six days had passed, and he had heard nothing. The only hope left was that the Moscow detective bureau would come up with something.

Istomin decided that he should telephone his contacts again. It also suddenly occurred to him that no one had told Valli anything. When Evgeny returned, Istomin told him to call if there was any change with Thomas and went to his study.

Floor to ceiling shelves filled with books on engineering, history, geography, and complete sets of the nineteenth-century classics—Pushkin, Gogol, Turgenev, Dostoyevsky, Tolstoy—lined two of the walls of the large room. The third wall, opposite the tall windows which looked out over the garden in the back of the house, was covered with oil paintings, watercolors and sketches Istomin had collected over the years: birches reflected in a quiet pond deep in a forest; three hunters at night around a campfire, one of them mimicking the ferocity of some creature with his mouth open and his fingers like claws while the others chuckled; a brace of Borzois stretched out in pursuit of a grey wolf glancing back, its red tongue lolling in exhaustion. In the corner near his desk stood a tall, carved birchwood gun cabinet that had belonged to his grandfather.

Istomin gave the operator the home numbers of two of the men who worked in the Moscow Governor General's administration, but they weren't in. Even though he didn't expect much from them, he left messages asking them to call back. The third man, a former captain in the Army's Adjutant-General Corps and now the editor of *Golos Moskvy* (Voice of Moscow), a popular daily that advertised itself as "knowing what happens in the city before anyone else," replied that he had quizzed the crime reporters on his staff, but, unfortunately, got nothing useful.

Istomin didn't relish calling Valli and steeled himself as he recited Thomas's home number.

She snatched up the receiver so quickly that she must have been sitting by the telephone. She also sounded completely distraught. When he told her about Olga's abduction and how Thomas was recovering after being wounded, he could hear her breathing heavily into the mouthpiece as though she was trying to get closer to him.

She dissolved in a torrent of gasping sobs when he stopped. Istomin tried to calm her, repeating that Thomas was recovering, all would be well with Olga, doing his best to sound as if he really believed it himself.

But it did no good. In between her bouts of weeping, Valli

poured out all the resentment and fear that had built up in her—her panic since the previous afternoon when Olga didn't return home after school with her father; her call to the Aquarium and shock when they said no one there knew where Thomas was; the sleepless night she spent not knowing what to do or how to comfort the younger children, who began to cry when they saw the state she was in. To make matters worse, she gasped between tears, Aquarium called her this morning to ask if Thomas was there, and she couldn't tell them anything because "she knew nothing, absolutely nothing."

Then, without pausing, Valli announced that she wanted to bring Mikhail and Irma to Istomin's house right away so they could see their father. Istomin replied, trying to be polite, that it was too early for visits because Thomas was still very weak and needed to sleep. She didn't want to listen, and her voice became shrill and demanding. In the end, the only way Istomin was able to mollify her was by promising to telephone as soon as Thomas woke up.

Talking to Valli also reminded Istomin that the staff at Aquarium couldn't have known anything about what happened to Thomas either, or that he was going to be absent for some time. He called the central office at the Garden, gave his title with his name, and asked that the senior maître d'hôtel be summoned to the telephone. When the secretary balked, explaining that Nikolay Ferapontovich wasn't in the office and that he didn't know where Nikolay Ferapontovich had gone, Istomin raised his voice and repeated who he was. After a fifteen-minute wait the man finally picked up.

Istomin didn't go into all the details, explaining only that Thomas had a serious accident, was recovering at Prince Istomin's home, and would return to the Garden when he was able. In contrast to Valli's recitation of complaints, the maître d'hôtel's reaction surprised and touched Istomin.

He began by gasping into the receiver. Then, his voice trembling with emotion, Stepanov assured Istomin that all the employees would "pitch in and do their utmost" to manage things in the way "our dear Fyodor Fyodorovich" would want and offered personally "to do anything, anything at all" to help. The only thing Fyodor Fyodorovich needed to concern himself with, the maître d'hôtel insisted, "was getting better as quickly as possible." Before ringing off, Istomin asked specifically that Markov, the Aquarium's director of security, be told what had happened. He also invited Stepanov to call or visit if he needed to be in touch with Thomas, starting tomorrow, when he should be able to receive visitors.

Unable to think of anything else he could do that evening, Istomin went to the kitchen, dismissed the housekeeper and other servants early, had a dinner of leftovers he found in the icebox and retired to his study.

To distract himself, he spent two hours continuing to read a new history of the Japanese War that had recently been published by a retired general. He added some long comments in the margins about the siege of Port Arthur—based on what he knew were certain facts—that contradicted the author's patriotic and inaccurate evaluation.

He then checked on Thomas again, heard his peaceful breathing, and went to bed.

CHAPTER THIRTY-TWO

After drinking the potion Zoya prepared, Thomas slept for forty-eight hours without dreaming or stirring. He began to awaken only when the rising sun sent a brilliant white bar of light creeping across the wall opposite the curtained window, and a faint noise sounded above him.

He opened his eyes. A bright red and brown butterfly was fluttering near the plaster medallion in the center of the ceiling, bumping into it lightly, then flying off again, as if searching for something. When it finally settled on a place it liked above Thomas's head, it froze, displaying brilliant purple eyespots on its rear wings. It was a male Peacock that had emerged unusually early in the season. With its furry body resembling a beak or a nose, it looked like the face of some fantastic creature peering down at Thomas.

He lay still for several minutes. The herbal smells of the banya still lingered in his nostrils. He ran the tips of his fingers carefully down his left side and touched the bandage across his ribs. The wound no longer ached but tingled and itched, a sign it was healing.

He felt changed somehow. It wasn't upsetting, and he didn't want to think about it now because something else was more urgent.

The image of Olga struggling with the man suddenly appeared in his mind. He felt as if a cold hand grabbed his heart and squeezed it.

He had to get up. Raising himself to a sitting position and swinging his legs over the side of the bed, Thomas paused on the edge, testing himself. The wound didn't hurt much when he moved.

When he stood up, he felt light-headed, but not enough to stop. Taking small, flat steps as if the parquet floor was wet and slippery, he shuffled to the bathroom and flipped on the wall switch. Bright light from the ceiling lamp flooded the large, white-tiled space, making him blink. He noticed a cheval glass in the corner and walked up to it to examine himself. Something clear that made his skin glisten covered him from head to toe and the white bandage around his rib cage was stained with a line of dark spots of dried blood. He untied the ends of the bandage and carefully peeled it off. A brown scab ran along the length of the entire wound, but its edges were only slightly inflamed.

Looking around, he noticed a folding metal screen at the far end of the room and behind it a deep zinc bathtub with a pile of towels on a stool near it. The sight made him yearn for a wash.

He turned on the hot water and stood for a moment, watching the thick stream breaking against the bottom of the bathtub. The sound of running water was familiar somehow and he tried to remember where he had just heard it, but the clouds of steam rising out of the bathtub distracted him before he could place the memory.

When Thomas returned to the bedroom, he dressed in the clean clothes he found hanging in the closet and put on a pair of slippers that were by the bed, mentally thanking Istomin for his thoughtfulness.

He also realized that he was very hungry and thirsty. The clock in the hallway showed it was only 6:07, which was probably too early for anyone in the house to be up. But he knew the layout of the first floor and made his way down the stairs, passing through the large dining room, with its mahogany table and chairs for sixteen under a large crystal chandelier.

When he entered the hallway leading to the kitchen, he saw the lights in it were on. And when he walked in, he saw

Zoya.

She was standing by the brass samovar she had just finished firing up and was looking straight at him, as if she was
waiting for him to appear in the door. Her dove was perched
on a shelf by the window and twisted its head toward Thomas
when he came in.

"How are you, my dear soul? How are you *batyushka*?"
she asked in her singsong fashion as she scrutinized him, her
pale blue eyes on her amber-colored face almost disappearing
amid the deep wrinkles that spread to her temples when she
smiled. It seemed to Thomas that her smile was so warm it
extended into a faint golden glow surrounding her small, grey-
haired head. She was wearing a long-sleeved, floor-length,
blue muslin dress buttoned to the neck, with a white, goat's
hair shawl on her shoulders.

"Very well, I'd say," she concluded after examining him.
"Thanks be to God! Nothing like a peaceful sleep after a prayer
to heal what ails you, my *solnyshko*!" (my dear little sun!).

Thomas walked up to her, extended his arms, and embraced her as carefully as if she were a small, fragile bird. Her
head came up only to the middle of his chest, and she was so
slight he could have enveloped her twice over with his long
arms. He felt her narrow back and angular shoulders move as
she embraced him in turn.

When he released her and looked down at her, she raised
her right hand and made the sign of the cross over his face.

"Thank you," Thomas said, taking her hand and kissing it.

"Thanks be to the Mother of God who spreads her protective veil over us and Saint Panteleimon the Healer," she replied with feeling.

Taking him by the arm she guided him to the table: "Come
sit, sit right here, *batyushka*," she urged. "You must be famished after all this time."

"How long was I asleep? What day is it today?"

"You slept two days and two night, two entire days and
nights," she replied, "and today is Friday, the day of Saint The-
odore the Miracle worker."

"Friday!" he exclaimed in a panic. "They took Olga on

191

Tuesday! What happened? Have the police found her? Did Vladimir Vladimirovich find out anything?"

"He'll be here soon," Zoya replied evasively.

Then, seeing Thomas's bewilderment, she looked directly into his eyes and continued with firm conviction: "You'll get her back, have no fear. But now you must strengthen yourself for what lies ahead so you can help her!"

Thomas didn't know where Zoya's certainty came from, but her tone was so persuasive that he felt his anxiety recede somewhat and sat down at the table. Zoya took off her shawl and draped it on a chair before turning her attention to the samovar, which was now hissing and vibrating on the counter like a small steam engine as the water in it began to boil. Taking a towel, she removed the angled pipe connecting the samovar's short chimney to the vent in the wall and set it aside. After spooning something that looked like dark, grainy molasses from a jar into a teapot, she filled it with steaming water from the samovar's spigot and set it on top of the chimney to steep.

She then turned to the big cast-iron stove, opened the oven door, reached in with a large wooden spatula and withdrew a pan that she transferred to the table. The delicious aroma of freshly baked bread and something savory filled the kitchen, mixing with the scent of charcoal from the samovar.

Thomas realized Zoya had gotten up before dawn to bake one of her celebrated *pirogi* for him. Using two towels to hold the hot pan, she turned it over with a practiced motion and tapped it sharply on a serving platter, releasing a golden brown, flat, rectangular loaf. After thumping it with a finger to satisfy herself it was indeed done and flipping it right side up, she cut some large squares from one end with a big knife, transferred a piece to a plate and set it before Thomas.

"Eat, my dear, please eat," she urged him, "this is just what you need now, together with the special tea I brewed for you."

Thomas was famished and the smell of the *pirog* made him even hungrier. He cut the steaming square with a fork, picked up a piece, and blew on it several times to cool it before taking a bite.

He recognized most of the filling—buckwheat groats mixed with forest mushrooms and onions cooked in fatback, hard-boiled eggs, fresh dill. But there was also something else that looked like big chunks of a white root he couldn't place. He knew Zoya always added herbs, roots, and plants to whatever she prepared, and that she gathered them in fields or forests or grew them in her own small garden in the back of Istomin's property. The *pirog* was as delicious as it smelled.

The tea she poured into a large cup and sweetened with two dollops of crystallized honey also had something unfamiliar in it. Dark and fragrant, it smelled of sweet, freshly mown hay, something smoky, and something else that was musty and spicy. When Thomas raised the cup to his lips, he saw small, round, transparent disks of oil floating on the surface, and when he sipped it, it tasted more like a rich, sweet and earthy broth than tea.

Zoya sat opposite him and watched him eat, her small face propped up on her palm in the immemorial gesture of a mother doting on the child she was feeding. When he finished the first piece Thomas gladly accepted another and drank two more cups of her tea, feeling as though its heat and flavors were coursing through his body all the way to the tips of his fingers and toes.

He was finishing the last bite when Zoya looked up at the door behind him.

"Vladimir Vladimirovich is coming," she said. "That's good, you both have much to do."

Thomas got up and turned around, looking expectantly through the doorway to the corridor. A moment later he was wrapped in Istomin's embrace.

"My dear friend! Thank God you are well! Let me get a good look at you!"

Taking both of Thomas's hands in his, Istomin stepped away with a happy and anxious expression. His handsome face was beaming, and tears glistened in the corners of his eyes as he looked Thomas up and down. He was about to say something but felt a sob rising in his throat. Giving up, he embraced Thomas again. Thomas leaned in, holding him, and patting his back.

For a moment Zoya looked at them, nodding her head slightly with a faint smile, then got up from the table and began to drape the shawl over her thin shoulders.

Seeing she was about to leave, Istomin stepped away from Thomas. He felt he should say something to thank her for the miracle she had wrought.

But Zoya seemed to read his mind, and although her smile didn't change, he saw an interdiction in her gaze and stopped. It was as if she had whispered, *No, no, none of this is from me.*

"Thank God, thank his Mother, and thank the saints," she said out loud.

Then, turning toward Thomas, she looked directly into his eyes again and repeated with the same tone of firm conviction as before: "You'll get Olechka back, have no fear. But now you must strengthen yourself for the trials that lie ahead so you can help her! And remember, the Mother of God will keep her protective veil over you."

"I'll go now, *batyushka*," she added, nodding, and repeated, "you've both much to do."

When Zoya walked out of the kitchen, it was as if a dam collapsed, and Thomas's anxiety flooded back.

"Tell me!" he asked Istomin, his voice ringing with urgency. "What do you know?"

"My dear fellow, I have nothing! Nothing! I'm sorry! I got what I could about this *Dickerman* from the American consul but couldn't find a trace of him in the places I checked."

"What about the police? And Markov?"

"Markov told me yesterday that the police had nothing new and that they're overwhelmed with the imperial visit. Even that detective they promised us has been reassigned. But I'll call Markov now to tell him he should come here to report whatever he has."

Thomas sighed wearily and rubbed his face with his hands. "What am I going to do?" he asked in a hollow voice.

Istomin looked at him with concern: "Maybe you should rest? I can't believe you're already up after what happened to you!"

"No, I'm fine and we can't wait." He looked up at Istomin. "What did happen to me? All I remember is fighting, that Southerner stabbing me, and the others seizing Olga."

"The doctor said he thought the blade was poisoned. Zoya agreed and said it must have been snake venom. She'd seen snake bites when she was still in Siberia, where there are poisonous vipers, if you can believe it—I would have thought it was too cold. There may have been something else as well."

Thomas shook his head in disbelief. "Amazing woman. She saved my life. How did she do it?"

"I don't really know. It looked like a ritual. I've heard that the Siberian peoples do something like this. She also said prayers and I heard the name 'Saint Panteleimon.' She had you put down on the bare earth, spread a salve over you, and covered you with tree bark and animal skins. She put herbs into the water for the steam in the *banya*. It was as if she wanted to evoke all living things. She told me before that the *banya* is a hallowed place because it combines the five primal things—earth, water, fire, air, and wood. It's also a 'threshold,' although into what, she didn't say."

"Ah!" Istomin added when something else came to him. "I remember she also whispered something like she did with the tiger in Ussuri. But ultimately, I don't know, I simply don't know."

Istomin remembered the white light that seemed to appear when Zoya put her hands on Thomas but felt a strange constraint and didn't mention it.

Thomas was listening attentively when something stirred in his memory.

"I dreamt I was dying but . . . I didn't care that I was. . ." he said, trying to recall the feeling he had when he heard the running water.

"And there was something else . . . I saw . . . some people . . . people I knew, my parents, and others. . . It was so strange, so strange." He struggled to remember more, but whatever it was had slipped away.

"The doctor was certain you would die. I feared it too," Istomin added with an apologetic tone.

"Yes, but I wasn't afraid to die," Thomas said quietly, still holding onto the little he remembered.

Istomin looked at him, not knowing what to say. It was all above his understanding.

"Zoya has a power," Thomas said after a moment's silence. "Back when I was a child, some people in Coahoma, mostly old but some younger ones too, were known as healers. Everyone believed they had some power. They'd pray to God and to Jesus—they were all strong believers—but they also did things, said things . . . The whites sure didn't have whatever it was! I saw the power once when a little girl was pulled out of a bayou. She looked drowned but an old man who lived near us saved her."

The recollection of the little girl snapped Thomas back to the present.

"Please call Markov now. I know it's early, but I need to know about Olga! He's a good man and won't mind."

CHAPTER THIRTY-THREE

Friday, May 29, 9:40 a.m.
Prince Vladimir Istomin's residence

Half an hour after Istomin called him at home, Markov arrived by cab, freshly shaved, in a formal black suit, and eager to begin. The former Okhrannik must have been waiting by the phone, ready to go.

"I'm very relieved to see you so well recovered from the attack, sir!" Markov said in a heartfelt tone and with his eyes glistening as he walked up to Thomas in Istomin's study and took his right hand in both of his.

They hadn't seen each other since the night they took Nikitin to the Ustyinsky Embankment to identify the dead girl. The news that Thomas had been nearly killed during the attack on his daughter upset Markov deeply. He knew he couldn't have done anything to prevent it, but he felt that a new tie had developed between them and that he was still somehow guilty for not having been more vigilant.

"I regret that all I can report now is some more troubling news," Markov continued, turning down the corners of his mouth to signal his unhappiness with what he was about to say.

"And no thank you, your excellency, I'd rather stand if you don't mind," he added, bowing to Istomin in response to his gesture of invitation to take a seat on the couch.

Markov knew Istomin preferred not to use his princely title. But he didn't approve of such new "democratic" tendencies. He thought a nobleman should act like one and pointedly continued to address him using the customary honorific. Moreover, even though the setting may have been informal,

Markov felt he was on duty, and experience had taught him it was better to keep a professional distance when reporting bad news. He also thought more clearly on his feet.

"Please tell us, Sergey Sergeyevich," Thomas urged him, leaning forward anxiously in his armchair. The security director's words and somber tone made him very anxious.

"Arkady Frantsevich, the Chief of Detectives," Markov began in a respectful tone befitting the famous personage he had the honor of knowing, "called to tell me the Germans are likely involved in the abductions of children that have been taking place in the city in recent weeks. Also, the Germans know you had been attacked on Tuesday, Fyodor Fyodorovich, even though this was not reported anywhere. It follows from this— eh . . . excuse me, sir, I know this is very painful for you—that the Germans were likely somehow involved in your daughter's abduction as well."

"Germans! My God! What Germans!? Do you mean some German gang?" Istomin exclaimed, his eyebrows arching in surprise.

"How can that be?" Thomas added, rising from the armchair. "I know who did it because I saw them. It was that American Southerner Dickerman! I told you how I threw him out of Aquarium! This attack was obviously his revenge. Were the other men with him the Germans?"

"I didn't know that sir!" Markov replied sharply, ignoring the question, and looking genuinely shocked. He had been rocking back and forth on the soles of his shoes as he spoke and stopped abruptly. "No one told me you recognized your attacker!"

"I'm sorry, it's my fault," Istomin interjected, rising to his feet in agitation. "I neglected to mention it when I called you."

"But if we know the attacker and his name, we should be able to find him!" Markov exclaimed, annoyed at what he saw as the amateurish meddling of this well-born gentleman.

"I apologize, Sergey Sergeyevich. I should have told you that I already tried to find Dickerman," Istomin explained. "I looked for him yesterday without success before I called Aquarium to tell Nikolay Ferapontovich what happened to

Fyodor Fyodorovich. I'll tell you everything I did yesterday in a minute. But please tell us what you have learned about German involvement!"

Markov suppressed his irritation. He had to remember he was now a retired officer of the Okhrana and an employee of a civilian.

Resuming his tone of calm authority, he continued: "Arkady Frantsevich has a detective who acquired solid evidence that German military intelligence was involved. How, we don't know yet. But they could only have been somewhere behind the scenes of the abductions and the attack on you. This is obvious because if they were directly involved in these crimes, they would know more about them."

"What on earth is going on? Why would this Dickerman be in league with German military intelligence of all things?" Thomas asked incredulously.

"We don't know, sir, but I assure you, we will find out," Markov replied. He then shifted to something that had been weighing on him and that he wanted badly to get out.

"I have to say that despite all the protestations of friendliness, and despite all the ties of kinship between our two empires, Germany is Russia's mortal enemy. This American's involvement with the Germans is a new and troubling development. But I will find out what they are all up to. I will get your daughter back! And I will find out if they also had anything to do with that poor girl's death on the Ustyinsky Embankment!" Markov announced, his voice ringing with indignation.

Thomas was struck by his vehemence, and the way he stressed the ties of kinship. For Markov the matter was bigger than just Olga's abduction. Thomas guessed he meant Tsaritsa Alexandra, who had been born a German princess and was suspected by many Russians of harboring traitorous sympathies for her German homeland. Markov evidently belonged to that camp.

"If you know about the involvement of German military intelligence, can't you arrest and question them if we can't find Dickerman?" Thomas asked. "Perhaps they could lead us to

Olga?"

"No, sir, I regret that would be impossible. This American is our best chance. German agents in Moscow work under cover of their embassy and consulates. As a result, they have diplomatic immunity, and we can't touch them. Moreover, we don't have any details about which Germans may be connected to the gang or how. And if they learn that we suspect any of them, they could all go into hiding and we'd never find out anything."

Istomin felt embarrassed by his failure to tell Markov about his search for Dickerman the previous day. He decided to make up for it by summarizing everything he had done, beginning with the American consulate.

Markov listened carefully, wrote something down in a notepad, and sniffed skeptically when he heard about Istomin's quizzing people at the Hippodrome.

"Thank you, your excellency. But I would have handled that part differently," he said with a note of displeasure. "Horse racing is a secretive world, as you say. However, there are ways to penetrate it without alerting a person that someone is looking for them."

Turning to Thomas, he asked: "Can you remember anything about this American from when he was at Aquarium? Some details that might help us? Nothing would be too small."

"He was just a very rude customer," Thomas replied, searching his memory, "we get those every once in a while, although it's never been an American before. He had money, he had an entourage—two women and another, younger man. And that younger man was also there when they took Olga, I remember it now. I broke his jaw, I think, judging by what it felt like."

"You what?" Istomin exclaimed. Markov stopped rocking on his feet again.

"I fought off two of Dickerman's henchmen before he stabbed me. I remember it clearly. Didn't I tell you? There were three or four men altogether."

"Are you sure, sir?" Markov asked slowly, letting a hint of

doubt creep into his voice. He had heard about Thomas's boxing from some of the Aquarium staff who had seen the equipment in his office but hadn't taken it very seriously.

"Yes, quite," Thomas replied and held up his fists, looking at the scabs on the big knuckles on both, as if to make sure it had really happened.

"Yes, I remember. I hit the two men hard and broke the skin on both hands. If it hadn't been for Dickerman's sword cane, they wouldn't have gotten Olga."

"Well, sir! That's something! Two men beaten, that's impressive!" Markov exclaimed, looking at Thomas with admiration.

"Perhaps there's some way to find these men through their wounds?" Istomin asked hopefully. "Canvassing hospitals, maybe?"

"Not likely, your excellency, scores of fights happen every day in Moscow, mostly when men have too much to drink. There's an awful lot of that in our ancient, white-stoned city," he added with a smirk, using the old epithet for Moscow. "Impossible to find or check them all."

Thomas, who had begun to feel light-headed after standing for a while, sat down in an armchair and leaned back. But Markov's mentioning drunken fights triggered something in his mind.

"I thought of something," he announced. Markov looked at him expectantly.

"I remember Dickerman ordered a lot of food and drink when he was at Aquarium. And he acted like a boor when I told him to leave. He knocked over one of the bottles on purpose, so it would spill all over the table. I remember it was something unusual—not wine or champagne, not vodka or the other usual drinks."

"Well, sir. Even if we could find that bottle, or anything else he touched, and succeeded in finding fingerprints on it, he's unlikely to be in our print registry. So we'd be no closer to knowing where he is."

"I was thinking of something else, Sergey Sergeyevich," Thomas said. "It might be useful to know what that bottle was, since it was unusual. Maybe it will tell us something."

"All right, sir, . . . if you can find out," Markov agreed. "Waiters were there too, I assume? Questioning anyone who dealt with Dickerman's party could be productive. Perhaps they noticed something. Can you identify them, sir?"

"Yes, of course, we keep track of staff assignments like that. In fact, I recall that a maître-d'hôtel was also overseeing the private rooms." The face of young Viktor Prokopenko bobbed up in Thomas's memory.

"Yes, we can certainly question the staff. We should also still have Dickerman's bill, which would list everything he ordered. Maybe that will give us a lead of some sort," he concluded, feeling a stirring of hope.

Thomas got up and walked to the desk with the telephone. "May I call Nikolay Ferapontovich at Aquarium?" he asked Istomin, who waved his hands dismissively to indicate it wasn't even worth asking for permission. "I'll have him verify who the waiter was in the private room," Thomas continued. "I remember Prokopenko, the maître-d'hôtel, because he called me to intervene. Dickerman was trying to get a young singer drunk. But I'd rather not involve her if we can avoid it. Too upsetting for her. I'll ask Nikolay Ferapontovich to see if he can find the bill as well. They are kept for a short time, for book-keeping, but after that the bills are discarded and it becomes harder to trace any particular customer's orders."

"Oh, and one more thing," Thomas said, looking at Istomin. "You won't mind if I have Prokopenko bring Strelka here, will you? She won't be a bother, as you know, and, frankly, I miss her."

The reaction of Nikolay Ferapontovich Stepanov, the senior maître d'hôtel, to Thomas's voice on the line was an exclamation of joyful surprise. He assured Thomas that he'd get to the task of finding the information on the bill right away and would of course have young Prokopenko bring the dog too.

An hour and a half later, a smart, lightweight cab with a hot-shot young driver in a trim black tunic and a cap tilted rakishly over one eye pulled up in front of the entrance to Istomin's house. Prokopenko got out, followed by Pyotr Golovaty, the bald, middle-aged waiter with a distinguished mien and a drooping moustache who had been on duty in private Room 3.

Strelka bounded out after them and ran up the front stairs, into the house and straight to Thomas's room on the second floor, as if she knew where he would be. She greeted her master happily, whining and jumping up to lick his face. On her hind legs, she was as tall as he was.

Markov reacted to the arrival of the two men with the enthusiasm of someone who has been offered a glass of cold water after being parched all day. He asked Thomas for permission to take the lead in interviewing them, implying strongly that his experience in this line of work made him the obvious choice, and smiled with satisfaction when Thomas agreed.

Meanwhile, Thomas scrutinized the long bill. He ran his eyes down the list until he came to the beverages and then read more slowly.

Dickerman's group had ordered quite a few bottles of wine for only four people, and they were all expensive—a good Pomerol, a vintage Montrachet, a Sauternes, and two bottles of Veuve-Cliquot. What Thomas was looking for was at the end. Instead of the usual after-dinner drinks, such as cognac or liqueurs, there was a bottle of "Alt Fitzgerald."

Old Fitzgerald, he automatically corrected the name in his mind. It was an American bourbon, which the waiter had mistakenly given a Germanic twist when he wrote down the order. Thomas included it on Aquarium's list of spirits because he liked it himself on occasion and also out of nostalgia. He could still picture the distiller's familiar advertisements in Chicago and Brooklyn newspapers, which claimed this was the last "Old Fashioned Copper Pot Distilled Whiskey" in the United States. But bourbon hadn't caught on with very many of his Russian and European customers and didn't sell well.

Thomas held up the bill and announced excitedly: "This 'Old Fitzgerald' whiskey is what Dickerman knocked over. I remember the smell."

Strelka, who had been lying on the floor by his chair, got up at this and turned her head toward him, as if he was going to go somewhere and she expected to follow.

The waiter Golovaty looked at Thomas. Something had occurred to him, and his face brightened: "Ah, sir, I remember now too! The bottle was nearly full and most of it spilled onto the table and the floor. We even had to have the carpet replaced. And there is something else," he added, his face spreading into a hopeful smile at the thought that he had recalled something that could be helpful, "the gentleman, uh, . . ." he paused to correct himself, "or rather, that older man I should say, asked me about the whiskey when he saw it on the beverages list. He wanted to know where we got it in Moscow. Although, to be quite precise, it was the other man, the younger one who spoke Russian with a Polish accent, who asked for him."

"And what did you do?" Markov asked, shifting forward like an old guard dog who'd caught the rustle of something interesting just around the corner.

"Why, sir, when I went to place the order for beverages with Mikhail Solomonovich—he's one of the sommeliers at Aquarium," Golovaty paused to explain, "I asked him. And he told me the only purveyor in Moscow was Eliseyev's."

"It's a special order from Eliseyev's," Thomas commented, referring to the celebrated gastronomic emporium on Tverskoy Boulevard. Aquarium Garden had become one of their biggest customers under his directorship, especially for imported goods.

"I can also add another small detail, I believe," Prokopenko added hesitantly and sat up. Everyone turned toward him.

"When I tried to intervene on behalf of Miss Solovyova, I heard the older woman say something like 'speaking for myself, I much prefer cognac because it's so much more aromatic'."

A silence ensued and Markov looked at the young man with his eyebrows raised, as if waiting for him to continue.

Prokopenko tried to explain: "I . . . I . . . believe the woman was referring to this whiskey because they hadn't ordered any other strong spirits. It wouldn't have made sense for her to compare any of the wines to a cognac. I remembered her remark because I'd never tried the whiskey myself and was curious about it. And from what the older woman said, it follows that someone at the table had praised the whiskey. So, this confirms that the older man must be very fond of it," Prokopenko finished lamely and blushed, realizing only when he was finished that he hadn't added anything new in his eagerness to be helpful.

When Thomas saw Prokopenko's embarrassment, he felt sorry for him: "Thank you, Viktor Aristarkhovich, a useful confirmation indeed!" he announced, reaching out and patting the younger man's knee.

"I agree," Markov said. He was pleased with himself for anticipating that the detail about the whiskey could potentially be useful. "So, we can ask at Eliseyev's if anyone ordered this whiskey from them after May 22, the night Dickerman was at Aquarium. Correct?"

"Exactly," Thomas replied. "And I'm guessing Dickerman wouldn't have ordered it at Aquarium if he was already drinking it in Moscow."

"Quite right, sir, that is entirely plausible," Markov agreed. Then, realizing it would be prudent to temper everyone's expectations, he added, "But it is a long shot . . . ."

"Nevertheless, it sounds promising," Istomin announced, looking from Markov to Thomas, "and I would be happy to go to Eliseyev's right now."

"Thank you, my friend," Thomas replied, shaking his head gently, "but I think it would be better if they saw someone from Aquarium. They might balk at revealing anything about their customers to a stranger."

Thomas turned to the young man: "Viktor Aristarkhovich, could I entrust this to you? Mikhail Solomonovich must be at Aquarium by now since it's almost eleven. Would you pick him up and then go to Eliseyev's? We would like to know to whom they sold this whiskey during the past year, but especially if there were any sales in the past week. Tell them the information is for me personally. I can't imagine that the list of customers will be long."

"We can take my automobile," Istomin offered. "I feel absolutely useless here now!"

The idea that he would have such an important role in the investigation, whatever its mysterious aim, thrilled Prokopenko. And being driven by Fyodor Fyodorovich's distinguished friend in his private automobile was a bonus.

"Thank you very much, Fyodor Fyodorovich, I would be happy to!" Prokopenko said, looking at Thomas eagerly. Turning toward Istomin, he added, "and it would be an honor, your excellency!"

"Very good!" Markov replied gravely. "And I will continue to try to get some inside information from Hippodrome. Gentlemen, we are beginning to make progress!"

CHAPTER THIRTY-FOUR

Stürmer had arranged his second meeting with Ivanov as early as he could on the day after the first, and he arrived at the new location—this time, the southern end of Tverskoy Boulevard, across from Malaya Bronnaya Street—fifteen minutes before the appointed time. The weather was clear and cool, with high clouds drifting across the brilliant blue sky. But Stürmer was too nervous to notice. He wanted to observe the Russian detective surreptitiously, to see if anyone was with him.

Fancying himself a skilled conspirator, he glanced around the stretch of lawns and trees and decided to stand near a tall growth of lilacs, expecting it would shield him from the Russian's view. The racemes were almost barren now and drifts of pale, faded flowers littered the ground in a slippery layer. Stürmer wrinkled his nose at the stale, sweet smell of decay.

But he miscalculated, and Ivanov spotted him first from a distance. Stürmer had not anticipated that his enemy, as he thought of Ivanov, might also try to approach him furtively and would come from an unexpected direction.

They greeted each other even more coldly than the day before, and walked as they talked, falling silent when passing anyone sitting on a bench.

Ivanov followed Koshko's instructions and told Stürmer that the police were not aware of any notable child abductions in the city. They also hadn't heard anything about Thomas being attacked, much less killed. If someone as prominent as Thomas had been injured, the news would surely have reached them. In any event, Ivanov added, the police checked and learned that Thomas had some sort of "accident" but was now recuperating well.

Ivanov watched Stürmer as he delivered this information. The German showed no reaction to the matter of the children, but his eyes widened when Ivanov told him about Thomas.

This bastard was hoping to hear something different, Ivanov concluded. *It was clear the Germans had some sort of interest in Thomas's death or injury. But why*?

Stürmer tried to conceal his shock with a show of sang-froid. He thanked Ivanov curtly for the information and handed him an envelope with his monthly retainer.

"We shall be in touch in due course," he added noncom-mittally, turned crisply on his heel, and strode off in the direc-tion of Strastnaya Square.

Ivanov watched his erect figure for a moment. It struck him that the man walked unnaturally, as if he was trying to correct his posture all the time.

Ivanov regretted that they couldn't put a *fileur* on the Ger-man. But there was nothing to be done and he headed back to headquarters to report to Koshko.

Stürmer had parked his Mercedes nearby on Sytinsky Lane and fought the temptation to run to it as he digested the shocking news from the Russian detective.

The fact that Thomas was still alive meant the operation Stürmer had nurtured meticulously for months was under se-rious threat, as was his career. Thomas knew who Dickerman was and must have seen him during the attack; he would tell the police, and their investigation would reveal Stürmer's in-volvement. And even though Stürmer couldn't be held by the Russians because of his diplomatic immunity, there would still be an international incident, the reputation of German military intelligence would be tarnished, and he would be the cause of it all. The only thing he could do now was shut down and liquidate everything in the Convent right away and turn himself in to Colonel Michaelis to face the disgrace and pun-ishment he deserved.

Stürmer started the engine and drove across Strastnaya Square between the statue of Pushkin, who seemed to be looking sternly at him, and the pointed belfry of Strastnoy Monastery before turning down Tverskaya Street. It was clogged with the usual traffic of cabs, wagons, and omnibuses, and it took him a quarter of an hour to get to Mokhovaya Street near the Kremlin, where he could at last turn toward the southwest and the Convent.

Nevertheless, he forced himself to delay before driving to the property. He made several detours into the quiet, narrow lanes off Prechistinsky Boulevard lined with old townhouses so he could stop and look in the rear-view mirror and make sure he wasn't being followed. When he finally pulled into the driveway in front of the Gothic mansion, he was not only panicked but fuming.

Maria Chernyshova, the Russian madam, as Stürmer thought of her, met him in the gloomy central hall after Stepan let him in. She was wearing one of her pastel-colored, girlish dresses with flounces and bows, and looked as if she was expecting company. Her hair was done up, and the scent of her floral perfume filled the air as she waltzed around Stürmer, showering him with light-hearted chatter about how nice it was to see him, asking him to come in, offering refreshments. But as she was taking his hat and gloves, she got a good look at the dark expression on his face and stopped abruptly, saying she would fetch Dickerman right away and hurried up the central staircase.

"Thomas is *alive!*" Stürmer shouted in English when he saw the Southerner coming down the stairs, pulling up his suspenders and with his shirt collar unbuttoned, looking as if he had just gotten dressed. "That means he saw you!"

Dickerman almost lost his footing on the last step and had to grab the banister to steady himself.

"*That's impossible!*" he exclaimed angrily. "There was enough poison on the blade to kill an ox, and I cut him good—I saw it and *felt* it!"

"Nevertheless, you fool, he is alive and recovering! Our information is certain!"

"How do you know?" Dickerman demanded.

"What difference does that make! You failed and he's alive! That means he can identify you, and you can lead the police to me . . . and . . . and . . . that means the entire plan has been . . .," Stürmer groped for the right word, opening and closing his mouth several times without making a sound, "it has been . . . exploded . . . *blown up!*"

Bartkow and Stepan heard the shouting in the hall and appeared in the door leading to the kitchen, both of their faces covered with purple bruises and brown scabs. The commotion also drew Hilda, who came down the stairs and joined Maria, who was watching the stormy encounter anxiously.

Stürmer looked at Bartkow and Stepan with revulsion and switched to Russian as he yelled at them: "Did you hear what I just said!?"

Stepan, his nose misshapen and swollen to twice its normal size, glowered at him from under his brow but said nothing. He hadn't understood what Stürmer yelled in English, but it was clearly nothing good.

Bartkow gestured weakly with a limp hand at his swollen chin and lips to show that his jaw had been wired and he could open it only a little. He also bit his tongue badly when Thomas hit him in the mouth, which made it even more difficult for him to speak and he slurred everything whenever he tried.

"You miserable swine! The two of you got beaten to within an inch of your lives by that one Black man, and he has survived! Your ineptitude destroyed our entire plan!"

"How were we supposed to know . . .," Stepan began to mumble.

"*Silence!*" Stürmer cut him off in a voice that was turning hoarse from strain.

Then, turning toward the others he announced, making a chopping gesture with his right hand: "This entire operation is suspended! You will do nothing, you will not leave the house, and you will wait for me to return with instructions!"

Dickerman had never seen Stürmer in such a frantic state—his face covered with red blotches, his body jerking as he waved his arms, his mouth working furiously.

But after the first few moments Dickerman's shock and surprise faded, and his mind began to race as he tried to figure out a solution to this mess. He had been in tight spots before and always managed to get out of them.

He also began to appraise Stürmer more coolly. He had never imagined the German was capable of such vehemence and wondered what was behind it.

Scrutinizing Stürmer's pinched face with its oversized mustache, Dickerman noticed his eyes—they were wide open and filled with fear, raw fear. When Stürmer ended his tirade and stood breathing heavily, Dickerman also saw that his eyes were glistening.

That milksop is close to crying, it dawned on Dickerman. *And all his talk about "further instructions" means he's scared shitless of someone who's really in charge.*

What sort of "consortium" is behind him? he wondered.

The faces of some of the tough characters he'd known in New Orleans and Nashville floated up in his mind's eye. *He sure as hell doesn't look like any mobster I've ever seen*, Dickerman thought.

When he first began to work with the young German, he noticed that he wasn't as commanding as he liked to pretend. But since he held the purse strings and was generous with money, it seemed reasonable to let him have his way. All that had just changed.

"Now, now, now, baron! Get a grip on yourself!" Dickerman exclaimed as he walked toward Stürmer, looking steadily into his frightened eyes, as if trying to pour his will into him. "We can fix this! I assure you—we can fix this! Everything is not lost!"

The moment Dickerman began to speak in his slow and forceful tone, he saw Stürmer hesitate, and his distraught expression slacken. It was as if he'd been hoping to be told he was wrong, or to have someone guide him.

I was right, Dickerman realized with a feeling of satisfaction.

"But how? How can we fix this?" Stürmer exclaimed, although in a weaker voice. "If Thomas is alive, he'll tell everyone about you, including the police. And . . . and that will lead them to me and . . . and to my . . . superiors."

As soon as he uttered the word, Stürmer realized he made a mistake. He was too agitated to think clearly. He should have said "colleagues" or "partners"—anything would have been better.

A malevolent smile appeared on the Southerner's face.

He noticed, flashed through Stürmer's mind.

Dickerman pressed his advantage and continued to persuade the German, speaking slowly and clearly, trying to bend him to his will: "We'll work it out, baron. Just listen to me and it'll all be all right. No one will be the wiser."

He then dropped his voice to a soft, confiding tone: "You have nothing to fear from anyone, do you understand me? We're in this together."

"Yes, yes, of course . . . if, if you are sure, Mr. Dickerman," Stürmer murmured weakly. He was now hanging on the Southerner's every word.

Dickerman watched Stürmer's transformation with amusement. "What we have to do now, my dear baron, is finish what I began," he concluded more somberly. "Do you understand me?"

"Finish . . . how . . . what do you mean?"

"Don't pretend to be dense. We have to get rid of Thomas once and for all. He's the only thing between us and success."

"But how can you say that? He knows you tried to kill him, and he surely told others! How can killing him now solve anything?"

Dickerman didn't reply but walked over from the staircase to an upholstered yellow silk settee by the wall and sat down. Leaning back comfortably, he crossed his thick thighs and let his right foot rock casually back and forth as he stared at Stürmer.

The last remnant of will appeared to drain from the German. "I'm sure you are correct, Mr. Dickerman. I fear I may have I reacted with . . . too much . . . too strongly," Stürmer said in a quiet voice.

Seeing the change and realizing he'd won, Dickerman sensed that now was the time to switch to magnanimity: "Don't worry about it, baron. We'll put it behind us. What we need to do now is look ahead. And for that we need to know where Thomas is."

"Yes. Yes, of course."

"You should go now and assure your . . . colleagues, whoever they are," Dickerman said, pausing pointedly, "that all will be well and we're going to take care of this little hiccup. Tell them there's nothing to worry about and that we can still open in a few days."

"And you," he turned to Maria, "go find out where Thomas is. First go to Aquarium. Then, if you have to, go to his apartment building. Bartkow has the address. I want to know today. Today, do you understand?"

He had spoken in English, but Maria understood enough to nod "yes."

"Make up an excuse why you need to know," Dickerman continued. "And take the carriage."

Maria looked flustered but nodded again and nearly curtsied.

Dickerman then walked up to Bartkow, who was standing meekly in the doorway to the foyer.

"Normally, this would be your job, but with your mug like that I don't want you anywhere near Thomas or anyone who knows him. He must have told people what he did to you and to him," Dickerman said, gesturing at Stepan with a thrust of his chin. "But have no fear, I've got something for you. And you won't need a pretty face for it."

"Whatever you say, boss," Bartkow replied weakly, sounding as if his mouth was full of porridge. But the idea of vengeance against the Black man had now hooked him too.

"I want you and him," Dickerman pointed to Boris, "to go to that big gun shop on Tverskaya, Zim . . ., Zim . . . something

. . ."

"Zimin and Nikiforov," Bartkow supplied the name, "I know it, it's on Tverskaya near Gazetny Lane."

"Yes, well, go there and buy three Smith and Wesson revolvers, .38 caliber, not .32. They must have them, they're popular. We want something with real stopping power. Understand? And don't let them try to sell you any of those automatic pistols—they're unreliable and jam. Also buy three boxes of cartridges. I want all of that here quick."

"Wha . . . what are you doing? Why do you want three?" Stürmer stammered, looking shocked.

"Because I already have a gun, I'm assuming you do as well, and these three don't," Dickerson explained sarcastically, as if he thought Stürmer was naive or an idiot.

"You do have one, don't you, baron? We're going to need all our guns because we're going to have ourselves one hell of a turkey shoot!"

"Yes, of course, I have a pistol. But I didn't think that . . ."

"What, you thought I was joking!" Dickerman interrupted him, raising his voice, and getting up from the settee. He stepped toward Stürmer to reinforce his words: "I told you, we have to finish this Black sonofabitch, and the sooner the better. And we're all in this, understand? Together! I don't want any more surprises."

Stürmer lowered his eyes. A heavy silence filled the hall as Dickerman surveyed the men and women for several seconds, shifting his gaze from one to the other.

"Alright, you all have jobs to do, so get to it." He took out his pocket watch and flipped open the gold lid. "It's almost 11:30. I want all of you back here by . . . let's say . . . 4 p. m. That should be plenty of time. And I don't want any excuses. Just results. Do you understand?" Everyone remained silent and avoided his gaze.

"You're on guard upstairs," he told Stepan and gestured so he'd understand.

A minute later the foyer was empty.

CHAPTER THIRTY-FIVE

Friday, May 29, 10:30 a.m.

When Prokopenko and Istomin left for Eliseyev's, Thomas went upstairs to his room to rest. However, he had no sooner taken off his slippers and lain down on the bedcover than a tentative knock on the door made him sit up.

It was Evgeny, Istomin's valet, looking apologetic: "I'm sorry to disturb you, sir, but your wife and children arrived and are asking to see you."

Thomas felt a stab of guilt. He'd been so preoccupied by Olga's abduction that he'd forgotten about Valli. He felt even worse that he'd forgotten about the little ones. But Valli hadn't forgotten him or that the children needed to see their father after everything that happened.

Telling Evgeny he'd be down in a minute, Thomas went into the bathroom and rinsed his face with cold water, then rubbed it briskly with a towel in an attempt to revive himself. He looked at himself in the mirror as he stroked his moustache lightly to neaten it and resolved he would have to try to make up his lapse to Valli.

When he walked into the living room, she and the children were sitting side by side on the large couch, with Mikhail in the middle. She was wearing one of her dowdy broad-brimmed hats and a sack-like flowered dress and was watching Mikhail as he explained to his sister in English, emphasizing the words self-importantly, "No, no, Irma! Papa was sick, but now he's better!"

The little boy's face brightened when he saw his father, and he slid off the couch and ran over to him. Looking up at his father with a smile, he wrapped his arms around his knees.

215

But Irma took advantage of her brother's absence and sidled over to Valli with a wary expression on her face.

Thomas reached down, wanting to pick up Mikhail, but a stab of pain in his side made him stop. He winced, kissed him on the forehead instead and straightened up.

Valli was watching him with alarm, clutching a crumpled handkerchief, her eyes rimmed with red from crying and lack of sleep.

"Frederick! What in God's name happened to you? What happened to Olga? Prince Istomin told me she was abducted! How could this have happened? No one tells me anything!"

Thomas approached her and took her left hand with his right. It was freezing. Her face had a dull, pale olive tint, and her distress moved him. "I'm sorry, Valli," he said. "Some criminals have taken Olga, but we're doing everything we can to get her back."

"Criminals! Taken? But how, why? What do they want with her? She was with you after school, and they attacked you too!" Valli began to tremble as the questions that had tormented her ceaselessly for the past two days poured out in a flood. She pulled her hand from Thomas's and dabbed at her eyes with her handkerchief.

It's become her usual accessory, flashed through Thomas's mind.

"Are they holding her for ransom?" she asked in disbelief.

"No, there hasn't been any ransom demand, at least not yet. And I know who did it because I recognized him and the other attackers. We're going to use this to find them."

"You know them!" Valli exclaimed. She looked so horrified that Irma became frightened too and the corners of her little mouth turned down. She looked as if she might start crying any second.

Thomas dreaded having to explain, but felt he owed it to Valli to be honest. "It was someone I threw out of Aquarium. An American and his group were abusing an entertainer. I couldn't let this continue. . . And the man . . . insulted me."

Valli gaped at Thomas, her open mouth moving as if she was trying and failing to draw a breath. "You mean this horror

216

happened over an insult! Olga is God knows where because you quarreled with a customer?"

"You don't understand!" Thomas started to explain, sensing at the same time that Valli would neither grasp nor accept what he was saying. He'd never been able to explain his American past to her so she really understood it.

"It wasn't a quarrel! I didn't start anything. The man is an American racist of the worst kind. I dealt with his type all the time in the United States, in Mississippi, Chicago, everywhere. I know his type . . .."

But Valli was no longer interested in hearing what Frederick's past life had to do with Olga's disappearance. Her resentment boiled over and all she wanted now was to hurt him for the repeated pain he had caused her.

"So, Olga is in the hands of some American criminal because of your pride!" she raised her voice. "You put your skin color above the welfare of your daughter?"

Valli stood up and looked Thomas up and down with a bitter expression on her face: "They told me you were hurt, but you don't seem to have suffered very much, to look at you!"

What she said was so unjust that Thomas felt as if she'd slapped him in the face. He couldn't understand how he had allowed himself to get involved in recriminations with her and lose sight of the only thing that mattered now—finding Olga.

"You don't know what you're saying, Valli! Calm yourself!" he cried, feeling his anger rise. Another second and he would lose all patience with her.

Valli was shocked at herself for saying what she did, and Thomas's reaction frightened her.

"Come children, we're going home," she announced in a trembling voice, pulling Irma toward her on the couch, and stretching her hand out to Mikhail.

"Valli, stop this right . . .," Thomas began when a movement to the side caught his eye.

Istomin's valet had appeared on the threshold of the doorway leading to the entrance foyer. He was holding a silver salver and looked hesitant.

"What is it Evgeny?" Thomas asked distractedly with

Valli's accusation still ringing in his ears.

"Excuse me for interrupting, sir, but there's a lady asking for you," Evgeny said in a diffident tone and walked over to Thomas to present the salver.

"A lady?" Thomas repeated, not understanding. He picked up the visiting card from the glinting surface and turned it around.

The engraved French script read, "TSIFFER, Mina Samoïlovna, La Reine de Versailles, Kuznetski most 17, Moscou."

This was so unexpected that Thomas froze and stared at Evgeny. He felt himself blushing.

"Please ask her in," he said after a moment and turned expectantly toward the arched doorway.

He heard the sharp click of heels on the foyer's marble floor and a second later Mina walked into the living room and stopped, facing him. Her expression was anxious.

After Valli's shapeless dress and haggard appearance, Mina looked to Thomas as if she was a being from a different world. She was wearing a trim black jacket over a high-collared white lace blouse and a narrow black skirt that swelled gently over her hips. Perched squarely on her head was a crisp straw boater with a black ribbon. A watch dangled from a long chain around her neck, as if she had stepped from behind the counter of her boutique.

"Fyodor Fyodorovich!" she exclaimed, and then continued rapidly in French, her voice vibrating with emotion, "I am relieved to see you are . . . you are not injured . . . or are much better. I heard you had a very serious accident. I hope you don't mind that I came unannounced. I tried calling Prince Isto . . . I mean Vladimir Vladimirovich before coming but was told he wasn't in . . . So . . . ." Mina stopped awkwardly in midsentence, feeling embarrassed and thinking that she had already been too frank.

"It's very kind of you to come, Mina Samoylovna," Thomas began, trying to sound calm. "I am much better now . . .."

He stepped closer, expecting her to offer him her hand.

But as he tried to make sense of her expression, he saw her eyes shift and widen when she noticed Valli and the children on the couch on the other side of the room, and she left her hand by her side.

With a feeling of utter hopelessness about what was coming, but also that he had no choice, Thomas stepped aside and turned toward the couch.

"Valli," he said in Russian, looking at her and glancing back at the visitor, "this is Mina Samoylovna Tsiffer." Then, gesturing toward Valli with his right hand, he continued, "my wife, Valentina Yakovlevna, and my children, Irma and Mikhail."

For a second, Mina's face registered disbelief. But then her years of experience of being on public view in her boutique and of dealing with the most varied clientele came to her rescue and she regained her poise.

She nodded to Valli, and said affably, "It's a pleasure to meet you, Valentina Yakovlevna." Shifting her gaze to Mikhail and Irma, she forced a smile, glanced at Thomas, and added, "What lovely children!"

But Valli was still so shocked and hurt by Thomas's indifference and coldness that she didn't even think of trying to be civil. Whatever connection there was between him and this Jewish woman made everything worse. All Valli wanted now was to get away.

"Come children, we're going home," she repeated, getting up from the couch and taking Mikhail's and Irma's hands.

Irma had been whimpering even before Mina arrived, and now began to work herself up to really start crying. But Mikhail, who had watched his father, Valli, and the new lady was bewildered and asked: "Are you coming home with us, Papa?"

The little boy's innocent question went through Thomas like an electric shock.

"No, Mikey, not right now," he replied in Russian. "I've got something important to do. You go with Auntie Valli and I'll come and see you all soon, OK?"

Thomas pulled the boy close to him, bent down, and kissed him on the head. Then, ignoring the tears streaming down Irma's face, Thomas kneeled next to her, embraced her, and kissed her on both cheeks. "It's going to be alright, honey," he whispered, and hugged her again.

Looking at Valli he added: "We're doing all we can now. I'll tell you about everything that happens as soon as I can."

Holding both children by the hand, Valli walked out without even glancing at Mina. Only Mikhail twisted around from the doorway to take one last look.

Thomas tried to steel himself as he turned toward Mina, feeling he had to say something but also that he couldn't tell her anything about what was most important. Not now, not after what had just happened.

"Mina Samoylovna, won't you please sit down?" he asked, gesturing at the couch.

"Thank you, Fyodor Fyodorovich," Mina replied coldly. "But I really must go. I'm pleased you are recovered. I found out from your young secretary, Ivlev is his name, I believe? He came to the boutique today and mentioned that you were badly hurt. I really didn't mean to intrude into . . . it's . . ."

Mina felt tempted to add something biting about Valli because of how insulting that woman had been, and also because she was Thomas's wife and he hadn't told her he was married. But she decided there was no longer any point.

Her impulse to come to see Thomas seemed foolish to her now. She had yielded to it because of how strongly she felt attracted to him and because she saw how he looked at her. Ever since the evening at Yar her thoughts kept returning to how kind and unusual he was, how unlike the other men she usually met in Moscow. She had been moved by the way he responded to the mysterious accident that happened to his employee. But she never imagined there was so much about himself he hadn't mentioned.

Thomas was silent as he walked Mina to the cab that was waiting in front of the house. When he offered her his hand to help her get in, she took it.

"Goodbye," he said to her when the driver turned around to see if his fare was ready. She replied with a faint, sad smile, turned away and looked straight ahead.

Thomas sighed as he watched the droshky turn onto Malaya Nikitskaya Street. He knew he had hurt Mina, but he also knew he never intended to deceive her. If the evening at Yar hadn't been interrupted and Olga hadn't been abducted, he would have made his position clear somehow, or as clear as he could.

He would speak with Mina later. No matter what came of it, she would know the truth of what had happened. But now only one thing was important.

CHAPTER THIRTY-SIX

Stürmer left the Convent persuaded by Dickerman that not all was lost, and he felt new strength and resolution as he drove to Michaelis' office to report what he learned from their spy in the Moscow police.

By the time Stürmer got to the river the leaden sky began to release a cold, steady drizzle again, and he had to turn on the windshield wipers and slow down as they labored to scrape away the wet streaks of dust that made it hard to see what was in front of him.

The thought of meeting Michaelis made Stürmer nervous, even though, on the face of it, the information he had to deliver was entirely satisfactory: the Moscow detective bureau was not aware of any rash of kidnappings of children, and it had no knowledge of an attack on the entrepreneur Thomas. Thus, from this point of view, the Convent was not in any danger.

But Stürmer was also preparing to lie to his chief for the first time. Or, if not lie, to withhold something important from him. As much as it annoyed Stürmer to admit it, he concluded that Dickerman was right about Thomas and it was essential to eliminate him. This was the only way to protect the operation Stürmer had put into motion and whose importance was paramount.

However, there was no way of knowing in advance what Michaelis would think of killing Thomas.

Also nerve-wracking—but exciting as well, Stürmer realized in a moment of illumination—is that now he would find out if he was a real soldier and could be as ruthless as a soldier would have to be in wartime. He had never fired at an actual person, much less killed anyone, and it was time to see how well he would do it.

Throwing his narrow shoulders back in preparation for the ordeal, Stürmer knocked on the door of the "Schmidt & Sons" office.

But a few moments later he was heading back to his automobile with a relieved expression on his face because the duty officer informed him that Michaelis had to go out unexpectedly. He would be back after three and asked Stürmer to telephone him then instead of coming back to the office.

Stürmer felt as if the fates had handed him a gift by removing a yoke from his neck. Dissimulating to Michaelis over the telephone would be much easier than being questioned face-to face and drilled by his unnervingly open left eye.

Once Stürmer was back in his apartment, he decided to get ready for what was coming and busied himself with his Parabellum Luger semi-automatic. It was standard German Army issue and he had enjoyed his training with it at target ranges in Berlin because the instructors had always praised his accuracy. But he realized that it had been nearly a year since he last fired it, and he rebuked himself for not having found the opportunity to practice more recently.

He took the weapon in its brown leather holster out of the locked bottom drawer of his desk together with a box of ammunition and a cleaning kit and laid everything out on the polished wooden surface. Because he had always been careful to keep the pistol spotlessly clean and well-oiled, he limited himself to looking it over with admiration, cocking it, and dry firing it once as he aimed at an imaginary enemy. He then forced eight cartridges into the clip and pushed it into the handle with a satisfying click. After thinking for a moment, he got a spare clip out of the drawer and loaded it as well.

At 3:15 Stürmer telephoned Michaelis. The conversation went better than he expected. He used euphemisms to conceal what he was talking about, in case the line was tapped, and thought he did a good job of avoiding any allusions to his earlier panic at the idea of attacking Thomas.

CHAPTER THIRTY-SEVEN

When Prokopenko, Istomin and Mikhail Solomonovich Berdinsky, the Aquarium's beverage manager and senior sommelier, arrived at the Eliseyev Emporium on Tverskaya Street and announced their mission to the manager on duty, they were received like honored guests. Fyodor Fyodorovich Thomas was one their best customers and his name opened all doors and books.

The three visitors were escorted to the office behind the wine and spirits department—the label "Wines of the Brothers Eliseyev" was famous throughout the Russian Empire—and assured that their inquiry would be treated with the discretion it deserved. An accountant was summoned and within ten minutes a list of all sales of Old Fitzgerald for the past twelve months was ready.

It was very short. Other than Aquarium's two orders of a case each time, last December and again in March, and seven individual bottles sold, apparently to walk-in customers who were curious about the exotic American liquor, only two other cases were sold. One was sent to 9 Arkhangelskiy Lane, which Istomin recognized as the address of the American Consulate. This could be eliminated from further consideration. The second was ordered on Saturday, May 23, together with eight cases of other spirits and a quantity of wines, and all were delivered that same day to an estate at 17 Kochkinsky Lane in the First Khamovniki District, care of a certain "M. Bartkow."

Berdinsky had been told little about the purpose of the visit to Eliseyev's, except that Fyodor Fyodorovich wanted him to clarify a matter pertaining to inventory. Why this had to involve young Prokopenko, and someone as distinguished as Prince Istomin was entirely unclear. But Berdinsky valued his position at Aquarium and decided it wasn't his place to question what the *khozyain* wanted.

All three visitors were so preoccupied with their mission they hardly noticed the cornucopia of enticements through which they were escorted by the manager on their way out of the store. There were glass-fronted displays of Havana cigars, Egyptian cigarettes, Turkish tobaccos; refrigerated cases filled with imported cheeses, meats, and tins of black, red, and golden caviar; and counters piled high with multi-colored pyramids of fruit.

When they were getting into Istomin's Russo-Balt, Berdinsky noticed that the prince and the young maître d'hôtel exchanged glances and seemed very pleased with themselves.

Thomas went upstairs after Valli and Mina left. Both had upset him for reasons that were related, but he knew he could not afford to deal with any of this now. After taking off his slippers, he lay down on his bed and managed to doze for forty-five minutes before the low rumble of the returning Russo-Balt in the driveway awakened him. He got up quickly. He still looked drawn, but his eyes were alert, and he reached the foyer as Istomin walked in with the others.

While coming downstairs, Thomas decided to leave it to Evgeny to tell Istomin about the visits by Mina and Valli. They could talk about all that later. A second later, Markov, who had been waiting in the sitting room, appeared as well.

"You were right, my friend," Istomin announced as soon as he saw Thomas. "Eliseyev made very few sales of that whiskey and only one seems to lead to Dickerman!"

"May I see, sir?" Markov inquired impatiently, stepping forward and extending his hand for the sheet Istomin was holding.

"Do you know the address, Sergey Sergeyevich?" Thomas asked, looking anxiously at the old detective.

"I do indeed. It's a quiet lane near the Novodevichy Convent. Parts of the area are built up very little. A good place if you want to keep out of sight. Some big estates were built there when the area was still outside the city's boundary."

"We should investigate the address as soon as possible, Sergey Sergey'ch!" Istomin said excitedly. "There's absolutely no good reason to delay. I'm prepared to go. In fact, I could go right now!"

"But under what pretext, your excellency?" Markov objected. "You can't just knock on the door and say you want to look around and question the inhabitants," he added with a note of regret, thinking of the days when he was a member of the Okhrana, and no doors were closed to him.

"No, no, of course not," Istomin agreed, realizing his error.

"We also don't know anything about the number of people involved," Markov went on, turning toward Thomas. "Although, judging by the attack on you, sir, there probably aren't many more than you saw."

Istomin was embarrassed because he had spoken rashly. He began to run through other ideas when suddenly one came to him.

"I can suggest an excuse that would work to get us into almost any building in the city!" he announced with an eager expression.

"Yes?" Markov asked, smiling politely, and trying not to sound skeptical.

"An engineering or building inspection! When I did some work for the city's building department, I was amazed at how easy it was for inspectors to get in anywhere they wanted. We were issued passes signed by the governor-general himself and they opened all doors."

"We're not going to have time for that, your excellency, if you don't mind my saying," Markov replied, still polite, but with a hint of tolerant condescension, as if explaining to a novice who still had much to learn. "The imperial visit will make getting official authorization very time-consuming. Everybody in City Hall is overwhelmed with preparations. We would also have a great deal to explain and there might be objections to our, . . . how shall I say it, . . . thinking of taking the law into our own hands."

But Thomas had an idea. "Do you have any of your old

authorizations?" he asked Istomin.

"I do, actually. I think I kept all of them," Istomin gestured toward a series of filing boxes on a low bookshelf. "Why?"

"Do they differ much?" Thomas asked.

"Do they differ? Well, no, I don't think so. They're quite standard in terms of wording and such." Istomin paused and looked at Thomas.

"Ah, I see what you are getting at!" he said, his face brightening. "We might be able to use an old one if we can change the date."

"Exactly."

"But that would be *forgery*, sir!" Markov objected, his eyes widening in alarm, "including misusing the signatures of some very senior figures!"

Thomas didn't answer him. Looking at Istomin with an urgent expression, he urged him, "Please get them!"

Istomin's papers were well organized, and he found the folder he wanted quickly. Looking through the dozen official documents printed on heavy paper watermarked with the imperial crest, he stopped on one for March 5, 1912.

"What do you think?" he asked Thomas, giving him the sheet. "Wouldn't a bit of careful erasing and precise penmanship allow us to change this to May 28, 1913?"

"You mean, yesterday? Yes, I think it could be done. But doesn't it have to indicate the address where the inspection needs to be carried out?"

Istomin looked at the document: "Well, this one doesn't for some reason. But I can always write it in, say, here . . . at the top of the text," he pointed with his index finger.

"Gentlemen! This is going too far!" Markov protested indignantly. "What you are proposing may be a state crime!"

"Sergey Sergeyevich, please!" Thomas implored him. "I agree that under normal circumstances we need to follow the law. But you're a practical man and you know my daughter's life is in danger. God knows what they've done to her and to Nikitin's daughter and whoever else they may have! If your scruples don't allow you to take part, you don't have to. I won't hold it against you. You know how much I respect you."

Thomas's voice vibrated with emotion, but he didn't show any anger. Nevertheless, Markov winced. He felt his honor and courage were at stake. He also wanted badly to be involved in anything that happened, rather than return to the tedium of the Garden with its pickpockets and grifters.

"Very well, sir . . . I will take part, then." He straightened up and raised his chin. "I believe I can still be of some use in this matter," he said with a sour smile.

Thomas ignored the subtle dig. Reaching out, he clasped Markov's right hand with both of his. "Thank you, Sergey Sergeyevich, I couldn't imagine doing any of this without you."

Istomin turned on his desk lamp, got a magnifying glass and set to work.

Fifteen minutes later the altered document was ready. The thick, creamy paper on which the authorization had been printed proved relatively forgiving when he gently scraped at the hand-written date with a razor-sharp penknife. After he blew away the small fibers, he chose a bottle of the same dark blue ink and wiped the nib on the rim to ensure the fresh ink would not run on the roughened surface. He held the sheet at arm's length: the changes were not noticeable. Thomas bent over the paper as Istomin worked, and patted him on the back when he was finished.

"If you don't mind, Sergey Sergey'ch," Istomin said to Markov in a cordial tone, "since the document names me as the building department's inspector, you will play the role of my assistant."

He was relieved when the old Okhrannik nodded.

"Shall we go pay our visit to 17 Kochkinsky Lane now?" Istomin asked, getting up from the desk.

"Yes, your excellency, without delay. But perhaps you could give me some pointers about what I should do when we're there to support our cover story."

"Quite right. Let us both take these," Istomin said,

opening another drawer and pulling out two folders with marbled cardboard covers and fabric ties. He inserted a series of sheets into each, some with writing and some blank, and handed one to Markov.

"We'll take my automobile, and I'll suggest a few things while we drive over. I'd be grateful for directions. I don't know the area very well."

"Of course. Start as you would for Khamovniki, and I'll direct you when we are closer."

CHAPTER THIRTY-EIGHT

When Istomin and Markov got to Kochkinsky Lane, they decided first to drive past the entry gate to number 17 and then go around the block to get a sense of the property and the area as a whole. The convertible top on the Russo-Balt was still up because of the rain and helped shield them from view.

No one was about in the streets and they could drive slowly without drawing attention. A tall, continuous wooden fence, freshly painted green, surrounded the large property, which was full of old trees, and they didn't see anything noteworthy until they reached the halfway mark. Markov called Istomin's attention to a metal gate streaked with rust that was secured with a shiny new chain and padlock. However, judging by the weeds and shrubs growing in front of it, it was little used.

"It looks like a rear entrance to the property. Useful to know. And someone bothered to make sure it's secure," the older man commented.

As they circled back to the main entrance, Istomin down-shifted, slowed down, and looked at Markov. Markov nodded, as if saying it was indeed time. He patted the left side of his suit jacket, reminding Istomin he was armed, just in case.

Istomin drove down the driveway and parked past the mansion's porte-cochère. He didn't like the idea of having the automobile hemmed in by the pillars supporting the overhang if they needed to leave in a hurry. When he stepped out onto the neatly raked gravel his heart began to race—the way it did when he was entering a new stretch of field or woodland at the beginning of a hunt.

Istomin hadn't expected the property to be as imposing or well-maintained as it looked, perhaps because he had imagined Dickerman as no more than a shady criminal. He exchanged glances with Markov, who also seemed impressed.

The rose-colored brick façade of the large building with its pointed arches and peaked gables looked weathered but well-scrubbed; the wood trim around the windows was freshly painted; the massive oak front door with its curving, forged-iron hinges in the shape of coiled serpents gleamed with varnish. As Istomin climbed the broad granite front steps, he noticed there were electrical and telephone wires entering the mansion through a front cornice, and when he looked over his shoulder, he saw a line of new conduit poles receding through the trees to the street.

What luck! The place has recently been renovated, Istomin thought with satisfaction. *I can make use of this for the inspection.*

The doorbell was activated by a pushbutton and when Istomin pressed it he heard a melodic cascade of chimes. *Also electric,* he thought. *All the latest innovations. And lots of money.* He glanced at Markov behind him and saw him purse his lips and nod, indicating he had also noted the modern upgrades.

A few seconds later the door opened to reveal a woman—slender, dressed in a dark dress, pale oval face with regular features, no jewelry, hair pulled back into a bun. She looked like a stern headmistress and her expression was both alert and wary, as if she didn't expect anything good to come from the unexpected visitors.

"Yes?"

"Good afternoon, madam. Moscow Building Department," Istomin announced. He removed his hat, pulled the authorization out of the inside breast pocket of his jacket, unfolded it, and handed it to the woman.

"We are here to carry out a mandatory inspection because of recent renovations to the property. I'm the inspector," Istomin said with a polite smile and handed the woman his card, which he had ready. "And this is my assistant," Istomin gestured with his hand toward Markov, who tipped his bowler to the woman and stared at her with an expectant expression.

"Are you the owner?" Istomin asked.

Hilda was flustered by the visit. She first squinted near-sightedly at the official-looking document, which had a seal at the bottom and was bewilderingly long and detailed. Then she raised the card to her eyes.

There were two engraved lines on it in Russian: "Prince Vladimir Vladimirovich Istomin, Engineer." The man who gave it to her was very distinguished looking and the card made an impression on her.

"No, sir. No, I'm not," she replied hesitantly.

Istomin held out his left hand for the document he had given her, and she automatically handed it back. After a second's confused hesitation, she stepped to the side. "Please, come in," she invited. "I'll get the owner."

Istomin and Markov followed her into the entry foyer. "Please wait," she asked and disappeared through an arched entryway into the interior of the mansion.

The richness of the architectural detail around them was impressive and the two men couldn't help turning their heads and craning their necks as they took in the stone floors, carved wooden paneling on the walls, and deeply coffered ceilings. A light smell of lemon oil filled the foyer, as if the paneling had recently been cleaned. Several brass electrical lights struggled against the somber setting, but the dark wood seemed to absorb the light and there were unpleasant shadows everywhere one looked.

They didn't have long to wait. A door slammed, the noise echoing somewhere inside the mansion, then they heard two voices arguing—the intonation wasn't Russian—and the sound of approaching footsteps.

Istomin recognized Dickerman from Thomas's description as soon as he walked in—short, corpulent, round-faced, thin-lipped, with hair brushed straight back, and a nose like a hawk's beak.

Dickerman eyed the two visitors as he walked toward them, looking entirely self-possessed. He stopped when he was still a few paces away and gestured to the woman in the dark dress who was following him to come forward.

"This is Mister Dickerman, the owner," she explained. "He

is an American and does not speak Russian. My name is Hilda Weber, and I will translate for him."

"Ah, an American!" Istomin exclaimed in English, "it is fortunate I speak the language."

An expression of surprise replaced the imperturbable expression on Dickerman's face. But he made no move to offer his hand to Istomin.

"Well then," he drawled, "that's wonderful—perhaps you would be so kind as to explain to me what this is all about . . . Prince Íz-tow-min." Dickerman hesitated over the unfamiliar name on the card and stressed it incorrectly on the first syllable rather than the second.

"Of course. As I told this lady," Istomin bowed toward Hilda, who was standing with her hands clasped in front of her and an unhappy expression on her face, "we are here from the Moscow Building Department to inspect the recent renovations to this property."

"This is the first I've heard of it. What exactly do you want to see?" Dickerman's expression became suspicious. Istomin realized he had to be careful if he was to get anywhere.

"All the main systems, Mr. Dickerman—water, gas, electricity, sanitation. We need to confirm that everything was done according to city codes and regulations," he replied, adding a note of weariness to his voice, as if going into detail would be too tedious. It was important to disarm Dickerman, so he wouldn't get the idea of trying to verify the inspection with the city's building department. "It'll be quick. We'd like to start in the basement, please, and work our way up."

Istomin noticed Hilda stiffen at this. Dickerman objected as well: "The basement is fine, as is this floor, but you cannot go upstairs."

"May I ask why? Don't you have utilities there too?"

"That's not the issue," Dickerman replied sharply. "My children are sick upstairs, and I can't let you disturb them."

Istomin felt his heart start to race again. He decided to try to push a bit further.

"Such a shame. I'm sorry to hear it. But we won't disturb them, Mr. Dickerman, I assure you. We don't even have to go into their rooms." He looked up at the ceiling: "Your second floor looks quite large, and we can inspect the other areas, such as the bathrooms."

"I'm afraid it is quite out of the question. They've got a fever and must have complete quiet. Doctor's strict orders," he concluded in a tone implying he wouldn't budge.

Istomin felt a swell of elation building inside him. Being blocked from going to the second floor meant their reconnaissance had succeeded. The thought flashed in his mind that he should have brought a gun; he and Markov could have strong-armed these two and run upstairs.

But then his military caution intervened: it was foolhardy to attack without knowing your enemy's strength or location. Who knew if there were others upstairs? Thomas said that at least four men had attacked him and Olga.

"Very well. We'll do a partial inspection. For now," Istomin replied in what he hoped was a matter-of-fact tone.

Out of fear that he might give away his excitement, he avoided looking at Markov. He wished he could leave immediately to tell Thomas. But like a stalker who sees his prey moving behind a tangle of branches and still must maneuver patiently until he can get a clear shot, Istomin understood that he and Markov had to finish the charade of an inspection so they did not alert Dickerman.

Hilda took their hats and left them on a side table in the foyer. For the next half hour, she led the way, opening doors and turning on lights, the two inspectors following and Dickerman bringing up the rear with his slight wheeze. In the basement, Istomin stopped several times to make detailed technical comments in Russian to Markov about water and gas pipe diameters, sewage lines, insulated electrical conduits, and load-bearing pillars, even pausing so Markov could go through the motions of noting it all down in his folder. When they passed a musty-smelling side room filled with wine racks, he noticed a dozen wooden cases of spirits arranged neatly on new wooden shelves—vodka, cognac, liqueurs. The label on one leaped out at him: "Old Fitzgerald. Old Fashioned Copper Pot Distilled Whiskey." He let his gaze linger on the room, hoping Markov would follow his lead but avoided looking at him.

On the first floor, there was little to inspect apart from the kitchen and the newly remodeled bathrooms, all of which were finished with expensive materials and had the most modern conveniences. When they passed through the butler's pantry and entered the dining room, Istomin noticed the wall-sized paintings on eroticized themes and glanced at Markov. The old policeman managed to maintain his poker face, but small frown lines appeared on his forehead. The paintings erased Istomin's last doubts about the aim of the establishment.

Enough is enough, he decided. Time to get out.

"We'll come back another time to inspect the second floor, but for now I am happy to tell you everything is in order," Istomin said, turning toward Dickerman when they returned to the foyer.

"You will receive an official report in the mail. Good day to you, sir. And you, madam."

After Hilda translated, Dickerman replied "And good day to you too, inspector," staring straight into Istomin's eyes and emphasizing the word.

Istomin sensed a threat emanating from the man and wondered if Markov noticed it too. Hilda opened the heavy front door and stood aside. Seeing that Dickerman was waiting for them to leave and wasn't going to say anything else, Istomin pivoted, put on his hat, and walked out. Markov settled for a curt nod to Dickerman and followed.

Once the Russo-Balt reached the street, Istomin turned left and stepped on the accelerator, going as fast as he could, passing slow moving carriages and vans, and cutting off cross traffic whenever he had a chance. He and Markov had exchanged glances when they were getting into the automobile, but no words were necessary.

CHAPTER THIRTY-NINE

After watching the two Russians drive off, Dickerman went into the library and spent several minutes walking back and forth over the expensive Isfahan rug that covered the floor, trying to figure out if this "inspection" was a problem or not. He pivoted so sharply that he left scuff marks on the intricate floral pattern.

Hilda had confirmed that Istomin used a lot of technical language she didn't understand but that sounded real, particularly when they were in the basement, and that the document she was shown looked official too. Dickerman wasn't entirely convinced but decided the visit wasn't worth worrying about. There were more important matters, like Thomas.

His daughter had become a problem as well because of her exceptional stubbornness and surprising ferocity. After taking a couple of sips from the first glass, she refused to drink any more of the drug-laced *mors*. She was as indifferent to Hilda's intimidation as she was to Maria's sugary manner, and when Boris was called in, she screamed that she'd attack him with her teeth and her fingernails if he so much as touched her. With all the other problems in the Convent, Dickerman decided that for the time being Olga would be kept under lock and key and separate from the other captives, who were now being allowed downstairs together.

There'll be time enough to rein in that little bitch when we've finished with her daddy, Dickerman concluded.

Maria was the first to return to the Convent from the errands Dickerman handed out earlier. She found out where Thomas was simply by going to the Aquarium office and claiming she was a singer and had business with him. The secretary gave her Istomin's address and telephone number.

By nature, Maria was a frank woman and honest in her own way. This was an extension of her libertinism, and she was accustomed to doing whatever she wanted and only when she wanted. As a result, the spying and duplicity disturbed her. She began to feel that she was being coerced into something incomprehensible and far more dangerous than she had bargained for. When Hilda let Maria into the mansion, she whispered that Dickerman was in the kitchen, then rolled her eyes in that direction to signal he was in a foul mood. Maria's anxiety increased even more.

Entering the kitchen warily, Maria saw Dickerman sitting at the table, eating a *kalach*, a ring-shaped white bread roll, slathered with butter and drinking tea, a large white napkin tucked into his collar and hanging between his widespread knees.

"At last! You're back! Well, what've you got for me?" he demanded without any preamble as he chewed, then bunched up his napkin and wiped his mouth.

Maria's English was halting but she could get by. "Thomas not home some days. He staying by friend. His friend important man," Maria emphasized.

"What do you mean, important? What're you getting at? What's his name dammit! Where's he live? Did you find out or not?"

"Yes, I got what you want, but, please, I not think it good have trouble with him."

"You . . . don't . . . think!" Dickerman hammered out, in a tone of disbelief about her sudden presumption. "What's his goddamned name?" he shouted.

"It's . . . Prince Istomin," she emphasized his title, "Prince Vladimir Vladimirovich Istomin. He lives at 17 Malaya Nikitskaya Street. Not far from here," she answered, dropping her voice to a whisper, as if speaking softly would lessen the impact of what she said.

Dickerman's reaction made her take a step back.

He turned red and started gasping for air, as if someone had punched him in the stomach. Scrabbling at his jacket pocket with his stubby fingers, he pulled out the "inspector's" business card Hilda had given him.

"Like this?" he asked, extending it to her.

Maria leaned in warily and peered at the engraved lines as if afraid they would bite her. "Yes," she whispered after a pause. "How you get?" she asked incredulously.

"Because he was just here!" Dickerman shouted, his eyes bulging as he tried to breathe. He stuck a finger into his shirt collar and tugged at it until a button popped off and rattled across the floor.

"I knew there was something fishy about his damn inspection! It's got to be the same man!"

"But why he come? What inspection?" Maria struggled to understand.

"They're on to us! That's why! It's got to be because they somehow found our address!"

Maria glanced over her shoulder nervously, as if someone might burst into the house any second. "You mean police? But what we to do? Maybe leave before anyone come!"

Her mention of the police made Dickerman come back to his senses. He paused to think for a second.

"Nah!" he said, shaking his head. "He didn't look like a copper. Not at all. But his assistant . . .." Dickerman let his voice trail off as he pursued the implications of what had occurred to him.

Although this "assistant" had the bloodhound eyes of a dick, the fact that he'd come with some guy who was a prince to scout the place meant he probably wasn't working with the regular police. This was good.

Dickerman stopped paying attention to Maria and waved his hand dismissively at her to leave him alone. He felt like an utter fool for having been taken in by the visitors and chalked it up as another mark against Thomas.

An hour later Stepan and Bartkow returned with the revolvers, ammunition, and a cleaning kit, which the old salesman in the store persuaded them to buy—"So you gentlemen can enjoy your revolvers for a long time!" They hadn't encountered any difficulty buying the guns. The only restrictions on firearms sales were for those adopted by the Russian military, and they didn't use American revolvers.

Dickerman opened the cardboard boxes and examined each gun with practiced hands—spinning the drum, cocking the hammer, aiming, and dry firing. He had always liked Smith & Wesson's Model 10, even though they were manufactured by Yankees in Springfield, Massachusetts.

"Do you three know how to use these?" he asked.

"I do," Bartkow said, but the two brothers shook their heads.

"All right, take them down to the basement," he told Bartkow, gesturing at the brothers, "set up some of those construction timbers that are down there and show them how to load and fire."

"I don't want you back here until you know what you're doing," he admonished Stepan and Boris, and waited until Bartkow translated before adding, "and try not to shoot each other!"

A few minutes later, the muffled sounds of gunfire started coming up through the living room floor, first hesitantly, one at a time, then, after a pause—they must be reloading, Dickerman guessed—came a fusillade of rapid fire.

When Bartkow and the brothers came back up ten minutes later, they reeked of cordite and the brothers' faces were flushed with excitement.

"You guys like what these guns can do?" Dickerman asked them with a grin.

"Yeah, boss. And they got the hang of it right away," Bartkow mumbled through his swollen lips, trying to sound enthusiastic.

The Golub brothers still had their fingers on the triggers of their revolvers.

"*My razreshetili eti kolody v chortovy drebezgi!*" (We riddled those logs to damned smithereens!) the usually silent and taciturn Stepan exclaimed excitedly.

He and his brother had used fists, clubs, and knives

during their past depredations. But a gun's devastating power was something new and impressed him greatly. It would allow him to wreak the vengeance he yearned for.

Stürmer returned to the Convent at half past three, earlier than he'd been told. Dickerman snorted derisively when he saw his outfit, which Stürmer thought would be a practical disguise, but which would have suited better a genteel hunt in Bavaria—knee socks and plus-fours, a belted tweed jacket with bone buttons, ankle-height hiking boots, and a hat with a chamois brush.

Dickerman was tempted to say something cutting, but changed his mind. He needed Stürmer to be composed, at least as much as he was capable of it. And seeing how well the German responded to being browbeaten, Dickerman continued to treat him like an errant youth who was being given a second chance. The news about the "inspection" shocked Stürmer, but when he tried to ask about it, Dickerman told him curtly to wait. He then summoned the entire gang to the living room.

"We're going to have ourselves a little council of war," Dickerman proclaimed as they all filed in and took seats on the couches and armchairs.

"But first, show me your weapon, baron," he asked Stürmer and watched with an ironic expression as the German reached inside his jacket, fumbled with the Luger in a shoulder holster and passed it to him. Dickerman hefted the gun, his eyes narrowing as he ran a finger over its cocking mechanism and handed it back.

"Looks kinda complicated. You ever shoot anyone with it?" he asked.

"No. No, I have not. However, I'm a crack shot. Of that I can assure you," Stürmer replied. He blushed at Dickerman's question and was trying to seem calm.

Dickerman didn't reply but reached under his jacket and pulled his own gun out of a holster on his belt. It was an older Smith and Wesson .38, nickel-plated, with ivory grips stained with use. He put it on his left palm and showed it to the others: "This has served me well many times. And yes, I have shot people with it, if you were wondering," he said, looking pointedly at Stürmer. "But only those that needed killin'," he finished with an unpleasant chuckle.

He then looked at everyone in turn to make sure he had their attention. "OK, listen up. We have to move fast. You translate since he can't talk too good," he instructed Hilda as he jerked his head in Bartkow's direction.

"A couple of Thomas's friends was just here, which means he knows where we are. But it wasn't cops, so that means they're not involved. Or at least, they're not the ones leading Thomas's pack. So, what we're going to do is go in hard and fast tonight and clean them all out before they figure things out."

No one moved or spoke. Hilda stared at Dickerman, Maria dropped her eyes to the floor in front of her. Only Stepan and Boris smirked, their eyes still burning with their new-found confidence.

"But we need to have a plan," Stürmer spoke up in a hesitant voice. "We don't know how many people Thomas has."

"It doesn't make any damn difference. There'll be five of us, and we've got these," Dickerman hefted his revolver before tucking it back in its holster. "I doubt Thomas has more than the two guys who showed up here. We're going to kill all three of them—Thomas, that prince of his, and the old cop. Once we do, any connection to us will be dead too."

Stürmer looked aghast: "Are you proposing we to this man's house go and just shoot everyone!" he exclaimed. "What if there are innocent people inside? What if someone sees us and reports us to the police? What if you're wrong and he has more men? This is sheer madness!"

Maria looked up at Dickerman. She looked terrified. Hilda followed what he was saying closely and looked serious but calm.

"Yes, that's exactly what we're going to do!" Dickerman replied and stood up. "We don't want any witnesses, and we're going to clean out Thomas's entire passel! It'll be just like the way we dealt with troublemakers like him back home in the South!"

"This is insane!" Stürmer exclaimed and jumped to his feet. "It goes against all the rules of war!"

"Rules of war?" Dickerman shouted back, then drew his revolver in a surprisingly quick motion, cocked it and pointed it at Stürmer's face.

"Rules of war!" he jeered. "I'll tell you what the rules of war are, you sniveling little coward! I've got a good mind to shoot you right here and now, you little piece of shit!"

Stürmer was trembling from agitation, his eyes fixed on the revolver's black muzzle in front of his eyes.

"We need him, boss!" Bartkow interfered, slurring his words, and wincing at the pain in his tongue.

Dickerman lowered his arm. He knew he shouldn't have gotten carried away like that, but his resentment against the German's pretensions had built up in him. When he saw how spineless he was he felt a flood of anger.

Pushing his feelings into the background, Dickerman changed his tone with chameleon-like facility.

"Well now, let's not get all worked up for nothing," he said.

He tried to smile as he put away his gun, but only an unpleasant grimace appeared on his face. "I was just kidding, baron! We gotta pull together now, all of us. Right?"

"Yes, of . . . cour . . . course," Stürmer stammered, mesmerized by Dickerman's aura of self-assurance.

"You two will stay here, obviously," Dickerman turned to Maria and Hilda, "to keep an eye on what's upstairs."

"As for you," he addressed the four men, "We're going in at 2 a. m., like the night riders back home, when everyone's asleep, and that Black sonofabitch and his pals won't know what hit em!"

Dickerman pulled out his pocket watch. "It's four now. You've got plenty of time to eat, catch some sleep, get ready. I want you all to be here at 1:30 sharp, ready to go. That's 1:30 tonight, got it? Make sure you check your guns. We'll take your car, baron. We're not going to do any sneaking around. We're going to go in the front door and start blazing. And do you know why it's going to work? Because we have surprise on our side! It never failed me before and won't fail us now."

CHAPTER FORTY

Friday, May 29, 1:45 p.m.
Prince Vladimir Istomin's residence

After racing home from Dickerman's mansion, Istomin turned the Russo-Balt into his driveway and braked to a hard stop in front of the house, throwing up a spray of gravel that clattered on the front steps. Leaving the automobile's door open, he strode rapidly indoors with Markov following at a dignified trot. The valet was in the front hall and was about to explain that Thomas had gone upstairs to rest after lunch, but Istomin was already on the stairs, taking them two at a time.

"We found Dickerman and his nest!" he exclaimed when he saw Thomas wasn't asleep on the bed. *"And I'm certain Olga and the other children are in the mansion!"*

Markov made it up the stairs a moment later, breathing hard. He frowned when he heard Istomin's exaggeration.

"Actually, your excellency, we should say in all honesty that we have good reason to believe the children may be there, although I agree it was a very successful reconnaissance," Markov interjected. He had seen too many hopes dashed during his long career and didn't want to be party to another grievous disappointment.

"Tell me," Thomas urged them, sitting up and lowering his feet to the floor. His heart began to thump when Istomin described the case of whiskey he saw in the basement. Dickerman's categorical refusal to let anyone go upstairs because "his children" were sick clinched it for Thomas.

"We have to attack the place as soon as we can," he with a determined tone. "From what you say, it sounds like your visit might have alerted Dickerman."

"Yes, unfortunately," Istomin replied, and looked at Markov, who nodded in agreement. "He looked as if he was getting suspicious, sir. I think we left just in time."

"I want to go now," Thomas announced. "How many guns do you have in your cabinet?"

"My dear fellow, I have . . . let me think . . . five, no six. And Sergey Sergeyevich has a revolver, but that's not the issue. We have no idea how many people Dickerman has with him. We saw only him and some woman, his housekeeper I assume. But from what you said about the attack when he abducted Olga, he had four other men in addition to himself." When Istomin finished, he glanced expectantly at Markov for support.

"I agree with his excellency," Markov said grimly. "We should wait until tomorrow. I can get my assistant, Ilyushin, to help. He served in the police and is experienced. And I think that under these extraordinary circumstances I could persuade Arkady Frantsevich to delegate a couple of men."

Thomas had gotten up from the bed and began to pace back and forth as he listened to the arguments. He knew Markov and Istomin were being prudent. Acting rashly could ruin everything. But the delay was deeply frustrating, now that he knew where to find his enemy, and probably Olga.

"Very well, we'll wait," he said. "Can you telephone Arkady Frantsevich for help, and your assistant? We should move as early as possible tomorrow. I'd say at dawn. Agreed?"

Markov nodded. "I'll get right to it."

Thomas turned to Istomin: "Let's go look at your guns."

The tall birchwood cabinet, its narrow double doors decorated with intricate scrollwork, stood at the end of a row of bookshelves in Istomin's study and looked like an innocent wardrobe. Istomin felt around the top until he found a key and unlocked the doors. The sweet, waxy smell of cosmoline floated out.

In a vertical rack were four long guns: two German Mauser hunting rifles—a .25 light caliber and a .44, which was heavy enough to stop a wild boar; and two French shotguns—beautifully engraved, Darne double-barreled side by sides, one 12-guage, the other 10. The stocks of all the weapons showed signs of wear but were clean and well-maintained.

"Take your pick," Istomin invited Thomas, gesturing with his right arm.

"I'll take the 12-guage if that's all right with you. I've got one just like it. We're likely to be indoors. If there's any shooting we'll have to move fast and hit them hard." He paused for a second, remembering. "Last time I used mine was when we went for geese near Kostroma last fall, remember? Now it seems like a lifetime ago."

"Yes. And you're right about close quarters. The shotguns would be best. I'll take the 10-guage then. It will give us even more firepower if we need it."

Istomin pulled the smaller Darne out of the rack and handed it to Thomas, then reached up to a shelf at the top of the cabinet filled with neatly stacked boxes of ammunition.

"How about these long cartridges with heavy buckshot?"

"All right. Heavier than what I've ever used for wingshooting, but they'll do real damage," Thomas replied with a serious expression on his face and took the box Istomin offered him.

The weight of the gun, with its smooth walnut stock, checkering on the grip, and dully gleaming barrel felt comfortable in his hands. He opened the breech lock and closed it with a satisfying metallic click. They were all familiar gestures.

"I think we should also take something for backup, just in case," Istomin said, pulling open a drawer at the bottom of the cabinet and revealing two revolvers in vertical slips.

"That Nagant is what I carried during the Japanese war. And the .455 Webley is, well, . . . a war trophy, let's say. It belonged to a Japanese officer." It pained him to remember the moment, but there had been no choice when he shot the man.

"How about the Webley for you and the Nagant for me?" he continued. "I had it on my hip for nearly two years."

"That's fine. I haven't fired a revolver since that affair in Budapest I told you about, but I remember how to use one."

Istomin handed the gun to him and found the right box of cartridges, but after looking at the label put it aside and got another.

"These are fresher," he explained. "Don't want to take any chances. I don't have holsters for either of them, but we'll manage."

Istomin suggested they strip the weapons down and clean and check them even though they looked spotless, and spread an oilcloth he kept rolled up in the gun cabinet on his desk.

They were finishing up and reassembling the guns when Markov came in to report about his telephone calls.

When he saw the guns on the desk he stopped and looked silently at the two men for a second, then raised his eyebrows and nodded. He didn't much like the sight of civilians handling firearms, but because of what he had just found out, there was no other way.

"Gentlemen! Ilyushin agreed to help. Sunrise tomorrow is a few minutes after 4 a. m. He said he'll be here at 3 a. m. and will bring his revolver. I regret I couldn't reach Arkady Frantsevich. I left a message with his duty officer, but I don't know when I'll hear from him."

"Very well," Istomin replied, "thank you Sergey Sergey'ch. That means it'll be the four of us. We should plan on getting there just before dawn. If you like, you can spend the night here," Istomin added. "I have plenty of room."

"Thank you, sir, but I'd rather go home. I'll need to talk to my wife. She would worry otherwise. But I'll be here tomorrow in plenty of time."

CHAPTER FORTY-ONE

Friday, May 29, 5:00 p.m.
The "Convent," 17 Kochkinsky Lane

Dickerman decided he couldn't trust Stürmer after his last outburst. The only safe way to handle him was to keep him close, at least until the Thomas problem was solved once and for all. He would also have to make certain Stürmer took part in the killings.

Nothing like spilled blood to create a bond, he thought grimly. *I might even get some leverage against whoever the hell his mysterious backers are.*

But now it was time to shift from the stick to a carrot. Dickerman knew that Stürmer's weakness and inexperience would make him susceptible to a bit of kindness. He found him sitting alone in the library with a book open on his lap. But the lights weren't on, and he wasn't reading.

Never mind, Dickerman thought, *I can play you like a Tennessee fiddle.*

The young German rose to his feet with an apprehensive expression on his face when he saw Dickerman entering. But this changed to a shy smile when he heard the friendly tone with which Dickerman invited him to spend the night in the Convent. Leaning in close to Stürmer and holding him by the lapel, Dickerman spoke so solicitously about how they were "a team" and "real comrades" who "were in it together" that Stürmer melted and agreed, despite the brutality with which Dickerman had treated him earlier.

"Good man," Dickerman announced heartily and clapped Stürmer on the back. He then asked him to come to the kitchen so that he could translate to the cook that she should serve them all an early dinner at six thirty. That way, Dickerman explained, whoever wanted to try to sleep for a few hours afterward could do so.

He also told the cook to serve everyone a drink at dinner—one generous shot of vodka or full glass of wine—and after that to make sure the liquor cabinets were locked. He needed the men to feel connected and drinking together always helped.

However, one drink would be enough. Dickerman remembered the disastrous consequences when the men in his Klan coven decided to "get good and liquored up" before they started a night-time raid on a Black church back in 1898 outside Baton Rouge. They did burn the church, but two of his men never made it back.

That evening, when everyone was seated around the dining room table, Dickerman raised a toast "to our being rich." Maria looked anxious but Hilda appeared to be taking everything in stride. Most important was the look of determination on the men's faces, and even Stürmer downed his vodka in one gulp.

After dinner, Dickerman went to a storage room in the basement and then to the carriage house behind the mansion to gather some equipment. He also got Stürmer to review the route to Istomin's address with Bartkow, who said it would take fifteen minutes to drive there when the roads are clear of traffic at night. Leaving the things he had collected on a table in the corner of the living room, he went up to his and Hilda's bedroom and lay down next to her.

He woke up two hours later without an alarm, feeling rested and clear-headed. When he went downstairs at half past one, he grunted with satisfaction. Everyone was already present. They were all standing. He didn't ask them to sit down.

"Show me your guns and ammo," he demanded, then, realizing he was too harsh, added "please."

The Golub brothers and Bartkow had their revolvers tucked into the front of their waistbands and opened their jackets to reveal them. They also drew handfuls of loose cartridges out of their pants' pockets. Stürmer pulled his Luger from his shoulder holster and showed Dickerman an extra loaded clip.

"Good. Mine is right here," Dickerman patted his right hip. "So, this is the plan. Translate what I say," he said to Hilda.

"We're not going to let anyone get away, understand? Our own lives and everything we've built here depend on it. You and you," he gestured at Stepan and Boris, "will use these to force open the front door." Dickerman turned around to the table behind him and handed Stepan a short iron crowbar with a chisel-shaped tip and a thick tire iron to Boris.

"Once the door is open, you drop the bars, and we go in with these in one hand and your guns in the other." He reached behind him and handed each man an electric torch.

"I'll be going in with you. And when we go in the front, you," he poked his finger at Bartkow, "go around to the back of the house and wait by the rear door. If anyone tries to get out, you drop them right there."

"You all know how to work these?" he asked, flicking his torch on and off. "Any questions?"

Bartkow was looking unhappy, and after shifting back and forth on his feet several times got up the courage to speak. "Why me in the back, boss?" he asked peevishly, still slurring the words, then looked at Hilda to translate for the others.

"Because we need their muscle with the crowbars, and I doubt you've ever used one," Dickerman replied, raising his voice. "And they know all about breaking down doors," he added, turning to face Boris and Stepan. "Am I right?"

The brothers nodded eagerly after Hilda finished translating.

"Your job is going to be important," Dickerman continued and put his right hand on Bartkow's shoulder, who flinched at the unexpected gesture. "You're going to be the one who guarantees our success, understand? Because you'll make sure no one gets away."

Bartkow gave a reluctant nod, but the tension in his face

eased.

"And one final detail. See this?" Dickerman held up a large, round, grey metal container with a screw-on lid. "Kerosene. When we're done, we pour it all over, toss a match and the whole place goes up in flames. Nothing and no one will be left. After that, we come back here."

"What if someone sees us?" Stürmer asked. He had tried to keep silent but couldn't help himself.

"At that time of night in that neighborhood, no one's going to be around to see us. And anyone in the house who sees us will be dead and there won't be any evidence left. Got it?"

Stürmer tried to seem calm, but he couldn't hide the fear in his eyes.

CHAPTER FORTY-TWO

Saturday, May 30, 1:50 a.m.
Prince Vladimir Istomin's residence

The night was cool, a bright half-moon floated in the sky, and clouds streaming across its surface made the light swell and fade. One moment the houses and trees lining Malaya Nikitskaya Street emerged into view and the next they were swallowed by darkness. The only light in Istomin's house came from the window of Zoya's bedroom facing the garden—a faint red glow that was almost invisible.

Zoya rarely slept more than a few hours on the best of nights and a disturbing, violent dream had awakened her. She got out of bed wearing a nightshirt that draped her tiny frame like a sheet thrown over a floor lamp, put on a warm robe and felt slippers, and moved to an armchair.

The dove that had been asleep on the headboard of her bed fluttered into the air and landed on her shoulder. Zoya didn't turn on the electric lamp on a small table near the armchair. She could see well enough by the light from the candle in the ruby-colored glass holder suspended in front of the icon stand in the room's eastern corner.

The day before, when Prokopenko brought Strelka with him to Istomin's house at Thomas's request, the dog had explored everywhere, sniffing and "making friends" with everyone, as Istomin's valet reported to Thomas with a smile. After checking with the cook, Thomas made up a straw-filled bed for her by the kitchen door that led to the back yard.

When Zoya got up in her wing several rooms away, Strelka heard her. She raised her head from the striped ticking and yawned widely, revealing two long rows of white teeth, then padded down the hallways, her claws clicking lightly on the polished wooden floors. When she got to Zoya's bedroom, she nosed the door open, walked up to the chair where the old woman was sitting and looked questioningly into her eyes. Zoya looked back and put her hand on the dog's head.

A moment later Strelka tensed, flattened her ears, and dashed out of the room down the dark hallway, through the kitchen into Istomin's part of the house, skidding on the turns, and up the stairs to the second floor. She stopped at the door to Thomas's room, sat down on her haunches and barked once, something she never did indoors.

Thomas opened the door a few moments later wearing his pajamas. He had been dozing fitfully when he heard Strelka bark and quickly got out of bed, realizing something was wrong with the dog.

"What is it, girl?" he asked, bending down and stroking her head, "what is it, did a bad dream wake you up?" he asked with a smile. In his haste, he hadn't turned on the lamp in his room, but enough moonlight was streaming in through the window so he could see.

The dog looked at him and barked once more, as if in reply, then trotted down the hallway to Istomin's door. She barked again, turned around and dashed down the stairs.

Thomas had never seen her act this way before. He went to Istomin's door and knocked.

"It's me. Are you awake? Something's going on with Strelka and I need to check downstairs."

"I'll be out in a second. I wasn't asleep and heard her," Istomin replied. A second later, a light appeared under the door and Istomin opened it. He was wearing a robe over his pajamas and looked disheveled but was fully awake. The bright lamp on his nightstand illuminated him from the rear.

"What is it?" he asked in a whisper when he saw the worried expression on Thomas's face.

"Strelka never acted like this. It's as if she's trying to warn us. We have to go downstairs and see."

As the two men were talking, on the other side of the house Zoya got up from her armchair, went to the corner of the room with the icon lamp, and stretching up with her right hand, pinched the flickering flame of the candle between thumb and forefinger. The room went dark.

Thomas had already turned around to go downstairs when he noticed that he cast a shadow on the floor in front of him because of the light in Istomin's room. He felt exposed and vulnerable. Speaking in a whisper, he looked over his shoulder and asked Istomin to turn the light off.

"All right," Istomin replied. He didn't understand what Thomas was afraid of but went back into his room and turned the switch. It took several moments before his eyes adjusted to the dark enough for him to make out Thomas's dark figure in the doorway.

"Do you think there's someone downstairs?" he asked, "someone Strelka doesn't know? Who can it be? There are only two servants in the house tonight—my valet and the cook, and she knows them both."

"I'm not sure. But we should get the guns out of the cabinet just in case. And let's keep the lights off so no one knows we're awake."

The two men descended the steps, holding onto the railing and listening for any noise.

CHAPTER FORTY-THREE

Saturday, May 30, 2:07 a.m.
Prince Vladimir Istomin's residence.

When the black Mercedes turned onto Malaya Nikitskaya Street, Stürmer slowed down and dimmed the headlights. Bartkow leaned out the front passenger window, searching for the entrance to Istomin's estate.

"There it is," he whispered when he saw it halfway down the block, "do you see the two brick pillars?"

Dickerman leaned forward and gave Stürmer a series of curt orders—extinguish the lights, turn off the engine, let the automobile coast.

The engine's soft rumble stopped as abruptly as if it had been cut with a knife and the Mercedes glided forward in the darkness for several long heartbeats, its tires rustling on the pavement. After it came to rest, the five men climbed out, taking care to shut the doors quietly and not make any other noise.

Walking in single file, they entered the driveway, with Stepan in the lead and Dickerman bringing up the rear. The light from the moon faded when a cloud passed over its face and they had to slow down. As they approached the looming dark mass of the house in front of them, they slowed down even more and started to step as lightly as possible because of the crunching noise from the gravel underfoot.

During the drive to Istomin's house, Dickerman went over what each man was going to do and Bartkow repeated it in Russian. When they reached the front steps, he signaled to Bartkow to go around to the back, then pointed at Stepan and Boris and gestured at the front door, indicating that they should get ready to force it open.

But to Dickerman's consternation, Stepan hesitated, turned toward his brother, and said something to him.

"What the hell's the matter?" Dickerman whispered and looked at Stepan's hands. He was holding a torch in one and his gun in the other, but the crowbar he was supposed to have brought was nowhere in sight.

"*I don't goddamn believe it! You forgot it in the car!*" Dickerman gasped. He felt as if he was going to explode with rage and was on the verge of telling Boris to just break the goddammed door open by himself, but abruptly came to his senses. What if he couldn't manage it on his own?

Gritting his teeth, Dickerman grabbed Stepan by the shoulder, spun him around and pushed him toward the street: "Well, don't just stand there you dumb shit! Go get it!"

The fool can't remember three different things at the same time, Dickerman fumed as he watched Boris's silhouette recede into the darkness, his arms outstretched for balance.

Inside the house, Strelka heard the whispering and the footsteps on the gravel by the front steps. She trotted into the foyer and stopped with her nose almost touching the door and her head tilted to the side. She seemed to be listening with preternatural attention, her whole body taut with anticipation.

When they got downstairs, Thomas and Istomin went to the library and retrieved the guns from the cabinet. Istomin took off his robe so it wouldn't get in the way. To keep their hands free, they put extra shells and the loaded revolvers into their pajama pockets, then cinched in the ties at the waist to keep the pants from slipping under the weight.

Moving together, their shotguns pointing forward, they began to walk slowly through the darkened rooms, navigating between the dark shapes of the furniture, and pausing to listen every few steps, still uncertain if anyone was in the house. Only when they emerged from the living room into the foyer, and a passing cloud allowed the moon to shine more brightly for a moment, did they see Strelka frozen by the front door.

Thomas crouched down and shuffled to the narrow, curtained sidelight to the right of the door, keeping his head low, then moved the fabric aside slightly and peered into the darkness. Holding his shotgun across his chest for balance, Istomin tiptoed to the door and pressed his ear to it.

CHAPTER FORTY-FOUR

While Dickerman—almost beside himself with anger and anxiety—waited for Stepan to return from the automobile, Bartkow crept around to the back of the building, pausing to listen, using whatever cover he could find: a tree, a copse of lilacs, a structure that looked like a log *banya*. The moonlight faded as he approached a row of large windows on the side of the mansion. He looked up and thought he saw shadows moving inside but the darkness deepened and he sneaked by. A moment later he was by the rear entry.

Bartkow climbed the steps holding his revolver in his right hand, tucked his torch under his right arm and automatically tried the doorknob with his left. To his shock, it turned, the latch clicked, and when he pulled, the door swung open.

They forgot to lock up! he exulted, what a stroke of luck! Now I can show Dickerman what I'm really worth!

Bartkow switched on his torch and stepped across the threshold. Something like a big striped pillow lay on the floor inside the door.

The diffuse beam showed a high-ceilinged space filled with shelves holding jars and boxes, a wooden table, a white enameled stove at the far end, and an open door that he realized must lead to the main part of the house.

In the foyer, Strelka cocked both ears and turned her head back toward the interior of the house. Thomas and Istomin noticed her movement. She whimpered but didn't bark or move from her post at the door.

"She heard something! And I think I may have seen someone moving outside a moment ago," Thomas whispered, bringing his lips close to Istomin's right ear. "It's hard to tell.

I'll stay here and keep watching, you go to the back of the house."

"Who on earth could it be? Thieves?" Istomin whispered in return, but Thomas just shrugged and shook his head in response.

Istomin made his way through the living and dining rooms, passing through shifting patches of grey and black that made it difficult to tell if he was facing a solid wall or an open archway. The only sound he could hear other than his own breathing was the slow ticking of the old clock on the second floor.

Holding his shotgun close to his chest so he wouldn't accidentally knock into anything with it, he came to the corridor leading from the dining room to the kitchen and the servants' quarters when he saw a pale beam of light playing on the floor at the far end. Someone was about to enter the corridor from the kitchen on the right.

Stepping as lightly as he could in his bare feet and holding his breath, Istomin tiptoed to the gathered portiere at the entrance to the corridor, got down on one knee behind the heavy fabric so it partially hid him, and raised the shotgun to his cheek. He slowly exhaled as he waited for the intruder to appear. A floorboard creaked, then another one, and Istomin thought he heard a metallic noise, like a gun being cocked.

A second later the intruder stepped into the corridor and the beam of his torch swept toward where Istomin was crouching.

Istomin filled his lungs with air and shouted as loudly as he could: "*Don't move! Get your hands in the air!*"

The light jumped crazily, then dropped to the floor with a clatter. A man's shoe and pantleg flashed into sight and a split second later three loud shots rang out in quick succession, the muzzle flashes illuminating the corridor and revealing a standing figure.

The man had fired wildly. Istomin heard the crack of bullets somewhere above and behind him as they hit the ceiling and walls. He exhaled, aimed down the middle of the corridor, and pulled the first trigger. The right barrel of his shotgun flashed and boomed, kicking him in the shoulder, the noise of the explosion amplified by the enclosed space. The intruder screamed as the heavy blast knocked one leg out from under him and he fell with a crash that shook the floor.

Jumping to his feet with his gun still pointing down the corridor, Istomin rushed toward the electric torch, which had rolled against the wall. He grabbed it and played it over the intruder's body, searching for his gun.

The man was curled up on the floor, moaning and clutching his left leg with both arms. His pants leg was shredded and soaked with blood. Istomin saw the revolver near the man's head; he stepped forward and picked it up.

On the other side of the house, Thomas stood bolt upright when he heard Istomin's sudden shout followed by the multiple blasts of gunfire. In the gloom, he made out Strelka twisting away from the door, her paws scrabbling as she tried to gain purchase on the slippery marble floor. Thomas started to follow her into the interior of the house but managed only a few steps before he heard a voice shout something outside. A moment later, two powerful blows shook the front door.

Dickerman had been peering through the sidelight, frustrated that he couldn't make anything out, when he heard the muffled gunshots inside the house. He jerked his head back in shock, as if the shots had been aimed at him, and staggered away from the door, almost losing his balance on the steps, and had to grab Stürmer's arm to steady himself.

He realized that it must have been something to do with Bartkow. His first reaction was fury at him for putting the raid in danger by losing the element of surprise and getting into trouble. But then Dickerman saw Stepan jogging back to the porch, glistening with sweat in the moonlight and carrying his crowbar. It occurred to him that they were still four men with guns, and that Bartkow must have distracted whoever was inside the house.

The shout Thomas heard was Dickerman ordering the brothers to break open the door.

They braced themselves, slammed the tips of their tools into the door jamb above and below the lock, and pulled hard. The wooden frame shattered as easily if it had been made of papier-mâché. The deadbolt popped out of its strike plate and fell to the marble sill with a clatter.

Raising his right foot, Stepan kicked the door open, sending it banging against the inside wall. He fished his torch out of his pants pocket, flipped it on, drew his revolver from his waistband and strode inside. Boris and Stürmer followed, with Dickerman behind them.

When the loud blows hit the front door, Thomas was only a few steps away, under the archway separating the foyer from the living room. He stopped abruptly, spun around and instinctively dropped to one knee.

The door crashed open a second later, and his target appeared before him as a stamping, multi-armed and multi-legged mass with waving torch beams that was silhouetted against the paler darkness outside. Thomas lifted his shotgun and fired into the right side of the mass, shifted his aim to the left and fired again.

Screams erupted in the darkness in front of him; two torchlight beams swung crazily, and two others fell to the floor.

Most of the heavy buckshot in Thomas's first round caught Stepan on the right side of his chest with such force he was thrown back against Stürmer behind him; the rest hit the German's left arm. Thomas's second round was a bit wide and hit the left side of Boris's face and neck.

Feeling as if he had been poleaxed, Boris fell to the floor, cursing hoarsely and pressing his left hand to his mangled cheek. Neither he nor his brother had fired their weapons. Stürmer was so disoriented when Stepan crashed into him that at first he didn't realize he'd been wounded too. He raised his Luger and emptied it blindly into the house. Only

Dickerman remained unscathed. The bodies of the three men leading the attack had shielded him from both shotgun blasts.

"We have to get away from here," Stürmer shouted to him as he staggered backwards through the door, his left arm feeling numb and hanging by his side.

Dickerman pushed him out of the way. He recognized the sound of a shotgun and realized that whoever had just fired twice was likely empty and would have to reload. The only hope of saving the attack was to stop him before he did. Dickerman crouched and darted forward, stepping over Boris and Stepan sprawled on the floor, his revolver in his right hand and the torch in his left as he searched for the man with the shotgun.

He stopped when the beam of light landed on a kneeling figure that was grappling at something at its waist with both hands.

Dickerman felt a gleeful rage when he recognized who it was. He thrust his gun forward, aiming for the Black man's head, when something flew out of the darkness with a loud snarl.

Dickerman felt powerful jaws clamp down on his left forearm. He dropped the torch and screamed, more from shock than pain, almost losing his balance as the weight of the animal pulled him down. Struggling to stay on his feet, he slammed its head with the butt of his gun, then stuck the muzzle into the furry mass and fired.

He heard a sharp howl, like the wail of an injured child, and the weight dropped from his arm. Before he could think, he felt someone grabbing his coat from the back.

"*Come! Come now! We must retreat to the automobile!*" Stürmer yelled, pulling Dickerman back toward the shattered doorway.

Horrified by the thought of what the animal's jaws had done to his arm, Dickerman twisted around. Following the German, he sidled between the sprawling limbs of the two bodies by the door, stumbled down the front steps, and ran awkwardly down the driveway to the estate's entrance.

Stürmer could barely move the fingers on his wounded

arm as he started the automobile. Then, wincing from pain and his eyes filling with tears, he put it into gear and accelerated down Malaya Nikitskaya. Dickerman was half-reclining on the seat next to him as he struggled to wrap a handkerchief around the bloodstained sleeve of his left arm.

CHAPTER FORTY-FIVE

When Dickerman's torch beam caught Thomas, he was yanking frantically at the Webley, trying to get it out of his pajama pants pocket, where it had gotten hung up by the hammer.

Thomas had heard Strelka's attack and the shot that silenced her, followed by the commotion of the gunmen escaping. A second later, he was on his feet with the revolver in his hand. Then, someone switched on the light in the foyer.

It revealed a horrific scene. Two men were on the floor by the front door, one lying flat on his back, unmoving and pale as chalk, his chest soaked with blood; the second curled up in a fetal position, trembling, his hands pressed to his face and neck, with blood seeping through his fingers and dripping onto the floor. The door was hanging crookedly, its frame shattered. Blood was splattered on the wall by the sidelight and smeared below it.

A step away from Thomas, Strelka was lying on her side, whimpering and scrambling with her legs as if she was trying to get up, her neck a mass of blood-stained fur.

All the gunfire, blood, and fury had scarcely taken a minute from the moment Bartkow discovered the kitchen door was unlocked.

When Istomin shined the flashlight down on him and saw him grasping his bloodied lower leg, which extended from the knee at an impossible angle, he realized he was no longer a threat.

The gunfire had awakened the cook and she ran into the corridor, holding the only weapon she could find, a coal shovel. Istomin yelled to her to stanch the man's bleeding, then rushed to the foyer, drawing his revolver as he went. He got there just in time to see dim figures running down the driveway and turned on the light.

"Are you all right?" he asked anxiously, seeing Thomas. He put his hand on his shoulder and looked him up and down for signs of blood.

Thomas nodded. His eyes were wide open and looked feverish. He was breathing heavily, but he was uninjured.

"I haven't seen anything like this since Mukden!" Istomin exclaimed at the sight of the bodies and the blood.

Thomas shook his head in disbelief. "The only time I saw this kind of horror was in Coahoma, when my father took me with him once to help at a farm that had been burned by the KKK. I never dreamt I'd see anything like that again."

Istomin looked around. He realized he had exposed himself and Thomas by turning on the light, and cried out in alarm, "We need to check if there's still anyone outside!"

Both men crouched down, cocked the hammers of their revolvers, and stepped over the two bodies onto the landing in front of the door. No one was in sight.

"Did you see Dickerman?" Istomin asked.

Thomas shook his head. "I couldn't see anyone's face. But he must have been here," he said.

"This guy," he pointed at Stepan with his revolver, "was part of the gang that attacked Olga and me. See, his nose is broken. The one you got in the kitchen was probably there as well. Is he still alive? I'll have to go and see him, maybe . . .."

"What's this?" Istomin interrupted, pointing his weapon at the grey metal container on the middle step. He raised it to his face with his left hand and smelled it.

"Kerosene," he said. "What the hell was this for?"

"They were going to torch your house after they killed us," Thomas replied through tensely drawn lips, "just like the damn KKK. To destroy any evidence."

"What barbarians . . .," Istomin started to reply when someone called out in a croaking voice:

"*Help me, for God's sake!*"

It came from one of the men lying by the door. Thomas

stepped back indoors to get a better look but didn't recognize him from Olga's abduction.

The second blast from Thomas's shotgun had just missed hitting Boris squarely in the face and he was lucky to be alive. Most of his right ear was gone, his right eye was swollen shut and caked with blood, his cheek was a bloody mess. Several of the heavy pellets had hit his neck, including his voice box, but missed his carotid artery. If it had been severed, he would have bled out in a couple of minutes.

"For God's sake, help me!" the man repeated, twisting his face up with a grimace of pain, his hands still pressed to his wounds. He sounded as if he was choking, and when he spoke air hissed from his punctured larynx.

But Thomas felt no sympathy for him and didn't reply. He walked over to Strelka and bent over her.

She rolled her eyes back toward him as far as she could and tried to turn her head but couldn't. Thomas moved to where she could see him more easily and knelt, stroking her head.

He remembered her as a puppy. How she'd been covered in blood when a horse had nearly trampled her to death and how he'd managed to save her when it seemed hopeless.

"What goes around, comes around," he whispered. "Thank you, girl, thank you."

Thomas heard movement and turned around. People were crowding into the foyer from the living room—Istomin's valet, the cook, and behind them, Zoya.

Her eyes were filled with tears as she shifted her gaze from the bodies of the two men to the dog. The faces of the valet and cook were frozen in amazement at the havoc in front of them. When Zoya started to shuffle forward, the others stepped aside to make way.

"What sin, what sin, my dear ones," she said softly and shook her head.

Thomas didn't know if she meant the attackers' violent intentions, or the blood he and Istomin had shed. For a clue, he looked at Istomin, who was watching Zoya intently with an odd expression of reverence, one that was difficult to reconcile with his usually decisive mien.

She means all of it is sin, Thomas realized. *What these men wanted to do and what we did.*

"We have to tend to those who are suffering. We have to help them all, poor souls," Zoya said in a resigned tone.

Then, turning toward Thomas, she spoke directly to him: "But you, you have more to do, my dear one, as I told you. And you too, *batyushka*," she added, looking at Istomin. "It is bitter, it is hard, but you must see it through to the end, to the very end."

Thomas and Istomin looked at each other without saying anything. There was no time to spare. Some of the attackers—who knew how many—had gotten away, and the only place they were likely to go to ground was their mansion. If the children were still there, they would be at even greater risk than before because of what Dickerman might decide to do with them after the mauling his gang had gotten.

Istomin hurriedly instructed his valet and the cook to take care of matters in the house as best they could: help Zoya minister to the two wounded men—the third one in the foyer looked dead—but make sure they didn't try to get away; see what they could do for Strelka. And also, call Markov at home to tell him what happened, have him inform the police, and ask him to get to the gang's mansion with his assistant as soon as possible. It didn't make any difference that it was the middle of the night.

Istomin and Thomas went upstairs to change, agreeing while on the stairs to wear dark clothing. They checked and reloaded their shotguns in his study and took additional cartridges. Thomas also made sure he could get his revolver out of his jacket pocket.

They were about to leave through the rear door when Istomin stopped, handed his shotgun to Thomas, and asked him to wait while he went to the front of the house. He came back a moment later with the tin of kerosene and the crowbar one of the Golubs tossed aside when they broke down the door.

"These could be useful," he said.

Thomas looked at him, waiting for an explanation.

"When Markov and I drove around their place, we saw that it's surrounded by a tall fence and there's a gated rear entrance. It looked like it hadn't been used in a long time, but it has a new chain and lock on it."

"At least we might be able to get to the mansion itself without being seen," Thomas replied.

"Right. And maybe this will help us as well," Istomin said, raising the kerosene container. "Do you have matches?"

Thomas patted his pants pockets and pulled out a silver matchbox.

As they strode toward the Russo-Balt, a final band of clouds passed across the face of the moon, leaving the sky clear and the pale light pouring down freely.

CHAPTER FORTY-SIX

When Dickerman and Stürmer got back to the Convent and stumbled in though the rear entrance, their bloodied clothes and wild-eyed appearance threw Hilda and Maria into a panic. The women panicked even more when they realized Bartkow and the Golub brothers were missing.

Both men collapsed onto chairs in the kitchen, but they were so distraught that initially neither one could answer the frantic questions the women threw at them.

Thinking the police were in pursuit and going to arrive any minute, Hilda tried to get Dickerman's attention by thrusting her face in front of his and shouting they had to use Stürmer's automobile to escape. They could go to Riga, she urged, where she had influential friends.

Maria felt so overwhelmed by the calamity and her yearning for cocaine became so strong that she had trouble thinking clearly about anything. She latched onto Hilda's idea about abandoning everything and fleeing and started to prattle about going to her place in Moscow, and after that maybe abroad, to Germany or France.

Only when Dickerman gathered his wits enough to shout that the police had not been involved, and, raising his bloodied arm, insisted he and Stürmer needed help, did the two women stop.

Hilda came to her senses first and told Maria to rouse the two maids. A few minutes later, wearing robes over their nightshirts, their hair in braids and their eyes filled with fear, one was in the kitchen cutting up a sheet for bandages while the second was clattering in the pantry, searching for a bottle of their highest proof vodka.

Hilda had some experience treating wounds herself—usually from knives but also bullets—because there were times in

Riga when she didn't want to risk summoning a doctor to her brothel to treat a client who'd gotten into an altercation. Using a pair of kitchen shears, she set to work to expose the wounds. Dickerman sat at the kitchen table and watched the procedure stoically, his lips pursed.

But Stürmer proved to have a low tolerance for pain and kept shifting in his chair, cringing and trembling, as the scissors cut through the sleeve of his bloodied jacket. Maria couldn't stand the sight of blood at all and used it as an excuse to escape to her room for the fix she craved.

Both men's wounds turned out to be less serious than either one feared. Strelka's teeth broke the skin on Dickerman's left forearm in four places, but the punctures weren't deep because the dog tried to hold, not maul him, and the tightly woven fabric of the jacket cushioned her bite.

Stürmer had only a half-dozen pellets embedded just below the skin in his upper arm and shoulder, which Hilda was able to pull out with tweezers. She dabbed at and cleaned both men's wounds with a vodka-saturated cloth, which caused Stürmer to pull back and make a loud hissing sound through his teeth. She then gave each man a small glass to drink to distract them and to quiet their nerves. A few minutes later they were neatly bandaged and feeling less hysterical.

Dickerman's mind raced from one possibility to the next as he tried to figure out what to do about their disastrous situation. Abandoning the Convent now, after all the effort and expense that went into it, was hard to imagine; so was giving up his lucrative operation at the Hippodrome. But it was also impossible to stay in the Convent because sooner or later Thomas and his friends, or the police, or both, would descend on them.

And where could he and the others escape, as the women insisted in their annoyingly shrill voices? Somewhere else in Moscow? Could drug-addled Maria deliver on her offer? Could they really lie low in her brothel? Or get to Riga, like Hilda said?

The idea of Riga made Dickerman grunt derisively—the place was a thousand kilometers away. And what would they do with the nine children upstairs, now that Bartkow and the Golubs were gone? Who would keep the captives from trying to escape? And how would they all travel anywhere? By train? Trying to control nine children during a long train trip was absurd. In automobiles? They had Stürmer's but taking everyone would require a caravan of two or three more and where would those come from? Even leaving the children behind was impossible because they would be evidence, living breathing evidence. And what about the servants? They'd have to come too because they could tell the police a lot.

It suddenly occurred to Dickerman that the captives could all be killed, despite the trouble that had gone into finding and collecting them. They could be buried on the grounds, and with no children, there was no proof of what Convent's purpose was. When things blew over and he hired new men, they could start a new collection.

But after a moment, Dickerman decided: no. Without Bartkow or the Golubs, who would do it? Stürmer or the women wouldn't be willing, and he couldn't imagine himself shooting all of them in cold blood by himself. One of his secret dreams about resurrecting the old family plantation and Ophite Hall was to have heirs of his own. There were some lines even he would not cross.

It seemed the only alternative would be to hide out in Maria's place in Moscow, if her offer could be taken seriously. At least it would buy some time. But how would they get there in the middle of the night, all sixteen of them, counting everyone in the house, even if it was only across town?

While Dickerman kept running into one dead end after another and getting increasingly depressed, Stürmer was feeling growing elation. Never had he felt so fully alive and fulfilled or known as clearly as he did now that he was a professional soldier and a warrior. Before this day, he had never fired his weapon to kill an enemy. But in his imagination the attack on Istomin's house was transformed into a prolonged and bloody battle against an unexpectedly large enemy force.

Stürmer decided that his wounded arm was a badge of honor. He remembered clearly how he had fired his Luger repeatedly. And although he did so into the darkness and without aiming, it now seemed to him he had unleashed what must have been a deadly fusillade. He recollected with relish the sounds of his pistol's blasts and the feeling of its powerful recoil in his hand. It occurred to him that since he fired so many rounds, he must have wounded or killed several of the enemy. In fact, this must be why he and Dickerman were able to escape. These thoughts filled him with pride.

Looking at Dickerman sitting morosely at the kitchen table across from him, his round face flushed, his deep-set eyes staring fixedly into space, Stürmer decided the American was a fool and responsible for the attack's failure because he knew nothing about tactics. By comparison, Stürmer concluded that he had acquitted himself quite well under the circumstances, and that his fear earlier that night, when he tried to dissuade Dickerman from launching the attack without a plan, was justifiable anxiety about the American's lack of foresight.

I always knew it would end badly and tried to tell him, but he wouldn't listen, Stürmer consoled himself. *I should have taken charge of everything myself from the start. Things would have ended very differently!*

Dickerman noticed the German looking at him with a smug smile. It angered him because he already felt guilty about underestimating Thomas and the catastrophic failure of the attack.

The thought was so humiliating it made him want to knock Stürmer off his high horse.

"Well, baron, we're up shit creek and there's nothing we can do about it except try to save our skins, like our ladies said! Good thing we've got your automobile for a getaway. I hope you won't mind our using it."

Dickerman succeeded in stinging Stürmer and saw the self-satisfied expression on his face fade. Pleased that he scored, Dickerman continued with what he imagined would hurt the German even more: "Too bad we have to give up all this! I hope your consortium won't be too upset with the losses."

Stürmer blanched. The idea of abandoning the Convent had not even occurred to him, and his immediate reaction was that he would rather die first. It would be the end of his career. Even worse—it would betray the trust Colonel Michaelis and German Military Intelligence had placed in him.

Feeling he had to live up to his position as a German officer and do whatever it took to forestall such a disaster, Stürmer drew himself up in his chair.

"How can you say this, Mr. Dickerman? We lost the first battle, yes. But the war is not over. This is no time to lose courage. We have to regroup and remedy the situation."

Dickerman's sneer collapsed, replaced by a perplexed expression.

"What the hell you talkin' about?" he asked in his shrill voice. "How're we going to do anything? That Black bastard is still alive and either he's going to be here soon, gunning for us with everything he's got, or the cops will be here. And what do we have left?"

Dickerman leaned in across the table and slapped his hand on it to accentuate his point. "We're down three men! So now it's just you and me!"

"We can't even get out of here without leaving a whole passel of living, breathing, two-legged evidence!" Dickerman continued. "You know how many?" he added with a malicious grin, "nine of those brats, the two maids, and the housekeeper! Twelve people, not counting us and the ladies! How're we going to get them all to Maria's, which is the only place we could go, in the middle of the night and with just your automobile?"

Stürmer was taken aback by Dickerman's vehemence. He'd been so preoccupied with himself he'd forgotten about losing Bartkow and the Golub brothers.

"Yes. Of course. Our losses are unfortunate. However, those men were ill-prepared for this kind of mission," he said in a dismissive tone, "so it is not surprising they are casualties.

There are always casualties in war. Perhaps they were only wounded and are prisoners. But I have other men who are well-trained and well-equipped."

Stürmer wasn't expecting the effect his words produced. Dickerson looked stunned, and the angry expression disappeared from his face as quickly as if it had been wiped off with a rag.

"What do you mean, baron? You can get men here now? With cars? And guns? Who are they?" he asked incredulously, his hopes soaring, like those of a man who has climbed the steps of the gallows only to see a messenger on horseback galloping up and waving a reprieve.

"You do understand that sonofabitch is going to come here to get his daughter, right?" Dickerman explained. "And he's not going to come alone or unarmed? In fact, he may be on his way already."

"I can telephone now, Mr. Dickerman, and three men with extensive experience will arrive here very fast. They have automobiles, weapons, and they will do whatever I order . . . whatever I say," he corrected himself.

"And what if cops come here instead, or if they come with Thomas? Can your men handle them too? Thomas and that prince buddy of his must've already called the cops. Or their neighbors did, with all the shooting they heard! The cops must be descending on that house right now like flies on shit!"

"Yes, perhaps, they are. But the city police are also distracted very much with preparations for the visit by the imperial family," he said, repeating something Michaelis had mentioned while explaining why this was a good time for German military intelligence in Moscow.

"So, I believe that any who may be summoned to Prince Istomin's house will be too busy to come here."

Stürmer paused as if he was assessing whether or not he should continue, then concluded with an arch and mysterious mien: "And, I have not mentioned this to you before, but there is a legal way to stop any police from entering this property. I have certain documents that ensure this."

Dickerman couldn't have been more surprised if Stürmer

had said he knew a way for all of them to grow wings and fly away.

Did the German manage to pay off the cops? flashed through his mind. He'd had suspicions before that the so-called "consortium" wasn't really a group of German "businessmen." Maybe they're gangsters big enough to pull off miracles. But this clearly wasn't the time to worry about such things.

"The hell you say!" Dickerman shouted excitedly and stood up. "I have no idea what you're talking about with these documents, but your guys are our only chance. *Call them now!* What're you waiting for?"

Satisfied with how Dickerman reacted, Stürmer also rose to his feet and proclaimed in a knowing tone: "Thomas and the prince defeated our attack and will want to launch a counterattack, as military history and tactics teach us. But if they show their noses here, they will have a surprise and it will be the end of them. It will also be the end of the entire problem you caused when you abducted the Black man's daughter."

Dickerman flicked an angry glance at Stürmer but said nothing. It pained him to admit it to himself, but what the German said was true. The only hope now was that Stürmer's men would arrive in time.

"We will be able to wipe the slate clean, Mr. Dickerman," the German continued. "With Thomas and Istomin gone, there is no defeat. Without witnesses, there is no crime."

"A nice fantasy, baron, but you're forgetting the Golubs and Bartkow, who could be talking to the police right now."

"You think they're alive? Perhaps. But what can they say? They will point their fingers at us, but we are unknown to the police, and, moreover, we will soon be gone. The police will find only this empty mansion and will be unable to do anything about it."

Dickerman swallowed the rest of his pride and gestured toward the interior of the mansion: "Please, baron, come this way. There's a telephone in the library."

Dickerman left Stürmer by the apparatus and went into the front hall to wait. He could hear him asking the operator for a number in Russian and then, after a pause, switch to rapid-fire German. Dickerman didn't understand what he said but noted with grudging admiration that his tone was curt and authoritative.

"They will be here in one hour with two automobiles. The third one is unavailable because it needs to be repaired. But with mine the two are sufficient for our needs," the German announced in a satisfied tone when he came out of the library. "We should instruct the ladies and the staff to get the children ready to leave. And I suggest we see to our weapons in the meantime," he added, reaching for his Luger in its shoulder holster. He was relishing the prospect of another battle even though his wounded shoulder was very painful whenever he moved it.

A few minutes later, Stürmer and Dickerman were sitting in the library in front of a low, marble-topped table, which was covered on one end with a stained kitchen towel and their guns, boxes of cartridges, and cleaning supplies spread out over it. On the other end was a tray with tea and sandwiches the housekeeper had prepared.

Neither man touched them. Dickerman settled for examining and reloading his revolver, but Stürmer cleaned his Luger thoroughly before inserting a freshly loaded clip into it. Both men moved awkwardly, trying to spare their injured arms.

Stürmer checked his pocket watch and announced his men would arrive in half an hour. All the other arrangements for the evacuation were going smoothly. Maria had delicately inhaled her usual dose of cocaine and now felt alert and energetic. Following Dickerman's instructions not to go into any details, she called ahead to her brothel and told the manager to turn away any late arrivals and prepare as many rooms as possible.

She helped Hilda, the maids, and the housekeeper get the children up and dressed. The six addicted to the *mors* were very groggy when roused and promptly fell back asleep on their beds. But Maria was in a hurry and didn't notice that Anya and Ibrahim were continuing to play-act at being drugged.

The maid assigned to get Olga ready decided not to wake her until it was time to leave. On her last attempt to enter the room, she'd had to back out quickly when Olga flew into a rage, grabbing her chamber pot and threatening to hurl it if the maid came any closer.

CHAPTER FORTY-SEVEN

Thomas and Istomin barely spoke as they drove to Dickerman's mansion, their heads swarming with images of the bloodied bodies and anxiety about what awaited them. It was unlikely Markov would arrive in time to help. The thought of what Dickerman might do to Olga if he was cornered made Thomas feel ill, and he had to struggle to suppress memories of the dead girl on the Ustyinsky Embankment.

The Russo-Balt sped along the nearly empty streets, its springs rattling on the uneven pavement and jolting the passengers so strongly at times that they had to clench their teeth or risk biting their tongues. There was little traffic in the pre-dawn hour. Once the automobile entered Khamovniki, it felt as if they had left the city altogether—the district was quiet, empty, and dark.

Istomin pulled the automobile under a big birch tree that grew over the fence at the rear of the Convent property, and he and Thomas made their way to the old gate, trying to avoid the brighter patches of moonlight and staying in the shadows as much as possible.

The houses on the other side of the street were far apart and showed no signs of life. The cool air smelled of lindens. At one point they froze when they heard a dog barking somewhere ahead of them. But when it stopped after a few seconds, they went on.

Istomin ran his fingers along the padlocked chain looped through the bars of both halves of the gate and slipped the tip of his crowbar into one of the links. Holding the lock with one hand so it wouldn't bang against the gate, he twisted the crowbar until he eliminated the slack in the chain, pushed down hard on the bar and watched the link pry open.

Thomas flinched when the rusty hinges squealed as he pulled one side open far enough to let them squeeze through; the hinges squealed again when he pulled the gate shut behind them.

Both men paused to listen, fearing there might be dogs on the grounds. But all they could hear was the soft rustle of young leaves and the distant, melancholy tolling of a bell from the Church of the Assumption of the Mother of God summoning the nuns of the Novodevichy Convent to service. It rang a dozen times and stopped.

Istomin led the way, his shotgun in his right hand and the kerosene tin in his left, Thomas following with his gun and the crowbar. Their feet brushed softly through the dew-soaked grass, which was thick between the widely spaced oaks, lindens, and birches.

As they approached the rear of the mansion, its fantastical silhouette of spires, gables and chimneys rose in the darkness ahead of them. There were lights in some of the windows on the first and second floors, although they were dimmed by drawn curtains. The window by what looked like the service entrance to the kitchen was dark.

The two men stopped behind a cluster of three birches growing out of a common base a dozen yards from the coach house, which was a smaller echo of the mansion, with the same lancet windows, peaked roof, and towering chimney pot. They listened again, thinking there might be dogs inside the house that could sense them and sound the alarm. But all was quiet except for Thomas's and Istomin's tense breathing.

The mass of birches cast a long shadow toward the coach house. Taking advantage of it, as if it was a magical path shielding them from view, Thomas and Istomin ran over to the small building, stepping as softly as they could on the gravel that replaced the grass growing between the trees. Their shotguns ready, they peered around the building's corner.

Its wide, barn-like doors were open, and something gleamed darkly inside. Moving warily and stopping every few steps to listen, Thomas and Istomin approached the doorway and entered. When they got closer, they made out a long, black automobile. A strong smell of petrol hit their nostrils.

Istomin put down the can of kerosene and ran his hand along the automobile as he walked toward its front.

"The hood is still warm," he whispered to Thomas, who nodded.

Istomin peered into the automobile through the raised window on the driver's side and after a moment opened the door, reached inside, and picked something up from the seat.

"Look at this. The driver was wounded," he whispered to Thomas holding up a crumpled white cloth. In the moonlight the blood stains on the handkerchief looked black. Something about them gave Thomas an idea.

"I know how we can get inside the house," he said in a whisper, and huddling close to Istomin, began to explain.

CHAPTER FORTY-EIGHT

Upstairs, on the mansion's second floor, Olga woke up with a start in her dark room. Her heart was pounding and she'd had a vivid dream, so vivid it was hard to believe what she saw wasn't real. She was in a forest of towering trees as thick as a man is tall, the space between them choked with underbrush, vines, and cane. She had never been in a place like this before, but she knew it was Coahoma, her father's birthplace, about which he had told her many times. The dream was upsetting because her father was looking for her, but the forest was so thick she didn't know how he would ever get through it.

Olga got out of bed and shuffled to the sink in the corner, her arms outstretched and groping, half-remembering, half-seeing where everything was. She had been in the Convent for three days, but the gang's plans had been in turmoil all that time, and she had spent much of the time locked in her room alone.

Olga turned on the cold tap and washed her face with big handfuls of water, over and over again, trying to escape from the lingering impressions of the dream and to calm her pounding heart. After toweling her face dry, she sat back down on the bed and listened to the house.

All was quiet in the hallway outside her room. She couldn't hear any sounds coming from downstairs or from the neighboring rooms. Despite this, her anxiety kept increasing and tightening, like a piece of fabric being twisted until the fibers begin to tear.

And then, as clearly as if someone had whispered it in her ear, she knew her father was coming to save her.

Outside in the carriage house, Thomas picked up the container of kerosene, unscrewed the lid, and being careful not to get any on himself, began to pour it into the automobile through the open door so it pooled on the floor near the brake and gear shift pedals. He then turned around, opened a rear door, and poured more onto the floor. The coach house began to fill with the liquid's sickening, sweet chemical smell.

While Thomas was pouring the kerosene, Istomin, holding his shotgun in front of him, crept along the outside of the mansion to the corner to see if there were any other vehicles by the front entrance. But the porte-cochère and driveway were empty and most of the windows in the front were dark.

Thomas saved a quarter of the container for the last stage. When Istomin returned and shook his head to indicate there was no one out front, Thomas bent over by the driver's door of the automobile, and, backing away, began to pour a stream of kerosene on the ground.

He stopped when it ran out after a dozen paces and cradled his shotgun in the crook of his left arm. Looking back over his shoulder to check if Istomin was in position, he got the box of matches from his pocket and struck one. He let it drop on the end of the kerosene trail and backed away toward Istomin.

A tall, bright yellow flame flared up almost silently and snaked rapidly toward the automobile, lighting up the space between the mansion and the coach house and filling the air with wavering curls of black smoke.

Istomin took shelter around the corner of the mansion. Thomas crouched down next to him.

They watched as the flame slithered to the automobile, climbed up to the running board and leapt inside. With a soft rush, a blaze erupted from the pool of fuel on the floor and seconds later the entire inside of the automobile was an inferno.

Thomas and Istomin drew further back behind the mansion's corner.

The automobile's fuel tank exploded with the roar of a bomb.

The men felt the sudden heat wave and saw the blast's flash reflected in the leaves of the trees around the mansion, which shuddered as if in a storm.

Debris from the shattered automobile and the coach house doors clattered down on the gravel in front of the kitchen service entrance.

After a second, like a painful afterthought, they heard the plaintive tinkle of broken glass from several windows facing the coach house that had been blown out by the explosion.

Moving in a crouch, Thomas and Istomin ran over and took up positions on both sides of the service entrance's landing, their backs pressed against the building, their shotguns cocked and raised.

CHAPTER FORTY-NINE

Hilda and Maria had just settled onto the couch in the library, across from Stürmer and Dickerman with their guns, when a thunderous explosion erupted at the rear of the property, shaking the entire building.

Everyone jumped. For several seconds, no one moved or spoke.

Then Dickerman and Stürmer leapt to their feet. Ignoring the women's frantic questions, they rushed to the back of the house. The kitchen windows facing the rear were shattered, and through the jagged glass they could see the carriage house engulfed in flames.

Thomas! flashed through Dickerman's mind.

Simultaneously he realized they had left their guns in the library.

Dickerman was about to shout a warning to Stürmer. But before he could utter a sound, the German ran to the service entrance, threw the door open and disappeared.

Istomin and Thomas saw the kitchen door crash open, followed by a slender man who stepped out onto the landing and froze, mesmerized by the sight of the roaring flames. He didn't notice the two men crouching on either side of the entrance, but the fire illuminated him as clearly as if it were day.

Thomas raised the stock of his shotgun, stepped forward and slammed it into the left side of the man's face.

Stürmer managed to glimpse something moving out of the corner of his eye, but it was too late.

He felt as if his head exploded, then everything went dark. He collapsed on the wooden landing like a rag doll and rolled down the steps to the ground.

Thinking someone else might come out of the door, Istomin stepped back with his shotgun ready, and waited for a moment. When no one appeared, Thomas told Istomin he was going in. Istomin nodded, stepped over the prostrate body, and followed him.

On the mansion's second floor, the noise of the blast made several of the addicted children stir in their sleep. Two of them woke up and began to cry.

But Ibrahim, who had realized something unusual was going on when he was told to get dressed in the middle of the night, jumped off the bed, carried his chair to the window and climbed up onto it so he could look down at the space behind the mansion. When he saw the flames rising out of the carriage house he grinned with delight. Someone must be attacking the gang that had imprisoned him and the others.

Who it could be, he didn't know. *But any enemy of that fat Iblis and the female shaitans is my friend*, he thought with glee, using the Tatar for "Satan" and "demons."

Ibrahim grew to hate Dickerman and Hilda and Maria more than he had ever hated anyone or anything in his life. During long periods of boredom when he was alone in his room or had finished his prayers, he tried to entertain himself by imagining scenes when he would jump out of a hiding place and beat them with his fists. It would be even better if he could get his hands on the long Circassian dagger his uncle had hanging on the wall of his bedroom above the leather goods shop.

In the room next to Ibrahim's, Olga, who had been waiting for something to happen, also sat up on the edge of her bed. Her window didn't face the carriage house, but the glass panes in it rattled sharply from the powerful explosion. She was sure all this was connected to her dream about her father.

Lowering her stockinged feet to the floor and feeling the darkness in front of her with outstretched arms, she walked to the door of her room and pressed her ear to it. She could hear nothing in the hallway, although it seemed to her that she could make out agitated voices downstairs.

A moment later she heard Ibrahim's muffled whisper calling her through the hole in the lighting fixture on the wall.

When the mansion was being remodeled, Hilda had suggested that spy holes be installed between the bedrooms as well as from the corridor into the rooms because of how useful they could be for watching clients. She had them in Riga, she said, and explained there were even special cameras that could be used to take photographs, which would be valuable for blackmail and other purposes.

Dickerman readily agreed to the expense. The concealed holes were in the brass lighting sconces on the walls between bedrooms as well as in the corridor walls. Their covers were cleverly camouflaged to look like acanthus leaves and could be opened or closed from either side with a simple mechanism.

But none of the gang members suspected that the children might discover the spy holes and use them to talk when they were locked up. Anya found hers by accident and in a rapid whisper told Ibrahim about it ten days ago when they were in the living room after breakfast and the Golubs were out of earshot. In turn, Ibrahim passed it on to Olga when she unexpectedly arrived. It was chance or good fortune, as the children thought of it, that Olga's room was between Ibrahim's and Anya's.

Prying up the leaf-shaped cover with her fingernail, Olga pushed it until it swiveled out of the way and clicked. It was too dark to see anything, but she felt a weak stream of air coming out and knew there was a shiny tube several centimeters wide running through the wall. When it was light, you could see the person on the other end, or at least their mouth when they were whispering. Now, with the spy tube open, she could hear Ibrahim clearly.

"I think someone has come to save us!" he whispered urgently in his light Tatar accent. "The small house in the back is burning. The flames are as tall as the trees!"

His words thrilled Olga. "I had a dream my father was coming!" she exclaimed. "Did you see anyone outside?" she asked.

"I can't see much. But I'll go look again."

A moment later Ibrahim was back. "A man is lying on the ground outside the kitchen door!" he whispered excitedly, "and the door is open!"

"Okh!" Olga exhaled, her heart sinking.

"I don't think it's your father. He looks like a white man, although it's hard to tell from my window."

"We have to try to do something to help!"

"How? We can't get out of our rooms!"

Suddenly Olga remembered how her heart was pounding after she woke up from her dream and realized what they had to do.

"We have to make as much noise as we can!" she whispered. "We can bang on the floor with the chairs, jump up and down, scream!"

"Why? The *shaitans* and the brothers and everyone will get very angry," Ibrahim said with a frown, even though the prospect of creating mayhem appealed to him greatly.

"Because that's how my father will know where we're locked up! And it'll be good if they're all upset because of the noise. It'll make it harder for them to do anything to him!"

"Yes, good!" Ibrahim exclaimed, adding the Arabic "*In-shallah!*" ("If God wills it!"). He clasped his hands together with glee, picturing how the noise would make the *Iblis* and the *shaitans* run around in panic. "You tell Anya and we'll start. If we all do it at the same time, it will be louder!"

Olga crossed her room groping with her arms until she reached the bed, climbed onto it, and ran her hands over the wall until she found the sconce. She opened the cover on the spy hole, put her lips to it and whispered, "Anya! Anya!"

While waiting impatiently for Anya to answer, Olga thought how sad it was that Masha, the blonde girl she liked who had been brought to the Convent just before her, but who seemed to be drinking all the *mors* they gave her, was on the other side of the hallway. They couldn't talk using the secret tubes. Masha also didn't have anyone near her who could help because her room was between Sergey's and Duya's, both of whom drank the *mors* and did whatever Maria and Hilda told them. Olga, Anya, and Ibrahim felt sorry for the others, but they feared betrayal and kept their discovery of the spy holes secret.

When Stürmer disappeared through the kitchen door, Dickerman didn't wait to see what happened. Panicking at the thought that Thomas was coming after him, he scuttled back to the library as fast as he could and headed for the table. His revolver was where he left it and he was relieved to feel its familiar weight when he picked it up. But the Luger had disappeared.

Looking around he saw Maria standing by the staircase in the central hall, her fists holding a handkerchief pressed to her mouth, her eyes round with terror.

Then Hilda stepped into view from behind the archway. She had the Luger and was holding it comfortably, the barrel pointed at the ceiling, her finger on the trigger, like someone who knew what she was doing.

She raised her finger to her lips, and whispered rapidly that she would hide behind the archway wall so the attackers couldn't see her when they came down the corridor. That was the only way into the library from the kitchen and the back of the house.

Pointing the gun barrel toward the front of the room and wagging it up and down, she indicated to Dickerman that he should conceal himself there.

Good girl! Dickerman thought, feeling hope stir. With Hilda's gun and ambush, the odds of fending off the attack from Thomas and whoever was with him improved considerably. And the resulting delay also might buy enough time for Stürmer's men to arrive.

Dickerman nodded to Hilda and ran his eyes over the front of the room. Two green winged armchairs big enough to conceal him stood on either side of the bay window and he went over to the one on the left. Grimacing with the pain because of his wounded arm, he pulled the armchair away from the window to make more space and crouched behind its high back. He could surprise whoever was coming into the library and shoot them by popping up above the back of the chair or leaning out from either the left or right. Hilda would have a straight shot at them from the side as soon as they entered the library. And if they got as far as the center of the room under the Venetian chandelier, it would be even better because then their backs would be towards her.

CHAPTER FIFTY

Thomas and Istomin entered the kitchen from the landing, crouching to make themselves smaller targets, shotguns raised to their cheeks, eyes searching.

Thomas had trouble restraining himself from rushing forward. With every step he was becoming more and more anxious that Dickerman would try to hurt Olga out of vengeance now that he saw he was under attack.

The lights were on in the kitchen and in the corridor leading to the interior of the house. But there was no one in sight. The only sound the two men could hear was the crackling of the fire in the carriage house behind them and the slow drip of the faucet above the kitchen sink.

Thomas sensed a trap. Dickerman had to be in the house, but who knew how many others might be with him.

Istomin and Thomas slowly entered the corridor leading to the front part of the house, trying to tread as lightly as they could and to stay close to the walls.

But they weren't able to be completely quiet. Every few steps the floorboards creaked softly, making them stop and hold their breaths, their ears straining for the slightest sound in front of them.

Dickerman heard the noises and knew what they meant. He leaned out to the left side of his chair, looked at Hilda, who was visible behind the archway jamb, and jerked his head toward the corridor, signaling he'd heard sounds of someone approaching. She nodded with a grim expression, lowered her pistol, and stepped back further so she couldn't be seen.

When Thomas and Istomin reached the end of the corridor they stopped to survey the space that opened in front of them. It was a large room with book-filled shelves along the walls, brown leather couches on the left and right, and a

Persian carpet in muted rose, green, and gray on the floor.

At the opposite end, near the leaded glass bay window, was a small table flanked by two large, winged armchairs upholstered in plush forest green. A wide archway on the right led to what Thomas guessed was the building's gloomy central hall, judging by the height of its vaulted ceiling. There was no one in sight and everything was quiet.

Thomas knew it was dangerous to proceed but he also had no choice. He took a step into the library and paused, letting his eyes jump over the space, from the furniture to the corners of the room and back again. He took another step. A floorboard creaked under him. He froze.

Dickerman heard the noise and guessed his target was only a dozen paces away. With surprise on his side, it would be an easy shot.

He took a deep breath and gripped his revolver with both hands. But just as he was about to lean out from behind the chair and open fire something crashed overhead. High-pitched shrieks and incoherent shouts followed, mixed with additional loud bangs that shook the ceiling and made the chandelier's crystal pendants jingle and shiver.

Thomas ducked and dropped to a squat. He looked up in bewilderment—it sounded as if the ceiling was about to fall through.

Dickerman was so disoriented by the noise that he thought something had happened to the attackers. As if pulled by an invisible force, he stood to look—forgetting the revolver still in his hand. He would curse himself forever after, never understanding why he'd done something so foolish.

"Hands in the air!" Thomas shouted in English, pointing the shotgun at his face.

The sight of Thomas's gun and its twin black muzzles, which looked like the giant nostrils on some monstrous face, paralyzed Dickerman.

Then he saw the Russian "engineer" behind Thomas approaching with his shotgun pointing at him as well and raised both hands.

Thomas narrowed his eyes at the revolver Dickerman was

still holding and came several steps closer, keeping his weapon pointed at his face.

"*Put the gun down!*" he shouted, "*or I swear I'll blow your head off!*"

Dickerman heard Thomas's command but didn't move. He was scarcely breathing because his attention was now focused on Hilda's stealthy movements. His anticipation swelled as he watched her step out from behind the wall of the archway, then extend her arm with the Luger pointing at Thomas's back. Neither Thomas nor Istomin could see her.

Thomas first, then the Russian, and it's all over, Dickerman thought.

Dickerman's silence and immobility unnerved Thomas. Taking another step forward, Thomas commanded, "*Drop that gun, I tell you!*"

Hilda pulled the trigger.

The Luger made a metallic click but didn't fire. She tried to squeeze the trigger again, but it didn't yield. The gun had jammed. In a panic, Hilda began to reach for the toggle with her left hand, but it was too late.

Thomas turned toward the noise and seeing a dark figure pointing a gun at him, fired.

The blast hit Hilda squarely in the midriff and lifted her off her feet. She landed on her back with a crash, her arms widespread, the Luger spinning away across the floor. Only when Thomas noticed her billowing black skirt did he realize it was a woman.

Istomin had looked away for a second when Thomas fired at Hilda but then advanced rapidly toward Dickerman, who was too paralyzed with fear to move. Holding his shotgun with his right hand and his index finger on the first trigger, Istomin reached out with his left and pulled the revolver from Dickerman's limp hand.

"*Get down on your stomach!*" Istomin ordered Dickerman, and watched the man obey, moving awkwardly because of his girth, as he got down on all fours and struggled to lay down on the lush Persian carpet.

"I'm going upstairs!" Thomas told Istomin in an urgent

tone. "You tie up this bastard and the one by the kitchen entrance, if he's still alive." Glancing at Hilda's sprawling body and the pool of blood spreading under it, he said, "She doesn't look like she's going anywhere."

Istomin nodded: "For God's sake, be careful! We don't know if there are any more of them!"

Thomas broke open his gun, pulled the spent shell out of the right chamber, slipped in a fresh one from his pocket, and snapped the gun shut. He strode to the staircase leading to the second floor. Keeping the stock pressed to his shoulder and the barrel pointing up the stairs, he climbed up.

When he got to the top he paused to look and listen. Nothing. No sounds, no movement.

To the right was a short corridor ending in a large window seat under a pointed arch. To the left, the corridor was long and had doors on either side.

Thomas turned left. He stepped silently on the deep maroon carpet, listening for the slightest sound. When he came to the first door on the right, he saw it had a card attached to it with a neatly written name, Sara. On the left was Fatima. Karina came next, then Duya, Masha, Sergey, Zina; Ibrahim was on the right, and, suddenly, on the next to the last door at the end of the corridor, Olga.

Feeling nauseous from anxiety, Thomas transferred the gun to his left hand, put his right on the doorknob and tried to turn it. It didn't budge. He put his right shoulder against the door and pushed, then pushed again, harder. It didn't yield, but he thought he heard a noise like a gasp coming from the other side.

And then, the familiar, dear voice he would recognize anywhere asked timidly through the door, "Papa?"

"Olga!" he exclaimed, no longer trying to be quiet. "Are you alright? I'm going to get you out in a second, baby girl," he cried in English. He hadn't used that endearment in years.

"Oh, Papa! I'm so glad you're here!"

Thomas tried his shoulder against the door again with no success. "Can you unlock it from the inside?" he asked, raising his voice. He was feeling frantic because he couldn't see her though she was just inches away.

"No, they always lock it. But the keys are in the little table at the head of the stairs," she explained. "I've seen them put there."

For a moment Thomas hesitated. He was tempted to blast the lock with his shotgun but decided it would put Olga at too much risk.

"OK, I'll get them and be right back," he shouted, leaning his gun against the wall.

A small drawer in the table had a ring with just four keys on it. The second one Thomas tried turned smoothly in the lock. A moment later Olga was hugging him, her arms around his neck, her eyes filled with tears.

Thomas burst into sobs of relief as he bent down, embracing her shoulders and stroking her head. He was so overwhelmed he couldn't say anything. He didn't want to let her out of his arms but forced himself and pulled away so he could see all of her.

"Are you really alright, darling? They didn't hurt you?" he asked looking at her dear face and holding her hands in his. "I can't believe what you've gone through!"

"I'm fine, Papa, really!" she insisted, with the trusting and truthful expression in her soft brown eyes he recognized and loved. "They didn't hurt me . . . not really. Not as much as some of the others."

"My dear, brave girl!" Thomas exclaimed through his tears. The thought that someone had injured her was like a stab to his heart. He reached out to embrace her again.

But this time Olga gently pulled away.

"Wait, Papa! We have to let the others out! A boy or girl is in each of these rooms!" she gestured with a sweep of her arm at all the doors. "Some of them are my friends. They also didn't drink the potion those witches were giving us. But some of the others couldn't help it and are in a bad way."

"What do you mean, potion and witches?" he began to ask, feeling his heart contract. But seeing the anxious expression on her tear-stained face, he put the questions off until later and picked up the key ring.

Olga wanted him to unlock the doors on either side of her room before the others, and he discovered the same key worked in all the locks. The three other keys on the ring fit doors that were not labeled and when he opened them, he saw lavish chrome and marble bathrooms.

During all his years in the United States and in Europe, where he had traveled widely and seen much, Thomas had never come across anything like what he found when he finished unlocking all the doors. It was no secret to him that there were some men, and women, who lusted after children, even very young ones. But this perversion always spoke in whispers and hid in the shadows, and he had never even heard of an establishment that put it on center stage in such an elaborate and costly way.

The condition and appearance of several children shocked Thomas. Despite all the noise in the building, six were still asleep and seemingly indifferent to what was happening around them. They were fully dressed for some reason, and when he turned on the room lights and unlocked their doors, they stirred languidly in their beds and looked up at him through their tousled hair, some with vacant expressions, others with expectant half-smiles. When he looked at their eyes and realized they were on drugs he felt a chill run down his spine. Now he understood what Olga meant by "potions." Somehow, only she and a few others managed to avoid being drugged.

As he looked at the children, Thomas was overwhelmed by the monstrous ambition of Dickerman's plans. He was reminded of an illustration he once saw in Mikey's school book showing "the peoples of the world." He also remembered what Markov said when he began his investigation. Dickerman didn't just abduct his victims randomly, which would have been bad enough, but assembled a collection to appeal to connoisseurs of the criminal and perverse. It made Thomas shudder when he thought how they were going to be used.

CHAPTER FIFTY-ONE

More than anything else now, Thomas wanted to get Olga out of this abominable place and bring her home, or to Istomin's house, which, he realized sadly, he now preferred to his own apartment.

But as the other children started coming out of their rooms, strangely quiet and moving listlessly, he saw Olga and her two friends approach a blond girl whose room was opposite theirs. Olga put her arm around the girl's shoulder with touching solicitude, the others bent toward her, telling her something, and it became clear to Thomas that he couldn't possibly leave any of them behind.

He was thinking about how he would manage it when he heard Istomin call his name. Turning around, he saw him approaching down the hallway, holding his shotgun in his left hand.

"*My God!*" Istomin gasped when he saw the crowd of children.

"Yes," Thomas replied, "it's hard to believe what Dickerman was planning here."

"Where's Olga? Is she all right?"

"She is, as far as I can tell. She's right here, comforting a friend. But tell me what happened downstairs," Thomas urged him.

"That woman you shot is dead. I hog-tied Dickerman on the floor with electrical cords from the table lamps and gagged him. He thought I was going to kill him and looks terrified. The fellow I clubbed at the rear entrance is still unconscious, but he's breathing, and I tied him up well. Oh, and I also found several women servants cowering in one of their rooms near the kitchen, two maids, and a housekeeper. There's also a woman who's all dressed up and who looks like she might've had something to do with running this place. But she was so terrified she was scarcely coherent, so I locked her in her room for now. That's it, no other men."

Thomas remembered how he shot the woman but it was hard for him to grasp that she was dead. The entire night was so extraordinary and his reactions so instinctive that little of what took place had fully sunk in yet. In a way, he felt oddly uninvolved, as if everything had happened because of someone else and not him.

Thinking of the dead woman made Thomas feel anxious about Olga even though she was just a dozen feet down the hall. He wanted her near him.

"I'll call Olga. She'll want to see you," he told Istomin.

"Olya! Vladimir Vladimirovich is here!" he cried, raising his voice.

Olga looked up, beamed, and started to walk over. She was genuinely fond of Istomin because of how he always took an interest in whatever she was saying, even when she was younger, but especially because he was her father's best friend. Standing on tiptoe, she put her arms around his neck and hugged him. He kissed her on the forehead in return, blinking rapidly to conceal the tears welling up in his eyes.

Seeing Ibrahim and Anya looking shyly at her father and Istomin, Olga called them over, then went back, took the hand of the tall blond girl who had been with them and returned with her as well.

"This is Masha," she told her father after introducing the two others.

"Nikitina?" he asked, and Olga nodded. The beautiful blond girl didn't seem to realize what was happening around her.

Thomas looked at her sadly. *Her poor parents*, he thought, remembering the horrible night when he had come to their house with Markov. *And what a blow it'll be to them when they see her like this. But at least she's alive, thank God!*

"Do you know what they gave her and the others?" Istomin asked Olga in a whisper, gesturing with his eyes at the five other children who were standing in the hallway as if waiting for something.

Olga shook her head.

But Ibrahim overheard him. "The *shaitans* make them drunk on vodka!" he spat out.

Thomas looked at the boy. He suspected the children were drugged with something else, but that wasn't important now.

"We have to get all of them out of here as quickly as possible," Thomas said looking at Istomin.

"Of course, of course," Istomin agreed.

"What time is it?" Thomas asked, pulling out his watch: "A quarter of four. Markov should be here soon. We're going to need him to help with the children and to deal with the police. This case is so big it'll have to go straight to Koshko."

"All right. Let's get them downstairs. We'll take them all to my house and start sorting things out. We'll have to get doctors and find their families."

"We're going to need more than your car, there are too many of us," Thomas said.

After all the bloodshed and turmoil, he felt relief at being drawn into the mundane matter of logistics.

It was more difficult than Thomas or Istomin imagined to get the drugged children to do anything. When Istomin announced to them that they had to come downstairs because they would be leaving this place, some looked at him with blank expressions, as if their minds were elsewhere, while others just smiled wanly but didn't move. Thomas wasn't sure how to behave toward them, but Olga and her two friends intervened. They took some by their hands and led them, and guided others by holding their shoulders and pushing them gently. Even so, it took a while to get everyone filing down the stairs.

At the last minute, Thomas realized he and Istomin should have tried to conceal what had happened downstairs. Hilda's body was clearly visible in the middle of the hallway, where the force of the shotgun blast threw her. She was a ghastly sight, lying on her back, arms and legs sprawling, her dead eyes staring at the ceiling. The pool of blood under her had spread across the glistening floor, and her mouth had fallen open, leaving a gaping black hole in her white face.

Thomas and Istomin stood in front of the corpse to block it from view as best they could and tried to hasten the children through the library toward the corridor leading to the kitchen. But the children still noticed the body and Thomas was struck by how they reacted to it more strongly than to anything else that happened since he let them out of their rooms. Some looked away or covered their faces with their hands so they wouldn't see, while others stared at the body and began to cry, although Thomas couldn't tell if it was out of fear or sorrow.

Olga walked by still holding the blond girl's hand. Both looked frightened when they saw the body and the girl's lower lip started trembling.

"One of the witches," Olga explained, then added, "she was really cruel."

Only Anya and Ibrahim reacted differently. She glowered at the dead woman from under her brows, and he muttered something that sounded angry in what Istomin guessed was Tatar.

"We should have thrown a blanket or something . . .," Thomas began to say to Istomin, when, suddenly, a wild shriek interrupted him. As Ibrahim was crossing the library, he had glimpsed Dickerman's corpulent figure, lying half-hidden behind the winged armchair.

"Hog-tied" was an accurate description of how Istomin had left him: his wrists were tied behind his back, his knees bent, and his ankles tied to his wrists. He was lying on his side and had what looked like a black necktie stuffed into his mouth. His eyes were crazy with fear.

Before either Thomas or Istomin could react, Ibrahim dashed between them and fell on Dickerman like an infuriated wildcat. Grabbing the Southerner by the throat with both hands he tried to choke him, but the man's neck was too thick for Ibrahim's slender fingers, so he fell to his knees and began to pummel his face with his fists, hitting him as hard as he could. Dickerman moaned and tried to twist out of the way, squeezing his eyes shut under the hail of blows.

Thomas and Istomin made a move toward the boy, but stopped.

Istomin felt himself getting caught up in Ibrahim's rage. "That's the way! Get him, *beat the bastard*! Beat him!" he started to mutter through his teeth as he watched, raising his clenched fist.

Thomas knew the attack had to be stopped but couldn't bring himself to put his hands on Ibrahim to restrain him. All he felt he could do was step closer to the boy and keep repeating that the police would deal with Dickerman and he would go to prison.

But the boy wouldn't listen and didn't stop his furious assault until he was too tired and his knuckles too bloody to continue.

He rose to his feet with a proud bearing, breathing hard, his black, almond-shaped eyes burning, the high cheekbones on his face flushed, and feeling as if he'd been possessed by the *jinn* of retribution.

"I wish I had my grandfather's *khandzhar*," he said to Thomas and Istomin, then turned back to Dickerman and kicked him hard in the stomach.

The other children watched Ibrahim's attack with the same anxiety and tears as when they walked past the woman's dead body. But Olga whispered something to him that Thomas couldn't make out and put her arm around his shoulders, while Anya started to dab at his bloodied hands with a handkerchief that she pulled out the pocket of her skirt.

They've bonded in this hellish place, Thomas thought. He felt moved and humbled by how self-possessed and resourceful Olga and her friends were despite everything they had endured.

As soon as Thomas and Istomin crowded into the kitchen with the children, Olga led Ibrahim to the sink and began to rinse his hands, making him wince from pain as the cold water ran over his skinned knuckles, while Masha searched through drawers to find something to use as bandages.

But the drugged children seemed mesmerized by the

different shaped jars, boxes and crocks filling the kitchen's counters and shelves. They started wandering around the room, running their fingers over the multi-colored labels, and scrutinizing them as if they were searching for something.

Thinking it might distract them, Thomas asked if anyone wanted a drink of water, but they all either ignored him or shook their heads without looking at him.

Thomas guessed they must be going through early symptoms of withdrawal, and that it wouldn't be long before their cravings grew stronger. Istomin was also watching the children with concern.

"I'll get my automobile, but what about a second one?" he asked. "Do you think it would be quicker if you called your garage to order one? Maybe it'll arrive before Markov gets here. There's a telephone in the front hall."

"At this time of night?" Thomas sounded skeptical. "I'm guessing if there's no night-chauffeur on duty in the garage, it could easily take . . .."

The sound of loud voices outside the kitchen door interrupted him.

"*Speak of the devil!*" Thomas exclaimed with relief, handing his shotgun to Istomin.

As he strode toward the open door, he called: "Sergey Sergey'ch, it's wonderful you're here, just in time!"

But it wasn't Markov.

CHAPTER FIFTY-TWO

Thomas walked over to the kitchen door and looked out-side. Silhouetted against the fire in the carriage house, which had burned through the roof and spread to the walls of the building, were three figures bending over the body lying on the ground in front of the steps. It took Thomas a second to recognize this was the man he had clubbed. Two of the men were untying him and he was stirring weakly. They were speaking German and addressed him as "*Herr Hauptmann*" (Captain, sir).

Thomas stopped on the threshold, dumbfounded. When he hit the man, they didn't have any idea who he was. Now Thomas realized all of them must be in the German military, even though they were wearing civilian clothes. This meant they were the intelligence agents Markov had mentioned.

One of the men noticed Thomas in the doorway, twisted around with surprising agility despite his stocky build, and drew a gun from inside his jacket.

Pointing it at Thomas's face, he asked in heavily accented Russian:

"Who are you? Did you attack this man?" The German narrowed his eyes and an angry expression appeared on his pale, sharply angled face.

"*Nein*," Thomas replied in German, shaking his head. Alt-hough he was shocked, he realized he had to stall somehow so he could figure out what to say and do.

"*Ich kenne ihn nicht. Ich bin hier nur um meine Tochter abzuholen*" (I don't know him. I'm just here to get my daugh-ter).

Not expecting a Black man to speak German or to hear anything about a child, the man with the gun peered at him.

"Your daughter? Who else is inside?" he demanded in a

skeptical tone, switching to German himself.

"Only other children and their doctor," Thomas invented, trying to steer the German in an unrelated direction. "Most of the children are not well and we are here to take them to the hospital."

"A hospital?" the man asked in a perplexed tone, looking uncertain.

Thomas saw that the German didn't know what had happened in the mansion and was trying to make sense of what he and his fellows had stumbled into.

Just then the two other men succeeded in hauling Stürmer to his feet. He was still unsteady, and they had to hold him by both arms to keep his legs from buckling. Stürmer's eyes were half-closed and the right side of his face was swollen with a big bruise from his chin to his ear.

"Captain, do you know this man? Is he the one who attacked you?" the German with the gun asked.

Stürmer tried to focus on Thomas's face, blinked several times with the effort and leaned forward to get a better look. He still looked wobbly but shrugged off the arms of the two men who had been supporting him.

"Yes," he said in a barely audible voice, then cleared his throat and said more loudly, "Yes! I didn't see who hit me, but it could only have been this Black man or his friend. Mr. Dickerman and I were expecting them to attack us. That is why I called you here, because of them. For assistance."

The German with the gun stiffened, took a step toward Thomas and gave him a backhanded slap across the face with his free hand.

"*Black pig!*" he cursed. "*That's for lying!*"

The blow surprised Thomas. But he also realized it wasn't worse than what he got in the ring when he didn't get his guard up in time. Thinking it would be good to look more injured than he was because it might buy him some time, Thomas bent over, pressing his hand to his face, as if debilitated by the blow. He looked through his fingers, trying to estimate if he could launch himself at the German before he managed to pull the trigger.

Suddenly, he heard Istomin's voice behind him:

"Frederick! What's the matter? Who are these people?" he asked in English.

Thomas glanced back over his shoulder and saw Istomin in the doorway. His hands were empty.

The two Germans standing near Stürmer pulled Lugers out of their shoulder holsters and pointed them at Istomin. Both were young with cold blue eyes, narrow faces, and short military haircuts, one blond, the other black.

"*Hands up!*" the first one commanded in Russian, striding forward. With all the guns trained on him, Istomin raised his arms. He couldn't understand what was happening.

"Turn around," the German continued, then walked up to him and stuck the barrel of his gun into Istomin's back.

Stürmer's face and head were still throbbing, but he was feeling stronger and thinking more clearly. Seeing that his men had taken control of the situation, he ordered, "Get them inside and keep them covered."

When Thomas went out of the kitchen, Istomin thought they wouldn't need their shotguns or revolvers any longer and put them all on a high shelf above the icebox so they would be out of the children's reach. Now, with the German behind him pushing him into the room with his pistol, Istomin's first thought was how he could try to grab one of his own guns without being shot himself.

Olga, Anya, and Ibrahim were facing the kitchen door when Istomin entered from the outside, expecting he would be followed by the man named "Markov" who was coming to help them. Their eager smiles faded when they saw a stranger holding a gun behind Istomin. And when Thomas walked in, his lip cut and bleeding, followed by two other strange men with guns, Olga gasped.

"Everyone over there," Stürmer ordered Thomas and Istomin, pointing to the corner of the kitchen by the stove.

"*You too!*" he raised his voice at the children, gesturing with his hand.

Olga took Masha's hand, pressed close to Anya and Ibrahim, and moved to the corner. But the rest of the children, whose confusion increased because of what was happening, didn't obey and began to shift from foot to foot nervously as they stared at Stürmer and the other strange men.

"Get them over there," Stürmer raised his voice, grabbing the red-haired boy named Sergey by the shoulder and pushing him toward the corner.

The boy bumped into the stove and would have fallen if Masha hadn't caught him by the arm and drawn him close to her. His eyes filled with tears as he began to rub his injured hip.

Stürmer watched impatiently while everyone was herded into the confined space, then ordered the man he called Schlanger to watch them at gunpoint and to keep his eyes on Istomin and Thomas. He told the two others to come with him and ushered them into the corridor leading to the front of the mansion, then followed himself.

The two men moved carefully, uncertain of what lay ahead, their guns ready, until they reached the library's threshold and stopped.

Stürmer saw Dickerman's trussed body on the floor first. "*Gott im Himmel!*" (God in Heaven!) he exclaimed and rushed over to him.

Stürmer bent down, but Dickerman's face was covered with so much blood it was hard to make out his features.

"Mr. Dickerman! Mr. Dickerman!" Stürmer called, gingerly shaking him by the shoulder, uncertain if he was dead or alive. Dickerman's obese body quivered, he moaned and opened his swollen left eye as much as he could.

"Untie, him, Gifter, quickly!" Stürmer called over his shoulder to the man behind him.

When Gifter didn't respond, Stürmer turned around, and to his irritation saw that neither he nor the third man, Rutschen, was paying attention to him. Instead, both were looking off to the side.

Stürmer stood up, followed their gaze, and felt the hair on the back of his neck stir.

"The bloody devils! I cannot believe they killed a woman! I know her, she is a German!" Stürmer exclaimed when he saw Hilda's spread-eagled body lying in the pool of blood.

"What shall we do, Captain?" Gifter asked angrily.

"Untie Mr. Dickerman. Take him to the kitchen and see if you can help him. And you," he addressed Rutschen, pointing, "give me that pistol."

Rutschen walked around Hilda's body, stepping widely to avoid the blood, picked up the Luger lying on the floor near it, and brought it back to Stürmer.

Flipping the pistol over in his hands, Stürmer recognized it was his. He held it in his right hand, pulled the toggle and cocked it. An unfired cartridge flipped out and rattled across the floor.

She tried to use my pistol to defend herself and they killed her, he thought bitterly as he hefted the Luger in his hand. He winced as he raised his wounded arm and slipped the pistol into his shoulder holster.

"Rutschen, you search the rest of this floor and the cellar to see if anyone else is in the building, and after that return to the kitchen. I will search upstairs and meet you there."

CHAPTER FIFTY-THREE

Ibrahim had beaten Dickerman's face so badly it looked like a raw slab of meat on a butcher's counter. He could hardly see out of either eye—his left was swollen shut, and blood from a cut eyebrow blinded his right. His nose was broken, and his lips swollen and split. Thick streaks of blood covered his cheeks and chin and gathered in the fleshy folds of his neck.

But the face bleeds easily, Ibrahim's fists were too small and weak to cause deep damage, and Dickerman looked worse than he felt. He had also feigned passing out on the floor after the beating in the hope no one else would attack him.

Getting up with Gifter's help and leaning so heavily on him that the German's legs almost gave way, Dickerman let himself be half-led, half-dragged to the kitchen. Once there, Gifter tried to help Dickerman into a chair, but Dickerman started repeating "water, water" impatiently in a hoarse voice and groping with his hands until the German understood and hauled him to the sink. Dickerman pressed his belly against its edge, felt for the cold-water tap, twisted it, and thrust his whole head under the stream.

The burning pain of the water hitting his broken skin made him groan out loud, but after a few seconds the cold stream began to revive him, and he rolled his face repeatedly under it as he tried to wash out his eyes.

He felt a wave of elation rising within him. When Istomin had tied him up he thought he was dead, but now the arrival of Stürmer's men changed everything. Letting the tap run, Dickerman lifted his face from the sink, gasping and snorting as water poured down his chest and belly, then groped for the soiled towel hanging on the wall.

Thomas and Istomin were in the corner with their backs against the wall where Schlanger had ordered them at gunpoint and watched nervously as Dickerman dabbed at his face and winced. The children were huddled together in front of them. Those who had succumbed to the drugs were shifting about restlessly, grimacing, hugging themselves, craning their necks, searching for relief.

When the German dragged Dickerman into the kitchen, Olga, who was standing in front of her father, felt him tug her arm and try to pull her behind him. Istomin saw what Thomas was doing and started trying to inch ahead of Anya to shield her from whatever was coming.

Ibrahim was paralyzed by Dickerman's sudden reappearance and stared at him with disbelief. The boy had tried to kill his tormenter. Seeing him in the kitchen covered with blood, and now standing in front of him, made it seem as if the *Iblis* had risen from the dead.

The cuts on Dickerman's swollen face were still oozing, but as he blinked repeatedly, his gaze began to focus, and when he raised his head, he saw Thomas behind the children huddled near the stove.

Dickerman's mouth started to stretch into a triumphant grin until a stab of pain from his cut upper lip made him stop and relax his features. The salty taste of blood filled his mouth. He thought of spitting it out into the sink but swallowed instead so he wouldn't have to move his eyes from what was before him. He could scarcely believe his luck. All his thoughts were now focused on how he would avenge himself against this damned Black sonofabitch. And not only him, but his fancy Russian friend too.

"Where's Stürmer?" he asked Gifter, who sat down on a chair next to Schlanger. Both men looked relaxed, their elbows on the table and knees comfortably spread, but with their pistols still pointing at the captives.

"I am here," Stürmer announced as he strode into the kitchen. It pleased him to hear Dickerman's question just as he entered. He thought the coincidence was a good omen, a sign that things were going his way and falling neatly into place, as he had always intended. Gifter and Schlanger rose respectfully to their feet.

Stürmer stopped and looked around the kitchen with a smug expression. He was standing as erect as ever. Were it not for his cut jacket, and the purple discoloration and swelling on the right side of his face, there was nothing to suggest he had been affected by what happened that night. He apparently forgot his shock over Hilda's death as readily as he forgot about Bartkow and the Golubs.

"I am pleased to see you are recovering, Mr. Dickerman, and that your wounds are not as serious as they seemed at first," he said in a confident tone, punctuating his words with a slight bow.

"But to answer your question, I was searching the upstairs. Sergeant Rutschen searched this floor and found the maids and cook in one of the rooms in the servants' quarters. Fräulein Maria, I believe is the . . . lady's name?" he asked Dickerman. "She was upset but has taken something and is better now. She is resting in her room."

"Excellent, my dear baron," Dickerman drawled, trying to sound chipper despite the pain in his cut and swollen lips. The night's events shook him to the core, and he was shocked by his bloodied and bruised appearance when he saw himself in the mirrored door of a kitchen cabinet. But he didn't want to lose any more face with Stürmer. He also realized he needed the German now more than ever and wanted to flatter him.

"Your men have turned everything around. You were absolutely correct to summon them. Your tactic was brilliant. It's also wonderful to see how efficient they are. I can see how loyal they are to you personally."

Stürmer beamed. Dickerman's words echoed what he was thinking himself, but he felt he should be modest. He settled for another slight bow as an acknowledgment and stroked his moustache with his right index finger.

"And now," Dickerman prompted him, "we eliminate all our problems. Do you agree?"

"Indeed, Mr. Dickerman, it is time for the clean slate."

As they were saying this, Rutschen walked into the kitchen with a stack of neatly folded bed sheets and dropped them on the floor in front of the captives.

Thomas started when he heard the German's remark about a "clean slate" and looked at the pile of linen on the floor with disbelief. He tried to think of something he could do, but a feeling of helplessness washed over him. The risk to the children if the Germans opened fire at him was too great. The thought briefly flashed through his mind to try pleading for his life, just to gain some time, but he realized it would accomplish nothing except satisfy Dickerman. He could never bring himself to do that.

Thomas glanced at Istomin. His jaw was tense, and his eyes were jumping from one German to the next, as if he was calculating something.

Maybe if we both rush them at the same time, one of us can grab a gun, Thomas thought. If only he could catch Istomin's gaze, he might be able to communicate the idea to him.

Thomas was about to clear his throat, hoping it would make Istomin look at him, when he heard Stürmer give Rutschen and Schlanger an order to get the children out of the way. As he spoke, he waved the barrel of his Luger from right to left to show what he meant.

Keeping their guns leveled at Thomas and Istomin, the two Germans started to pull the children out of the corner one by one, grabbing them by their arms or shoulders and pushing them toward the kitchen's entrance. The drugged children moved jerkily. Seeing how they were being manhandled, Anya and Masha walked over to join them on their own.

Only Olga and Ibrahim were left in the corner with Thomas and Istomin. The two Germans were about to reach for them when Dickerman, who was watching the process with satisfaction and relishing the anguished expression on Thomas's face, felt a surge of anger at the prospect the two would get away.

What the hell! he thought.

"Wait a minute, baron, would you, please? Would you be so kind as to do me a favor and include these two in our clean slate?" he asked, pointing to Ibrahim and Olga. "I want to make an example out of this little slant-eyed bastard so none of the others ever dares raise a hand against me again . . . or any of us. And as for our trouble-making mulatto miss, well . . . with her daddy here and watching . . . I can't think of much else that would upset him more."

Thomas felt his heart stop.

Pleased by the respectful way Dickerman had spoken to him, Stürmer waved to the two men to wait. He enjoyed wielding power and decided it would be politic to grant Dickerman's request.

"Yes, why not? We probably won't be able to use them later, given how they behaved," he replied calmly.

Thomas's mind reeled at what he had just heard, and he wrapped his arms around Olga's shoulders. She looked up at him. He saw her lips move as she tried to say "Papa, papa," but no sound came out.

"Spread out the sheets in front of them," Stürmer gestured to Gifter and Schlanger.

Suddenly, Istomin took a step forward and shouted to Dickerman: "Let the two children go. We'll pay you for their lives."

Dickerman flinched and looked up at Istomin with a mixture of surprise and annoyance. His head was beginning to throb. He was thinking that the sooner it was all over the better.

Thomas wasn't expecting what Istomin offered but immediately joined him: "He's right. We can pay you a lot. Name your price and let both children go."

"You've got a lot of money, do you?" Dickerman asked with a sneer. "Well, this ain't about money, boy, but about something you'll never understand!" he said with distaste, rubbing his forehead and turning away from Thomas.

"Shouldn't we just get on with it, baron, before anyone gets here?" he asked and sighed wearily.

Stürmer had listened to Dickerman and Thomas with curiosity but said nothing. Instead, he pulled out his pistol and nodded to Rutschen and Schlanger.

Thomas watched the Germans with horror. He felt as if his soul was being rent. A mute appeal rose within him like a

311

scream that goes unheard in a nightmare.

Keeping their guns trained on Thomas and the two children, Stürmer and his men backed away into the middle of the kitchen.

CHAPTER FIFTY-FOUR

But as the four Germans raised their weapons and spread out so they would have clean lines of fire, it appeared to Thomas that their movements were slowing down. It was as if someone took what was happening before his eyes and started to stretch it out like a piece of elastic.

When Schlanger put his left thumb and the knuckle of his forefinger on the toggle of his pistol and prepared to pull it back to confirm a cartridge was in the chamber, it seemed to Thomas that the time it took would have been enough for him to walk out of the kitchen, go around the entire house, and return.

As time slowed further, Thomas's vision grew, and his hearing sharpened. He felt a sense of calm settle over him like a gossamer shroud. He remembered what Zoya said after he awakened from his deep sleep and now felt he understood what she meant.

Looking up, Thomas noticed a small white moth fly in through the kitchen door and followed it with a sympathetic gaze as it flitted about the ceiling before settling in a dark corner and carefully folding its wings.

He could tell that the pistol of the German standing closest to the kitchen table hadn't been fired in several weeks and emitted a faint smell of graphite and gun oil.

The slow murmur of water from the tap Dickerman left on at the sink sounded familiar. Thomas' recent dream came back to him—how he was walking across a field and came to a stream with sun gleams rippling on its surface, and how, looking across it, he saw all those he loved.

The three Germans and Stürmer were now lined up and ready. The one on the left was aiming straight at Thomas's face, the muzzle's black hole trembling slightly as each beat of the man's heart reverberated through his arm. Dickerman got to his feet and was leaning forward in anticipation, wheezing with his mouth open. Thomas could feel Olga's shoulders trembling under his arms and sensed Istomin's despair and the tears streaming down Ibrahim's face. An upsurge of pity filled him, and he was about to assure them they don't have to worry because all would be well when he heard loud shouts and stamping feet.

With a wrench, as if a wave had unexpectedly appeared and plucked him from a calm shoal, Thomas felt himself borne back into the flow and roar of time, and when he turned toward the kitchen door where the noise was coming from, he saw a crowd of men rushing in.

"*Drop your weapons! Hands up! Now!*" a commanding voice cried out in Russian, and Thomas recognized Markov, red-faced, his eyes bulging, his right arm extended and pointing a large caliber snub-nosed revolver. A half-dozen other armed men, most wearing police uniforms and carrying rifles, followed him and surrounded the Germans.

Like a man roused from sleep who must struggle to reenter the waking world, Thomas tried to make sense of the cascade of events around him. He watched with bewilderment as Markov and his assistant Ilyushin pulled the pistols from the Germans' unresisting hands and hand-cuffed them. A pale Stürmer advanced on the police sergeant in charge, protesting that he and his men had diplomatic immunity and he had official documents to prove it. But the police sergeant only shook his head and replied with a grin that he forgot his glasses and couldn't read German anyway.

Thomas felt Olga wrapping her arms around him and hugged her back as he stroked her head. When he searched for Istomin, he saw him blinking rapidly and pressing Ibrahim's head to his chest. Two of the police officers, whom Thomas recognized as patrolmen from Triumphal Arch Square near Aquarium, set down their rifles and with expressions of concern on their flushed and mustached faces were trying to tend to the children cowering against a wall.

Markov put himself in charge without asking anyone's

permission and Thomas happily watched. The four city police officers and their sergeant, whom Markov enlisted on the strength of his old connections, rounded up the four Germans, Maria, and the servants, and telephoned the night desk at central police headquarters for a horse-drawn prison van.

Markov sent Ilyushin to bring Istomin's automobile around to the front of the mansion. Using it and one of the two automobiles Markov commandeered from a garage, half an hour later the nine children, Thomas, and Istomin, were rolling through Moscow on the way to Istomin's home.

The city's streets were still dark, but dawn was breaking. The eastern edge of the sky was turning a lovely opalescent pink and there wasn't a cloud in sight.

With Olga by his side, Thomas let himself sink into the leather seat and stopped resisting the fatigue washing over him as his heart expanded with a feeling of immense gratitude.

CHAPTER FIFTY-FIVE

Saturday, October 23, 1913, 7:45 p. m.
Otradnoye Estate, Kostroma Governorate

Istomin had already been sitting for close to an hour in a rocking chair on the colonnaded portico of his family's ancestral seat near Kostroma waiting for Thomas to arrive. Thomas had telegraphed the day before to confirm that his train from Moscow's Yaroslavl Station was due in at 6 p. m., and Istomin had dispatched his Russo-Balt, with Ivan, the junior clerk from his estate behind the wheel, to meet him.

The sun had gone down at six and Istomin felt cold. *There will be frost tonight,* he thought as he buttoned up his overcoat and looked up at the clear night sky.

Myriad stars covered it, like diamonds scattered over a black velvet mantle, and a crescent moon, a sliver of silver, hung in the east, shedding its pale light on the forest that began beyond the expansive mown field in front of the house.

Istomin inhaled deeply. The mysterious dome overhead; the silence accentuated by the distant, flat ringing of a hammer in the village smithy; the air scented with the inebriating smells of fallen leaves and autumnal decay. These were all balm for his soul.

He got up and strolled along the portico's edge, skirting the four white columns supporting the neoclassical pediment. When he looked down at the intricate brick pattern at his feet his thoughts turned toward the past. His ancestors had walked here—his great-great grandfather, who started construction of the manor house in 1753 and named it *Otradnoye* (Place of Happiness); his great-grandfather, whose portrait by the celebrated Levitsky hung in his study; his grandfather, whom he remembered well and who died when he was a boy; his father; and now him.

This is home, Istomin thought for the second time since he had come outside to wait for Thomas.

Moscow still called, with its Kremlin, ancient churches and monasteries, crooked side streets, distinctive speech, squalor, riches, music, theaters, and museums. But after everything that happened in Moscow in May, Istomin started to feel more strongly than ever before that his roots were in *Otradnoye*. Only here did he find a unique peace and satisfaction, even though, when he was being honest with himself, something was still missing, and it troubled him that he couldn't quite put his finger on it.

A moment later, Istomin saw the Russo-Balt's distinctive, white headlights flash as the automobile rose and dipped across the new bridge he built over Voskresensky Brook, which ran between the forest and the edge of the mowed field before turning south toward the Volga twenty kilometers away. The headlights turned from the main road leading to the village and flooded the allée of old birches his great-grandfather had planted along the drive to the manor house. Istomin squinted into the bright light, walked down the front steps of the portico with a broad smile, and a moment later was clasping Thomas's hand and embracing him.

"Well, well, better late than never!" he greeted him in a mock gruff tone as they exchanged three kisses on the cheek.

"Yes, sorry about that. We were delayed leaving Moscow, there was some police trouble at the station. But I'll tell you about it later," Thomas replied and looked around as he inhaled.

"My God, the air here is like a *tonic*!" he exclaimed. "And I'm very glad I was able to come."

"Me too, my dear man, me too," Istomin replied enthusiastically, shaking his hand again. "But come inside, you must be hungry and exhausted. How long is the trip by train now? I usually drive."

"Almost twelve hours, even though it's only 350 kilometers or so. I feel all right, but yes, I'm famished!"

"How is Olga? How are the other children?" Istomin asked, leading the way inside and holding the front door open. He was going to ask about Valli as well but stopped himself.

"She has some emotional scars but is handling them well. The little ones are fine. I try to spend as much time with them as I can. More than before. I have to admit that . . . Valli has been a great help with her . . . and with the little ones," Thomas said looking up at Istomin with an embarrassed smile. He wanted to talk about his relations with Valli, but not now.

"I'm very glad to hear it. Olga is a strong young woman," Istomin replied.

Then, seeing Thomas's reticence, he got back to practicalities: "Let me take you to your room, which you already know, so you can freshen up. I also have a surprise for you!" he concluded with a smile and squeezed Thomas's upper arm.

Thomas inspected the renovated bathroom attached to his bedroom and didn't hesitate when he saw that in addition to hot running water there was now a shower above the big copper tub. Fifteen minutes later, feeling completely refreshed, he changed into comfortable and softer country garb—a raw silk shirt, blue velvet jacket, tooled Moroccan slippers—and descended the steps to the living room.

Thomas found Istomin sitting in an armchair under an electric torchère that seemed out of place in the high-ceilinged living room, filled with antique, straight-backed furniture made of Karelian birch and portraits of family members on the walls. Some were so old that the benignly smiling subjects were depicted in powdered wigs and crinolines. He put his newspaper down when Thomas walked in.

"Feeling better?" he asked.

"Much," Thomas replied.

He could see Istomin was excited by something. Eager to please his friend, Thomas asked, "So, what's the surprise you have for me?"

Istomin's smile grew even wider. He reached over the arm of his chair and pulled up a wicker basket that had been on the floor on the other side.

"Here it is!" he proclaimed, handing it to Thomas by the handle.

The basket was covered by a white linen cloth embroidered with green oak leaves and when Thomas held it up, he had the impression the cloth moved. Bewildered by what it could be, he raised the fabric and gasped.

"A puppy! A borzoi *puppy!*" he exclaimed with delight. Putting the basket on the floor he slipped his thumbs under the little dog's forelimbs and lifted it up: "A little bitch, and she's cream with a brown flash on her muzzle, just like Strelka!"

Thomas's delight was so genuine that Istomin teared up with pleasure. "Yes, now you have a new Strelka, Strelka the Second, like an empress!" he said with a laugh.

The puppy whimpered and began to stir. Thomas shifted her to the crook of his arm and bent his face down to her muzzle, whispering "Shhh . . . shhh . . . shhh" to calm her. The little dog stopped fidgeting, raised her head and licked Thomas on the cheek.

Both men burst out laughing.

"Where on earth did you get this little beauty?" Thomas asked, setting the puppy down on his lap and stroking her head.

"There's a fellow in our district, Antonov, an eccentric, old-fashioned landowner who's also a borzoi fancier and breeder. He uses his dogs to hunt wolves and . . ."

Seeing Thomas raise an eyebrow at this, Istomin stopped to assure him: "Yes, yes, we still have them around here, believe it or not, although mostly in the northeast corner of the district. In any event, I found out that Antonov had a litter of six pups last month and he let me choose the one I liked as soon as they were all weaned. I had told him about what happened to your Strelka, you see, and he was very moved. He thinks the world of this breed. I assured him you'd be a good owner."

"Thank you, Vladimir Vladimirovich," Thomas said, his voice filled with emotion as he reached out and clasped

Istomin's hand. "You can assure Antonov I will treasure her. You know that the head of that veterinary clinic on Trubnaya Square really did everything he could to save Strelka and operated on her. But she lost too much blood."

"Well," Istomin said sadly, "you saved her life and she saved yours, but it apparently wasn't meant to happen more than once."

Both men were quiet for a moment. They knew they would talk about everything important later, but it was hard to keep the past from flooding back uninvited.

Their silence was broken by Istomin's valet Evgeny, who came into the room and discreetly cleared his throat to get his master's attention. When Istomin looked up, Evgeny bowed to Thomas, saying it was a pleasure to see him again, and announced that the cook was prepared to serve dinner whenever Vladimir Vladimirovich was ready.

Istomin understood the hint. The cook had been waiting and was eager to serve the special dinner she'd prepared.

"Well, let's go in," he said, getting up and stretching out his left arm toward the dining room. "We'll leave *Strelochka* (Little arrow) with Evgeny for the time being, if you're agreeable."

"What a nice name, Strelochka!" Thomas exclaimed. "Maybe that's what I'll call her! The 'Second' sounds too grand. You don't mind keeping an eye on her, Evgeny?" Thomas asked, setting the little dog in her basket.

At *Otradnoye* Istomin liked to eat only what he considered traditional, simple Russian dishes, all made with what was grown and raised on his estate. When he discovered Thomas was also enthusiastic about country fare because it reminded him of his youth on a Mississippi farm, Istomin made a point of keeping a note of his favorite dishes. As a result, the previous day, after consulting with his cook, Oksana, a stout, middle-aged woman of the people originally from Cherkassy in the Kiev Governorate, Istomin built the dinner around their shared tastes.

"We're starting with borshch, my friend, the kind you like with marrow bones," Istomin explained, "so we're not having separate *zakuski* first, if that's all right with you.

"Not only is it all right, but the idea of Oksana's *borshch* makes my mouth water!" Thomas replied enthusiastically.

He couldn't think of anything he'd like more to start with on a cold autumn night than some of the deeply flavored marrow in the bones that had been simmering for hours in Oksana's rich vegetable and beef soup. When scooped out onto a piece of freshly baked rye bread and sprinkled with coarse salt, the marrow's unctuous richness was the perfect accompaniment for iced vodka.

Oksana, wearing a brightly colored headscarf and a clean white apron, brought in a steaming tureen filled with the crimson borshch and insisted on serving it herself, adding the traditional accompaniments: a tablespoon of sour cream and a heaping spoonful of cooked buckwheat stirred into each bowl.

"Eat it like that, dear sir," she urged Thomas in her soft and lilting southern Russian. "It's just the way you liked it last time!" she said, looking at him with a benevolent smile.

"Except we don't have fresh dill, it's not the season," she added apologetically.

In response, Thomas got up from the table and to the cook's embarrassment took her hand and kissed it. Then he proclaimed he had never eaten borshch better than hers anywhere, including Moscow and Kiev, and that her serving it herself more than made up for the missing dill. Oksana turned pink with pleasure and waving her hand dismissively at Thomas' extravagant praise retreated to the kitchen as Istomin grinned from ear to ear.

The friends' high feelings lasted through the main course, roasted grouse, which Istomin hunted himself and hung for two days to deepen the flavor. With it he served a hearty Crimean red. For dessert Oksana brought in a fragrant butter tart made with blackberry preserves she cooked and canned herself in August.

Both men knew they had much to talk about that was painful, but it would also be best to leave it for after the meal.

Otherwise, they would hardly notice, much less enjoy, the food and drink.

Thomas explained how he had been forced to put off his visit because business was going so well that he couldn't get away until things started to quiet down for the winter. Lina Cavalieri's summer concert tour at Aquarium was an enormous success and exceeded what he hoped for. The diva had already signed a contract to return for a longer engagement the following year. Even better was that Tsarev hadn't supported Martynov's push to restructure their three-way partnership, and Thomas was able to buy out Martynov's share of the business. He had begun to think of buying out Tsarev as well, perhaps next year, and maybe even expanding to another property.

Istomin knew Thomas would want to see Zoya, and hadn't asked about her only because of how difficult it was for anyone whose life she had touched to talk casually about her. To ease Thomas's mind, Istomin volunteered that Zoya was going to return in three days from the Trinity Monastery of Saint Sergius. She had been invited to go there on a pilgrimage by an immensely grateful merchant's family from Kostroma after treating and saving their only child, a seven-year-old boy who'd been bitten by a rabid dog and declared beyond help by the doctors.

When dinner was over, Thomas followed Istomin into the living room, where two armchairs were positioned on either side of the fireplace.

"As I told you in my last letter," Istomin began in English after sitting down and crossing his legs comfortably, "there's much I don't know because of the secrecy surrounding the investigation and trial. The city's newspapers hardly mentioned them. So, I'm eager to hear about everything that happened after I left Moscow. Tell me first, please, about what happened to those poor children."

Thomas didn't answer but waited for Evgeny to finish pouring each of them a snifter of Armenian cognac. When the valet left, Thomas lifted Strelochka out of her basket onto his lap and gently stroked the silken fur on her head. She looked up at him, yawned, and fell asleep.

"I called the Morozovskaya Children's Hospital last week and they told me that things were finally looking up for all six of them," Thomas replied. "But frankly, it's a shame the city's medical authorities didn't let Zoya finish what she was doing."

"Yes, I remember. I was still there before they were taken away. Their craving for the narcotics dropped noticeably because of her. And that sexual . . . I don't know what to call it . . . that revolting erotomania the gang induced in some of them was beginning to fade."

"It's all because of the Germans," Thomas said angrily and shifted in his seat, causing Strelochka to stir on his lap. "Everything would have been different if it hadn't been for them and the scheme they cooked up."

"Why do you say that?"

"Markov was able to find out a lot of what went on behind the scenes. He told me, in strictest confidence, that the Ministry of the Interior and the Okhrana got involved in the investigation because all the Germans turned out to be intelligence agents. Spies and saboteurs, in other words. It became a matter of 'highest-level foreign relations,' as Markov's friends in the Moscow police hinted to him."

"I had no idea. That's appalling."

"Yes, it is. But that's not the end of it. Because the Interior Ministry got involved, the Moscow Board of Health found out about the entire affair and the Board's doctors intervened. They weren't about to let the children be treated by someone like Zoya or stay anywhere except a hospital. The children's parents didn't help either when they started claiming Zoya was a sorceress."

"Not all that far-fetched, actually," Istomin replied with a sad smile. "Although, of course, these people have no idea of what they're talking about. Given what happened, it's a good thing the church authorities didn't get wind of anything.

"Yes," Thomas replied. "In any event, the head doctor at the Morozovskaya Hospital told me the children no longer have to be restrained and have stopped begging for drugs. But the doctors haven't been very successful with the . . . erotomania you mentioned, especially with three of them who seem to have become as addicted to this as to the drugs themselves. The doctors don't really understand it. They're talking about sending them to the Alekseyev Psychiatric Hospital. Maybe they'll have more luck there."

"I'd put more faith in Zoya, if they let her," Istomin said.

"Me too," Thomas agreed.

Istomin sighed, uncrossed his legs, and drained his glass before continuing. "You said Olga was doing well, which is wonderful."

"Yes, it's very fortunate she was seized later than the others, if I can use the word 'fortunate' at all for this nightmare. You know, she was a kind of afterthought, because Dickerman was trying to avenge himself on me. As a result, the gang didn't have time to try to drug her the way they did most of the others. And without addicting her to drugs, they weren't able to start their vile practices either. She knows what was done to the others, but I'm certain she herself was not touched."

"That's a relief!" Istomin replied.

Thomas paused, thinking about something, then went on, "It's ironic that all this dreadful business had a positive effect. It brought Olga and me closer together. And I got to know her better, how she thinks, what she feels. Do you know she asked me to take her to see the imperial family when they arrived in Moscow on the 6th? That was only a week after the night with the attacks and the guns."

"Really? I'm surprised she would care," Istomin replied in an indifferent tone.

"It surprised me too, but she explained it to me in a way that made sense. She said she'd been born in Russia and felt Russian, Moscow is her home, and the dynasty's 300th anniversary was a major event. She didn't want to feel left out of what the people were celebrating."

"Well, not all the people!" Istomin exclaimed. "I for one

was glad to have left Moscow before the 6th, and also to have missed all the hoopla in Kostroma when the Romanovs were there a few days earlier."

"Yes, I read about that. But Olga wanted to see the procession from the Alexandrovsky train station to the Kremlin, and, you know, I'm glad I went. It made me hopeful in a way. I know what you think of the monarchy . . . But what I found moving was the reactions of the enormous crowds of people who came out. There was a feeling of unity, of shared feeling. That means a lot. This included well-dressed city types, and merchants, and a lot of peasants and simple folk, of course. People were cheering, crying, holding their children up. They were singing 'God Save the Tsar' over and over again, church bells were ringing. Despite the crush of the crowds and the excitement, everyone was very friendly. We were in Triumphal Square. Some of the people who saw Olga stepped aside to let her get closer to the line of soldiers along the route so she could see better. I recall one old woman even stroked her head as she passed by and urged her not to be shy. I'll tell you honestly, I felt I was getting swept up by it all."

"My friend, I'm glad it went so well for you and for her," Istomin said, looking annoyed. He seemed to want to say something else, but changed his mind, and instead returned to the children.

"What about Ibrahim, the Tatar boy, and that black-haired girl, Anya?"

"Ah, well. At least for those two the ending was happy. Despite his delicate appearance Ibrahim is a tough young fellow and appears to have gotten out of all this horror without any lasting damage. He's from a devout Muslim family, you know, and he's back with them now. He thought that what happened to him and the others was something like a struggle with demons in Tatar folklore. And he felt he won because Allah was on his side. He'd heard stories about demons since childhood. Not so wrong, actually," Thomas concluded, thinking how different the world seemed to him now in comparison to just a few months ago.

Istomin smiled faintly at Thomas's words. The world had

changed a lot for him too.

"Anya also comes from a strong family, Old Believers, and is doing well at home," Thomas went on. "And Nikitin's daughter, Masha, is recovering as well, although it's a slow process. You remember her, don't you? I told you about her abduction that night at Yar, which was the first I heard about this entire horrible business."

Istomin nodded, "Indeed, I do."

Istomin reached for the bottle Evgeny left on the side table and leaned toward Thomas.

"Some more?" he offered.

"No, thanks, it's very good, but I'm deeply satisfied and happy now, and don't need anything else."

"I don't think I'll have any more either then," Istomin replied, slapping the cork with his hand, and setting the bottle down. "I want to have a clear head for what I want to ask you next. You can guess, I'm sure."

"Yes, of course. Dick-er-man," Thomas pronounced the name syllable by syllable as he exhaled. "You know there was a military trial because of the German involvement?"

Istomin nodded.

"What wasn't mentioned in the papers is that it was conducted behind closed doors—all very hush hush. And I am pleased to tell you Dickerman got twenty-five years in a hard labor camp in Yakutia," Thomas said in a satisfied tone.

Istomin sat up, and his eyes flashing darkly. "*Bravo! Bravo!*" he exclaimed. "That is *justice!*"

"It is. He'll end his days there, given his age and condition, and he'll be forced to think about his punishment and what he did every day for the rest of his miserable life."

"Very, very satisfying to hear this. Justice!" Istomin exclaimed again, clapping his hands, and rubbing them together. "You must have seen his face when the sentence was pronounced," he asked Thomas eagerly. "How'd he look?"

"No, actually, I didn't see him or the trial. The Okhrana did the same thing with me they did with you. They interviewed me at length before the trial. Markov told me my testimony was read at the trial, as was yours. But I wasn't called to testify in person."

"Huh!" Istomin exclaimed at the unexpected news. "I was surprised I wasn't called but certainly assumed you'd be, since you were central to the whole case. They really were keeping it all under wraps."

Istomin paused before continuing, "I'll tell you frankly, I don't much like the smell of this."

"What do you mean?"

"I wouldn't be surprised if there was collusion at some high level to hide the scandal. You know of course that Kaiser Wilhelm and our beloved Tsar Nikolay Aleksandrovich are related, they're cousins of some sort," Istomin said with a wave of his hand, not wanting to parse the tedious genealogical details.

"And the Tsaritsa was born a German princess. So, I suspect that with all the foreign delegations sent here because of the 300th anniversary, our *anointed emperor* or his advisors might have decided to sweep the scandal under the rug," he said stressing the pious epithet ironically.

"But go on," Istomin continued, "what about the other members of the gang?"

"Well, let's say that . . . that part of the sentencing . . . varied," Thomas replied hesitantly, as he tried to find the words to characterize what had happened. "Maria, the woman who was arrested in the mansion with Dickerman, also got twenty-five years because she perverted the children personally, if you can believe it. The man you wounded who came into your house through the kitchen, the Pole, recovered, but he'll limp for the rest of his life. He got only twenty years in Yakutia because he was an underling. So did the thug I wounded in the face, the one who came with Dickerman to force his way into your house."

"Did the police make any trouble about the two we killed? That woman and the second thug at my house?"

"No, it was so clearly self-defense they just noted the details and left it at that."

"Well, so far, so good. But you haven't said anything about the Germans themselves!"

"They . . . got . . . off," Thomas said his voice dropping. "All of them, even though they initiated the whole thing. And the reason is exactly what that leader of theirs, Stürmer, was going on about when Markov and the police arrived. Do you remember?"

"Of course. Stürmer was claiming some sort of diplomatic immunity."

"Unfortunately, it worked. Three days after they were arrested, they were all on a train to Berlin. Again, Markov told me all this in confidence. The Okhrana tried to question them while they were being held in Lefortovo Prison but didn't get very far. The Germans knew they'd get out and clammed up. The Okhrana also ordered their commander who was in Moscow, a colonel no less, to get out of the country. That's all the Okhrana could do. Most of what came out about the German involvement was from Dickerman, who thought he could soften the judges by confessing whatever he knew. He even confessed things no one suspected, such as that he'd been drugging horses at the Hippodrome for months. A sideline of his, apparently."

"What a foul, disgusting louse!" Istomin exclaimed. "But what really angers me is that the Germans were able to get off without punishment," he continued bitterly.

"Oh, they managed to get away from Russia, yes. But Markov doesn't think that's the end of their story. Their child-prostitution plan was a catastrophe, their accomplices are all either in prison or dead, and they spent a great deal of money with nothing to show for it. Also, the Okhrana found out about the whole operation, even if it couldn't intervene. Markov says that's not something the German General Staff is likely to look upon very kindly."

"We can only hope. And did the investigation find out what the hell their perverse plan was for?"

"Blackmail. Again, this is what Markov says—but he has his sources. And whoever the targets were, they would have been expected to give up a lot of information or pay a lot of money, judging by what the Germans spent on their mansion."

"What a filthy affair! I thought the Germans were a nobler people. I was obviously naïve."

"I didn't know you disliked Germans so much."

"I didn't. Before. But if they're prepared to do this to us now, worse will come later. Of this, I'm sure. And there are other signs," Istomin said sternly.

"I sincerely hope you're wrong. I've lived in Germany and know lots of Germans, including members of Hedwig's family. Some others, too, that I . . . met recently," Thomas replied, thinking of the new act from Berlin he had hired.

Istomin noticed Thomas's hesitation but said nothing, and shifted to a conciliatory tone: "Of course, of course. It's foolish to generalize too broadly."

Thomas had been sitting comfortably in his armchair as they talked, when he suddenly lifted Strelochka from his lap, put her back in the basket, still asleep, and stood up.

Istomin thought at first there had been an accident with the puppy, but Thomas tucked his hands into his pockets and began to stroll back and forth across the living room. He seemed to be taking his time, as if trying to compose his thoughts, and Istomin watched him in silence.

"I need to tell you something I can't tell anyone else," Thomas finally said, turning toward Istomin and looking searchingly into his eyes. "You're the only one who can understand what I'm talking about . . . because you were there. It's about my guilt. I feel guilty because I, I, killed two people that night . . . one of the men who attacked your house and that woman in the mansion. And I can't get over the great sins I committed."

Seeing Istomin shift in his armchair and prepare to object, Thomas raised his right hand: "I know, I know what you're going to say. I did it in self-defense. And I was trying to free Olga from people who tried to kill me and were hurting her and the other children. All that's true. But even so, I've never felt before as strongly as I do now that killing, any killing, is a sin."

Istomin's gaze softened at Thomas's words, and he settled back, listening.

Thomas walked back to his armchair and sat down.

"You've been to war, and you've killed people yourself and ordered others to kill. But I never killed anyone before. And I hope to God I'll never do it again. I'm not saying this just because I know what it says in the Bible about 'Thou shalt not kill.' It's more real for me than that. When I think about those two I killed, I get a feeling that's hard to describe. I think I can actually see in my mind something of what happened when those two died. How can I put it? What I see, what I have a vision of, is like a powerful, funnel-shaped spinning. Do you understand? It's like when you're on a country road, and it's dry, and wind makes dust spin on the ground, and you see a little whirlwind form and rise up, sometimes high up into the sky. It's like that. Something from the earth to the heavens. Connecting them. Except the whirlwind I see is bigger and darker, and I know somehow it's a human soul being ripped out of the body and carried away. I've never felt anything like this before, but I know it's about great suffering. It's like a howl of unspeakable suffering. That's why I know killing is always a sin, even when one thinks one has to do it, as I did."

Both men were silent for a minute, each lost in his own thoughts.

"You could ask Zoya about it when she returns," Istomin said in a quiet voice, reaching over to pat Thomas's arm, "if you feel it's right to talk to her about it."

"I will, definitely. But you, you've never experienced anything like this?"

"No. Not in Manchuria. Not now in Moscow. Not even in Manchuria, I should say. If I hadn't killed the Japanese during the one battle in which I had to fight, they would have killed me and my men. I'm not proud of what I did, but I don't regret it, even though I regret the war itself very much. As for those thugs who worked for the Germans and abducted innocent children off the street, they had it coming! That holds for the dead woman and the man!"

Thomas shook his head. "I know our hands were forced by

Dickerman and his gang, but for me the pain remains."

"Maybe that's the price we pay for being human and for having a conscience. We can't be whole and embrace all of totality," Istomin replied and reached for the bottle of cognac.

"I think I will have some more after all. And you?"

Thomas extended his glass and watched as the amber liquid filled it.

"There's another thing I wanted to tell you that's related to the first, in a way," he said after taking a big sip of the liquor, savoring its bouquet, and swallowing it slowly.

"When I came close to losing Olga, I realized more strongly than ever before how important my children are to me. How important my family is to me. They were always important, I'm not saying they weren't. But now they've become so important I feel almost overwhelmed by the need. My marriage to Valli has failed, as I'm sure you noticed. It's my fault. I admit it and I regret it. I shouldn't have married her when I did, after Hedwig died, I didn't really love her then and I don't love her now."

Istomin listened without saying anything, his head down and his eyes fixed on the long tongues of flame rising from the birch logs in the fireplace. What Thomas was saying was resonating for him in a new way and he wasn't used to it yet.

"I don't want to pretend any longer that my marriage to Valli can last, that I can make it work in some reduced or limited way. It pains me that I'm hurting her. But I need a woman I can love and who will love me. One who could help me be myself, help me become what I feel I must become. We must be able to fulfil each other. I also need a woman who can be a mother to my children, and maybe even have more children."

"What about Mina Samoylovna? Did you see her again? Is there anything for you with her?" Istomin asked, looking up.

Thomas felt himself blushing but concealed it by continuing in a calm tone. "No, I'm afraid that's over. She's a lovely woman, as you know, but it all . . . it somehow didn't take."

"What do you mean?"

"She's an enjoyable companion, and she's a good person.

And I was able to explain to her how . . . about the . . . mistakes I made. That time when she came to your house when you were out. I think she believed me. You remember, I told you about it," Thomas said, looking questioningly at Istomin.

Istomin nodded.

"But what it comes down to in the end is that I don't think she wants to be a mother. Or, rather, doesn't have it in her."

"I liked her."

"I know you did," Thomas said, looking closely at Istomin. "And she noticed it, I think."

Thomas continued to look silently at his friend for a moment, thinking he might want to say something about Mina.

But when he didn't, Thomas decided it would be better to switch the subject.

"You left Moscow shortly after giving your deposition to the police. So, did you have a chance to see Vera again? Her chorus was still performing, as I recall."

"How curious that you'd ask me about this today," Istomin replied, shifting in his chair, and looking uncomfortable.

"Why curious?" Thomas asked, surprised by his friend's reaction.

"Because I've changed in the last few months, ever since all that horror in Moscow."

"How? Are you all right?"

"Yes, I'm fine. But my situation with Vera . . . or, rather how I feel about her, because there really wasn't any situation, is really . . . very much like what you said about Mina Samoylovna."

Thomas was struck by how Istomin turned his gaze away from him to the burning logs in the fireplace again.

"Vera is one of the most beautiful women I've ever known," Istomin said in a quiet voice, as if he was reluctant to speak but felt he had to get something off his chest.

"And she's very charming. The problem is she wants something from life that's entirely different from what I discovered I want and need. The last time I saw her in Moscow she told me that she's hoping to get a part in a motion picture. She auditioned for Khanzhonkov's studio. It went well, apparently, because she photographs well, which is the hardest part. For her it would be wonderful, and I hope she succeeds. She wants something glamorous that will make her famous. Adoring crowds and all the rest. But she's not ready for what I need, for what I've discovered about myself since I came back here."

Istomin hesitated for a second and his expression became more thoughtful as he continued. "In the last two months at *Otradnoye* I've come to the same conclusion as you. I feel now in a way I never felt before that I need to start a family of my own."

Thomas was moved by how his friend's emotions kept changing. An abashed and vulnerable expression appeared on his handsome face.

"But that's *wonderful*! *That's really wonderful news!*" Thomas exclaimed. He got up, stepped toward Istomin, pulled him to his feet and embraced him.

"Thank you, Frederick. You don't think what I'm saying is absurd? That I'm too old and set in my ways?"

"Too old? You're only what? Thirty-eight? Thomas calculated, remembering Istomin was three years younger than him. You're dans *la force de l'âge*, or in the prime of life, as the French say!"

"Thank you, dear man. I'll tell you, it's a great relief to hear you say that," Istomin admitted with a shake of his head. "After everything that happened in Moscow, when I came back here, I felt the pull of family in a new way. It feels very strange. I don't know why, but I do."

"Oh, I do!" Thomas said eagerly. "How can you not? Didn't you tell me your great—I forget how many times great it was—grandfather built this place? And your people have lived in Kostroma for hundreds of years before that?"

"Yes, since the 15th century," Istomin replied pensively, "before even the Romanovs, from what I've read."

"Well, my friend, what you feel is the pull of the land, of the past, of your ancestors' bones that have become part of the soil and the trees and the grasses and everything that lives and grows here!"

"Do you think . . . Do you suppose Zoya had anything to do with this feeling of mine?" Istomin suddenly asked.

Thomas got up from his chair and started pacing around the living room in excitement.

"I don't know. It's possible. In some ways, she's like a tuning fork, or maybe better to say, a compass needle. What she does to you, for you, somehow aligns you with something deep and true."

"And powerful."

"Yes, and very powerful," Thomas agreed.

"Maybe my decision about Valli has something to do with what Zoya did for me. Because I, too, want the same thing you have here at *Otradnoye*. I want to feel attached to the land, to the country, to the people. I want a new home. I need a new home. And I can't have any of this without a family. It wouldn't be real without one. A family is what would root me here."

"It's what you lost in Coahoma, in America," Istomin said sadly.

"Yes. Yes, it is. And I'll never be able to go back, I think. That's lost forever, or at least in my lifetime. Probably in the lifetime of my children too. I'd never be able to live there the way I can here."

"Ironic, isn't it, that this will be your new home. Russia and America aren't exactly similar countries. Or the best of friends."

"Perhaps," Thomas replied. "But what is it that can transform a new place where you live into a real home?"

"Love?"

"Yes. Probably love. At least that's what I hope."

NOTE TO MY READERS

Frederick Bruce Thomas, the main character in this novel, is not someone I invented. He really existed—although his life was filled with so many improbable twists and transformations that it reads like fiction. Born to former slaves in Mississippi in 1872, he traveled to Europe in search of freedom, became a multimillionaire impresario in tsarist Moscow, fled Russia to escape the Bolsheviks, and reestablished himself in Constantinople as the "Sultan of Jazz." Thomas was famous during his lifetime, but after his death in 1928, he fell into oblivion for the next eighty-five years—until my biography, *The Black Russian*, returned him to public memory.

I discovered the facts of Thomas's extraordinary life by doing research in dozens of archives and libraries across five countries—the United States, France, England, Russia, and Turkey—and I strove to be as thorough as possible. Even so, I realized when I finished that there might be parts of his story I was unable to recover—adventures that left no trace in the kinds of old documents and publications I found. Thomas's remarkable personality, and the turbulent times in the exotic countries where he lived, make it easy to imagine that this was the case.

The story above is the first in a series inspired by his life. It can be enjoyed without reading *The Black Russian*, although I hope, of course, that at some point you may want to read the biography as well.

ACKNOWLEDGEMENTS

I am grateful to the following individuals—whose anonymity I have chosen to preserve—for their advice and assistance: NA, SA, SA, DB, RB, JD, CM, EM, GP, DS, and ST.

If they see their initials, they will recognize themselves. Otherwise, they will remain known only to me—and perhaps to Zoya Pavlovna Shchyogoleva, still residing at the *Otradnoye* estate, Kostroma Governorate, Russian Empire.